FACE TO FACE

Face to Face: A Novel of the Reformation

Published by:
1517 Publishing
PO Box 54032
Irvine, CA 92619-4032

Publisher's Cataloging-in-Publication
(Provided by Cassidy Cataloguing Services, Inc.)

Names: Mantravadi, Amy, author.
Title: Face to face : a novel of the Reformation / Amy Mantravadi.
Description: Irvine, CA : 1517 Publishing, [2025] | Series: Reformation novel series | Includes bibliographical references.
Identifiers: ISBN: 978-1-964419-30-5 (paperback) | 978-1-964419-31-2 (hardcover) | 978-1-964419-32-9 (ebook) | 978-1-964419-33-6 (audiobook)
Subjects: LCSH: Reformation—Europe—Fiction. | Church history—16th century—Fiction. | Luther, Martin, 1483-1546—Fiction. | Erasmus, Desiderius, -1536—Fiction. | Melanchthon, Philip, 1497-1560—Fiction. | Word of God (Christian theology)—Fiction. | Interpersonal relations— Fiction. | LCGFT: Christian fiction. | BISAC: FICTION / Religious. | FICTION / Historical / Renaissance.
Classification: LCC: PS3613.A5825 F33 2025 | DDC: 813/.6—dc23

Printed in the United States of America.

Cover art by Zachariah James Stuef.

Praise for *Broken Bonds: A Novel of the Reformation* (Book 1 of 2)

"Amy Mantravadi has taken one of the most consequential yet inaccessible controversies of the Reformation—over the freedom or bondage of the will—and rendered it in living color, three-dimensional depth, and an emotional charge that grabs you by the throat. Civilization and salvation are at stake, yet we experience the stakes through the intense, ever-shifting relationships between the three men at the center of the debate. An ambitious undertaking, deftly executed!"

—Rev. Dr. Sarah Hinlicky Wilson, author of *Seven Ways of Looking at the Transfiguration* and *A-Tumblin' Down: A Novel*

"This is a wonderful and weird book, which will delight and edify lovers of theology, history, and the history of theology. *Broken Bonds* is a thoroughly researched and exceptionally well written recreation of one of the church's pivotal dramas that does not shy away from exploring the humanity and complexity of its central characters. *Broken Bonds* is a compelling book that every reader will benefit from."

—Matthew Lee Anderson, Asst. Professor, Baylor University Honors Program, author of *Called into Questions*

"I cannot get over what Amy has pulled off in *Broken Bonds*. Historical fiction of the highest order, jammed with excitement and grit and detail, yet with a depth of theological understanding the genre almost never possesses. This helps tremendously given the period she's chosen to bring to life, The Protestant Reformation. Events and people I thought I knew well take on a whole new dimension and urgency in her hands. I was gripped from start to finish. A major achievement, and one that I hope finds a wide readership. Bravo!"

—David Zahl, author of *Low Anthropology*

AMY
MANTRAVADI

FACE TO FACE

A NOVEL OF THE REFORMATION

BOOK 2 OF 2

FIFTEEN-SEVENTEEN PUBLISHING
1517.

Contents

Primary characters

In Wittenberg:

Philipp Melanchthon, Professor of Greek
Katharina, his wife
Anna, their daughter
Philipp, their son
Martin Luther, Professor of Theology
Katharina von Bora, Former Cistercian nun
Justus Jonas, Provost of the All Saints' Foundation
Johannes Bugenhagen, Pastor of St. Mary's Church
Famulus Koch, Live-in assistant to the Melanchthon family
Wolf Seberger, Live-in assistant at the Black Cloister
Eberhard Brisger, Former prior and housemate of Martin Luther
Lucas Cranach, Artist and Court painter
Barbara, his wife
Anna, their daughter, one of several children

In Basel:

Desiderius Erasmus, Scholar also commonly known as Erasmus of Rotterdam
Johann Froben, Publisher
Gertrude, his wife
Hieronymus, their son
Justina, their daughter
Johann Erasmus, their son
Christoph von Utenheim, Bishop of Basel
Jan Łaski, Polish diplomat living with the Frobens

Margarethe, Housekeeper to the Frobens
Johannes Œcolampadius, Vicar of St. Martin's Church
Bonifacius Amerbach, Heir to the Amerbach printing legacy

Elsewhere:

Friedrich, Elector of Saxony
Johann, Younger brother and heir apparent of Elector Friedrich
Andreas Bodenstein von Karlstadt, Former pastor in Orlamünde
Thomas Müntzer, Radical preacher formerly of Allstedt
Charles V, Holy Roman Emperor

In loving memory
Joanne Blackston Mantravadi
1938-2022

"I would have despaired unless I had believed that I would see the goodness of the Lord in the land of the living."

—Psalm 27:13[1]

"You have known the alien feeling
In the calm of candlelight;
Gloom-embraced will lie no more,
By the flickering shades obscured,
But are seized by new desire,
To a higher union lured."

—Johann Wolfgang von Goethe,
"Blessed Longing"[2]

---

[1] All quotations from the Christian Scriptures in this work are taken from the following translation: *The New American Standard Bible* (LaHabra, CA: The Lockman Foundation, 1995).

[2] Von Goethe, Johann Wolfgang, "Blessed Longing," in *The Essential Goethe*, ed. Matthew Bell (Princeton: Princeton University Press, 2016), 39.

"Who then devised the torment? Love.
Love is the unfamiliar Name
Behind the hands that wove
The intolerable shirt of flame
Which human power cannot remove.
We only live, only suspire
Consumed by either fire or fire."

—T.S. Eliot, "Little Gidding"

Prologue

17 April 1521
Free Imperial City of Worms

Martin Luther kneels before a small wooden crucifix, hands clasped in prayer. He gazes upon the image of Christ in agony, sensing the kinship of suffering. Outside, he hears the distant cries of his supporters, but within this tiny room perched high in the tower of St. Johannes Church, all is silent. It is nearly four o'clock—the hour is almost come.

Today, I die.

He shifts his hands, pressing palm against palm, kneading his flesh to the point of abrasion. Blood pumps steadily through his neck and into his ears. He can sense it in his skull, his wrists, his belly. In his mind, he rehearses the arguments he has pondered since his departure from Wittenberg but struggles mightily to direct the course of his thoughts. The longer he waits, the more his fears awaken. Muscles tensed, limbs tingling, he strives to regain control.

This is what the end feels like.

Soon, a man will ascend the stairs and knock upon the ancient oak door to his right. Martin will be summoned to answer for his beliefs before Emperor Charles V, the most powerful ruler in Christendom. Since Martin has no intention of recanting, the result is almost certain: he will suffer the same fate as a long line of heretics before him. The rulers have promised him safety, but they made the same promise to others before him, and promises to heretics need not be kept. The Elector sent word before he entered the city gate: Martin will be found guilty and sent to the stake. Away from his home and those he loves, he will die surrounded by his enemies, his flesh consumed by the flames. But the work of reform must not die with him, and for that reason, the way he dies will be just as important as the way he has lived. He thinks of his friends back in Wittenberg.

Everyone is counting on me. I must defend the gospel. I must do it for their sake. They must see with what power this gospel is filled—that it will sustain them in the trials to come.

The door opens and his heart suffers a jolt, but it is only Dr. Hieronymus Schurff, clothed in a black robe and flat cap indicating his role as Martin's legal counselor. A professor at the University of Wittenberg, Schurff possesses a mind equal to the task before them, but in this moment, Martin values most highly the man's utter self-confidence and unwillingness to be moved. Schurff steps around the straw mat on the floor and stands beside the small table and chair that suffice for the room's furnishings.

"They will be in momentarily," Schurff informs him.

Martin nods but says nothing, for speaking seems a tremendous effort. His stomach is cramping. He fears he will be sick.

Now comes a thunder of footsteps ascending the stairs. There is a fierce bang on the door, sending a faint vibration through the floorboards. Martin feels it like a mallet pounding the drum of his heart. Schurff opens the portal, and the imperial herald enters with a great staff in his hand, along with Ulrich von Pappenheim, master of the imperial cavalry. Martin rises to his feet, struggling to believe that the moment has truly arrived.

"Brother Martin," Pappenheim greets him. "You are summoned to address the court of His Imperial Highness, Emperor Charles. Follow me," he concludes, turning on the spot.

With so few words am I summoned to death? Martin wonders. *Lord, strengthen me. Allow me to speak the words.*

They begin the descent, stepping carefully on each of the triangular stone slabs—the uneven stairs constructed centuries earlier. It is a great kindness to Martin's body: the releasing of nervous energy, the harnessing of anxiety for some useful purpose. And yet, each step brings him closer to the end of his earthly existence, and by evening he could be in the presence of his Creator. They cross the small yard that separates the church of St. Johannes from the cathedral. It is strangely empty, for the dignitaries are all in the bishop's palace and the crowds have been kept on the other side of the buildings.

Martin glances to his left and sees rows of headstones placed haphazardly among the cobbles: the final resting place for the parish's congregants.

Here, he thinks. *It will happen here—away from the people. They will tie me to a post with chains, then cover me with wood up to my chest. No further: they will want to see my pain.* This provokes his tears, but he forbids himself to weep.

"I cannot guarantee the security of your person on the street, so we will cut through the alley," Pappenheim announces.

A lie, and no mistake. They do not fear for his security, but their own. The street is full of Germans who treasure Martin as a national hero, but he will not be allowed to see them. Instead, the group happens upon a few partisans of the papal nuncio Aleandro. Having awaited Martin's passing, the men spit at him and shout insults in Latin and Italian. One of them pushes Martin, drawing a reproach from the herald.

"Are you alright?" Schurff asks, gripping Martin's arm.

What a question! To inquire after the mind of a dead man is far more cruel than kind.

"You are damned, Luther!" one of the Italians shouts. "You are fuel for the fire!"

Martin averts his eyes, his frame shaken and off kilter. *Keep going. Keep walking,* he urges himself, but he trembles fiercely.

While he traveled cross-country, he felt the strength of support—the consolation of Christian love. For a time, it held his fear in check, but now he has entered the citadel of Satan. As he weaves through dark passages, he sees different eyes staring at him: not bright spheres filled with compassion, but rings of onyx that bind him in judgment, goading him toward his fate, the sentence of death already passed. He has never beheld such hatred in the human gaze, and he knows they are imagining the cries of agony that will burst from his lungs, the stripping of his skin and blackening of his flesh, the destruction of all he is. *How they must hate me to wish such an end upon me! They would repay me fear for fear.* He shudders at the thought. They are now in the bishop's palace: yes, they have reached the door. Pappenheim lends him a final word.

"Speak not until they address you, and then only reply to those questions you are asked. The more you say, the worse it will be for you. Everything must be spoken in both German and Latin. Wait for both before replying, and do not fail to respond in kind. Hold yourself like a man and give respect to your betters. Despite any temptation to do so, do not stare at His Imperial Highness. Do not address him. Do not show your back to him unless explicitly dismissed. You are at his mercy; therefore, do nothing that might earn his wrath."

Martin nods in acknowledgment, but he has struggled to grasp the instructions. His thoughts are darkening—his heart pounding. As they stand waiting to enter, every second is torture. Much as he prefers not to think of it this way, he is an actor about to take part in a play, and his performance matters greatly. He must speak the words with strength. Only then will he lay the necessary foundation for what must come after him. If he should faint, vomit, or piss himself before the lords secular and ecclesiastical, it will be seen as proof that he is a false prophet in league with the devil, and he feels as if he might do all three. His thoughts are pulled downward. The light is fading.

Into your hands, I commend my spirit, Lord God, he prays, but feels none of the confidence of those words. He is powerfully aware of his smallness—his vulnerability. The doors open.

Here is a room worthy of an emperor, with a marble floor and dark linenfold panels on the walls. On either side, the princes of the Empire and bishops of the Church sit in expectation, along with an army of clerks and minor officials. At the far end of the room, a grand dais stands crowned with a scarlet canopy on which the double eagle of the Holy Roman Empire is displayed in gold. Seated upon the throne is Charles of Hapsburg, Lord of the Netherlands, Duke of Burgundy, Archduke of Austria, King of Spain, King of Italy, King of Germany, and Holy Roman Emperor, to say nothing of his territories in the New World. Heir to the Caesars of old, he is the image and substance of power on earth.

In the middle of the room and at the center of attention is a simple oak table bearing a stack of newly bound books. Standing beside it is Johann Eck, assistant to the Archbishop of Trier, who upon this day will act as prosecutor on behalf of the imperial majesty.[1] He is a tall man, his limbs impossibly long and lanky, his slender fingers

---

[1] This is not the Johann Eck with whom Luther debated at Leipzig in 1519, but another man of the same name.

clasped together at severe angles, as if he intends to slash Martin with the sharp blades of his knuckles.

The room is filled with chatter as Martin is led forward. The tension surging through his body, he strives to focus on Eck and the table of books. He will not look upon the Emperor, nor will he glance at his own Elector, Friedrich of Saxony. He has only strength enough to focus on one thing, so he directs all his energies to the questions he will receive and answers he must give.

They have reached the middle of the room. The herald initiates the proceedings. Now comes the hour of Johann Eck: a man seemingly equal in age to Martin, with dark eyes and hair to match. There is a firmness in Eck's features and a confidence in his long gait as he rounds the corner of the table and speaks in a commanding voice.

"His imperial majesty has summoned you here, Martin Luther, for two reasons: First, that you may publicly acknowledge that the books which have been published under your name"—here Eck gestures to the volumes on the table—"are truly yours. Second, that you may declare whether you wish to retract anything in them."

Martin struggles to reconcile what he is hearing with what he expected to hear. It seems he has been suffering under a misapprehension: the Emperor is not interested in discussing the content of his teachings. His only concern is to get Martin to the stake as soon as possible, regardless of whether his teachings are in line with Scripture. *They will not let me speak. They will not let me die well.*

With this revelation comes a change in Martin's body. The fear that has brewed for hours releases, rushing through his limbs, surging into his chest. His heart begins pounding with wild abandon. His pulse rushes dangerously fast. Darkness—terrible darkness! *Am I dying?! Here, before all the world, am I dying?!* He feels an intense pain in his chest: growing, spreading. *My heart is seizing!* His breath is short—his body leaks sweat. He cannot bring himself to speak.

Schurff notes his distress, and evidently stalling for time, demands, "Let the titles of the books be read!"

Sighing deeply, Eck retrieves a listed index from one of the volumes and begins reciting. "Commentaries on the Psalms, Commentaries on the Epistle to the Romans, Disputation on the Power and Efficacy of Indulgences, A Sermon on Indulgences and Grace…"

Martin feels the crush of impending doom. *How am I still standing?* His body is overcome. *I have failed. I am a dead man.* Every breath is a gripping pain, every beat of his heart a death knell.

Schurff whispers into Martin's ear, placing a hand on his shoulder. "Are you alright?"

"Something is wrong with my heart," Martin says softly. "Can we call for a recess?"

Schurff's eyes widen in alarm, but he quickly recovers himself. "Repeat the question to them, stress its importance, and beg time to think."

Martin nods his head even as Eck finishes reciting, "Prelude on the Babylonian Captivity of the Church, Against the Execrable Bull of Antichrist, and the Assertion of all the Articles Wrongly Condemned in the Bull." With this, Eck slams the book shut in his oversized hand and inquires again, "Are you, Martin Luther, the author of these works, and do you recant their contents?"

Martin's legs wobble. He grips his hands, one intertwined with the other, attempting to release the pain. He is speaking now—doing exactly as Schurff instructed—but he cannot manage much more than a whisper. Yes, the books are his, but the matter is grave, concerning the salvation of souls. He hears the creaking of wood as those upon the benches strain to hear. Then Martin does precisely what he was warned not to do: he stares at the Emperor on his throne, ensconced in grandeur.

"I beseech your imperial majesty for time to think, that I might satisfactorily answer the question without doing violence to the divine Word and endangering my own soul."

The Emperor looks at him in confusion, even after Martin repeats the statement in Latin, but Eck is visibly furious. As Martin's interrogator departs to consult with his fellows, Schurff whispers, "Now we must wait and pray."

Martin does pray, beseeching God to give him a second chance. His pulse is still racing—his chest aching. He longs to hide from the hundreds of eyes fastened upon him. *Failure! You will die a failure!*

Eck approaches him again, fists clenched, eyes burning. He berates Martin. "You do not deserve to be granted more time for consideration, but out of his innate clemency, his imperial majesty grants you one more day for deliberation."

Within minutes, Martin is ushered back to his room high in the tower, and as the door slams behind him, he breaks down in tears, clutching at his chest, gasping for breath. *What was that?! What happened?* He notes that his pulse is slowing—the pain is drifting away. It seems he is not dying: his heart is functioning normally. *The terror—it was only the terror.* He feels a great fool. *How will I face them all again?*

Even as these dark thoughts trouble him, there is a knock on the door. He does not want anyone to see him like this, so he calls out, "Who is it? I am occupied!"

"It's Jakob," comes a reply in the unmistakable voice of his younger brother, one of the few persons on earth to whom he would grant entrance.

Martin opens the door and is immediately embraced. He is wrapped in Jakob's arms—cloaked in the warmth of brotherly affection.

"Martin. Oh, Martin!" Jakob exclaims. "How I have trembled for you!"

Martin shuts the door behind them and looks upon this man who is so much the image of himself, though seven years younger and with far more hair.

"My brother! My soul!" Jakob exclaims, gripping his shoulders. "How fortunate that they allowed me to see you!" Then Jakob's smile fades. "You make no reply to me. Tell me, brother, what demon tortures you?"

Ashamed, Martin breaks away and walks toward the lone window with its circles of thick glass rimmed in iron. Below is the church's central building, a decagonal chapel crowned by a dwarf gallery on which figures of beasts support the stone columns. He stares at them until they blur and meld together, taking on a kind of perverted life, winged demons ready to torture him. Again, his pulse increases. He can see men gathering in the yard and knows they are speaking of his performance—or lack thereof—and speculating how long it will take him to recant. He is meant to be answering his brother, but he is just on the edge: a single breath away from that chasm into which he so recently fell. Still, he must speak.

"It happened again, Jakob," he whispers.

"What happened?"

Martin turns to face his brother, his body tingling with shame. "The terror. I had the terror."

"You still have those?" Jakob asks, brows raised.

He nods and begins pacing the room in a tight circle, unable to take more than two paces in any direction before hitting a wall. "This one was worse than any before. You remember how they used to torment me. Father would call me a coward."

"I remember," Jakob replies solemnly, "but I never thought you a coward."

"I could feel it starting before I entered. Then when I saw them all—" He ceases walking and looks upon his brother with aching eyes. "I couldn't make it stop, Jakob. I tried! I prayed. I attempted to be calm, but I couldn't make it stop. Such pain in my chest! I thought I was dying!"

"Is that why you asked for a delay?" Jakob asks, stepping nearer.

"Yes," he admits, resuming his circuit of the room. "When I saw the Emperor, when they showed me the books, as Eck was going on and on, I could barely make sense of what he was saying. My thoughts were spinning—descending. I felt the hand of death upon me. That was all I could think about: death. My heart was racing. I was short of breath."

Jakob grasps Martin's arm, stopping him in his tracks. He speaks soothingly. "It's over now, Martin. I am with you. Thank God I can be with you!"

Martin shakes his head sadly. "I wish it were over, but I must repeat the whole thing tomorrow, and this time they will brook no delay. I will have to answer them."

"Do you doubt your answer?"

"No!" he cries in all sincerity. "I'm sure that is what they all think, but nothing has happened to change my opinion. You must believe me, brother! I was prepared to make a bold statement—to place a seal upon my faith. But then the terror struck, and I was barely able to speak."

Jakob sets his face like flint and speaks with authority.

"It's the devil, Martin. He raises the image of death before your eyes to make you doubt yourself."

Then he has succeeded, Martin thinks, *for I doubt myself entirely.* With a deep sigh, he admits, "Yes, you are right. He presses on me so hard sometimes. But Jakob, I am no equal to the martyrs of old. What mettle they were made of, I cannot imagine. I shake so violently! I have come very far, but I fear that I will fail the final test. When I think of those flames—" His voice gives way. His eyes are moist. "What if they break me, Jakob? What if they pull the word from my mouth? 'Recanto.' I am only a man, and pain is an enemy like no other."

Jakob nods thoughtfully and begins pacing, hands clasped behind his back. After a period of silence, he faces Martin.

"You are the Doktor of Theology, not me, but perhaps I might offer you a word of wisdom from the example of our Lord. When did he defeat the devil?"

"When he said, 'It is finished,'" Martin replies. "On the cross, when he suffered and died."

"Maybe," Jakob agrees, nodding. "But you know when I think he won?" Here he moves closer to Martin, who shrugs his shoulders. "In the garden—in Gethsemane, when he said, 'Not my will but yours be done.' When he told the apostles, 'My soul is overwhelmed with sorrow to the point of death.' When he begged them to keep watch with him and not to fall into temptation, because he was tempted there in a way we cannot imagine. His trial, his death—they were still to come, but the moment he said, 'Not my will but yours be done,' it was inevitable. He had faced the devil and won. Even so it is with you, brother. If they drag you to the flames—which I pray they will not, for it would break my heart and I do not know who could replace you—"

"Melanchthon will replace me," he interjects, remembering the last words he gave to his fellow professor before departing Wittenberg: *I will not be a great loss, provided you remain.*

"Be that as it may," Jakob continues, "if they do take you there—if they strip you and lead you where you do not want to go, your task will already be finished. The battle happens here. This is the final temptation, then everything else is inevitable. That's why you were suddenly struck by the terror. The devil attacks you here, but you are not as weak as he thinks. You stand before an emperor, but you do not stand alone. We are with you to the end: everyone who loves you, all the people of Germany. And the Lord is with you. He will enable you to speak."

Martin is moved by his brother's words. They lend him comfort, but he doubts. "What if the terror strikes again?"

Jakob takes hold of him. "Let it! Let it wash over you. Breathe it in—feel its power. It is the fierceness of the storm, but it cannot command you. In that very moment when all hope seems lost, you will be captured by something greater than yourself. Remember what mother used to say to us? 'Do not rush to tear down in doubt what you have built in faith.' She wasn't right about everything, but she was right about that, so listen to your mother!"

Martin manages a chuckle. The fear is lifting, but for how long? He must have faith in these words—in the promises of God.

"Thank you, brother," Martin says. "You always knew what to say to me—back then, when I was too afraid to tell anyone else, when it was the middle of the night and my thoughts were darker than the sky, and you would calm me with your sweet, small voice. Many years I have walked through strange and fearsome lands, and now my time grows short. Pray for me, and may God help me."

Jakob takes Martin's face in his hands and speaks to him in brotherly love.

"Almost finished. It's almost finished, Martin. I wish I could stay with you. Just know, if they do take you away, and you do not see me, I am still with you. I will always be with you, to the very end."

Tears in his eyes, he tells his brother, "I love you, Jakob. I love you all."

The night brings Martin no rest. He dreams of maggots burrowing down to his bones—of his extremities blackening and falling off, of locusts chattering curses in his ears. Then he awakes to a day full of equal peril. The morning is composed of anxious prayers, the midday a sweating torment. Then comes the afternoon, and Martin sits at the small table in his chamber, waiting to be summoned for a second time. He stares at the trencher before him on which lies a single piece of dark bread dry enough to break his teeth. No matter: he has nothing approaching an appetite. He channels his breath, closing his eyes, recalling the words of his brother. His legs bounce rapidly as he clasps his palms, grasping at the minimal flesh that still clings to his bones. A thought enters his mind: *I will be consumed in seconds. There's naught of me to cook.*

He remembers a woman in Eisenach whose skirt caught fire while roasting a goose on the spit. To his great surprise and perverse fascination, she revealed that once the top layer of skin burns away, a person feels little pain. Why this should be, he is not certain, but he dearly hopes it is true. He places his head in his hands, and as he feels his thin line of hair, he remembers the final humiliation of Jan Hus: the shaving of his tonsure before the fool's hat was applied. *I do not think that will bother me,* he tells himself, but he isn't certain. Some things cannot be known until they are felt.

The door opens and Pappenheim enters. No longer standing on ceremony, he simply utters, "Brother Martin, it is time."

Martin nods in acknowledgement—rises to his feet. He feels the tension in his legs but bids them hold him upright. He is moving forward now, as if in a dream, through the same labyrinth of passages as the day before, at the end of which he will find not a garden filled with bursts of color but the table holding his books, and behind it Eck waiting to question him as the Emperor looks down from above, surveying the earth like the Greek gods of old, marveling at the frailties of those who are merely human.

In this moment, Martin thinks of what his life might have been like if he had followed his father's wish and married Anna Reinicke. He would be in his home in Mansfeld now, reading his law books, the voices of children echoing in the halls, comfortable and perhaps even content. Well, he would be alive in any case, and that would be something.

Or if he had listened to Staupitz and risen through the ranks of the Augustinians—if he had just left well enough alone, he might have been sent to Rome and the Church of Santa Maria del Popolo, there to spend his days raising glasses of Italian red to the heavens, one after the other, the weather almost as sublime as the money that would fill his pocket. Instead, he is here, about to accept the fate of a notorious heretic: a fate from which so many have tried and failed to save him.

He is made to wait for two hours. Could this be a strategy to throw him off balance? If so, it is working. His anxiety builds by the minute. The sky grows dark, and all hope seems to fade. He feels a chill in his bones but remembers the words of Christ: "But when they hand you over, do not worry about how or what you are to say, for it will be given you in that hour what you are to say."[2] He clings to the promise.

When the time comes, he enters a larger hall than the day before packed with even more officials. He looks again upon the young Emperor Charles, but instead of fierce majesty, he sees a man too small for his heavy garments, with a comically projected chin and a mind incapable of grasping the higher truths of God. Not a god, but a man, and one who will be subject to divine justice, even as he, Martin Luther, will be. Why could he not see it the previous day?

I have less to fear than you, he thinks.

Eck begins addressing him again. "Answer his majesty's question: Do you wish to defend these books acknowledged to be yours, or do you retract?"

Martin's heart beats strongly, even as before. The surf is pulling him under, but he remembers something a sailor once told him: *You do not fight the current, for even the strongest man will expend his strength. You allow it to capture you—to carry you whither it will—and sooner or later, you will find yourself bobbing up to the surface, free to breathe the air again.*

He chooses to believe it. He pictures himself breathing in the fear and releasing it—imagines the Spirit of God filling him from top to bottom, empowering him to stand. He grips his left wrist with his right hand and remembers that he is one with Christ, and Christ will not abandon his own. Then he looks at Eck with a fierce intensity.

You are not fighting fair, he thinks, *so I will not fight fair.*

Softly but clearly, Martin says, "I ask your most serene majesty and your lordships to deign to note that my books are not all the same kind."

With this request, he sets off on a long explanation, separating his books into categories, holding the room in sway. This is not what Eck expected: Martin can see it in the cleric's lowered brows and persistent frown. *You sought a quick kill. You will not get one.* He continues with his explanation, weaving back and forth, refusing to grant Eck an opening.

---

[2] Matthew 10:19. All scripture references in this book are from *The New American Standard Bible*, 1995 edition (La Habra, CA: The Lockman Foundation).

He speaks of the tyranny of the pope. He quotes Scripture. He draws attention back to his teachings themselves, demanding that the authorities distinguish between them. Every time Eck opens his mouth to cut him off, Martin launches on a new point. He speaks of his duty to God and his allegiance to the German nation. With each sentence, his confidence increases along with Eck's frustration. The very weight of the room has shifted, and the balance is in Martin's favor. Finally, he concludes, "I have finished."

Eck crosses the space between them, stopping within a single pace of Martin's position. With a look surely intended to obliterate, Eck cries, "You have not answered the question! What is more, you call into question things that have already been either condemned or dictated by councils of the Church. You think you can dismiss his imperial majesty with a horned response?[3] Tell us simply: do you wish to retract, or do you not wish to retract?"

Even as Eck speaks, Martin hears the words of Scripture in his mind. *By faith, when he was tested, Abraham offered up Isaac. He considered that God could raise the dead.*

He closes his eyes briefly. He can feel the tension releasing.

And you were dead in trespasses and sins. He has made you alive together with him. You were buried with him in baptism.

Now as he stares into the scowling face of Johann Eck, Martin feels an inner peace, for he knows he is loved by God and made righteous by his Son. *You do not know that Eck. You are the one who has reason to fear, not me.* The Scriptures are clear and beautiful, offering good news to men. No one can convince Martin otherwise. And though Eck looks upon Martin to kill, he is fighting against the force of the moment. It is time.

"Since your serene majesty and your lordships require a simple answer, I will answer neither horned nor toothed," Martin says.

And in his mind, Martin hears the words, *Let us hold fast the confession of our faith, for he who promised is faithful. Abraham was justified apart from works. Faith was credited to him as righteousness. God was not ashamed to be called his God.*

He speaks again, his voice gaining strength and projecting to the far corners of the room. "Unless I am convinced by the testimony of

---

[3] A "horned" response is overly complex and obscure—pedantic.

Scripture or by clear reason—for I trust neither pope nor councils alone, which have often erred and contradicted themselves—"

Oh, the fury in Eck's eyes! He is the one trembling now.

With the strength of voice gifted him from on high, Martin Luther releases the fire that has burned so long within him, concluding, "My conscience is captive to the Word of God." And with a confidence that seems almost divine, he proclaims without hesitation, "I will not, and I cannot recant anything, for it is neither safe nor right to go against conscience." He repeats the statement in Latin. A chorus of whispers erupts.

Then he is seized by his frail humanity. The fear and trembling strikes anew. He concludes not in strength but in that weakness that looks for salvation, speaking in his native tongue alone. "Here I stand. I cannot do otherwise. May God help me."

Applause breaks out, beginning with the Saxon delegation and rippling through the crowd. The imperial herald beats his staff upon the marble floor, while Eck turns a deadly glare upon Elector Friedrich to make sure he is not joining the verbal tumult. There are cries of, "Silence!" in both Latin and German, and the noise begins to taper off, but Martin Luther casts his eyes to heaven, overcome by the grace he has been granted. Against the power of the devil and the principalities of earth, he has done what he came to do. He whispers, "It is finished."[4]

[4] This was not the end of the interrogation, though for all intents and purposes, the business was complete. Eck pressed Luther to reconsider his statement, only to receive a repeat of the points already made. The assembly was finally ended on account of the late hour.

4 years later...

Spring

22 March 1525
Wittenberg, Electorate of Saxony

Martin Luther sits in the small lecture room at the Black Cloister, thoughts spinning furiously. It is strange how a space can become an absence: the gray walls are bare, stripped of their saintly ornaments in the year of purgation, and the student's benches are pushed back against the far wall.[1] There is no one to disturb his contemplation—likewise, no one to save him from it. Seated in a simple wood chair, he stares out one of the windows that overlooks the garden. The winter's frost has gone, and the persistent herbs are making their reappearance despite being untended for years. Rosemary and borage, lavender and mint—like him, clinging to life with little nourishment and in constant danger of extinction.

They seek my life to kill me.

With a sigh, he glances down at the sealed letter in his lap. There is no need to open it, for its author—Georg Spalatin, chaplain and secretary to Elector Friedrich of Saxony—has already delivered the message in person: Andreas Bodenstein von Karlstadt's request for shelter in Electoral Saxony has been denied.

Martin's old colleague and current adversary had dreamed of becoming a peasant, but it seems those peasants who have had the misfortune of making Karlstadt's acquaintance are now threatening his life. Although he claims not to care for the physical world,

[1] While Luther was away at the Wartburg Castle in 1521-2, the Black Cloister was emptied of its images under the influence of Gabriel Zwilling and others. This was during the period of Karlstadt's ascendancy in Wittenberg.

Karlstadt's concern for his earthly existence is evidently great enough to justify the humiliation of writing to Martin for help after previously denouncing him to his face. Too little and far too late: the Elector has grown even wearier of Karlstadt than Martin has.

Karlstadt didn't deserve a reply, Martin thinks to himself, *and yet I made his case to the Elector. I suppose I will get no thanks for that.*

Alas, the days are evil! The French king has been taken captive by the Emperor's forces at Pavia. The change in the weather has given new life to the peasant rebellion, which now burns freely throughout the southern German lands. Just as Martin feared, it is Thomas Müntzer who provokes the flame, filling the heads of the common folk with wild visions, bidding them forsake all earthly things before the immanent Day of Judgment. *What a hold he has over them, a very devil of hell leading them in chains to their own destruction!* Once Müntzer was willing to sit under Martin's teaching. They never talked much, but he remembers seeing Müntzer standing in the congregation, attention rapt, devouring every word that exited his mouth. *And now he calls me a heretic. He hates me in the depths of his bones.*

In an attempt to vindicate himself, Müntzer has released a pamphlet calling Martin "Doktor Liar," the "Wittenberg pope," a "puffed up, wily dragon" driven by "raging envy" and "bitter hate," a man of "unspiritual soft-living flesh."[2] Martin's chief sin is that he offers his congregants complete forgiveness of sins, the totality of divine grace, without condition or threat of expiration. For this, Müntzer dubs him an arch-heathen. "I would prefer to smell you roasting in your arrogance in a pot or in a cauldron by the fire, smitten by God's wrath, and then stewing in your own juice."[3] A Christian must always be questioning his faith, testing it through trial, pursuing the new outpouring of the spirit. In perhaps the cruelest blow of all, Müntzer brought up Martin's old mentor, Johann von Staupitz. "He has now deserted you."[4] Was that truly necessary?

Müntzer spits upon baptism, calls every peasant with a scythe a rightful judge of the state, and objects that Martin has not endorsed

---

[2] These insults are all found in "Vindication and Refutation" in *The Collected Works of Thomas Müntzer*, trans. Peter Matheson (Edinburgh: T&T Clark, 1988).

[3] Müntzer, 348.

[4] Ibid., 347.

Erasmus' position. "You have conjured up such fantasies from your Augustine; truly a blasphemous thing: to pour contempt on man's free will!"[5]

What might a man do who thinks he must earn his salvation? Martin wonders.

The one piece of good news is that Landgrave Philipp of Hesse has, thanks to the influence of Philipp Melanchthon, declared himself an ally of their cause and will introduce religious reforms in his territory.

All this, and I must still answer Erasmus, Martin fumes. *Oh, how he must be loving this! 'I told you, Luther. I warned you. The world is falling apart!' He dares nothing and gains every man's praise.* Yet, somewhere within himself, Martin feels the tension like a constant cramp. Erasmus' very existence seems like a rebuke of his own. The man is playing a double game, penning words of friendship while coming for all that Martin holds dear.

Even as these thoughts perturb his innards, Martin's assistant, Wolf Seberger, enters the room with a hammer still in hand and announces, "You have a visitor, Herr Doktor."

"I hope it is Doktor Amsdorf," Martin replies, "for I sent him on an errand some time ago, and he is long overdue to return."

"Coming up now," Wolf assures him, pointing with his tool in the direction of the stairs. "You must be patient, Doktor!" With this mild rebuke, Wolf exits the room and leaves Martin to his brooding.

Nikolaus von Amsdorf is Martin's former colleague in the theology department and now a pastor in Magdeburg. The errand in question is a visit to Katharina von Bora, the last of the former nuns whom Martin has aided, to inform her that her intended, Hieronymus Baumgartner, has announced his engagement to a 14-year-old girl of wealth and high status. *An unchristian betrayal of trust! An offense to manhood itself!* Martin dispatched Amsdorf to break the news to her, not trusting himself to handle such a sensitive subject. Now his friend enters the room clothed in a brown coat and boots with a scholar's cap on his head. Amsdorf's beard has lately developed a will of its own and is quite a sight to behold.

---

5 Ibid., 345.

"Nikolaus!" Martin says in greeting, setting the letter on the floor and standing to embrace him. "Good afternoon to you!"

"Not very good, actually," Amsdorf replies grimly.

Martin examines the folds of his friend's face, attempting to discern whether he is serious or in jest. "I'm sorry?" he finally blurts.

"What the devil were you thinking?!" Amdsdorf cries, his eyes alight with anger.

Martin backs away if only to spare his ears. "Be more specific."

"What the devil were you thinking, trying to put her with Glatz?"

The force of this accusation is palpable, knocking Martin's spirit out of joint. Dr. Kaspar Glatz, a former colleague of them both, had offered to marry Katharina von Bora if Baumgartner proved untrue. Martin mentioned it to Katharina, but not Amsdorf: one of many reasons the harsh judgment catches him off guard.

"What?" he asks in confusion.

"I've just been to speak with Fräulein von Bora, hoping to encourage her after that good for nothing Baumgartner broke his solemn pledge to take her as his wife, only to find her in distress once again because you're trying to force her to marry Kaspar Glatz!" Amsdorf complains, pointing an accusatory finger in his direction.

Martin settles back into the chair, shaking his head. "That's preposterous. I am not forcing her to do anything. It is because she was treated so poorly by Baumgartner that I hoped to find her a new arrangement. Glatz is a good worker and has a decent income now. He told me of his regard for her, so I made the suggestion. Where's the harm in that?"

"He was the crank of the department, and you know it!" Amsdorf blurts, his face twisting in frustration.

"Oh, he's not that bad!"

"He's a miser who cannot take correction from any man, and I pity the woman forced to abide him!"

Martin has seen errant students receive such a harangue from Amsdorf, but it is the first time he has been so unfortunate as to experience one himself, and he can hardly make out why.

"Truly, you exaggerate, and I'm glad Kaspar is not here to hear it," Martin concludes.

"I do no such thing!" Amsdorf declares, pulling a chair over from the corner and planting himself directly in front of Martin.

"Fräulein von Bora discerned these things in him quickly. How much more should I know them after I had to share a room with him for six months?"

"But knowing Glatz, he will have guarded that room against dirt and vermin from dawn until dusk."

"Ha!" Amsdorf scoffs. "Well, she's refusing him, and good for her!"

Martin's stomach lurches. *Refusing the only man who is willing to have her?!* It makes no sense, even if Glatz is, in Amsdorf's words, a crank. Martin has spent two years attempting to find places of safety for the escaped nuns of Marienthron. It has taken up much of his valuable time, and now this woman is shoving his kindness—that is, Glatz's kindness back in his face.

"I don't see how it could possibly be good for her," Martin concludes. "She is out of options and about to be out on the street. Nikolaus, do you know what happens to women in her situation? Nothing good, I assure you!"

"As it so happens, she sees another option, and I think it has merit—"

"Truly, it does not do for any woman to be so fastidious. I know she comes from a noble house, but really!" he interrupts, his frustration increasing the more he thinks about it.

"If you would allow me to finish," Amsdorf begs, speaking calmly, "she was at pains to stress that she is not as fastidious as you say. In fact, she suggested a possible solution."

Martin breathes deeply, attempting to regain control. "Very well. What is it?"

"She will have one of us," Amsdorf asserts matter-of-factly.

Now Martin truly suspects his friend is speaking a foreign tongue. He stares at Amsdorf for a moment, straining to comprehend it, then finally asks, "I beg your pardon?"

"She will marry me, or she will marry you."

Dear God! I did understand him. Martin's pulse quickens—his every fiber is on edge. He has a sudden sensation as if Katharina's eyes were fixed upon him, searching, beseeching. Struggling to wrap his mind around it, he inquires, "She said this?"

"Yes. She told it to me straight. Of course, I cannot marry her," Amsdorf asserts, his jowls shaking along with his head. "The Lord has not called me to that. But perhaps—"

"No!" Martin cries, feeling panicked. He senses how quickly events are moving. Before his mind's eye, she is approaching him, moving closer with every breath. But he will not be drawn: he wrenches his thoughts from her grasp. *I must stop this thing in its tracks.*

"You will not even consider it?" Amsdorf asks, frowning.

"The whole thing is ridiculous!"

Amsdorf crosses his arms and leans back in the chair. "That's rather unkind. I thought you believed her to be an honorable woman."

"No, it's not that. It's just—She turns things around!" Martin charges, gesturing broadly. "This is not how these things happen. Women don't just demand to marry someone and expect them to do it!"

Amsdorf tilts his head and looks at Martin oddly. *How can I make him understand?* Martin wonders. For reasons he cannot fully comprehend, he feels in great peril. He thinks back on every interaction he has had with Katharina. *No, I must not use her Christian name. She is Fräulein von Bora.* Did he somehow imply to her that he was interested in marriage? Did he imply that he was interested in her? *If so, I am the scoundrel.* But if it were so, she would not have suggested the possibility of marrying Amsdorf—right? *Might she be in love with me?* The question bothers him too much to consider. He berates himself for thinking it. *It cannot be true. It's ridiculous. After all, she offered to marry Nikolaus.*

"To be fair, she did not demand to marry you," Amsdorf explains. "She didn't even say she wanted to marry you. She just said that she would."

"But see, isn't that odd? It feels very odd to me!" Martin asserts.

"You have some great experience with the female sex of which I was not previously aware?" Amsdorf asks with a chuckle, clearly rejoicing in Martin's discomfort.

"You know I do not, although I was raised with sisters. But why should either of us be preferable to Glatz? We are both far older, and I have the sentence of death hanging over me like the sword of Damocles."

"No time like the present, I suppose," Amsdorf quips, taking the whole matter far too lightly for Martin's preference.

"It is no joke, Nikolaus! Have you forgotten those Jews who were sent to kill me earlier this year? Paid a fine price, they were, to slip a poison in my drink!"[6]

"No, I have not forgotten," Amsdorf concedes, his eyes sad and voice low. "Shameful business."

"Then you see my point. The spies of the devil are everywhere, and I cannot say how long the Lord will preserve me from their hate. I live every day in the shadow of death!"

For a moment, they simply stare at each other, Martin slightly out of breath. And in the silence, she is there again in his thoughts, her hazel eyes unwilling to let him go. Hoping to banish her, he shakes his head and comments, "I still say she is overproud for refusing Glatz."

"Say it if you must, but I cannot fault her for refusing to do what I myself would not do in her situation," Amsdorf concludes.

Martin glares at him. "Then perhaps you are two of a kind. Are you certain God isn't calling you to wedlock?"

"Quite certain, though not on account of any flaw in the lady. She seems quite clever and has a good character, for she values men of character."

"And is that what we are, Nikolaus?"

"Go over and speak with her yourself," Amsdorf suggests, motioning with his hand. "Perhaps you will understand her better."

"Absolutely not! I don't want her getting any ideas." The thought of it terrifies him: having to see her, having to be seen by her. *Obviously, I can never talk to her again.*

"Have no fear!" declares Amsdorf, raising a hand to signal calm. "As I said before, she does not expect that either of us will marry her. I think she just wanted to prove that she isn't unreasonable. But you know what she's like. You lived together, didn't you?"

A new wave of panic crashes upon Martin's being, coating him in its flow. *Of course! That is what people will say if they hear of it.*

---

[6] Luther received a warning in early 1525 that a Jewish doctor had been paid to assassinate him. A Jewish man was later arrested in Wittenberg under suspicion of the same, though he did not fit the physical description given to Luther earlier. Two Jews were held in Wittenberg in connection with the alleged plot. Luther requested that they not be subjected to torture, and they were eventually released.

"Not like that! For the love of God, never put it like that!" Martin demands. "We were two people out of a dozen living in the Cloister. It was for the space of a fortnight while I found them all homes. Nothing improper happened!"

"Well, of course not!" Amsdorf exclaims, his brow furrowed. "I never meant to imply otherwise!"

"But your choice of phrasing was dangerous!" Feeling a need to drive the point home, Martin repeats, "It could be very dangerous for me!" Then fearing to appear selfish, he adds, "It could be very dangerous for us," at which point he realizes he has used the word 'us' for himself and Katharina, and his pulse surges again.

Amsdorf shrugs. "All I meant was that you have seen a bit of her character."

Martin sighs deeply. "I know she has a wealth of opinions and presumes to know what others are thinking. She is far more direct than I would have thought possible for one of the sisters."

"Yes, I like that about her," Amsdorf says with a smile. "She has a fine spirit."

"Then marry her," he replies, glaring in response.

"I almost wish I could, but I think out there is some man who will make far better use of her than you or I could. She will do him a world of good. No need to speak on it further. I will leave you to your thoughts." Amsdorf rises from the chair and concludes, "Have a good evening, friend."

"You too, friend, but I bid you: do not trouble me any more about this. I have enough troubles as it is."

Amsdorf nods thoughtfully. "My father used to say there is no trouble like woman trouble. It seems he was right."

As soon as Amsdorf departs, Martin leaps to his feet and begins pacing the room as if the floorboards have done him a great wrong. *Honestly, of all the things! As if I don't have enough to worry about!* Another lap around the room. *Her family didn't want her: I sent her to the Reichenbachs. The Reichenbachs didn't want her: I sent her to the Cranachs. Baumgartner didn't want her: I sent her to Glatz. Now she is refusing Glatz! Can she not take a hint?!* He feels a pang in his chest. *I am being unkind.* He makes a further lap, sighing deeply. Somewhere deep inside him, a question: *What are you afraid of?*

With a grunt, he pushes it aside. *I am not afraid. I am annoyed—deeply annoyed!* He kicks the wall in frustration. No matter which way he views the problem, there is only one possible answer—at least, only one he is willing to allow. *I must speak with her and convince her to marry Glatz. That is the only way this ends happily. Too long, I have bitten my tongue and played the gentleman. I will confront her before she destroys herself. Yes, that is the kind thing to do.*

He stops in front of a window and stares out at the city wall. Beyond it, the silver thread of the Elbe weaves its way through the Saxon countryside, its banks meandering in and out, in and out. *I don't understand, God. What am I doing wrong? Why does everyone find fault?*

The sun is dipping in the sky. He closes his eyes, breathes deeply, attempts to find his peace. The bells of St. Mary's toll one…two…three…four…five o'clock. *Breathe. Breathe.*

Suddenly, he remembers—he looks down at the floor. There is the letter from Spalatin and the memory of what is at stake: a spiritual infection striking Germany with a fever of apocalyptic expectation. At first, the demands of the peasants were reasonable enough, but now they have been stoked by Thomas Müntzer and his fiery visions. The spirit of Allstedt is spreading. Thousands have already succumbed. The swarm is building, letting off a continual buzz that reverberates in his ears. Already, the blood of those slaughtered seeps into the soil of Germany, and from the ground a cry rises to the heavens, demanding justice. If something is not done and fast, the state itself will become sick, and Müntzer will have created a beast he cannot possibly control, for when men yield to no authority, there is only one possible result: a sea of blood rising like the tide at midday, drowning all Germany in its depths.

I must go to where the disruption is, he thinks. *I must preach to them before it is too late—before all we are is broken.* It worked once before: he returned to Wittenberg and restored the people to their senses, only it was not he who did it at all. The Lord in his mercy allowed it to happen. How long can one depend upon the mercy of the Lord to save a people from themselves? He must hope there is still a chance.

As he looks out the window again, his spirit troubled by war and a woman, he thinks of the biblical Book of Amos, the lectures for which he has just published. One particular verse has always made him uneasy, and current events are painfully calling it to mind. He whispers into the silence: "If a trumpet is blown in a city will not the people tremble? If a calamity occurs in a city has not the Lord done it?"[7]

1 April 1525
Wittenberg, Electorate of Saxony

Philipp Melanchthon awakes far too soon. This night has been no kinder than those before it. Every hour without fail come the shrieks in the dark, the quickening of his pulse, bidding his muscles press against exhaustion, praying the sleep will be longer next time.

He takes his crying son in his arms and hastens the babe to his wife, who rouses herself to bare her breast, from which their son will struggle to drink. When the milk finally lets down and young Philipp receives the nourishment that will keep him alive at least an hour more—*Please, Lord! An hour more!*—Katharina's lids grow heavy. Then, in her weariness, her eyes fully close. She is passed into that other world: a place of dreams she has seldom visited of late. When the babe is finished, Philipp lifts him away, placing his son's head on his shoulder, holding him upright as he sleeps. They will remain this way for half an hour, father and son, praying that the milk stays down—a trick learned from the boy's Oma.

As the minutes pass, Philipp's spirit quakes. It is in these moments, when the world is still and he is alone with his thoughts, that the devil does his best work. Perhaps it is a delusion born of the darkness, but he feels emptied of hope, a creature of the night, his mind struggling to find its proper function, his pleas to heaven growing more desperate with each hour of sleep that is snatched from him, never to return.

He chides himself. *You lose hope because he will not sleep. You should simply be thankful he does not sleep eternally.* For he remembers what the midwife Maria told him shortly after Philipp's birth: the words are etched upon his soul. "The child lives, yes, but he is not out of danger." She cut a path through his heart, infusing it with terror.

---

[7] Amos 3:6.

"Children born early—they have problems, Doktor. Some struggle to walk, others to talk. Few live as long as one would hope, and fewer still have what you might call a normal life."

Since that moment, he has lived every day in fear, wondering when they will see the tell-tale signs of which Maria spoke. Young Philipp's continuing struggles to eat, his tiny size compared to other infants—everything seems a harbinger of woe. If he cannot keep milk down, he will not grow. If he does not sleep, he will not grow. They have been told as much by many observant women in town. So much depends on these brief hours of slumber, not the least of which being his ability to hope.

Lord, you know what we need. We are teetering on the brink of despair. Please, I beg you—allow our Philipp to sleep that we may do the same.

With greatest care, he lays his son in the old wooden cradle carved with flowers, a Krapp family heirloom. The babe remains asleep.

Oh, thank God! Thank God! His wife will have her rest. Perhaps he will even enjoy the same. It is a small victory in the ongoing conflict for their collective well-being.

Then a gurgling sound. Instantly, the entirety of what young Philipp has just consumed is expelled from his throat, soaking him in barely digested milk. He begins fussing, pushing against the cloths that swaddle him, rocking to the left and right. Now, as his father leans down to retrieve him from the cradle, the babe is wailing, his cries rising and falling in plaintive bursts. Katharina awakes with a start.

"What's wrong?! Is he alright?"

Despair filters through Philipp's body, seizing him with fearsome hands. *Lord, do you not see how much we need this?! Do you not see?!* But he bids himself be calm. *It is only the terror of the night. It is only the exhaustion breaking down your will.*

Working quickly by the light of the moon, he unwraps the cloths around Philipp's body, wipes off his little face, wraps him in a new set of cloths, and attempts to soothe him back to slumber, patting him rhythmically on the back. When a minute or two of this does not achieve the desired result, he turns back to his wife and says, "I think he is still hungry."

She inhales deeply, evidently attempting to steel herself. Again, little Philipp is placed on her breast. Again, he struggles to gain a proper latch. Katharina begins crying.

"I can't do it, Philipp! I can't do it!" she exclaims, sniffling heavily.

He places a hand on her shoulder, her skin cold to the touch. "Yes, you can! Look, he's drinking now. It's working."

"No, I can't do this—all of this! I can't be a mother, Philipp. I just can't. I'm hopeless! I can't do anything right."

"You are doing wonderfully," he insists.

"No, I'm not," she moans, her voice breaking into a wail even as she holds their suckling son in her arms.

Philipp embraces his wife, stroking her hair, attempting not to give way to tears himself.

"We had plenty of difficult moments with Anna, but we got through them," he says. "The Lord carried us through them. He will carry us again."

She shakes her head. "It's different this time, Philipp. It's so much harder."

In his heart, he knows her words to be true. Attempting to raise young Philipp has been far worse than anything they suffered with their first child. Everything about him seems fragile, as if the slightest error on their part might be the end of their son. Knowing his own physical difficulties—the meandering curve of his back, the continual bouts of insomnia—Philipp has wondered if he is somehow at fault: if he has passed along weakness to his son. *But what can I do? Can I stand in the place of God? It is he who kills and makes alive.* He must not worry about the future. He must consider only the moment in which he resides.

"It is harder than last time," he agrees. "But as I believe that the sun will soon rise, I believe that you are a good mother, Katharina Melanchthon. There is no woman on earth I would rather have raising my son. It will get better. Your mother is coming to help today. It will be alright. Please believe me: it will be alright."

She buries her face against his shoulder. Voice muffled, she says, "I don't know, Philipp. I just don't know."

"Well, I do," he assures her.

They cling to each other until their son quits suckling, overcome once again by sleep. Katharina burps him, then holds the boy upright against her shoulder.

"Let me take him," Philipp suggests.

"No, you need your sleep," she says, still a bit congested from the effort of weeping.

"Don't worry about me. I will hold him until he goes back down."

Too tired to put up much of a fight, Katharina hands the babe over and settles back onto her pillow for sleep. But Philipp has no intention of putting their son in the cradle: he is not willing to take that chance again. He will simply hold the boy upright until he wakes.

Philipp rises from the bed and exits the room, swaying back and forth, patting his son slowly. They move to the stairs and descend, weaving their way down to the ground floor. Bounce, pat, bounce, pat: he continues the rhythm as the stairs creak and groan beneath them.

You lied to her.

The thought strikes him suddenly. He is robbed of breath.

You don't know that everything will be alright. You know nothing at all.

He walks into the kitchen, holding young Philipp close, feeling the warmth of his little body—the gentle breathing of a babe in slumber.

You knew this would happen. Why did you think you could be a husband? Why did you think you could do any of this? Your work is suffering, just as you feared. And if this child should die, you will succumb to grief. It will break you.

They move back into the passage. Fatigued well past the point of pain, he rises to defend himself.

I was right to do it. How could I live without my Katharina? I did not know love before her—before these children. Not a love like this. It was God's will. It is God's will.

As he arrives in their sad excuse for a parlor, the taunting voice returns, only this time it targets a different sore spot.

You failed. Martin trusted the work to you, and you failed. No wonder he is distant from you. He is cutting you out.

Philipp can hold back the tears no longer. They fall silently down his cheeks. He knows it is a lie: Martin is not cutting him out. In any case, the work of reform does not truly belong to either of them—it is much bigger than that. But what of Erasmus' offer to carry on his work in Basel? Might it still stand? If something does go wrong between him and Martin, Philipp will need a place to go. *But we are nowhere near that. Surely, we are nowhere near that.*

The faintest hint of light is filtering through the windows: two facing the street and two on either side of the hearth. *Is it morning already?* Then as if in answer, the bells of St. Mary's sound one… two…three…four…five. Only an hour until Philipp's mother-in-law arrives to help. Thank God the semester has not yet started, or he would have to give lectures this morning!

His relief is interrupted by a knock at the front door. Not wishing to wake his son, Philipp manages to suppress a groan. *Who could be calling at this hour?!* As classes are not in session, it is probably not a pupil seeking correction of his Greek. Walking to the door, Philipp adjusts his son's position to avoid waking him, struggling mightily to defend the sleep granted to Katharina. He cracks the door open and finds Martin Luther standing there, lantern in hand.

Good Lord! Did he know I was thinking about him? No, that's impossible.

Martin opens his mouth to speak, but Philipp raises a finger to his lips to indicate silence, then opens the door fully to reveal the sleeping baby. His colleague nods in acknowledgment and whispers, "I thought you might be awake."

"Sadly, yes," Philipp whispers in return, "but what can be so urgent?"

"Do you mind if I come in?" Martin asks.

Philipp does mind—exceedingly—but it would be impolite to refuse. Therefore, he steps to the side and allows his colleague to enter.

"You can leave your flame there," Philipp whispers, indicating the place on the floor where they keep their own lantern. "Do you want something to drink?"

"No need," Martin mutters.

Without speaking another word, they move into the parlor, where the trestle table is still set up from the night before. They sit in two of the four chairs, and Philipp begins brushing some crumbs off the board in front of them.

"No need," his colleague repeats.

Leaning back in his seat, Philipp attempts to fully rouse himself. There is some light from the windows and lanterns, but much is still cloaked in shadow. Martin's face is partially obscured, but in his eyes is a reflective glow, as if the fire has entered his pupils.

"Count Albrecht has invited us to the opening of the new school in Mansfeld," Martin informs him.

Philipp bids his tired mind to process this information. Mansfeld is not just any Saxon town, but the home of Martin's forebears, who settled there to participate in the smelting business. Thus, Count Albrecht is well-known to Martin, whose interest in the school is a particular one.

"Very good," Philipp responds quietly. "When does it open?"

"In two weeks."

Philipp's eyes bulge. "Two weeks? I can't possibly make it in two weeks."

"Yes, you can," his colleague insists.

"No, I can't, and neither can you. It is the start of the semester. We can't miss that. Plus, I must help Katharina with the baby."

Although he can't quite make it out, Philipp suspects Martin frowns as he asks, "Can't her family help with the baby?"

Spoken like a man who doesn't have children, Philipp thinks. "Since we're talking about things that can and cannot be done," he retorts, "can't you go to Mansfeld alone?"

"No, Philipp!" Martin objects a bit more loudly than Philipp would prefer. "You are the one who is always talking about the importance of setting up these schools."

"I thought you agreed with me about that."

"Of course, I do, but this is your moment of triumph, not mine. It will only take a week. Your family will be fine."

Philipp feels a surge of anger ripple through his bones, the product of exhaustion as much as true offense. "Really? Can you speak for my family?"

"They made do without you last year," Martin argues.

"That was different."

"How?"

Philipp points to the baby in his arms, his face scrunched in annoyance. "Philipp wasn't born. It has been very difficult caring for him. You want to know why I'm holding him now? Because it is the only way he will sleep reliably. My poor wife is at the end of herself."

"It sounds as if you are at the end of yourself," Martin mutters softly.

"Then you know why I can't go," he argues. "I cannot tell my exhausted wife that I am abandoning her for a whole week." And in the dark of his mind, another thought: *What if Philipp were to die while I was away? I could never forgive myself.* But surely, his son will live longer than that. *He must. He will.*

Martin nods. "Your concern for them is admirable. Nevertheless, you must come. There is considerable sympathy for Müntzer in that region."

"And?"

"And we must go and make a show of strength to counter him."

Philipp hears footsteps in the hallway. Koch has evidently arisen for his morning chores, but he will have to wait for a greeting.

"We cannot respond to every crisis with our persons, Martin," Philipp argues. "At least, I cannot."

Martin sighs dramatically—overly so, in Philipp's opinion. "This is not just some minor crisis. It is a threat to all our work! Our enemies will throw us in the same boat with the radicals: they are already doing so."

"And I am happy to do what I can from my desk," he replies, his own frustration reaching a crescendo.

"Philipp, you must simply—"

"No!" he cries. "You always do this!"

"Always do what?" Martin demands to know.

Bully me, Philipp thinks, but elects for something less inflammatory. "You try to force me one way or another after I have already stated my opinion."

"I dare say you need someone to push you in the right direction from time to time."

Philipp grunts in displeasure. "I am not the only one who needs an occasional push."

"What is that supposed to mean?" Martin asks, scowling.

"When are you planning on replying to Erasmus?" he dares to inquire.

Martin sighs long and hard. "I will get to it when my time is free. I have been consumed by this business with Karlstadt and the other prophets of doom."

Philipp shakes his head bitterly, and in the weakness of his flesh and exhaustion of the moment, he longs to unleash a biting reply. *Why can't you see how important this is? Why do you treat him like a nothing? Or do you believe I am a nothing?*

Philipp's fuming is interrupted by a loud crash in the kitchen. They both look in the direction of the noise, but their view is hidden by the wall. Now the sound of dear Anna's voice rises in a loud cry that grips Philipp in the bowels. The image of his beloved daughter covered in blood flashes across his mind. He instinctively leaps from his seat, still holding the baby, and rushes into the next room, where he finds her lying on the floor with an overturned stool beside her. She is weeping and wailing, harnessing the full power of her lungs, filling the house with her lament.

"Anna! What are you doing down here?!" he cries.

It is the wrong question to ask first and reflects Philipp's own guilt as much as anything. *I should have known it was her. I should have gotten up to check.* He bends down to attend to his daughter, but realizes he has one too few hands to lift her. Then he hears the voice of Martin beside him.

"Give me the baby."

Philipp nods and places his son in Martin's waiting arms, then scoops his crying daughter off the floor. She clings to him, covering his shirt in her tears.

"Are you hurt, Anna?! Can you tell me if it hurts?!" Philipp inquires desperately.

She is too upset to respond. He presses lightly on each of her limbs to discern if it increases her distress. *Why is she down here?* She must have left her bed and walked past his sleeping wife, then descended the stairs and entered the kitchen. There, she got it in mind to reach something and tried to use the stool as mama always does, leading to this disaster. He can find no obvious injury to her body. Her tears are letting up slightly.

"Papa," Anna whimpers.

"Yes, love. Does it hurt?"

"Where Philipp?" she asks, her nose completely stuffed.

Where is Philipp? he translates. He turns to see that Martin has departed along with his son.

"He is with Doktor Luther," Philipp replies, patting her back softly. "Anna, it is still very early. You should not be downstairs."

She sniffles once and then again, rubbing his beard, her spirit growing calmer.

"Papa!"

"Yes?"

"Is Oma coming?"

"Yes. She will be here soon. Come—let's go see Doktor Luther."

"Doktor Luther," she repeats, pronouncing the words deliberately, evidently enjoying the way they sound.

Father and daughter arrive in the parlor to find Martin cradling young Philipp in his arms and gazing at him peacefully—lovingly. Philipp has seen Martin hold many little ones this way: every woman in town wishes to have her child blessed by the famous Doktor Luther, and of course Martin dotes on all the Cranach offspring. Somehow it does Philipp good to know that the man who can be savage in print can also show such compassion to the most vulnerable. *He might have been a great father,* Philipp muses.

"He is awake," his colleague concludes, looking up at them, "but he does not fuss. He is staring at me—probably working out whether he should be afraid of me or not."

"Hello, Doktor," Anna says rather impressively for one so young.

"Hello, young Anna," Martin replies quietly, nodding his head. "Do you share your father's aversion to sleep?"

Her brow wrinkles. She is evidently attempting to work out the meaning of 'aversion.'

"Your papa is a very good papa," Martin informs her. "I always knew he would be, even though he denied it."

Such praise ought to cheer Philipp, but he finds himself thinking, *How good can I be? I cannot by my own power add a single day to my son's life. I cannot cause him to walk. I have nothing to give.*

With a sigh, Philipp sets Anna on the floor and holds out his arms. "I can take the baby again."

"But we were just getting to know each other!" Martin objects, holding out a finger for young Philipp to grip.

Anna moves to the small chest in the corner and opens it to retrieve two dolls of straw that her mother made for her. As she sits down to play with them, Philipp takes a seat as well—closes his eyes and exhales. *What a night it has been! What a day it is already turning out to be!*

"I will respond to Erasmus—you have my word," Martin says, prompting Philipp to open his eyes. "The matter requires great care. That is why I have not rushed it. I must wait for the right moment when I am not troubled by other things."

"Does such a moment exist?" Philipp asks knowingly. "For myself, I find no such peace. Sometimes I think there is more of hell on earth than heaven."

Martin nods thoughtfully. "I understand if you cannot come to Mansfeld, but at least check to see if it might be possible. I would love for you to meet my family."

"They were at our wedding," Philipp reminds him, "though I suppose I was too busy to speak with them properly."

"You have not met the Ludhers until you have met them in their native land," Martin assures him, chuckling at the thought.[8]

That does sound entertaining, Philipp thinks. *God only knows from what kind of roots this tree of fire is sprung.*

Now young Philipp begins pressing his face against Martin's chest, rooting back and forth amid muffled grunts.

"Oh. Oh dear," Martin mutters. "Does he think I'm his mama?"

"I'm afraid so. I suppose I will have to wake Katharina after all." Philipp shakes his head, pained by the thought of it. "I so wanted her to rest. Night after night, I beg God to grant us a bit more sleep, but—"

He cannot continue. He closes his eyes, inhaling deeply. *Lord, I long to see your goodness. Let me know you are there.*

"Have you spoken to Bugenhagen?" Martin inquires.

Philipp looks at his colleague, who is staring back at him, eyes full of concern.

"If not," Martin continues, "I would recommend that you do."

"For absolution?"

"Well, that too, but he and Walpurga had a difficult time with their little one. They might know something for you to try, or perhaps there is someone in the congregation who can help you for a time."

---

[8] Ludher was the original family surname. Martin changed his surname around the time of the indulgence controversy, a common practice among scholars of that era.

Philipp nods in gratitude. "Thank you. That's a good idea."

Martin hands little Philipp back to his namesake and rises to depart. "Let me know if you will be coming to Mansfeld." With that, he retrieves his lantern and exits the house, leaving Philipp standing there with his son in his arms as the door closes.

I suppose I should be glad that he wants me to come, though I doubt it is for the personal benefit of my company, he thinks.

The light is pouring through the windows now. He can clearly see little Philipp's face: his tiny eyes staring back, lips slightly parted, nose crinkled.

"I love you, son," he whispers, "even if things are difficult now—I love you."

Then a thought like lightning strikes his soul: words he has long known, but which have taken on a new and fearsome resonance. *Take now your son, your only son, whom you love...*

In a time long before stories were written, the Lord appeared to Abraham and commanded him to offer his only son as a sacrifice—this despite the prohibition against murder and God's promise that Isaac would be the father of a great nation. *What must have entered Abraham's mind as he traveled to Moriah, questioning all he knew of God and his goodness?* It was not the loss of his son that provoked Abraham's greatest horror, nor even the denial of the promised inheritance, but the loss of his faith: the annihilation of his being, the suffocating grip of non-existence. For it was not merely Isaac whom he would put to death on that hill, but his faith itself.

There at the end of his hope and the destruction of all he was, Abraham clung to a single word: a word that Philipp now whispers.

"Resurrection."

A concept unknown to man! A reversal of all that had been! Yet, this was all that remained of Abraham's beliefs—that the God who called him to destroy the promise was also a God who could raise the dead. So, he mounted the hill in fear and trembling, placed his son on the altar, and raised the knife to slay.

As Philipp stands holding his namesake in his arms, he wonders if God will ever make such a request of him. *And if he does, will I pass the test?*

10 April 1525
Basel, Swiss Confederation

Erasmus of Rotterdam stands upon a great height, the wind beating against his face, a pang in his stomach as he looks down, down, down to the cobbled yard below. He is perched at the summit of Basel's cathedral, nested in one of the twin towers upon its west front, but the fearlessness of birds is not gifted to him—he was not made to dwell among the gods. He moves back from the obscenely low rail, wondering how Bishop Christoph convinced him to climb the endless stair and stand at this perilous height. No, not a climb: he crawled up the narrow steps, clinging to the rope with white knuckles as if it were the thread of Fate herself. Thrice, he thought himself a dead man, and that was only the beginning! He must still endure the descent. But who could endure it?

What possessed them to build such a thing?!

The bishop begged leave to remain below on account of his age and infirmity, but now Erasmus sees the truth: it was fear of the fall that kept Christoph from climbing.

"Look—There is Froben's house! Hello, 'Old Faithful'!"

No, Erasmus is not alone. He has been accompanied on the ascent by Jan Łaski, a Polish priest and diplomat who has recently taken up residence with the Frobens. Although their relationship started poorly, Erasmus has come to accept the Pole's odd jokes and quick temper in exchange for his undying loyalty and firm friendship.

"Why do you stand so far away?" Łaski inquires. "Come and look!"

"No, thank you," Erasmus begs, leaning against the tower's exterior—clinging to the illusion of control. "I can see well enough from here."

Łaski bends well over the rail, peering down at the passersby. *You fool! Don't blame me when you fall over,* Erasmus thinks, but finds himself too petrified to speak.

"Cholera!"[9] Łaski exclaims. "There is the fishmonger who sold me those rotten herring! Ej! Ej! Spójrz na mnie!" Straightening up, he asks, "Do you have anything we can drop on him?"

---

[9] In addition to being a terrible disease, this is a common exclamation in Polish.

Erasmus' mouth opens slightly and his brow furrows as he grasps for something approximating an appropriate response. *I thought the Poles were a reasonable bunch!* He finally offers an indignant, "No."

"Cholera! Pity, that. Come, let's have a look from the other side!"

Łaski rushes off to view the Rhine, while Erasmus remains with his back pressed against the rows of red stone, looking not at the city below but the hills far beyond. Their curves rise softly from the green earth, as if a giant had laid himself down to sleep. Somewhere beyond are the Alps, hidden beneath the gray haze. Was it the giants that carved them out, dragging their feet to form the mountain passes? No, he thinks not: it was the pressing of earth against earth. Century after century, the stone beneath them fracturing, sending tremors through the ground, pressing upward into jagged peaks. It must have been a time long ago, before the grass grew and the river took its course, or perhaps it was that ultimate rending of the earth: the bursting of the watery caverns of the deep.

The beauty that captures him is therefore a relic of a strange and violent age—an hour of calamity that swept away humanity in the torrent. He remembers the words of God to the prophet Haggai: "Once more in a little while, I am going to shake the heavens and the earth, the sea also and the dry land."[10] Was that a promise or a threat? Erasmus felt the shaking of the ground during his time in Italy. *What if it were to happen now, while I am standing atop a tower likely to crumble?* Once again, he is thinking about the fall.

"Przyjaciel! Come and see!" Łaski calls from around the corner.

Erasmus sighs and makes his way ever so cautiously to the tower's eastern end, always keeping a safe distance from the rail—but there is no safe distance from the fall. *Kyrie eléison. Christe eléison.* He looks down on the cross-shaped roof crowning the cathedral, its many-colored tiles dazzling in the midday sun.

"There is the cloister," Łaski says, pointing, "and there is old Bishop Christoph's house!"

"Charming," Erasmus mutters, still unwilling to approach the edge.

"Do not tell me you are scared of heights, my dear Erasmus!" his friend chides playfully.

---

[10] Haggai 2:6.

He scoffs loudly. "Of course, I am scared of heights! It is a natural instinct of man. We are helpless against the pull of the earth. Every man fears the fall."

"I should think it is more the landing that creates concern," Łaski quips.

"Ha! The landing is instant death. It is the fall that fills one with terror."

Łaski strokes his beard thoughtfully, staring off toward the East. Though in holy orders, he has not practiced his trade for some time and is clothed as one would expect for a Polish noble: a tall, rounded cap with a single feather; a short-sleeved, fur-lined outer cloak; and beneath, a red tunic and shoes with curled toes. The shoes as much as anything make him appear exceedingly foreign.

"There is the precious river, carrying water to the Germans," Łaski mutters.

Erasmus dares to step closer. "It will be filled with blood ere it reaches the sea," he murmurs, thinking very much of the ongoing rebellion that is sweeping through the lands to the north.

"Are things that bad?" Łaski asks, his voice hushed. "One hears the most fearsome reports, but who would dare believe them?"

Erasmus laughs softly—ruefully. "That is the thing about terrible news. It has a way of forcing itself on you whether you believe it or not. Do you wish to see something fearsome? Watch a man collide with the truth."

His companion offers no reaction to these words but continues to stare into the distance. "They say Bavaria is caught up in it as well as the Rhineland, and the rebels will soon be in Thuringia. A preacher leads them: a man of fire."

"Thomas Müntzer," he confirms, his voice filled with disgust. "My spies have little to tell me about him except that he spent some time in Wittenberg before he became a preacher."

"He is no Lutheran!" Łaski objects. "The Lutherans do not seek the overthrow of government."

Erasmus looks at his companion long and hard, attempting to pry into the recesses of his thoughts—the bottomless pit of his desires. Although Łaski was a committed Romanist when he arrived in Basel, Erasmus has begun to suspect the Pole of having more sectarian sympathies. Łaski has spoken more than once with Œcolampadius, and Erasmus could not help but notice a letter from Ulrich Zwingli among Łaski's things. *Quite a turnaround for a man who once blamed the Germans for robbing him blind!* Of course, Erasmus has also corresponded with Zwingli, so perhaps there is nothing to worry about in Łaski's change of tune. He may simply be learning to live among the Germans,[11] even as Erasmus has been forced to do. But given the number of friendships lost in recent years—No, it is better not to think of it. *I must trust someone. What choice do I have? I must have some faith in my fellow man.*

"How I wish it would simply end!" the Pole exclaims. "Do you think it might end soon? After all, these rebellions rarely last long."

Erasmus gazes at the winding river, its waters shimmering in the midday sun, and remembers how close he came to death only a few months previous: the unspeakable pain he felt attempting to pass his latest stone. More than that, he remembers a dream that terrified him—the burning, the fall. Now, Erasmus feels a sharp pain in his chest: he inhales with great effort.

"The peasants will be beaten, sure enough," he concludes. "Their corpses will rot in the fields. But that will not be the end, for Pandora has opened the box, and who on earth knows if the hope that remains is false?[12] When every man is a lord unto himself, it will be an end indeed: the ending of Christendom! Today they deny that Christ is in the Lord's Supper. They reject the baptism of children and the veneration of the saints. Tomorrow, they deny God himself. Mark my words! How long until men decide there is no need for the sacraments at all? They have already dispensed with most of them. How long until they see no need to attend Mass when they can sit at home with the Scriptures and interpret them as they like? For every man will have a Bible someday: we've made sure of that. Why bother with the Church and its teachings? Why bother with God when you control it all? It is a sad day when any man with a pen becomes a god

---

[11] Erasmus tended to refer to anyone whose first language was German or who lived in German-speaking regions as a "German," whether or not they lived within the borders of the modern state of Germany or the former kingdom of the same name.

[12] In Greek mythology, Pandora opens a box holding a variety of evils, all of which are unleashed upon the world. The only thing remaining in the box is hope, which depending on one's interpretation is either a blessing or a curse.

on earth and every fool with a book thinks himself infallible. It will be the ending of society. War will give way to war. Men will worship their own flesh and seek consolation in their coin, though both will soon be destroyed."

Łaski swallows hard, his features as strained as Erasmus' were after approaching the rail. "You really think it will be that bad?"

He sighs, shaking his head. "Not tomorrow, perhaps, but someday, unless these new prophets are shown for what they are: men of straw with feet of clay. It is utterly unfair. Men lend their ears to fools, while the words of the wise are scorned. The more education a man has, the more he is mistrusted. Yes, there will be an end, but not the kind you seek."

A new gust of wind catches Łaski's coat and offends Erasmus' sense of balance. For the smallest fraction of time—no more than the blink of an eye—Erasmus feels as if he will fall. It is only a passing thing: a single breath of fear. Even so, the peasant uprising is likely to pass as quickly as all rebellions before it, but another will come after it, and then another and another. Each breath leads Erasmus closer to the final hour. In the end, no man can escape the fall.

He is there again in his mind's eye: wrapped in the talons of the foul beast, plummeting with a reckless fury, consumed by the darkness as much as the heat. The memory of fear lies deep within his breast. He cannot escape it by any power in his possession.

"I know how the end will come!" Łaski suddenly declares. "It is written in the second epistle of Peter: 'But the day of the Lord will come like a thief, in which the heavens will pass away with a roar and the elements will be destroyed with intense heat, and the earth and its works will be burned up.'[13] The first time with water, the second with fire. Oh, that I might be found righteous on that day!"

Erasmus does not respond. He is far too deep in thought. The roar! The heat! "*But by His word the present heavens and earth are being reserved for fire, kept for the Day of Judgment and destruction of ungodly men.*"[14] He can scarcely believe it, and yet there it is before his mind's eye: an endless space of charred earth still licked by the fires that continually burn, the whole of human history turned to charcoal,

[13] 2 Peter 3:10.

[14] 2 Peter 3:7.

the last of man put to death. There he wanders like a vagrant, the lone remnant chosen of God, but not for salvation. It is his curse to live on—to dwell forever in this place of the dead. The waters are tainted, the mountains laid low. The air smells of sulfur, deadly to the touch. Ash! Eternal, suffocating ash!

"Are you well, Erasmus?" Łaski asks. "I hope I have not troubled you by speaking of these things."

"What, of the inevitable destruction of the entire world in a firestorm of wrath?" He scoffs for effect. "Why should such things trouble me?"

"I do not yet know you well," Łaski admits. "I cannot always tell when you are joking. You are the first Dutchman I have met."

"And by the mercy of God, perhaps I will be the last!" he chuckles.

"But you are well, Erasmus—right? You would tell me if something were wrong."

I would not tell anybody if something were wrong, he thinks, but chooses instead to say, "If anything is wrong, Pan Jan, you will be the first to know!"

Łaski's eyes are alight—he smiles broadly. "You are learning our language, Herr Erasmus!"

"I would not go so far as to say that. In fact, 'pan' is the only word of your tongue that I can reasonably pronounce."

"It is better than I can do with Dutch."

Erasmus grins knowingly. "You will have no need of that tongue around me, Pan Jan. I am well rid of the land of my birth."

"Bad memories, eh?"

He stares out into the distance, his heart knotted within him. "Something like that."

As Erasmus gazes upon the beginnings of the Black Forest, he thinks of the bands of peasants marching across the fields, of the French king kept in a Spanish prison, of Luther taking up his pen to write a reply that will shred Erasmus' flesh with pointed teeth. And then last of all, he thinks of a night at the monastery in Steyn: a night when he dared to trust and learned he could depend on neither man nor God. He thinks of the icy waters taking hold of him. He hears a voice upon the wind.

God loves you, Brother Erasmus! God loves you!

For a moment, he savors it: the prospect of love. He imagines what it would be like to trust it fully, feeling the sweet release, knowing himself called by God's name. But there is no release and no comfort in his bones. Another voice has taken precedent. As he watches the waters of the Rhine following their appointed course, he is captured by a phrase that perfectly expresses the absurdities of fortune in an age when the earth is shaken and the world changed: *The river runs backward.*

12 April 1525
Wittenberg, Electorate of Saxony

Martin Luther stands before the main entrance to the Cranach home, its double doors a brilliant shade of yellow, the lintel above decorated with painted vines and fruits. He has put off this visit for weeks, but now shame, sharp and bitter, has forced him to the door. He must speak with Katharina von Bora and convince her to marry Dr. Kaspar Glatz. A delicate matter under any circumstance, but he is still shaken by the alternative she proposed to Amsdorf: that she would marry one of them instead.

Her odd declaration induced such discomfort in him that he has been hesitant to address the matter. When preaching from the pulpit, he has avoided meeting her eyes. When passing her in the street, he has found something else to occupy his attention. He is a coward, no doubt, but the whole business disturbs him profoundly. Now, as he stares at the brass knocker in front of him, a voice in his head asks a question that has been gnawing at his soul: *What are you afraid of?*

He sighs and whispers, "I don't know," taking the knocker in hand and pounding it twice.

The knob turns—the door swings inward. He inhales swiftly, pulse quickening. It is the matriarch of the house, Barbara Cranach, who answers, a great relief as it means he will have a bit more time to prepare himself for a difficult discussion.

"Herr Doktor! We did not expect you. Come in!" she says.

When he has crossed the threshold and entered the foyer with its white and black tile floor and grand marble staircase, his hostess inquires, "Have you come to see Lucas?"

"No," he responds quickly, removing his cap and turning it over in his hands. "I must speak with Fräulein von Bora."

His mouth seems to burn after speaking her name. The mere pronunciation of the syllables has committed him to a path he would rather not take. *I am in control,* he reminds himself. *I can do this. I have done things infinitely more difficult than this. It is not as if there is any danger to my person.*

Barbara nods and offers, "I will call her for you."

"Wait!" he requests.

She moves a step closer to him. "Yes? What is it?"

He continues fumbling with his cap, shuffling it in a circle with his fingers. "I know you have said before that I should be willing to address her directly, and that is true, but what I have to discuss is a sensitive manner, and I must insist that there be another woman present."

"I think that is a good idea," Barbara says, nodding eagerly. The emphatic nature of her statement is a shock to Martin's bones, for the woman seems to know more than she is letting on—perhaps even more than he knows about the situation.

Did Katharina tell her what she told Amsdorf? he wonders. *I don't like it. I don't like it all.*

"Let us walk together," Barbara concludes, leading him up the stairs and into the very hall where they enjoyed their Christmas feast a few months prior. She directs Martin to the pair of chairs by the hearth, in which he has so often sat with her husband, taking his ease in their cushioned depths. As he lowers himself into one of them, she pulls another chair over from the dining table and sets it across from the others. Then with a smile, she walks over to the kitchen door and cries, "Käthe! Visitor!" He stares down at his hands as Barbara takes the seat beside him, straightening her skirt and folding her hands in her lap.

"We will just wait for her then," she concludes.

He nods but says nothing. *Remember why you are here,* he urges himself. *A woman is in danger. You must convince her to marry Glatz. It is the only thing that will keep her from an awful fate.* Again and again, he repeats these words to himself, impressing them upon his will, strengthening his resolve to do what must be done.

Now Katharina von Bora enters the brightly painted room with its marble columns, brushing some flour off what appears to be a new gown. She had always worn the same one before—a donation from a sympathetic Wittenberger—but now it seems the Cranachs have paid for a better one in a dark brown shade. He is amazed that he can make this observation, as he gives little thought to clothes. Katharina locks eyes with him and pauses mid-step, the shock written on her face.

"Doktor Luther," she says quietly, bowing her head. "Frau Cranach did not tell me it was you."

"Come, sit across from us," Barbara instructs, motioning to the open chair.

Katharina approaches tentatively, looking at each of them in turn before planting herself in the seat. Martin finds himself very affected upon seeing her again. *It is true what Glatz said,* he thinks. *She is a fine woman—clever, resourceful.* But there is also fear within him, great and terrible. He reaches a conclusion. *I must not let her starve on the street. I must find a way to convince her.* His eyes trace the edges of her face. He remembers the first time he saw her, clothed in a garment meant for a woman twice her size, for in those days, she was extremely gaunt. She looks much healthier now. Her whole aspect seems better. *I cannot let her go back to that again.*

"Doktor, do you wish to start?" Barbara asks.

He realizes he has been staring rather than talking—not that he truly knows what to say or how to begin. Nevertheless, he must try.

"Good day, Fräulein von Bora," he offers. "How have you been?"

"Alright," she replies. "And you?"

"Well enough."

Katharina nods, and they fall silent. *That will not do,* Martin chides himself. He takes a deep breath—proceeds into more dangerous territory.

"You can have no doubt why I've come."

"Is this about what I said to Doktor Amsdorf?" Katharina asks. Her voice is soft, but confident.

"Yes," he confirms. "He said you are unwilling to marry Doktor Glatz. Is that correct?"

"Yes," Katharina answers, once again firm but properly respectful.

Swallowing hard, he continues. "He also said you told him something which I must admit I found rather extraordinary, so much so that I would like to hear it confirmed from your lips to avoid any misunderstanding."

Now Katharina's eyes dart to the floor. Her hands are folded in her lap—she rubs her thumbs one against the other. "If he told you I offered to marry one of you, then it was correct."

He breathes deeply, absorbing the force of her answer. He had been clinging to the possibility that he had misunderstood, for it would make the whole business easier. Now he must proceed onto even more treacherous ground. It will be almost impossible to prevent her from being harmed—from a disappointment that will crush her spirit.

"Did you really say that, Käthe?" Barbara asks before he can respond.

Katharina nods, eyes filled with sadness. Martin thinks she looks a bit embarrassed: her cheeks are suspiciously pink. He does not wish to press, but he must do so. She must understand the way things are. To leave her in doubt would be cruel.

"May I ask why you said this?" Martin inquires.

"Because it is the truth," Katharina answers quietly. "And as I am certain you believe me a fool for refusing Doktor Glatz, I thought I would make clear that I am willing to marry." A short pause—her breathe comes quickly. She whispers, "And as our Lord said, 'You do not have, because you do not ask.'"

As she speaks these words, she stares directly into his eyes, and he sees something there that terrifies him: desire. *I am asking you, Doktor Luther*, she seems to say. *I seek to have you for my own.* How he longs to look away! He feels as if she is gazing straight through him—no, straight into him. Her twin irises are great whirlpools threatening to draw him in, appealing soul to soul. His very sense of balance is offended. *I must put an end to this now,* he tells himself. He clears his throat—coughs once, then again. His bowels are knotted, but his resolve is firm.

"Well, I am sorry to tell you this, Fräulein, but neither Doktor Amsdorf nor I have any intention of marrying," he informs her. "It is Doktor Glatz who has made the offer."

Katharina nods her head, casting her eyes downward. She sniffs slightly, closing her eyes. *It is as I suspected,* he laments. *She is feeling ashamed. She is hurt.*

"Are you alright, Käthe?" Barbara asks, leaning toward her.

When Katharina does not answer, he continues, "I am sorry for any disappointment this has caused, but I assure you, Doktor Glatz will be a good husband, far better than either Nikolaus or I could be. He is closer to you in age and less caught up in the disputes of the hour. He has more money. He will take excellent care of you."

Katharina shakes her head grimly as Barbara reaches over and hands her a kerchief. He is sorry to see her in this state, but thinks, *At least I have things under control now. At least the worst is over.* The younger woman wipes her eyes and inhales deeply, then looks at him with real determination.

"I am sorry, Doktor Luther, if I upset you with my comment, which must have seemed highly presumptuous," Katharina explains. "I accept your answer and will not speak of the matter again. But this you must know without any doubt: I will never marry Kaspar Glatz."

What frustration fills him to see her sitting there, having suffered a wound to her pride but still seeking to impose her will! She looks at him not in weakness, but strength, refusing to be intimidated, unwilling to look away. Well, he has not come to intimidate her, but he must persuade her, or else she will be in grave danger. His mind fills with images of her: visions of possible futures.

She is alone in an alley clothed in rags, curled up in a ball, trembling in the winter cold. She is standing outside a house such as they used to have in Wittenberg, her hair limp and exposed, waiting for some man to purchase her form. She is lying dead in a field, having fallen at last in exhaustion, with no one to find her—no one to comfort her. *No!* he swears to himself. *No, it must not be.*

"I did not want to have to do this, Fräulein. Must I tell you what awaits if you take this path?" he asks.

Katharina breathes solemnly, her eyes cutting into him—refusing to surrender an inch. "I am perfectly aware what awaits me if I 'take this path,' as you say, Doktor. If you knew me better, you would understand that." A brief pause. She inhales again and speaks with conviction. "But perhaps you do not wish to know me."

Do you think me heartless?! he cries internally. Her apparent implication causes his spirit to combust. He has it in mind to chide her—to defend himself—but Barbara anticipates him and instructs, "Käthe, tell the Doktor what you told me."

Now Katharina looks at Barbara with fearful eyes, her determination a thing of the past. *Something is happening, but I cannot think what,* Martin reasons.

"It is alright," Barbara assures her. "Tell him your story. He will listen. He will understand."

Katharina looks at him with a piercing gaze, studying the features of his face, seemingly attempting to judge the truth of Barbara's statement. He feels a tightening of his chest muscles. At length, Katharina seems to reach a conclusion and says, "Very well, but I will only proceed if the Doktor desires to hear it."

Both women stare at Martin. He wishes he could melt into the floor or shrink down to nothingness—anything to escape such an awkward situation. But there will be no running away from this. Uncertain what awaits him, but knowing it would be rude to refuse, he responds, "Yes, of course. Whatever you wish to share, please share it."

Something in Katharina softens. She closes her eyes, breathes deeply, and whispers, "I remember the smell."

"The smell?" he asks, thoroughly confused.

"Yes," she replies with a nod. "The smell of fir branches freshly cut. My mother would bring them into the house for Christmas. We didn't have much money, but we had the trees from which we received our name.[15] She would hold me in her arms by the fireside, whispering words of love in my ear, while my father wrestled with my brothers. I remember the sound of her voice—the color of her hair, just like mine.

"I remember the sound of weeping when she died—when she was taken from us. My father wept so! I had never heard such a sound before. I remember the failed harvest: the plants wilted and brown, dry to the touch. The pangs! The deep ache of hunger, day after day. My father didn't know how to live alone. That is, he had us, but he was alone. So, he married the only woman who would have him: a widow with no dowry and children of her own. They knew nothing about money. What little we had, she demanded. And as for me, she barely knew me. So, it was easy, you see. It was easy to send me away.

---

[15] "*Bor*" is the German word for a fir tree and the root of the surname Bora.

"My father took me in the cart. 'Here you will learn,' he assured me. 'They will teach you to read German and Latin.' But I didn't care about that then—I wanted my home. It was raining when we said farewell. Not a long farewell, mind you: a swift kiss on the cheek. He drove away quickly so I wouldn't see him cry, but I was crying. Yes, I was trembling. I was six years old, unable to spell my own name. I never saw any of them again."

His heart is pained as he hears this description. He might have guessed at some of the details, but he sees now how much the loss of her family still haunts her. "I tried writing to them, as you know," he says quietly. "I received a reply."

Katharina nods. "Yes, from my brother, though not the kind one—not Hans. From him I have never heard a thing. A pity, for he had the most of my mother in him."

"Did they write to you at school?" Barbara asks, her voice tender.

"Once a year for three years, then year four another letter came from the abbess in Nimbschen," Katharina explains. "I was no longer to live among my friends in Brehna, receiving a good education. During my absence, the family had sunk even lower. My father turned to drink to remove his pain. Thirty groschen was all that was left.[16] Insufficient for Brehna, but just enough to earn me a place among the Cistercians. They don't believe in luxury, as you well know, Doktor. It doesn't take much to feed a Cistercian. And so, at age ten, I was sent to the cloister for thirty pieces of silver. I never heard from my father again."

As Martin listens to the words pour out of her, it seems to him a lament of the ages, as if he is hearing in her voice the sound of thousands of women crying out as one. It is so different from his own experience: entering the monastery in a burst of religious passion,

---

[16] It is difficult to determine the relative value of this amount, as coins in the Holy Roman Empire were variable depending on the region. However, if we are to take this "groschen" as a *Kaiser-Groschen* (also known as a *Schilling*), then it was worth 5% of a *Guldengroschen* (also known as a *Gulden* or *Guilder*). Dr. Luther's salary at the time was 100 *Guldengroschen* per year, so the amount paid for Katharina's entrance into nunnery at Nimbschen was equivalent to 1.5% of Luther's annual salary. If thirty Guldengroschen were paid for her entrance, then it would still only amount to 30% of Luther's annual salary, a pittance for the lifetime expenses of a noble woman.

going against the wishes of his family. For Katharina, it was exactly the opposite. He feels a fierce anger for what she has suffered.

"Even so, do noblemen dispose of their daughters, though there is nothing noble about it," he comments grimly. "From here, your story is familiar to me, I think."

"The common details, perhaps," she replies with a nod, "but there is more, Doktor. You cannot know it until you have felt it. I have said the Cistercians don't believe in luxury. I should have said they don't believe in colors."

He shakes his head slightly in confusion. "Colors?"

"Yes," Katharina explains. "The buildings were built of dark rock, or else of mud and straw. They were full of shadows inside, for windows were expensive, and plaster was viewed as an extravagance. I remember the first day I arrived, I asked the sister who was leading me, 'Why aren't there any pictures?' The school in Brehna was full of them, you see. There was a cross in every room—tales of saints and biblical heroes. I felt they were my friends, always there to comfort me. But it is not the Cistercian way: everything must be plain. Colors are a distraction from contemplation. There was only clear glass in the church. I remember thinking, 'How can this sad place become my home?' The roofs would leak with every rain. It was so cold in the winter. How the wind would howl against the walls! We had no proper bedding and no fires in our rooms." Here she seems to shudder reflexively, as if the cold is still with her. "Two of my aunts were there: my father's sister, Magadalene, and the abbess, Mother Margarethe, relative of my mother."

"Was that a comfort at least, to have family with you?" he inquires, attempting to find any ray of light in her dark tale.

Katharina closes her eyes as if in pain, shaking her head. Then opening them again, she speaks, her voice catching in her throat. "Oh, that it might have been, Doktor! But my father was the failure of the family, you see. They knew how little he had paid to place me there: quite an embarrassment to donate one's daughter on the cheap. As for the abbess, she had never forgiven my mother for marrying a man who brought the family low. They saw in me a chance for redemption—that is, I could redeem myself from the failures of my parents. It was a great burden for one so young. Mother Margarethe had many troubles. I came just after the inspection. The whole place was subject to—"

"The brothers of Pforza. Yes, I remember," he inserts reflexively. "It was Abbot Baltzar at the time, no?"

Katharina smiles ever so slightly. "See, you do know something about me after all." He feels his mood lighten, until he recalls the somber nature of what they are discussing. *Guard yourself, Martin,* he implores.

"Yes, Abbot Baltzar was the one who visited Nimbschen and found it not to his liking," she continues. "The nuns were not chanting well enough. They were failing to remain properly silent—for of course, we could not speak most of the time. We had to sign words with our hands. The abbot especially reminded my aunt of the requirement of poverty. He would walk past their tables at supper time and watch them eat. Afterward, he would line them up and place his fingers around each sister's wrist, like so"—here she demonstrates for him—"and if he could not cover one nail with the other, he would slap the wrist"—here she demonstrates again, a sharp sound that seems to reverberate down his spine—"and berate them for falling into the sin of gluttony. He would call to their minds the holy Anna. You know the one. 'Leave me not,' they called her in Augsburg, but among ourselves we called her the 'holy skeleton.'"

"Yes, I met her once," Martin recalls ruefully. "They claimed she hadn't eaten in twelve years. Even then, at a time when I was most fervently devoted to Rome, I doubted the tale."

Katharina crinkles her nose in disgust. "Oh, she was a fraud and no mistake![17] On account of her lie, we were meant to feel gluttonous for having a small piece of fish. It put terrible pressure on Mother Margarethe. She could do nothing against the will of the abbot. Then there were the gatekeepers."

"The gatekeepers?" Barbara inquires, leaning forward.

Katharina nods. "Yes, monks of Pforza. Two of them there were—always two. They held the keys to our buildings. Day and night, they watched us, reporting back to Pforza. We were never allowed

---

[17] See, for example, Lyndal Roper's assessment on page 53 of her book *Martin Luther: Renegade and Prophet*: "[Anna] was unmasked…by the duchess of Bavaria, who discovered her secret stash of luxury food, such as pepper cakes and pears; it turned out that she emptied her stools out of the window." (Random House, 2018 trade paperback edition)

out, of course. The whole property was surrounded by a ditch on one side and a wall on the other, and we were far from the nearest village. Very few pilgrims would visit, and even the ones who did could not walk among us, for we were kept behind a screen. There were people who worked the land, of course, but we saw very little of them. The gatekeepers would say we were 'precious treasures to be guarded from harm,' but they should have said we were prisoners to be kept from escaping. Naturally, I was miserable when I first arrived. I hated being woken in the middle of the night to say the prayers. I hated the hunger, the silence, the loneliness. I was the youngest person there until Ave came. I was so afraid of the gatekeepers. Every day, after I had eaten, I would go to the toilets and vomit."

This revelation pierces something within Martin. "What?" he stammers.

Katharina shrugs, her eyes growing moist again. "I knew they would be lining us up again—placing their fingers around our wrists. Gluttons go to hell, you know. My abbess didn't like it when I refused to eat, so I learned how to do it from one of the older sisters." Here she motions with her fingers as if to shove them in her mouth. "At least half of us did it. I would have kept at it were it not for Sister Magdalene."

A sudden tremor races through his breast at the mention of this name. *Staupitz.* He is alight with memory. It has been a very long time since he remembered the ostensible reason for his visit to the Cranach House, so rapt is his attention.

"Do you mean Magdalene von Staupitz?" Martin asks, referencing one of the nuns who escaped with Katharina.

She nods. "Yes, Sister Magdalene. If it hadn't been for her, I probably would have done myself an injury. I was that unhappy. She helped me see that there was value in that life—that I could learn about God and grow in love for him. She made me believe that God loved me, even if it felt like no one else did. She was like a mother to me more surely than the Mother Superior. Did you know we are related?"

"What—by blood?" he inquires, shock setting in. After all, Magdalene von Staupitz is the sister of the late Johann von Staupitz, the man to whom he owes so much, whom he considered a second father, and who pulled him out of the depths of despair before ultimately abandoning him.

"Yes. We are some sort of cousins," Katharina explains. "Knightly families tend to be closely connected."

He cannot think what to say in response. It is a strange coincidence that Katharina should have a connection with that family even as he does. Stranger still, her connection is even stronger, for it is bound in blood. The way she sits there talking of Sister Magdalene: he has spoken similarly of the woman's brother. The name Staupitz has long had a powerful hold on his heart and hearing her say these things now moves him deeply—so deeply, he dare not say. It is almost as if something of himself were being reflected back: the same, and yet different.

"I came to appreciate the way of the sisters," Katharina continues, unaware of the turmoil in Martin's heart. "I found a way to live, if not happily, then at least with a sense of purpose. I committed myself to the path of righteousness, but always within me there was a shred of doubt, like a splinter embedded in the skin. Rather than working its way out, it seemed to move deeper and deeper, entering my bloodstream, tearing at my insides. It was as if I were bleeding inwardly! Only I could feel the weakness of my spirit.

"You see, since I was a girl, as long as I could remember, I wanted to be a wife and mother. I had no pretensions of greatness or dreams of living in a palace. To do what women had always done—to have a family of my own: that was my desire. Even after spending five years among the sisters, I could not shake this longing. I spoke of it to no one, but as the day grew close for me to take the vow, I felt such fear inside me. The day before I was to be consecrated, I asked to speak with my Mother Superior. Somehow, weak as I was, I found the strength to tell her that I did not believe God ever called me to be a nun—that I was made to be a wife and mother. And she…she…"

Katharina can go on no longer. She covers her face with the handkerchief, crying softly. Martin looks over at Barbara and mouths, "What should we do?" She mouths in reply, "Just wait." At length, Katharina recovers and proceeds with her tale.

"After I told her this, she said to me, 'Sister Katharina, you are mistaken. Your mind is still too much in this world. Do you know why your father sent you here? Because he is a drunk who cannot put two groschen together to save his life. If you do not take the vow, we can keep you here no longer, and where will you go then? Back to your family? They cannot provide for you. Will you seek a husband? What man would have you? There is no dowry, Sister Katharina. There is no man who will have you. God has brought you to the one place where you can be assured of food and shelter, and where you can be certain that no man will mistreat you, for the brothers who protect us are not like the men of the world. You have no choice: you must take the vow. You ought to be more thankful for what God has given you. Here you will follow the path of salvation. You will be wed to a far better husband. If you succeed, you might even stand among the saints. If you rebel, if you turn away—there is nothing but darkness.'"

Katharina closes her eyes and shakes her head briskly back and forth, her brow furrowed, cringing at the thought of these words. Martin feels the instinctive urge within himself—the longing to move toward her and comfort her. It is the desire of any human being whose heart is filled with compassion, but he has rarely felt it so fiercely. Yet, he must remain seated and silent. It is Barbara who places a hand on Katharina's, attempting to call her back from the darkness of these memories. This slight touch seems to calm Katharina, and she is able to continue.

"Were I to be given such a speech now, I would know how to counter it, for I have learned that there is something worse than hunger in this world. But I was still young—I did not know. I believed her. I believed them all. I entered the church and made my vow before God. I had no choice. Everything was going well—I had resigned myself to it.

"Then came something dreadful that I shall never forget all my days. They sat me down in the chair to have my hair shorn: the casting off of worldly vanity. I didn't know why, but the idea of it terrified me. Even before they began, I was nervous. I could hear them cutting"—here she mimes with her fingers—"and I saw my hair begin falling to the floor: the hair that was the color of my mother's, which she used to stroke when I was crying. As I watched it fall, lock by lock, I was trembling—shaking violently. I heard the Mother Superior say, 'Hold still, child!' I could not help it. I started weeping, right there in front of everyone. Although they did not mean it so, I felt that I was being shamed. I began to feel the cool air on my neck. There was none of it left. Sister Magdalena came over to comfort me. They told me it was normal to be upset—that I would be over it soon and we all looked the same. We only had one mirror. It was a week before I dared to look in it, and when I did, I was horrified. I remember staring at my reflection and thinking, 'I am no longer a woman.' They took that from me."

Here she pauses for a moment to catch her breath, the bitter tears escaping her eyes. Again, Martin feels the yearning to reach out to her in her distress. It is a good ten seconds before she continues.

"In time, I moved on. What choice did I have? I was eventually placed in charge of the infirmary. I loved the work. Helping others allowed me to feel something of the joy I was denied. But I would still weep on occasion when no one was watching. I tried to remember how long it had been since I had seen a child. I longed so much to hear a babe laugh. Then one day, I was tending the herbs out in the field, and a little girl came toddling around the corner of the building. Her parents had brought her to our church, and she broke free of their grasp. I saw her for just a moment before she was retrieved. She smiled at me, and I smiled back. I felt joy and sorrow, both at the same time. I realized in that moment that despite all the work I had done to make myself forget, a person cannot forget certain things. It was my first sign that everything was not alright, despite my best efforts."

With this, Katharina pauses, staring off into the distance. It is just as well, for Martin feels he needs a moment—no, perhaps a month to breathe. He has always known her to be direct and open, but this is a level of openness one does not typically find even in the confessional. How his heart burns within him to hear what she has suffered! He briefly glances over at Frau Cranach, who has placed a hand on her stomach as if to steady herself.

"I have not told you the worst of it yet, Herr Doktor," Katharina continues, looking into his eyes again. "We received a new gatekeeper: a younger brother replacing an older one. Right away, we noticed how different he was. He never chided us for eating—never questioned the quality of our chants. When one of the sisters grew upset, he would comfort her, placing a hand on her shoulder, making the sign of the cross. We had been starved of kindness for years, so it was wonderful to have someone who treated us well, or so we thought."

"So you thought?" he repeats, frightened of what might come next.

Katharina nods, the look on her face grim. "I will never forget the day. My dear sister—I will not say her name, as it is not mine to reveal—came to me in the infirmary, face red, eyes filled with tears. This was not unusual, as I helped many sisters suffering from melancholy. But there was something different about her distress that sent a chill of fear through my body. I saw it immediately in her eyes. She told me she had been bathing. When she stepped out to dry herself, the door to the room opened. She cried out in shock. She had locked the door, you see, but there was one person who had the key. He did not touch her. He just stood there staring while she was naked, shivering, shaking. He told her, 'Do not be afraid. You are pure.'

"I told the abbess what had happened straight away, and to her credit, she complained to the abbot, but of course he wouldn't believe her. He said she was failing to keep her charges in line. That was when Mother Superior began requiring that one of us stand outside the room at all times if anyone was changing. We could no longer walk alone, even to prayers. I felt afraid to sleep at night, knowing who had the key. It was as if we had been specially prepared for what happened: penned in, cut off, denied sustenance, forbidden to speak. It was a dark time, and once again, I questioned whether I was truly meant to take the vow. I have said there are things worse than hunger, and perhaps I have described one.

"We were told to rejoice in God every moment, but there was nothing to remind us of his goodness. I longed for colors from the depths of my soul: to hear the laughter of a child, to taste the fruits of summer without fear, to pass a night in peaceful dreams, to feel grass under my bare feet, to follow the river wherever it might lead. I felt I was no longer a woman, and I knew nothing of men. I knew nothing of anything that did not exist within those dark walls. They lied to us, Doktor. They lied to us when they told us it was the path to salvation. What pain was bred of that lie! Then, a light from above. The Lord heard our prayers, and we were granted hope."

"What hope was that?" Martin asks.

Katharina tilts her head slightly, her brows lowered. "Why, you, Herr Doktor!"

With these words, she strikes him powerfully. For years, he has known his own pain and suffering—alone in the dark, desperate for light. He never would have thought, in the depths of his despair, that God would make of it a healing balm for others like himself. But now, as he sits mesmerized by her tale, he realizes the full power of words to kill or make alive: that he, in his terrible weakness, could sit down with a pen and simply write what God has declared, and that it could reach across great distances and bring life and hope to others. He knew it, of course, but now he feels it in his soul.

"We heard of you from the start—even before you posted the theses," Katharina explains, "for Sister Magdalena received news from her brother and would tell us all of your efforts. It was Herr Koppe who first brought us one of your writings. We would pass them around at night and read them by candlelight."

"Which ones?" he asks.

"All of them, or perhaps most of them. The German ones were easiest, naturally, but some of us had enough training in Latin. For myself, I could understand most of what you wrote. In the Lord's providence, my time at Brehna had allowed me not only to read them to myself, but to my sisters as well. But the one I treasured above all was what you wrote for the debate in Heidelberg."

Martin shakes his head in disbelief. "You were able to get that as well?"

She breaks into a smile, a lovely sight after so much sadness. "Yes, but it smelled awful. Herr Koppe would bury them below the fish, you see. I admit that I did not understand the parts about Aristotle, but the rest of it I loved. I would always ask to borrow that one again to read it. I ended up learning it all by heart. 'The love of God does not find, but creates, that which is pleasing to it.' When I understood that, I understood the gospel, and I knew I was loved by God. Several of my sisters had the same discovery, but we were afraid to speak of it to our abbess. We knew she would not approve. I remember when we heard that you were gone to stand trial before the Emperor. How I trembled for you! We all did. We prayed for you with great fervor, both day and night.

"Then came the awful day when we learned you were dead. Of course, you were not dead, but we all thought you were. I remember I had to go out that day to hang some of the clothes to dry. I was all alone. There was no sound but the birds flying and dancing in the sky. I longed to fly with them, but my heart was heavy. I did not understand why God would take the one who gave us hope—the one who spoke the words that made me believe. And I wept for you that day: I wept bitterly to think of what they had done to you. But then, a miracle! We learned that you were still alive. Soon after that, we received your treatise on monastic vows, and I believe that was the end for us. Our collective will was set.

"We knew what it would mean to leave. We were deep within the territory of Duke Georg. He would put us to death if he caught us. He had already done so with others. But when we heard of the work that was happening in Wittenberg—that the gospel was being preached—we all felt that God was leading us to flee. This is where, I think, the story is well known to you."

"I remember receiving your letter," Martin says, nodding. "It took me by surprise. I had no idea that even cloistered nuns were reading my works! When I heard of your plight, I naturally wanted to do whatever I could to help you."

"Because that is who you are, Herr Doktor," Katharina replies. "You are a shepherd who cares for the sheep. I sensed it from the first time I read your work. For too long, we had been preyed upon by wolves. It was Easter Eve. The other sisters were all asleep, and most importantly, so were the gatekeepers. We went quickly—quietly. We took nothing out of that world, not that there was much to take. I remember the fear hanging upon me like a dread weight. My heart was pounding. I knew that if the plan did not work—if they caught us—we would all perish. And yet, I pressed on, putting one foot in front of the other, praying to God in fear and trembling, for there are some things worse than death.

"We had to climb the wall. That was the part that scared me the most. Herr Koppe helped us. He threw the knotted cord overtop, and we climbed it in turn. It took a long time for all of us to make it over. I remember standing there, every sound placing me on edge: the snap of a twig, the distant bark of a dog, even the chirping of the crickets. When it was my turn to scale the wall, one of my feet slipped part way up, and I very nearly fell and injured myself. I don't know how I held on, but I suspect I was held—that God himself bore me in his arms. When we were all on the other side, Herr Koppe had us lay flat in the back of his wagon and stretched the canvas over our heads. We were able to breathe, but the air still smelled of fish. It is a terrifying thing to be confined in a space like that: in the dark, with no room to move, breathing in the pungent air. I was surprised how much it bothered me. I laid there for many hours—so long that I lost all sense of time—fearing every moment that I would suffocate. And I knew that at any point, we might be stopped, and we would all be dragged into one of Duke Georg's prisons—but we were not stopped. The angels of God cleared the way for us.

"When we finally arrived in Torgau and breathed the free air again, it was a beautiful Easter morning. For the first time in fourteen years, I was looking upon a world of color. There were children running through the streets—people of all types rejoicing in the day. And though I had no money to my name and still feared very much for my life, I felt in that moment that I too was resurrected."

With this, Katharina falls silent, her eyes fixed upon him, anxious perhaps to hear his response. But he is lost for words, overwhelmed by the bravery they all displayed, and perhaps equally struck by the bravery Katharina has shown in sharing this with him, opening her heart, allowing him to know her fully. He is deeply unsettled by it, so much so that his whole body seems to tingle. It feels as if everything has changed since she began speaking, although he cannot say how. *Is this the same woman whom I knew before? Could it possibly be? Or am I the one who has morphed?* Having received no words from him, Katharina begins speaking again, her voice soft as the gentle rain, yet filled with a fire that causes his heart to burn within him.

"I know very well what people think of me: that I have the bearing of a duchess without any of the substance thereof, I am over proud, I grasp for what I cannot have, I suffer no correction, I think myself clever, I am a nightmare, et cetera. Perhaps that is what you think of me as well, though were I being quite bold, I might suggest that it is exactly what they say about you, Herr Doktor." Here she smiles a bit mischievously. "But now that you know the sad history of my life—the full story, such as it is—you can perhaps accept that it is not due to pride that I refuse Kaspar Glatz. I am not attempting to live out some aristocratic fantasy. I know exactly how dire my situation has become, but I would rather starve than be bound to a man of poor character, for that would be a false comfort—the filling of the stomach but the emptying of the soul. It would be a second bondage not unlike the one I knew before, which I swore to myself I would never accept again. For too long, I made the mistake of saying nothing. Now I see that I must state my desires clearly and openly.

"I have risked everything to come to this place where I may hear the gospel proclaimed, and read the Word of God, and know the fellowship of those who share my faith. And though I have sunk so low in the eyes of men as to be fit for nothing but the bottom of a boot, I would not raise myself in their estimation at the price of my dignity. To bind myself to Glatz would be a violation of my conscience. I will not do it! If then I have lost your good opinion, which I doubt in any case I ever possessed, then I am deeply sorry for it, for it was you who pointed me to the truth of the gospel, saved my life, and allowed me to enter a joy unknown. Your opinion matters more to me than any other. But I have risked life and limb, and I will risk the loss of your favor if I must. You know what it is to starve yourself, even as I do. You know there is something worse than death. I tell you now, I am not afraid to starve again."

Martin sees her now as a woman transformed: no longer the frail thing who entered the Black Cloister gaunt and ill, but something brilliantly alive. Such passion he has rarely encountered. Her firmness of purpose cannot but amaze. There is only one possible thing he can say in response.

"Very well," he utters, his voice little more than a whisper. "You will not hear another word from me about Kaspar Glatz."

Katharina presses her palms together and bows her head. "Thank you, Herr Doktor. You are a good man. Truly, a good man."

He cannot find the truth in her words, for he feels anything but good in this moment. *I did not really see her—I was blind until this moment.* It fills him with shame. And yet, while he respects her enough to honor her choice, he finds himself wishing more than ever that her story could end differently. She seems, of all people on earth, to deserve the fulfillment of her dreams. He trembles to think of what awaits her in the life she has chosen. It angers him that it could not be otherwise.

"You are brave, Fräulein, and far stronger than most men," Martin acknowledges. "You do not make yourself clever—you are clever. I never doubted that. Your love for our Lord and passion for the gospel is admirable. Perhaps I have misjudged you in other ways.

After all, we do not know each other very well. But honorable as your intentions may be, the fact remains that you cannot live in your present state forever. I fear for you."

"She is no burden to us, Doktor!" Barbara assures him. "Indeed, she relieves our burden!"

"You would keep her on then?" he asks, turning toward Barbara. "To help tend the house and care for the children?"

"If Käthe desires it, she is very welcome to remain with us—forever, if necessary." Here Barbara looks at Katharina with a loving smile on her face. "She has become part of our family."

Katharina smiles in return. "Thank you, Frau Cranach. The kindness of this house is beyond any I hoped to receive. You are true Christians, as are you, Herr Doktor. I know your burdens are heavy. You have granted me far too much of your time as it is."

"It is no trouble," he insists, embarrassed that his minimal help should be recognized at all.

"I should go," Katharina concludes. "The children will be wanting to play."

"Thank you, Käthe. Feel free to give them those sweets!" Barbara calls after her as she rises from her seat and departs the room, leaving Martin and Frau Cranach sitting alone.

He stares at the ground, his mind captured by a thousand thoughts and feelings. *How did it come to this?* He is shaken by Katharina's revelations, and while one part of him wishes to move on from the experience as quickly as possible, another part seeks to remain in that place of inner conflict, wrestling with what he has heard. But to do so, he fears, would be a thing beyond his control.

"You are deep in thought, Doktor," Barbara concludes.

He shakes his head sadly. "I did everything I could for her. I wish it had ended differently."

"The Lord's work is hidden from us. We do not yet know his purpose with Fräulein von Bora. You have been faithful to his command. You saved those girls from death, sparing no effort." Now she places her hand on Martin's. "Let us relieve you of this burden. There is no need to strive any longer. We will look after her."

Again, he shakes his head, utterly dissatisfied. "I just can't help feeling that I have failed her. She would never have left the cloister had she not read my words and received my promise."

Barbara sits up straighter in her chair and speaks with an air of authority. "This is her choice. You must respect it. She does not fault you, nor do I."

Sighing deeply, Martin concludes, "Thank you, Frau Cranach. I must be going now."

"You will greet the children first?"

"I think not. I do not shun their company, but I am weary of body and mind." His voices trails off—he stares into the flames. "Just restless."

"Be off then and take our blessing with you," Barbara concludes, granting him a smile.

He rises from the chair, his body feeling somehow heavier than usual. It is the weight of his cares, a burden as great as that of Atlas. There is an answer staring him in the face. He is certain it is visible to Barbara as well. *It's impossible. Yes, surely, it is impossible.* He isn't a man like other men, however much he may long to be. He turns to face her, his voice soft and tremulous.

"I cannot marry her. You know I cannot. I have little money. The house I live in isn't mine. I do not have long to live. It would not be a kindness."

"Oh, Doktor!" Barbara says, compassion written on her face. "You need not convince me. The children love her. Our garden has never looked better. I tell you again, let us handle it."

"Right," he concludes with a quick nod, feeling intensely embarrassed. "Good evening."

With that, he departs the house, bidding himself to forget the whole thing. *She will be alright. They will take good care of her. There is nothing more you can do. You are going to die.* But in his heart, he wonders how long it will be before he feels right about this—before he can possibly absolve himself. Every time he thinks he knows who he is and what he must do, the world seems to shake his foundations. For he lives every moment before the face of God, the one who breaks and remakes, who bends men to his will. As Martin blows out the last candle before retiring to bed, the turmoil still fresh within him, he whispers a question in the dark.

"Who am I?"

22 April 1525
Mansfeld, Electorate of Saxony

Philipp Melanchthon gazes up at a sky the color of ash. A mix of grays, both light and dark, it swirls and glides, casting doubt over the day's activities.

"I think it will rain," he mutters ruefully.

He is standing on a cobble street that cuts through the middle of the town of Mansfeld. One could follow this road out the gate and up a hill to the gleaming castle or walk in another direction and enter a land of dirt and fire, where men penetrate deep into earth, ripping it open to retrieve its treasures. He saw it all as they approached the town: mountains of slag choking out the green grass and billows of black smoke rising to darken the sky. This is the business of smelting, which has made the name of Mansfeld and that of Hans Ludher. Wherever Philipp goes in this town, he can smell the fumes and see the faint soot that colors every surface. His throat is irritated—his cough frequent.

Despite his protestations, he has accompanied Martin Luther to the latter's hometown to celebrate the opening of a school that will operate by the principles of the New Learning. It is a moment of great triumph, but it comes at a time of high anxiety. The news grows worse by the day: peasant risings across Germany, nobles overthrown from their seats, lists of demands, an increasing number of dead. The situation has deteriorated to such an extent that he saw no option but to bow to Martin's wishes and accompany him to Thuringia. Young Philipp's health has marginally improved—the immediate threat to the boy's life seems lessened—but his father still feels the sting of guilt leaving his wife to tend the children alone.

The political situation is now so bleak, it is uncertain whether the center will hold: if the institutions of government and the military might of the princes can withstand the breakdown of order occurring throughout their lands. Hanging over them all is the threat of a violent anarchy driven by unchecked passions—a chaos inflamed by false promises of a spiritual kingdom to be built on earth, if indeed there will be any earth remaining, for Thomas Müntzer is predicting its imminent destruction. What would remain of civilization in such a hellish heaven?

Philipp attempts to set these fears aside, for the most anticipated part of his visit is about to occur: he is to attend a family dinner with the Ludhers. Not only Martin's parents, Hans and Margarethe, will be in attendance, but also Martin's brother Jakob with his family. Most of the Ludher children perished long ago. *What sorrow they must have known!* Philipp thinks. *I pray to God that all my children outlive me.* But the chances of that are slim given their concerns about young Philipp. *Oh, my son, how I wish I could take your suffering upon myself!*

Now Martin joins him outside the inn where they have been staying along with other members of their party, the Ludher home not being large enough to accommodate them all. Throughout their journey, Philipp has noted that his colleague seems on edge, succumbing more quickly to anger and often staring off into the distance, oblivious to those around him. *What is going through his mind?* Surely, some of this angst is related to the war, and Philipp would love to believe that his fellow professor is considering how to respond to Erasmus. But there is another potential source of tension: Martin's relationship with his father has never been perfect, and now they are set to meet again.

"We should get going," Philipp says. "The clock just struck five, and I believe we are soon to be deluged."

Martin grants him perhaps the first smile of the trip. "I hope you have prepared yourself, Master Philipp."

With that, Martin turns on the spot and begins walking the short distance to his family home, while Philipp trails behind, wondering what type of preparation he was meant to undergo. *Am I making a terrible mistake? What kind of people are they?* He is familiar enough with the way his own family behaves, and he has accustomed himself to the more jovial Krapps. What awaits him at the house of Ludher? *You have not met the Ludhers until you have met them in their native land,* Martin had warned him.

They are passing the finest houses in the city—brick constructions belonging to the smelting masters. From obscurity, Hans Ludher worked his way up to become a leading citizen of the town and master of his own fate. But now, as Martin tells it, the industry is run by businessmen in Nuremberg, and even the smelting masters are subject to their will. Increasingly, it is falling to Jakob Ludher to take up the mantle of their father and harvest what is left in the ever-diminishing veins of silver.

They halt before a red brick home two-and-a-half stories high, with stables and pens behind it and a shop for smithing and carpentry. It is not the house in which Martin was raised, but it has served the family for more than two decades.

"Here it is," Martin announces. "In such a place dwell my antecedents."

It seems to Philipp a very normal house, or at least normal for this social class. There are people pouring out the front door now: Jakob Ludher and his three sons have come to greet them.

"Martin!" Jakob calls, moving to embrace him. He then turns to Philipp and says, "Doktor Melanchthon! It is a pleasure to meet you again and receive you at our home. These are my sons Miles, Veit, and Martin," he adds, patting them each on the head in order of age. "My wife Barbara is inside with our daughter Anna and our fifth child, who is still inside her."

"And I thought I had my hands full with two," Philipp remarks.

"You'll get there, professor!" Jakob replies with a smile. He is very like his older brother in looks, though he wears a beard and dresses in apparel befitting his rank: a short brown jacket and gray cap, with tall boots rising almost to his knees.

"Onkel Martin!" Miles cries, a boy of about ten years of age. "Come inside! Oma made fried herring."

Martin's face lights up. "With mustard?"

"Yes, and there are noodles as well. Come in and help yourselves," says Jakob.

They walk through the front door and into the common room, where a long wooden dining table is set not only with metal dishes—proof of their prominent status—but also great platters of food: the previously mentioned fish and noodles, along with lettuces, breads, a plate full of bratwurst, boiled eggs, cheese, and a cake soaked in honey. The walls are brick, but inside they are covered in dark oak panels—also suggestive of a certain amount of wealth. Over the hearth is an icon of Saint Anna, the patron saint of miners and guardian of the community.

Philipp is immediately met by Frau Ludher, who is clothed in a simple black dress over a white collared shirt, her head wrapped in white cloth that trails down her back. Her skin is wrinkled and sags around her chin, while her brown eyes seem wizened. This is the woman, Martin has told him many times, who makes a habit of carrying large bundles of wood on her back and striking the ground with a righteous fury until it surrenders to her hoe. Philipp looks at her hands clasped together, which show callouses worthy of a common laborer rather than a wealthy wife.

"Welcome, Doktor Melanchthon!" she greets him, bowing her head. "It is an honor to receive you in our humble home."

"The honor is mine!" he replies quite earnestly—perhaps too much so.

"Do you wish me to take your cap and set it aside?"

"I'll keep it with me, if you don't mind," Philipp responds, not wanting her to go to any trouble.

She grants him a smile, and he feels emboldened to speak what is truly on his mind.

"I have so many questions about Martin's upbringing," he says quietly, leaning in.

Frau Ludher sighs deeply, as if she has received the question a thousand times. "Of course, boy, but you must remember—I was very tired."

"Yes, that's fair," he replies. "Tell me, was Martin always this difficult?"

She snorts. "Worse."

"Worse?! That is difficult to believe."

"You must remember: he had three brothers." Here she holds up the corresponding number of fingers. "When they put their minds together—well, you can imagine."

Philipp chuckles. "Indeed, I can. What was it like when Martin was born? Did the sky ring out with thunder and lightning? Did the crows circle and wail?"

Frau Ludher closes her eyes, her brow furrowed in thought. "I remember he was born on the 10th of November, late in the evening. I was long in labor with him. He wasn't ready to enter this world. As it turns out, the world wasn't ready for him either."

"Do you know the year of his birth?"

She pauses to consider, opening her eyes and staring at the ground. "I can't remember. My Jakob will know."

"1483, Mother," Jakob calls from his place at the table, "and I was 1490."

"And there were four more children between them, one of whom we lost during pregnancy," Frau Ludher adds.

"My word!" Philipp exclaims.

"Yes, I was always pregnant in those days," she says, rolling her eyes. "Now you understand why I was so tired, perhaps?"

"I knew you were Martin's mother. That was explanation enough," he assures her.

Soon, Philipp is seated at the table with Martin on one side and Jakob's eldest son, Miles, on the other. Directly in front of him is the pile of fried herring. The smell of mustard offends his nose. Whether from that or the soot in the air, he sneezes violently, leading to a chorus of chuckles.

"Are you alright, professor?" the boy to his right asks.

"Yes, yes. Quite alright," Philipp assures him.

Another of Jakob's children sitting across the table, young Anna, asks, "Do you sneeze a lot?"

"I suspect I sneeze as much as the average person," Philipp answers, thinking, *These are the questions I can look forward to from my own Anna soon enough.*

"Is it because your nose is crooked?" the girl inquires.

In an instant, he is transported back to his childhood, attempting to play with other children in the street but failing at their sport. *Why is your nose so crooked? Did somebody punch you?* one asks. *Your face looks funny,* another says. *Are you a dwarf? Why are your shoulders crooked? Did your mother drop you? Are you ha..ha..happy to sssssee us?* He has carried these questions for years, and they still bite, even after he has achieved great things—even after a lovely woman has borne his children.

Uncertain how to answer, he is spared by the entrance of Hans Ludher. He is a large man: not tall, but broad, and made more so by his thick, fur-lined coat. His clean-shaven face reveals a chin very like Martin's—their noses are virtually identical. Hans' gray hair reaches below his chin, but it is the eyes that capture Philipp's attention: dark as the slag heaps, but fiery as the furnaces. Here is a man who has fought many battles. Instinctively, Philipp stands and greets him.

"Herr Ludher, it is an honor to see you again!"

Hans looks at him with a frown. "Sit down, boy. I'm not your king."

Thoroughly embarrassed, Philipp's gut spasms. He retakes his seat immediately, even as Hans settles into the great armed chair at the head of the table. Martin leans over, pats Philipp on the back, and whispers in his ear, "Welcome to the Ludher home!"

Joke aside, Philipp feels mortified. Never at ease around strangers, he begins to understand why Martin advised him to be prepared. Now Frau Ludher places a metal pitcher full of beer on the table and a very tall glass with silver rings etched around it, each about two finger lengths apart from top to bottom.

"At the request of my grandson, Miles, we begin with the tipple game!" Hans announces.

The room lights up with exclamations, some more enthusiastic than others. Philipp breathes deeply, staring at the glass, the tension in his limbs increasing. He has seen vessels like this before, typically being used by his students. He knows how the game will be played: the glass will be filled with beer, then each man at the table must sip down to the next line. He must hit it exactly, for if he goes too far, he will be forced to proceed to the following line. His students tend to play until one of them falls down drunk, but given the mixed company and formal meal, Philipp guesses they will only go until the glass is emptied.

"How about it, Doktor?" Hans asks, looking at him pointedly. "Are you man enough to play our game?"

"It is not a question of manliness," Martin insists, turning toward Philipp. "You can skip the game if you wish."

"Oh, go on! Play!" urges young Miles, prodding Philipp's right arm.

Philipp looks from one person to the next, tortured by indecision. On the one hand, he has absolutely no desire to play. On the other, it would be a way to show his hosts that he embraces them and their way of life—that he is neither haughty nor weak. In the end, this impulse wins out.

"I will play," Philipp announces.

This is met by cheers from the children and a nervous look from Martin, who evidently has little trust in Philipp's stomach.

"Can I play, father?" Miles shouts across the table.

"No, you are still too young," says Jakob. "When you are a man, then you can play."

Thus, the game begins. The glass is filled to the brim with beer, and Hans Ludher raises it to his aged lips, perfectly meeting the mark in a single gulp, as if he has played so many times that he senses the amount in his bones. He reaches past his grandson Veit and places the glass on the table next to Jakob, who proceeds a bit more carefully, stopping midway to check his progress. The boys begin pounding the boards, chanting, "Drink! Drink! Drink!" When Jakob has finished, he extends the glass to Philipp, who takes it in nervous hands.

"On you go, then," Hans urges him. "Don't be afraid."

"I am not afraid," Philipp declares, raising the glass to his mouth.

He begins with a mere sip, even as he saw Jakob do. Surprisingly, the beer tastes excellent. He would have expected something second-rate to be used for this game, but he can tell that the Ludhers value their drink highly. Checking on his progress, Philipp sees that he is still quite far from the mark, so he takes a longer sip, swallowing hard, even as the children pound the boards. When he examines the amber liquid again, its surface covered in foam, he sees to his horror that he has gone too far.

"Oh dear," mutters Jakob's wife, Barbara.

"Sorry," Philipp says automatically, though he has not truly done anything wrong.

"Go on. You'll get the next one!" Jakob assures him.

With great trepidation, Philipp begins drinking again, stopping several times to make sure he is not downing it too quickly. He manages to meet the line exactly and can therefore pass it on to Martin, who much like his forebear is able to reach the line in one perfectly timed gulp. They keep rounding the table, the boys gleeful, each man going no further than the mark. When there is only one portion of beer left, Hans finishes it off with a flourish, pounding the glass on the table.

"Round one complete!" Jakob announces.

"Round one?" asks Philipp, suddenly alarmed. "How many rounds are there?"

"As many as it takes," Martin informs him with a knowing glance.

Oh no. I should never have begun. I'll be the one to drop for sure! Philipp wails internally. He looks on in misery as the glass is once again filled to the brim.

"Is something wrong, professor?" Hans inquires.

"No, no. I'm perfectly fine," he lies as the glass is slid across the table to Jakob.

The next time it reaches Philipp, perhaps on account of his anxiety, he again overdoes it and must drink down to a second line. As he passes the glass to Martin, he feels the first tingling in his fingers—the heat upon his neck. If he keeps imbibing at this rate, he will soon be properly drunk, an experience he has only been so unfortunate as to have once before. *It is too late to back out. I am committed.*

As the game continues, the others are forced to take extra drinks as well, but it is Philipp who suffers the most. Round and round the glass goes. Soon he must proceed to the fourth line before they determine he has not overstepped the mark. His vision blurred, he struggles to judge his intake. He doesn't bother to speak, for he knows he will either stammer, slur, or both.

Miles shouts into his ear, "Are you alright, professor? You look ill."

Philipp places a hand on his temple, the pain reverberating through his skull. On a more positive note, he can think of no reason not to continue. A burp. Another. *My burps taste like burps,* he thinks. Oh, it is his turn to drink again! As he does so, beer spills out of his mouth and into his beard, but who cares? They are cheering for him. That is what counts. But that pounding is so annoying!

"Shtawpit!" Philipp bellows.

The children are looking at him oddly, or maybe he thinks they are odd, or maybe he looks odd. He cannot be certain. Is Martin drinking now? No, it is Hans. *So tired. I just want to sleep.* Another burp. His legs are weak—everything is weak. Is the table weak? He takes the glass in his shaking hands, raising it to his lips. He is muttering something in Latin, or is it Greek? He swallows a gulp, two gulps, three gulps. Then suddenly, his insides are on fire. Yes, he is about to explode! Martin places a hand on his shoulder.

"Are you alright, Philipp?"

Without speaking, Philipp rises to his feet, nearly falling over in the process. He stumbles toward the front door, grasping wildly for the knob. When he eventually finds it, he thrusts the thing open and staggers out into the yard, colliding with the fence surrounding the chicken coop. He looks at the hens, feasting on corn. They are multiplying before his eyes, splitting and joining. *Oh, no!*

There outside the Ludher home, Philipp Melanchthon is violently ill, spewing everything he has drunk onto a rather stunned hen who takes to the air in fright but only makes it a few feet before having to land. The smell is atrocious. Unable to stand any longer, Philipp collapses in the dirt below, lying on his side, waiting for his strength to recover.

It could be worse, he thinks, attempting to comfort himself.

Then, the deep rumble of thunder. The clouds above release their burden. Philipp is pelted—soaked from head to toe.

"Nothing," he whispers. "Nothing could have prepared me for this."

He senses one of the women bending over him. "Herr Doktor, do you need a physician?"

"Sleep," Philipp mutters. "Let me sleep."

22 April 1525
Mansfeld, Electorate of Saxony

Martin Luther glares across the table at his father and brother. Philipp has just fled the room, about to be ill, and a very pregnant Barbara Ludher has followed close behind to make sure it is nothing more than common drunkenness. As Martin considers the events of the past half hour, he shakes his head in disgust.

"We shouldn't have made him do that. He is an honored guest."

"How did we make him do anything?" Hans protests. "He chose to participate of his own free will."

"No, Martin is right," Jakob concludes. "He felt pressured. I hope he will be alright."

Hans scowls at them both. "There is nothing wrong with him a good night's sleep won't cure. Now, pass me the fish!"

As they begin placing food on their plates, Martin broods over recent events. *Why did we have to play the game? Why did Philipp feel he had to join?* One question particularly needles him: *Why did my father treat him that way? Philipp was just trying to show respect. He isn't from here. He does not know our ways.*

It is not the first time that Hans Ludher has sullied an otherwise pleasant event. Martin has often been left to stew about his father's comments, his temper nearing the boiling point. Even the delicious fried herring does little to soothe the ache he feels inside. The entire trip has been a trial, each day bringing news of further disturbances throughout the land. He has written a tract responding to the peasants' demands, some of which seem more reasonable than others. If they refrain from further violent acts, there may be hope for a compromise. But if it is true that Müntzer is prodding them forward, the end is likely to be bloody. The rebellion is close now: perhaps within a single day's march. *How safe are we really?*

Then, seemingly from nowhere, Martin's brother asks, "What ever happened to the vestal virgins guarding your hearth? Have they all found hearths of their own?"

Jakob refers, of course, to the escaped nuns. Martin mentioned something about them once or twice, and it was naturally a subject of some interest. Everybody loves the tale of nuns smuggled out of the cloister, though after hearing Katharina's story, Martin doubts he can ever think of it with anything but horror. That recent encounter has been reverberating in his mind. The more he thinks of it, the more confused he feels. Not only that, but the memories are morphing and twisting, combining with his fears about the insurrection. Although there is no obvious connection, the two subjects seem to be feeding off one another, adding fear to fear. So, to hear his brother raise the matter without any prompting seems a thing most unnatural, as if some otherworldly force had planted it in Jakob's mind. It makes Martin uneasy.

"Almost settled," he replies. Then looking down at his food, he mutters, "One remains."

"That is quite a look on your face!" Jakob declares. "Is there a story there?"

Martin had not realized he had any particular look on his face. Was it his frustration that revealed itself, or his fear? He has been racking his brain these past few days, attempting to come up with another eligible man for Katharina: someone of high character who could match the fire she possesses. But every time a name comes to mind, he finds himself thinking, *Not good enough. Not nearly good enough for her.* She has earned so much of his respect that he has failed to identify an unattached man who can match her achievement. *Is that not suspicious?* a voice in his head suggests, but he pushes it away.

“Let us just say that despite my best efforts, she is still without a suitable husband,” Martin concludes.

“Perhaps she needs a better matchmaker than you,” Jakob says with a smirk.

Martin takes a quick look up and down the table. Everyone else is caught up in their own conversations or very much focused on the food. Leaning forward, he speaks quietly. “I made her a match. She refused it.”

“Ah,” Jakob mutters. “Maybe she will find her own husband then.”

“She has tried to do so, but without success.”

“What’s her name?” his brother asks, brow furrowed.

“Katharina von Bora.”

Suddenly, Jakob’s eyes are alight. “A knightly family! Good Lord, whoever refused her is an idiot!”

Martin groans quietly, looking back down at his fish and aggressively spearing a bite with his fork.

“Wait,” his brother says, recognition seeping into his voice.

Martin looks up at him hesitantly. He is only a single breath away from a conversation that must not happen. *Has he worked it out? How has he worked it out? Did the devil himself put it there?!* His shoulders, his neck, his head: all are harshly tensed, for the danger to him is great. He sees the smile on his brother’s face and desperately seeks to wipe it off, but what can he say? He reaches frantically for something—anything—to divert attention, but his mind is a panicked blank.

“Eat your fish!” Martin finally commands.

It is too late. Jakob is smiling from ear to ear, mouth slightly agape, a twinkle in his eye. “She asked you, didn’t she?”

Martin groans deeper this time, tearing at his piece of bread and muttering, “Shit…shit shit shit…”, under his breath.

“My God, it’s true!” Jakob declares, shaking his head in wonder. “I can’t believe it!”

“Can’t believe what?” Hans calls from the head of the table.

Martin locks eyes with his brother in desperation. *Please, I beg you, don’t say anything that will get me in trouble!* For he knows that if his father hears of this thing, he will seize upon it like a dog would a bone, refusing to loosen his iron jaw.

Jakob smiles mischievously, turns to their father, and announces, "Martin has had an offer of marriage!"

"Really?!" Hans exclaims, looking to Martin for confirmation. "From whom?"

Martin glares at his brother and grumbles, "I really don't think we should be talking about this."

Jakob is undeterred and proceeds to push him fully over the cliff. "From Katharina von Bora—a woman of mystery, for Martin has never spoken of her before."

"Because there is nothing to tell!" Martin insists, truly angry.

It is too late—much too late. Martin sees it in his father's eyes, bursting with expectant flame. There can be no turning back.

"Bora is a noble house," says Hans, and while his manner may not reveal it, Martin can tell that his father is very excited. "Son, do you mean to tell me that a woman of noble descent has offered to marry you?"

"I did not mean to tell you that at all," Martin retorts.

"And yet, miraculously, it slipped out," Jakob surmises, looking very much as if he has found nothing so amusing for the past year.

"Well, this is tremendous!" Hans declares, pounding the table with his palm. "When will the wedding be?"

Martin sighs deeply. "There is to be no wedding, father."

Now, it happens: the morphing of his father's countenance. In an instant, Hans Ludher moves from near elation to extreme perturbation, his face wrinkling into a scowl. "What? Why not?!" he demands to know.

"We are not getting married," Martin replies, shrugging his shoulders.

Hans pounds the table again, but for a rather different reason. "Why the devil not?! Is there something wrong with her?"

Martin thinks for a moment. Is there anything he can legitimately list as a serious fault? A week ago, he might have thought so, but now everything that comes to mind seems so minor—even unfair. His own faults are much greater in comparison.

"Not as such," Martin responds quietly. "It's just—I am not going to marry at all. That is the end of the matter."

"Like hell, it is!" Hans yells, his fury causing Martin's heart to pound. "Now, you listen to me, son, because I've been listening to your excuses for twenty years!" Here Hans points at him accusatively.

"First, it was that you wanted to complete your schooling before marriage. Then you went and made yourself a monk. Then you unmade yourself, or perhaps they unmade you—I never did understand that part. But you still insisted that priests shouldn't marry. Well, that didn't last long! You are quite happy now for other priests to marry, but still you refuse. So, what excuse is it now, son? Because from what I can see, you're just pulling them out of your ass."

"That is not fair," Martin insists. *My reasons are perfectly legitimate, aren't they? Yes, surely they are!*

"Is there something unnatural in you?" Hans sneers.

"Unnatural how?" Martin asks, filled with trepidation.

"You fear the touch of a woman?"

A ripple of shame moves through Martin's body, not because he believes his father to have hit the mark, but simply because it hurts to be accused of such. He found plenty of women attractive in his early years. In his flesh, he might have desired their touch, but he worked very hard throughout his time as a monk to put that part of himself to death. *No such compunction holds me back now!*

"It's nothing like that," he assures his father.

Then suddenly, Martin realizes he has been thinking about Katharina. He cannot help it: his father put the image in his mind. He imagines her touching his hand, his face—wrapping him in her arms. The sensation seems to envelop him. Since she made her very odd declaration that she would marry him, he has been striving not to imagine what it would be like to agree to her proposition, and for the most part he has succeeded. But now, in an attempt to insult him—to cut him deeply—his father has forced him to have the thoughts, and he wants to run from them.

Hans is still bellowing at him. "Well, then tell me, son! Tell me! I've worked my whole life to build up this name—our name. But will you pass it on? No. It means nothing to you."

"That is not true, father!" he insists, raising his voice to meet Hans' level. "The name means a great deal to me."

"If that were true, you would respect me. You wouldn't have run off and left us all to rot!" his father cries.

They have come to it: the original sin. Martin has tried to make amends. There have been times his father seemed almost over it, but here again it rises like the many-headed hydra, impossible to kill.

"I have admitted that I was wrong to depart as I did," Martin says more softly, "but consider that because of me, there isn't a man in Christendom who doesn't know our name."

"Right: Luther, not Ludher," Hans responds, his tone scornful. "And why do they know it? Because they think you're a heretic, an idiot, a subject for hatred or amusement. You bring us notoriety, not respect!"

The conversation has gone on so long and intensely that Martin has practically forgotten there are others at the table, but now his brother joins the fray. "Father, can you not see that Martin has done extraordinary things? You gave birth to a genius. You cannot expect him to be like other sons. The hand of God directs him."

Hans scoffs. "Always so quick to defend him when he left you to do the work that was beneath him."

"I certainly do not think your life here beneath me," Martin argues, "but it is not the life to which I was called. I cannot honor you by dishonoring God and refusing his summons."

His father is red in the face, nose scrunched, fists clenched. "Why can't you just marry this girl? Don't you want children? What's wrong with you, boy?! After everything your mother and I have done for you!"

Breathe, Martin bids himself. *Breathe. Softly. Breathe.* When he has regained his calm, he says, "Father, it is quite possible that I will be executed."

"Oh, that would please you, wouldn't it? A famous, glorious death! You would light the fire yourself!" Hans charges, yelling with such force that his jowls tremble.

Martin shakes his head, on the verge of tears. Something fierce rises within him. He speaks as one possessed, but not by the devil.

"How little you understand me! I want to live, father! I want to please you. From the time I was a boy, all I wanted was for you to be proud of me. Nothing would please me more in this life than to give you descendants to pass on the name you gave me, but even if I did, you would not be proud of me. You would approve my deeds, but my own thoughts and feelings would not weigh in your estimation. So, you must forgive me for honoring instead the will of a Father who knows me fully yet loves me truly and gives me a name which was purchased for me with his own blood. That blood speaks a better word even than yours!"

Hans Ludher leans back in his chair, hands planted on the table, a sly smile on his face. He scoffs and shakes his head in something like disgust.

"So sure of yourself! You defy the world, but I know the truth. You have doubts—terrible doubts." Now he leans forward, speaking with the force of a whirlwind. "And you should, boy! You're still the same scared, pathetic little thing I would hear crying at night on the other side of the wall because you thought the devil was out to get you. Every time you got scared, you'd crawl into a ball! You'd lose control." He presses on, seething, speaking to wound. "I remember when you used to wet yourself. Never knew up from down, you did. You thought you could be tough then, standing up to me, and you still think you're tough. But I know who you are and what you are, and you don't intimidate me with your books and your fancy cap. You're still the boy who wet himself and cried all night. You don't know if you're right or not. You're stumbling along just like the rest of us, but too proud to admit it. Damn you and your pretension!"

With these words, Martin suffers it all over again: the ache, the despair, the torment of losing his father's love. He feels as if he has been split open, his bowels ripped from his belly, his heart caught in a vice grip.

"Father," he whispers, unable to speak further.

"Get out of my house!" Hans screams, rising to his feet, pounding the table with his fists.

"Father, please!" Jakob cries in desperation.

Now Hans plants his fists on the table and bends forward, coming within inches of Martin's face. His voice is like a thunderclap. "I said get out!"

"Very well," Martin replies quietly, nodding his head. "I shall obey you." Without another word, he rises, setting his cloth on the table, placing his cap on his head.

"Son!" his mother cries, rising from her seat, and Jakob joins her, calling, "Come back, Martin!"

"No, let him go!" Hans orders.

Martin pays no attention to any of them. He heads straight for the door and makes his exit, slamming the thing behind him. As he walks into the muddy yard, the rain pummels him. In desperation, he grips his left wrist and speaks to himself.

"I belong to Christ. I was baptized. I am one with him."

Again and again, he repeats the words. It is not the terror that strikes him this time, but simply the pain—overwhelming, unsettling, vicious! *How many times must I be broken and remade?* He continues to recite with his eyes closed, allowing the words to perform their work. He is calmer now. His pulse has slowed. It is only the patter of the rain he hears now: yes, the gentle patter of water drops, now running along the cobblestones, making for the low ground. With the rain flow his tears, fallen silently to the earth. He breathes deeply, his lungs expanding and contracting.

Then he catches a scent upon the wind. It is the smell of molten metal—of smoke rising endlessly from furnaces that burn with fierce rapacity. In an instant, he is transported to a great fissure in the earth: a darkness stretching into depths unknown. He is suspended above the abyss, clinging to a rope, unwilling to make the descent.

"Quit your sniffling, boy! There's work that needs doing." The voice of his father fell upon him from above. "Now, hold on tight!"

Martin dared for a moment to gaze downward past the undulating walls of rock to the point where light could no longer penetrate: the utter darkness of the underworld. The air was musty—he feared to breathe it in. What creatures might lurk in places where light feared to travel? Goblins? Devils?

"I'm lowering you now," his father called. "Remember, look for the vein!"

The vibration of the rope pulsed through Martin's hands and into his chest. He was moving further into the deep, the light dwindling with each foot he descended. The walls of earth pressed close together: too close for an adult to easily fit. He heard a trickle of water. His heart was beating so hard, his chest ached. He could hear the pressing of blood into his skull.

Turning his face back to the light, he bellowed, "Father, let me up! There's nothing here!" The sound did not echo but was merely absorbed by the rocks that closed in around him.

"Almost there!" came the distant voice, faint as a bird call high above the earth.

Martin pinched his eyes shut, overcome by terror. "O Maria, salve me! Sancte Mater, salve me!"

Then he heard something new: a faint cheeping sound gradually building into a high-pitched drone. The air around him began to swish, as if disturbed by some unearthly force.

"Father! Save me! Father!" he cried, his whole body twisted around the rope, clinging to it with all his might.

A thunderous roar! An entire legion of demons taking flight! They rose from the depths of the abyss, colliding with his body, their wings beating against his skin. He no longer knew up from down or dark from light, but only the abject terror of his situation. When he was finally pulled back to the land of the living and assured that it was only a flock of bats, he refused to believe it. Still, he denies it.

Now, as he stands upon solid earth with the raindrops striking him, he wonders if it was truly the darkness he feared, or if it was the voice of his father that lent the chill to his bones.

"I have been young," he whispers, "and now I am old, but still the same tune plays."

Suddenly, he hears the splash of footsteps in puddles. He looks over to see his sister-in-law approaching, a cloak held over her head. Then he remembers: *Philipp!* Somewhere amid his fight with Hans, he forgot that his colleague had been taken ill.

"How is he?" Martin calls to her.

"Very unwell," she answers, stopping in front of him. "He is back at the inn now, fast asleep. I've just come from there."

"You should not be out here. Get yourself inside," he instructs. "I'll see to him. Have no fear."

She nods in appreciation and heads back into the house, leaving Martin to suffer the pangs of guilt. *I should have never put him in that position, and now I've abandoned him. I must set it right.* Even as the thoughts pass through his mind, the rain slows markedly. The clouds break, and a hint of sun falls from heaven to earth. He closes his eyes—attempts to relax every muscle of his body. Now, he hears the door opening behind him and turns around to look. It is his brother walking toward him, arms crossed, a smile on his face.

"What's so funny?" Martin demands to know. After all, they have just finished one of the more painful conversations of his life. "Have you so quickly forgotten our father's words?"

"I am sorry about that—truly," his brother replies. "But we've seen it before. He's playing the same old tune, and it will not bring you down now, even as it didn't before. I have a far more pressing question for you, and I will not allow you to squirm out of it."

"Oh really? What's that?"

"Is she pretty?" Jakob asks, stopping just in front of him.

Why, God, why? Martin moans internally. *Why must it always be her?* Having failed once again to escape this subject, he rolls his eyes. "You've been too much at the drink."

"So, she's hideous?"

"I didn't say that."

"Ah! So, she's pretty, then?"

"What does it matter if she's pretty or not?" Martin asks in frustration.

Now his brother frowns. "It would matter to me. It matters to you too. You just don't want to admit it."

Martin sighs deeply. "Is it possible that I am more mature than you, brother? That I focus on the inner person?"

"Only God can create a beautiful woman, Martin," Jakob says in all seriousness. "Who are you to sneer at the gift of God?"

A good point. I cannot deny it, Martin thinks, but insists, "I do not sneer."

"But you do not answer my question."

"What question?"

Jakob shakes his head in amusement and slowly repeats, "Is she pretty?", emphasizing each word.

The question seems to grip Martin in the chest. How should he answer it? Should he think of Katharina as he first saw her, gaunt and destitute, her skin sallow and eyes sad? Or should he think of her the last time he saw her, full of life and health, the color returned to her face, her eyes latching on to his, her words flowing forth with an almost musical quality? Should he think of the many times she has annoyed him or the time she moved him so deeply that he surrendered to her will?

"I've never really thought about it—"

"Liar!" Jakob accuses.

"—but upon further reflection, I suppose most people would say she is pretty, yes, not that it's any of my business. I am a poor judge."

His brother smiles, looking very much like a cat that has just had its fill. "We shall see whether it becomes your business. Do not spurn the gifts of God, brother. Do not make things more difficult than they need to be."

They fall silent. Martin's spirit churns within him. Jakob's words, offered calmly and with the knowing presumption of a little brother, have softened his resolve far more than the bellowed threats of his father. *Am I making things more difficult than they need to be?* he wonders. *Am I, after all, a man like other men?* His fear seems to lessen. He feels able to make a concession.

"Look, I know what you're about. I'm not an idiot."

"That remains to be seen," Jakob retorts.

"I will take the matter to God in prayer. I will give it the consideration it deserves. But I cannot make myself other than I am through mere exertion of will. The Lord must direct me in this matter."

His brother nods. "I suppose that is fair."

Now, young Miles comes rushing out of the house, running up to his uncle and embracing him. Martin holds the boy firmly to himself, realizing just how much he has needed a hug from someone who loves him.

"Onkel Martin!" his nephew cries, looking up into his eyes. "You're leaving?"

"Yes, I'm afraid I must."

"When will we see you again?" Miles whines, moving back toward his father.

Here Martin thinks of the war, the ongoing difficulties with Karlstadt, the need to respond to Erasmus—everything that fills his life with turmoil. *At least Müntzer does his evil in the open. The same cannot be said for Erasmus.* Always, the struggle continues without a moment's relief.

"I don't know. It depends on how things go," he concludes, then looking lovingly at them both in turn, he says, "I wish I could see you always."

Now Miles adopts the same mischievous look his father has so perfected. "I will slaughter you again at dice!"

"You rascal!" Jakob cries. "Come here!"

For a moment, Jakob wraps up his son and messes his hair. Miles responds by kicking backward into his father's shin, loosening the older man's grip and allowing himself to break free. The boy runs off gleefully, returning to the house where he is likely to stuff himself with the cake his Oma has made. Martin watches this all with a powerful sense of longing, though he cannot say exactly for what. Is it for the fellowship of family, the love of a father and son, or something else entirely? These days, he is full of all sorts of longings—a desperate yearning that he doubts can be fulfilled on earth.

With tears forming in his eyes, Martin whispers, "I'm sorry, Jakob."

His brother frowns in confusion. "For what?"

"That I left the work for you alone. I did not know at the time that it would only be you, but I'm so sorry."

Jakob's expression softens—he moves closer. "Martin, look around you. I have a good life here: a wonderful wife, four beautiful children, another about to be born. The business is difficult, yes, but we manage. I am happy. God has blessed me abundantly. And I could not be prouder of you. Truly, I could not be prouder. But I do worry about you, for I see the burdens you carry. I see what it's doing to you." Now, Jakob takes a deep breath, his face set, his purpose firm. "I know you fear what it would mean to bind yourself to this woman or some other woman of your choosing, and I do not deny the dangers you face. But what if God in his mercy and abundance of grace wishes to grant you a gift that will bring you tremendous comfort in this life, even as my wife has given to me? If that is the case, then you must not be afraid to accept the gift, Martin. I want you to be as happy and blessed as I have been, for the goodness of God is all around you, if only you would see it."

Martin is overcome with emotion. He wants to tell Jakob how much he loves him—how proud he is to have him as a brother. He wants to tell Jakob, *It was you who saved me at Worms.* That it is his influence, unknown to the wider world, that continues to strengthen Martin's faith. And in this moment, it is Jakob and no other who has nudged Martin to the brink of a decision that could change his entire life, for as skilled as Martin is in philosophical debate, he can think of no effective argument to counter what his brother has just spoken. But he is afraid—far too afraid to speak of it or contemplate all it means.

"Thank you, Jakob," Martin finally says. "Pray for me."

"I will," Jakob replies with a nod. "You know I will."

"I love you, brother."

"I love you too."

1 May 1525
Basel, Swiss Confederation

The air is thick with humidity as it enters Erasmus' lungs. He takes it in through his nostrils, flowing up and down, in and out. He becomes one with the air of this place: the land of the dead.

He is standing just outside the Preacher's Church of the Dominican Order: the church outside the wall. A member of the city council—one loyal to Rome and especially fond of the Dominicans—has insisted on having his new child baptized here instead of at the cathedral. So, the great and the good have been forced to make the trip on this Monday morning, though Erasmus notes that few of the new faith have been included in that number. Any chance to escape the foul air of the city is normally a blessing, but today he finds himself wishing very much to have one more wall between himself and the rest of the world. Having quickly tired of the dull conversation, he exited into the walled cemetery where he now stands, breathing deeply, wondering when the gathering clouds will release their burden.

It seems fitting to stand among the dead when every day brings fresh news of war: a rebellion the like of which has never been seen in the Empire, stretching through the forests and hills of Germany, threatening death to anyone with the faintest link to nobility. The peasants heed nothing but the call of crazed prophets who send their sheep to be crushed beneath the wheel of Fate. They are close now—very close to Basel. The thought of it horrifies him. It would be better to say less about his digestion and more about the lack of it these past few weeks. The troubling of his spirit has become the torment of his flesh.

As he stands upon a gravel path, his gaze passing over the rows of headstones and scattered hawthorn trees, his eyes fasten on the wall to his right, the entirety of which is covered in a mural depicting the Totentanz: the Dance of Death. Here, the rich and poor alike are portrayed, from the emperor down to the peasant, each man and woman pulled by a skeleton to meet his or her end. His godson Johann Erasmus once informed him, "You have the nose of the herald and the hair of the lawyer!" Though the mural was composed of brilliant colors in the beginning, exposure to the elements over many decades has left it faded and gray, but still fearsome. He looks upon the image of Adam and Eve taking fruit from the Tree of the Knowledge of Good and Evil.

The first lie—the first doubt, he thinks. *That was when man learned to fear.*

Erasmus is not alone, for there is another standing closer to the wall. Though he can only view the man from the back, Erasmus recognizes his old colleague, Johannes Œcolampadius, who has recently refuted Erasmus' *On Free Will* with a volume being devoured by the Lutheran camp—if indeed they can still be called "Lutherans," for they take no authority but themselves.

Œcolampadius is studying the mural intensely, bending forward to inspect its details. *My presence is unnoticed,* Erasmus realizes. He has it in mind to re-enter the church and endure the agony of whatever conversation he might find there rather than suffering an audience with this man who has so greatly angered him. But now he sees Œcolampadius placing a hand over his face—his shoulders rise and descend, his whole body shakes. *Why is he weeping?* Erasmus wonders. He feels a twinge of pity in his chest. For the sake of the fellowship they once enjoyed, he moves toward Œcolampadius and calls out to him.

"What hope will you gain by standing among the dead and gazing upon their strange dance?"

The awareness of his presence seems to shock Œcolampadius out of his grief. He inhales sharply, attempting to stifle his tears. "The only hope that ever a man can possess: Christ himself, and his resurrection."

"You speak wisely," Erasmus says quietly, "and yet I see fear in your eyes."

"Would you claim that fear and faith are opposed?"

"Good Lord, I hope not!"

Œcolampadius smiles and shakes his head, his beard lightly swaying. "And there is that word again: hope."

Sighing deeply, Erasmus declares, "Enough with your obfuscation! What is troubling you, Johannes? I have never seen you so downcast."

Œcolampadius looks back at the Totentanz—the mass of men drawn into the waiting clutches of death. He whispers, "There has been a massacre."

"Massacre?!" Erasmus cries, his mind immediately conjuring images far worse than anything that could exist in life. "Where?! What have the rebels done now?"

Œcolampadius speaks haltingly, as if straining for the right words. "I heard of it from my honored forebears. The town of Weinsberg—the place where I was raised, which I love as surely as my own flesh—has been laid low. A great slaughter! Everything plundered! My parents were fortunate to escape, but many were less fortunate. I wonder if anyone I knew in those early days is still alive. How it grieves me to think that my youth has been destroyed along with the loves of so many!"

"Oh, Johannes!" he exclaims, voice reduced to a whisper. "This is monstrous. Who could have done it?"

His former colleague shakes his head bitterly. "I don't know exactly. There are only scattered reports. It is part of the war, of course, though what the perpetrators were hoping to gain through this, I cannot say. Why Weinsberg?! It is a town of little significance, but for the count. To think of those poor souls cut down! I know what you think of me, Erasmus. Your friendship has turned to hate. You will not forgive me my associations. But pity me, I beg you, for our former friendship! See that I too am a man of flesh and blood, with a beating heart now wounded!"

How those eyes plead Œcolampadius' case! They latch onto Erasmus, drawing him back, begging him to remember. Despite all that has passed between them, Erasmus feels a desperate longing he can hardly describe. He yearns for what they had when they sat together through the long hours of the night, producing a work that would shake the foundations of Christendom. He wants to share drinks and jests: to know the fellowship of a mind not so unlike his own. Looking into those eyes, Erasmus feels something within himself loosen. He speaks with conviction. "I do not hate you."

Œcolampadius smiles sadly. "But you do not wish for me to call you 'friend': that much you made clear in your letter."

And just like that, Erasmus remembers what it is about Œcolampadius that annoys him. The man stubbornly refuses to play the game by which polite society operates. *When your adversary offers a truce, do not remind him why the war started.* This is certainly one of the principles upon which good conversation is built, and Œcolampadius has just violated it, regurgitating the source of their conflict: the growing divergence of opinions. *You betrayed me.*

"I do not wish you to call me your friend in print when it could be seen to link me with your ideas," Erasmus explains yet again. "That is all. I offer friendship to every man at my door."

"Every man but Hutten?" Œcolampadius asks pointedly.

Ah, yes! Ulrich von Hutten, a late defender of Luther, but more to the point, a foulness of a man horribly lacking in good sense. Pursued by the laws both of men and nature, Hutten arrived at Erasmus' doorstep half-dead and covered in pustules, demanding sanctuary from a man he had repeatedly slandered. No one in his right mind would have admitted such a guest, and Erasmus is not about to accept criticism for his refusal.

"Every man who is not rotting from the French disease will receive my hospitality," he replies drolly. "I have not stopped writing to you, have I? Surely, I would have ceased if I were half as cruel as you say."

Here Œcolampadius looks squarely at the ground, like a dog caught eating the cake. "You have not forgiven me for Farel."

You're not wrong, Erasmus admits internally. After all, it was Œcolampadius who sheltered and promoted the vile Frenchman, even as Farel was producing libelous pamphlets condemning Erasmus. It is a deep wrong and one not easily got over.

"There no one could blame me," Erasmus asserts. "I know you feel compelled to take in every exile and rogue who happens upon these parts, but really! I warned you, Johannes! I warned you!"

Œcolampadius breathes deeply, looking as if he might weep again. "Come, let us reason together, friend. You have suffered loss, as have I. Does not our grief bind us together?"

He makes it sound so easy, this restoration of relationship. But Erasmus will not be like the false prophets of old, proclaiming peace when the world is at war. He steps closer to Œcolampadius, staring him down.

"Tell me, friend: Why did you find it necessary to attack my diatribe *On Free Will*? Is not Luther able to defend himself?"

"I did not attack you!" Œcolampadius cries, as if offended by the suggestion. "I disagreed with you. Principled disagreement is no crime!"

"You treated me very harshly, sir."

"Well, how else would you have me respond when you attack the chief source of certainty that a man can have?!"

Something has been spurred within Œcolampadius. He is circling round for a pass of fierce intensity. He takes one step closer, his feet treading upon the departed, the Dance of Death continuing behind him. Then he releases a fire exceedingly alive, which would strip the flesh from Erasmus' bones.

"At what cost do you buy this 'free will', or what expense does it place upon your soul?" the younger man cries. "To know the world a spinning chaos, in which man in his weakness must struggle in vain to stem the tide? It will crush the life from every moment of your existence to walk with such a burden on your back! There is nothing so alone as being without the certainty of faith and communion with God."

Even as Œcolampadius unleashes this torrent of words, a thousand images pass across Erasmus' mind, or perhaps it would be better to say a thousand feelings. Gray columns, red and blue glass, candles burning, the smell of incense! Kneeling upon ancient tile still wearing the sweat of another. His whole being twisted in on itself. Reaching, grasping, screaming! *Smite me!* The fierce assault of silence. Alone—yes, utterly alone.

Erasmus breathes the memories in but refuses to grant them sway. He focuses on the words proceeding from Œcolampadius' mouth, and soon a storm is fomenting within Erasmus, breaking upon the walls, longing for release. With a certainty that could please even Œcolampadius, he responds.

"And yet, here we stand, having seen what the doctrine of the bound will produces, and I find myself far less assured of things both temporal and eternal. The whole world is in an uproar! You have just said that your own hometown is filled with blood, and any day the peasants may set fire to Basel as well. The denial of free will is the chief source of human despair! It robs every action of meaning. Why shouldn't a man cut down his neighbor if his deeds are not weighed in the balance? Why should he make any effort to please God? The great mass of men live as prisoners of Fortuna here on earth, unable to alter their destinies. If you remove eternity from their grasp as well, what is left to goad them out of bed in the morning? Nothing! This breakdown of societal order is no accident, but certain proof of the error of your claims. Men who believe themselves righteous will commit all sorts of unrighteousness!"

Œcolampadius absorbs this harangue, tears falling softly down his cheeks. "Oh, Erasmus! I wish you could see! You were like a father to me."

How Erasmus hates those words! He detests the very sound of them as they escape Œcolampadius' lips. *Father? Father?!* Only fools lend such devotion to their tutors. *What teacher could possibly live up to the demand created by that title?!* He senses the yearning within Œcolampadius—the need for approval. *Absurd, pathetic, cloying!*

"You ought not have made me so, for I never sought that role!" Erasmus replies sternly. "I am incapable of playing it!"

A pair of moist eyes stare back at him, honest and true, yet robbed of their power.

"I pity Weinsberg," Erasmus concedes, "and I am grieved to see you brought low, but sooner or later you must face the fact that the very ideas you cherish are driving the world mad. Now, I will leave you to your death musings."

Just like that, he departs Œcolampadius' company and walks back into the church, angered by what he has heard. *Nothing! I owe him nothing! What was that verse in Malachi? Ah, yes. 'If I am a father, where is my honor?' These men honor me with their lips, but their hearts are far from me!*

He enters one side of the sanctuary and exits immediately out the other. Now he is heading in the direction of the St. Johann Arch, preparing himself for the smells that will greet him when he stands again in the city's interior. So intense is his brooding, only the sound of a familiar voice keeps him from his intended course.

"Erasmus! Herr Erasmus!"

He whips his head round and sees Bonifacius Amerbach running toward him upon the dirt road: heir to his father's printing business, a man in his twenties with enthusiasm to spare, for he has not yet learned the cruelties of life. *Finally, a man whose company I honestly enjoy!* Amerbach is sporting a brown beard now, with a blue velvet coat and cap to match. Embracing Erasmus, the younger man declares, "Oh, blessed Rotterdamer! Prince of scholars! You did not think to leave without listening to my prattle?"

"What you do is not prattle," Erasmus says. Looking back in the church, he mutters, "For the others, I offer no such recommendation."

Amerbach laughs heartily, patting him on the back. "Are you headed back to Froben's?"

Seeing the light in the young man's eyes, Erasmus takes a deep breath, attempting to shed his disquiet. "Yes, by God's will. Come with me. Johannes will wish to see you."

"Why isn't he here with the rest of us?" Amerbach asks, brow scrunched.

With a grim chuckle, Erasmus replies, "Because he was clever enough to devise a good excuse. Come! Let us get within the walls before the peasants hang us!"

They walk side-by-side beneath the broad arch of St. Johann, turning onto Peter Alley, then pass some of the finest houses in town, their white-washed walls adorned with brightly colored shutters and doors. The road is covered in cobbles now, which undulate beneath their leather-clothed feet, causing Erasmus' weary soles to scream.

"Was that the Totentanz I saw you admiring?" Amerbach asks.

"I wouldn't say I was admiring it. I've seen better ones elsewhere," Erasmus responds, catching his first whiff of something rotten.

"You were having quite the discussion with Œcolampadius."

That sounds rather like an accusation, Erasmus thinks, but seeing the lack of tension on the younger man's face, he offers, "The rebels have destroyed his hometown. I thought it only fitting that I should offer him some encouragement."

"And did he take courage from your words?"

They are forced to part ways as a cart full of sheep is pulled between them. Rejoining their paths, Erasmus laments, "He takes nothing from my words. No one does anymore."

"Oh, speak not so, dear Erasmus!" Amerbach cries. "You are the best of us!"

He shakes his head grimly. "Yes, well, I forgot I was speaking with the most optimistic man in Basel."

Between some of the houses are garden plots pressed against the wall. There are children playing in them, enjoying the return of warmer temperatures. Rays of light peek from between gray clouds, soon to be blocked completely by a storm, if the ache in Erasmus' bones is any indication. His mind is far from Amerbach now—rushing across the plains of Germany. There he sees things that grip him in the bowels.

"Erasmus?" Amerbach asks, concern in his tone. "Is everything alright?"

He looks over at the much younger man. *Perhaps I can speak something of my angst to him.* Every fear Erasmus acknowledges is a gift to anyone who might wish him ill, but he does not think Amerbach falls into that category.

"It is the war," Erasmus explains quietly. "Always the war. Forever the war."

Amerbach nods sadly. "I too have been hearing the reports. Do you know anything about this prophet Müntzer—the one they say is leading them?"

"No man is leading them: that is the problem," Erasmus argues. Then as the anxiety swells within him, he releases the totality of his grief. "Oh, Bonifacius! How those great piles of dead appear before my mind's eye! I see war sweeping on without end, as a fire whipped up in summer's heat, consuming the kingdoms of Christendom, pulling the righteous and the damned alike down into the sea of blood, poisoning this continent until at last we can say, 'The very world we knew is dead.'"

The road curves as they walk past St. Peter's Church. The sadness in Erasmus' heart is echoed in Amerbach's eyes.

"No doubt the ancient Romans thought as much when Alaric was at the door," the younger man muses.

"They were not wholly wrong."

"But the ending of one world was the making of another: of the world we know now."

Breaking and remaking! Perhaps such things must occur, but Desiderius Erasmus has no desire to witness them.

"For a thousand years the writings of the Greeks lay dormant!" he cries, needing his friend to understand. "What was lost was only regained by the strivings of generations. A millennium of seeking out manuscripts through war and plague and financial ruin! Entire lives devoted to gaining a few more words of Plato and Aristotle, or a single treatise of Origen! Always grasping, always reaching for one more treasure to be snatched from the fire! And still it seems too little, for men would count the very riches of heaven cheap."

Amerbach is quick to the mark. "A great struggle in which you have played no small role!"

He shakes his head in frustration. "Then can you not see what it is I fear—what haunts my dreams both in sleep and waking?"

They have come at last to 'Old Faithful.' The green door stands before them, waiting to receive.

"Even so, faith is tested," Amerbach concludes, placing a hand on his shoulder. "It will be the testing of you, Erasmus. But you have something of gold about you that may yet be saved, even through fire."

"One day, these misjudgments will catch up with you," he replies, falling back upon self-deprecation.

Amerbach smiles and knocks on the door, which after a brief wait is answered by Margarethe, still wearing an apron covered in what appears to be the juice of some fruit.

"Welcome back, Your Malignancy!" she greets Erasmus, then surveying Amerbach's visage, inquires, "And who might you be?"

"Bonifacius Amerbach, recently returned from abroad," the visitor replies, removing his cap and bowing his head. "And am I speaking to a Fräulein or a Frau?"

Margarethe makes another study of the young man with her eyes, taking in the stitching of his garments and, if Erasmus does not mistake her, paying special attention to Amerbach's codpiece.

"It's Frau to you," she concludes. "Now, are you coming in or staying out?"

"In, thank you, Margarita," Erasmus responds quickly, hoping to discontinue the conversation before something more unsavory is uttered.

As they enter the main foyer, the boards creaking beneath them, Margarethe says, "Herr Froben is up in his study—take the stairs behind me. Herr Erasmus, that boy Sebastian came by to say he lost one of your letters again."

"What!" Erasmus cries, pulling at his hair. "That is the third time, Margarita! The third time!"

"Well, don't force your complaints on me! It's he who needs an earful!" she reasons.

Sighing deeply, Erasmus leads Amerbach in the direction of the stairs, where they almost collide with Froben's teenage daughter Justina, who is returning from the courtyard behind the house. She is dressed in a gown the color of the boundless sea, with a white silk covering on her head. Erasmus thinks he catches Amerbach standing up straighter in the corner of his vision. Without making eye contact or saying a word, Justina cuts in front of them both, lifting her skirt and ascending the stairs.

"And a very good day to you!" Erasmus cries after her, receiving no response.

"What on earth was that?" Amerbach asks, staring after her.

"That is the bane of our existence," Erasmus replies through gritted teeth.

"She's beautiful," Amerbach mutters breathlessly. "Does she go out?"

Erasmus swats him on the back of the head. "Not in that way, fool! She's practically a girl."

"She was a girl last time I met her," Amerbach explains as they ascend together, "but that was most definitely a woman I saw just now."

"You would not think that if you heard her speak," Erasmus mutters.

They make the turn down the passage and enter the open door to Froben's study, where they find the man of the house with a glass of wine in hand, studying the shelves full of books.

"My liege!" Erasmus declares, drawing Froben's attention. "We have just come from the blessed event which you could not possibly make on account of your excessive workload!"

Froben smiles wryly, swirling the wine in his glass. "I had business with this goblet," he claims. "Perhaps the two of you are about to become busy as well."

"Yes, please!" Amerbach exclaims. "I'm parched."

Soon they are all standing together, goblets in hand, sipping the fruit of the vine, their silence greater than the finest speech of other men. At length, Froben shakes his head, sighing in frustration.

"What is it?" Amerbach asks.

"I don't understand it," says Froben, staring down at the floor.

"Don't understand what?" Erasmus asks.

Froben lifts his head and looks Erasmus in the eye, his face painted with sadness. "Why?!" he cries, the guttural noise echoing from his throat. "Why would they do it? Why would they throw it all away—this precious moment in human history?!"

Although he has not named them, Erasmus knows of whom Froben speaks: not only the peasants in an uproar, stabbing and biting at will, but men who ought to know better—who have received the best education and supped at the finest tables, yet given way to passions far beneath themselves, whipping the lower classes into a frenzy, cursing the very learning that empowered them. *Professing to be wise, they have become fools.*

"How long have we worked to pull ourselves out of the morass of ignorance?" Froben asks, gesturing with his hands, working Erasmus' heart like a pile of clay. "How long have we been slaving in the dirt, borne down by pestilence and disease, without the light to guide our way? And now the light has come to Christendom: the kings have brought peace, the academies triumph, the wealth of human knowledge is available as never before." He shakes his head, overcome by grief. "They're throwing it away. They're throwing it away over nothings, rushing headfirst into war, heedless of whom they hurt, without an ounce of humility. We had a golden hour, Erasmus! Was it not golden?!"

Erasmus feels the sting of these words in his bones. In his mind, he wishes to say that the greater portion of men are led by lies, and always for the benefit of the liars. But in his heart, he knows that things are not as simple as that. Noble as their efforts may be to restore good learning, there are realities he must acknowledge—if not to the men who call daily for his head, then at least to the man he trusts as well as any other.

"Friend, no one thought it more golden than I," Erasmus explains, shaking his head sadly, "but you forget: not all that shines is gold. One man's triumph is another man's disgrace. There are always two sides to history. Old resentments fester and stir, and always the devil does his work. Some say war is the natural state of man. I could think of nothing less natural than to take up arms against one's neighbor, but I cannot deny the evidence."

Froben presses on, fiercely animated by what he feels. "We had a moment—a single moment in time to make things right! Now the hour is seized by thugs and miscreants!"

"Perhaps there will be other moments?" Amerbach asks timidly.

"Yes," Erasmus agrees, but finds he must offer a somewhat grimmer assessment. "Perhaps when the rain has come and washed the blood away, when the birds have had their fill and the bones are collected and ground up, when the last death-mad man is dead, perhaps someone will be left to read what we've written." As he speaks the words, he can see it: the great cities of the earth lying in ruins, the streets littered with the remains of the dead, the rivers running red.

"If it has not all become food for fire," Froben mutters.

"Indeed," Erasmus agrees, nodding his head. "And they will read it and build upon it, a single layer at most. Then the cycle will repeat again and again until the end of time—until the Judgment Day."

"Is that what business we are about?" Froben asks desperately. "Will we never equal the greatness of Athens?"

Erasmus interlocks his arm with Froben's, for from one another they may gain the courage they both lack. Within the crook of his arm, Erasmus feels the slight pulsing of Froben's flesh, and he senses that their fears are the same. *Not the sort of kinship one would prefer, but perhaps the deepest connection of all.* He knows he must offer his friend words, if not of comfort, then of something less than terror.

So, he says, "You forget that Athens was burned to the ground before ever there was a Parthenon, and as soon as the Parthenon was raised, the great plague came upon them. That is the way of humanity: two steps forward, but always one back." It is the most he can conjure at the moment—less than hope, but more than despair.

"But that is the way of Christ!" Amerbach contends, bouncing upon his toes, so great is his excitement. "The pilgrim way is fraught with peril. Never does it run straight, but there is strength for the journey, if only we would seek it out." He looks at one man and then the other, beseeching with eyes full of love. "My esteemed friends, we are pilgrims only—always pilgrims."

Froben nods sadly. For him, this exhortation seems to work its magic. Amerbach walks toward the windows, taking a draught from his goblet, satisfied with the speech he has just given. But Erasmus fidgets in his shoes, feet longing to stretch, toes constricted and burning. Many years he has spent upon that road of which Amerbach speaks, never knowing which way led to light and which to darkness. *Oh, to be young and unburdened! To experience these tumults with peace in one's heart!* For if he had eyes to see, Amerbach would know that the days of pilgrimage are over—that men move no longer toward the things of heaven, but further inside themselves.

Erasmus looks aimlessly into the distance, thoughts buzzing, heart restless in the extreme. Another young man, equally earnest, occupies his thoughts: one whom he once believed to be the hope of Germany. *A man more learned than any of these new preachers, but they would claim him for their own.* Perhaps the rising tide of violence will help Melanchthon to see—will allow him to finally understand the true nature of these radicals. The very thing that causes Erasmus misery may be a blessing for society, for if Melanchthon turns back to the light, if he takes up the mantle Erasmus wishes to leave for him, there may yet be some hope for the future. Thus, Erasmus closes his eyes and wills a message over the ancient hills of Swabia and Thuringia, into the flatlands of Saxony, along the twisting path of the Elbe, and within the very walls of Wittenberg. There he appeals mind to mind, as if such a thing were possible.

Oh Philipp! Can you not see? When the foundations are removed, the house crumbles, and you have removed the chief stone. You have allowed yourself to be led by lesser men. May you see before it is too late. I will be waiting.

4 May 1525
Seeburg, Electorate of Saxony

Martin Luther awakes with a start, his heart pounding. Someone is attacking him—perhaps more than one person grasping at his flesh, attempting to tear him out of bed. He strives to adjust his vision to the light coming from—well, what is it coming from? Torches! Yes, flaming torches!

He falls to the floor, his body crashing upon the wood boards, the pain seizing him as surely as the rough hands that pull him up by the arms.

"Your hour has come, Luther! You will burn!"

Still, Martin's eyes struggle to fight through the blur around him. *What is happening?! Who are these people?!* He can just make out their hateful faces scowling at him as he is dragged across the floor and out into the courtyard. Here is a crowd full of scoffers—the sound of drums beating along with his heart, counting down the final breaths he will take before he is consumed.

"You are damned to hell, Luther! Damned to hell!"

Farmers waving the implements of their trade. Mad preachers pointing at him and cursing. A bishop holding up a crucifix and spitting on his face. It is the whole world turned against him, and he is gripped with terror, desperately longing for the warmth of love from a human soul—any soul that might show him grace.

His vision is clearer now. He sees a raised scaffold on which a stake and wood have been prepared. Here at the base of the steps is his old opponent, Johann Eck, holding up the bull of excommunication.

"Burn, heretic! Despair!" Eck cries.

Now, as Martin is dragged upward, his knees banging on every step, he sees Andreas Bodenstein von Karlstadt holding his guilder aloft. "You have betrayed the gospel!" he charges, thrusting the coin at Martin. "Go to meet your Judge!"

In vain, Martin searches for a face that wishes him well, but the chants are thunderous. "Burn! Burn! Burn!"

Next comes Thomas Müntzer holding a blood-soaked sword. "The hour of judgment has come!" the mad preacher cries, the light in his eyes demonic. "Too timid—too weak! You will pay for your cowardice!"

Now Erasmus of Rotterdam stands before him, a book in hand, lending his sight to the words on the page rather than Martin's suffering. At the last moment, the Dutchman's blue eyes meet his own, boring into Martin's being. "All will be lost. Yes, I will come for it all."

They have reached the stake. Standing beside it is an old man in a dark cloak who holds a torch in his wrinkled hand, prepared to set the wood alight. Martin squints to make out the face, attempting to synchronize the nose, the mouth, the eyes. All is hidden in shadow. Then to his horror, the man throws back his hood to reveal the face of Hans Ludher.

"Father," Martin whimpers.

"Oh, no you don't!" Hans bellows. "Don't you dare call yourself my son!"

It is happening quickly now: they have stripped Martin down to nothing but his braies. He is pressed against the stake—the chains wrapped around his body, cutting into his flesh. His father steps forward to incite the flames. The crowd is rejoicing in the torment he will endure.

Then a soft touch upon his shoulder. His chains fall to the ground. A voice: "Follow me."

He sees a figure—female, he thinks—clothed all in white, with auburn hair. *An angel! God has sent me an angel!* He cannot make out the angel's face, but he follows close behind, stumbling and straining.

They slip through the crowd effortlessly, impervious to the forces of hate. He feels his terror melting—his strength returning. They have entered a peaceful meadow full of wildflowers of every imaginable color. The angel is beautiful to behold, glowing softly in the light of the sun. She—for he still senses it is a female, though he had never thought angels were sexed—seems almost lighter than air, unburdened by the weight of the world. He breathes in the scent of lavender—hears the faint buzzing of the bees. But the angel looks as if she might continue without him.

"Stop!" he pleads. "Please, stop!"

The angel pauses but does not turn to face him. She stares off into the distance, her tresses flowing in the wind. He feels himself invigorated by her presence: called to communion with their mutual creator. A joy he has seldom known filters through his being. He is in the land of the living. Indeed, he has never been more alive.

"Who are you?!" he begs to know. "Please, let me see your face!"

She turns slowly. Her features sharpen. A pair of hazel irises stare back at him.

Then suddenly, the scene disappears. Martin opens his eyes and sees the wood beams high above. He is back in his room, the last place he remembers being before falling asleep. The clarity of wakefulness washes over him.

A dream, he realizes. *It was all a dream.*

He pushes himself up with his forearms. His upper body is drenched in sweat. Now he swings his legs over and sits upon the edge of the bed, staring out the lone window in this tiny room. The sun is rising—the birds are singing. He has been traveling for almost three weeks now, and every day has brought news of the rebellion: lords surrendering to the insurrectionists, Müntzer hissing and cursing, and then the thing that nearly stopped his heart.

In the town of Weinsberg, on Easter Sunday, a band of rebels waited until the Count and his servants had gone to church. Grasping the opportunity, they invaded the castle, slaying its guardians and taking the Countess and her child captive. Next the rebels pillaged the town center, seizing the Count himself and anyone with links to him, from his chamberlain down to his cook. One man was stabbed and thrown from the church tower despite begging for mercy. The rest they drove into a field—twenty-four men in total—and demanded they run the gauntlet with the townspeople and Countess watching. Some scurried to their death, while others were cut down for refusing the humiliation. The Count and several others were impaled with lances, then dragged naked through the streets in celebration. Many of the townspeople later followed them in death.

When he heard of it, Martin was filled with a fury he has seldom experienced. He recognizes the hand of the devil in this present darkness, for he has known that searing touch in the throes of battle and felt it cold as ice upon his chest.

These are no simple peasants seeking relief from taxation, he thinks. *These are insurrectionists attempting to bring down the government. If they will do that in Weinsberg, then there is no one they will not kill and no law they will not break to impose their will.*

Ever since he received the news of Bloody Easter, his dreams have been haunted, growing worse by the night. Now, he has suffered the most fearsome yet, but it is not the hateful voices that shake him to his core, but the sight of the angel. No, not an angel: a woman of human flesh even as he. Someone told him years ago that men dream of what they fear. Whether that is true, he knows not, but he is quite certain it was Fräulein von Bora whom his mind conjured in the depths of slumber. *Is it a sign—the answer to my prayers? Should I marry her? But how can I when the angel of death is at the door?*

"What would you have me do, Lord?" he prays in his solitude. "The devil is pressing on me—pressing so hard!" Even as he speaks the words, he senses the darkness hanging over him, as if the sunshine streaming through the window were a cruel deception. There are now thousands upon thousands of rebels armed to the teeth, many of whom would not hesitate to slay him for his perceived crimes.

They are coming. They seek my life to kill me.

Suddenly, he hears a fist colliding with the door. A shiver runs from his neck down to his tailbone—he looks in the direction of the noise. Still, the door is assaulted. Again, again, again! Like the drumbeats in his dream, the hand of Fate seems to strike at his soul. *Could it be the angel of death? No, surely not!* And yet he feels himself transfixed, unable to move for fear of the unknown.

"Open up, Martin!" calls the voice of Johannes Agricola. "I must speak with you."

So, not the angel of death, then, he concludes. It is only his former student and sometime secretary, who has been traveling with the company. They took up this lodging in the village of Seeburg the previous night. Martin has preached every day in a new town, hoping to make the people see reason and refrain from violence. But everywhere their party travels, they encounter men wild in the eyes, driven mad by prophets who promise them heaven on earth at the mere cost of human blood.

"Come in!" he calls to Agricola, fearing very much what the urgent message might be.

Now Agricola strides through the very door Martin recently saw in his dream, but thanks be to God, there is no screaming crowd on the other side: only the passage leading to the other rooms. Johannes stops short to avoid hitting the end of the bed, so small is the chamber. The young man with a bare face looks at Martin from beneath a flat cap and speaks with an accent as familiar as his own, for they are sons of the same town.

"We have received word from the Elector's court," Agricola begins, his tone grave. "The rebels have formed into a massive band and are moving north. They are within a day's ride of our position. Duke Georg and Landgrave Philipp have called the Swabian League to arms. They join with the Elector's forces and will ride to meet the enemy. But that is not all, Martin."

"Really?" he asks in disbelief. "I should have thought that would be enough."

Agricola shakes his head sadly. "Spalatin has sent word: the Elector is close to death."

A pang in Martin's heart. This man, Elector Friedrich of Saxony, is the one who has protected him for years and allowed for reforms in the churches. He will be succeeded by his younger brother, Duke Johann, who is a good bit more enthusiastic about reform than his uncle. Therefore, all should be well, but it is still a blow to lose Friedrich. The Elector's relative, Duke Georg of Saxony, opposes all reforms and is keen to increase his power in the region. Might the day come when he challenges the new Elector for control of the territory in which Martin resides? Might all the reforms be brought to an end as he, Melanchthon, and their friends are dragged to the scaffold?

Remain calm, Martin, he charges himself, but he cannot help feeling that his little world—the place where he has managed to find refuge from the murderous desires of his enemies—is in grave peril.

"He has also sent this message to you specifically," Agricola continues, his face strained. "He bids you end your preaching tour and return to Wittenberg with all haste, for the Elector cannot be certain of his ability to protect you or anyone else under the circumstances. There have been threats against your life, Martin: very real threats. We must ride!"

Martin rises from the bed—walks over to the window. There he stands with arms crossed, his mind tormented by visions of angry peasants coming to hack him to death. He will be the first sacrifice upon the altar of this new society, but how many others will perish before men have said "enough"? He can almost hear the taunting voice of Erasmus: *I told you so. I warned you.*

"I am glad at least some of the princes are taking it in mind to oppose this," Martin says, attempting to make his voice strong, "for too many others have laid down the sword of justice that God calls them to bear, allowing these insurrectionists to rampage through the country and pillage the sacred places of this land. You say the rebels have formed an army. Who rides at their head?"

Agricola moves closer to him—speaks solemnly. "They say it is Müntzer riding beneath a rainbow flag, staking claim to promises of God that are in truth lies of the devil."[18]

He nods in recognition. "Once with water, but never again: the next time will be with fire."[19]

A fierce burning starts in Martin's bowels, rising into his chest, stretching into his arms and down his legs. His muscles tighten, unwilling to let go of life. His heart pumps like a furious bellows. Thoughts of death, violent and twisted, consume him. A surge of pain from feet to forehead. The need to move—the need to do something! This is what it feels like to be clay in the hands of a potter. Martin closes his eyes, pained by all he is hearing. He speaks softly.

"Even so does the devil appear as an angel of light, but it is in his nature to devour. He devoured Müntzer first, and now he draws legions of men into the very jaws of hell."

"Too right," Agricola agrees. "It will take us a bit to prepare the horses. Then we must flee, Martin."

He turns to face Agricola, nodding his head. "I must first write a letter to my brother by marriage, but after that we will depart. A pity, for I wished to visit the lake."

"You may have time if you walk quickly. I will leave you alone with your thoughts."

With this declaration, Agricola departs in haste, shutting the door behind him.

"If you leave me with my thoughts, then you do not leave me alone," Martin whispers.

He reaches into his leather bag to retrieve his writing implements. *One piece of parchment or two?* He thinks one will do. There

---

[18] The peasants who fought with Thomas Müntzer carried a flag that featured a rainbow against a white background. It also included text in Latin and German reading roughly, "Let the word of the Lord remain forever, which is the sign of the eternal covenant of God," a reference to God's designation of a rainbow as the sign of his covenant with Noah (and by extension all creation) in Genesis chapter 9. A replica has typically been displayed at the St. Marien Museum and Müntzer Memorial in modern-day Mühlhausen, Germany.

[19] In the Bible, the rainbow is a sign that God will never again destroy the earth with a flood (see Genesis 9:12-16). St. Peter writes in his second epistle that the earth will be destroyed a second time with fire (2 Peter 3:5-10).

is no desk in the room, so he sits upon the edge of the bed, placing a book in his lap for a hard surface, and begins writing, the ink flowing in quick slashes. But as he does so, he finds himself utterly distracted, unable to break free from the fears that capture him.

In his mind is a scene of apocalyptic fury: an army of the devil marching across the green fields of Germany, with the fool Müntzer on his farmer's horse and the spirit of chaos driving them on. They come not only for him, but for all that binds society together.

Could this be it? he wonders. *Could this really be the end? The peasants are in a murderous fury. The Turks are at the gates. The Antichrist is on the throne. The plague comes in its season. What will be left when the storm is passed?* he wonders. *Could this really be the end? Or are there horrors greater than these stored up for coming generations?* He cannot be certain, but it feels like the end. The planets are in alignment, and soon the stars may fall. "Have faith, Martin," he charges himself. "Have faith in the Creator, for only he can make the heavens and earth anew. Whenever the end comes, it will come on his terms. For the gospel will reach to the farthest corners of the earth, and only then will the end come."

He writes a few paragraphs, but it is no good. His spirit is far too strained within him. So, he sets the letter aside and departs the inn, walking in the direction of the lake, where he hopes very much to bring order to his spinning thoughts.

The weather is fine this morning. He walks beneath a blue sky. But he is not fooled: this is the realm of fire, and if the princes do not crush the rebellion, not only he, but everything he sees will be subjected to flame. He hears a loud cawing and turns to look at the small house on his right, where a group of crows are perched upon the thatched roof. *No doubt they believe they are the lords here,* he thinks, *and when the men are all dead, they will be.*

Sometimes birds are more than just birds. As he watches, they rise in a flurry, dark wings beating against the air, caws echoing across the countryside. In an instant, he feels himself transported to a time four years ago: a period when he wrestled face to face not with God, but the devil.

He remembers traveling through the Thuringian Forest, the Emperor having honored his promise of safe conduct from the Diet of Worms under pressure from the princes. It was a brief reprieve from the certain sentence of death: another chance to say farewell. But death had summoned him nonetheless, and they would meet in the end.

He remembers the wood—the soft green of the beech trees, the red-gray rock formations, the spruces swaying gently in the breeze. Crunching leaves under wagon wheels. Beside him sat his colleague, Nikolaus von Amsdorf, who like Martin was party to a great secret: the Elector intended to hide his most famous subject away. This word was passed to them, but Martin did not know if he could trust it. How was such a thing to be accomplished? Might the Elector have made some deal with the emperor to turn him over in exchange for bountiful reward? And who was to say if the Elector would reach him first?

Martin knew not whom to believe, or whether any man remained true. He could only endure the hours of travel, jostled continually by crevices of the earth, driven toward an uncertain end.

Then came a cracking sound in the brush. Suddenly, men fell upon them on all sides. The horse pulling their cart reared upon its hind legs, whinnying in fright. *They have found me away from the crowd,* he thought. *They will kill me without a trial!* For surely the Elector's men would not fall upon them so. A rough bag was thrust over his head. Darkness: wretched darkness! Sounds of a struggle. Metal striking metal. He could hear Nikolaus shouting something incoherent: whether urging him toward courage or haranguing their captors, Martin could not say. He was dragged away—loaded into another cart. Mile after mile it traveled, weaving left and right until he lost all sense of direction. *Death has come for you. It is drawing you to the scaffold.*

Be with me, Lord! he prayed, his hands clasped and bowels clenched, anxious sweat seeping from his pores.

How long they journeyed in the dark, he could not say. Weary beyond weariness, he succumbed to slumber—a foolish act, but he could not fight it. He felt as if he had no fight left at all, but the greatest battle of his life was about to commence.

The first thing he knew upon waking was the warm light of the sun streaming through a window and striking his face. He squinted against its glow, attempting to make sense of his surroundings. *Where am I? Is this a prison?* He was lying upon a proper bed: a fine four-poster! *That does not seem likely for a prison.* He realized he was naked from the waist up, clothed only in his braies. *My clothes! Where are my clothes?* He sat up and examined the room. It was clearly a bed chamber, and yet something about it was not quite right: the air felt too stagnant. All four walls were covered in wood panels, save for one small portion of stone where there was a simple hearth too small, he thought, to provide any real warmth. There was a desk and chair, a small wardrobe, a chest, but no sign of any of his things. *Where am I?!*

By this point, he was properly panicking. His pulse raced as his heart contracted and expanded. He attempted to calm himself, recalling the promises of Scripture, but it was no use. His breath was coming rapidly—he was hyperventilating! His limbs tingled and strained. A suffocating darkness descended upon him. Uncertain what else to do, he bolted from the bed and ran to the window, where to his surprise, he saw that he was very high up: above even the tops of the trees. Before him, the forest stretched to the horizon.

"A castle," he whispered. "A fortress upon a hill."

He stared at the trees for a moment: the multitude variations of hue in those leaves. *I know these trees.* The Wartburg Castle! Yes, the very fortress that watched over him during his boyhood days in Eisenach. It belonged to the Elector Friedrich. *So it was his men after all. But why the deception? Does he intend to carry out the Emperor's edict?* These were pressing questions, yet he found himself distracted by the absence of his clothes. In vain, he searched the empty wardrobe for his Augustinian habit. The chest revealed clothing, but not his: it was apparel fit for a knight. He turned to look at a door that he guessed led to a passage. *Could there be someone guarding the other side?* He went up to test this theory, but found the thing locked. Turning on the spot, he ran to a smaller door on the opposite wall. It too was bolted shut.

So, I am a prisoner, then, he concluded bitterly.

Uncomfortable remaining in such a state, he donned a shirt from the chest: one far finer than any he was accustomed to wearing, with decorative edging around the neck and wrists. He was about to retrieve a pair of boots when the door to the passage suddenly swung open, and a bearded man entered wearing the insignia of Elector Friedrich, his velvet clothes covered in the gold and black stripes of the House of Wettin.

Once the door was closed behind him, Martin asked, "Have you brought me here to kill me then?"

"Perhaps we should begin with 'good morning,'" the man suggested. "I am Hans von Berlepsch, steward of the Wartburg."

Martin shook his head in frustration. "I stand here wondering how many minutes remain until my death, and you jest with me?! Tell me now: Why has the Elector brought me here of all places?"

"To protect you, Doktor!" the steward declared with a smile. "He takes far greater concern for your safety than you do."

This, at least, was a relief. Martin's muscles relaxed slightly.

"Well, don't just stand there in your underthings!" Berlepsch charged him.

"What else would you have me do?" he asked, exceedingly annoyed. "You have taken my clothes."

The steward chuckled. "We have given you new ones! Right there in the chest: put them on!"

Martin looked down at the knightly garb, then back at the steward. "You mean for me to wear this?"

"Yes, and you had best forget your name. You are 'Knight Jorg' now." When Martin merely looked at him in confusion, the steward explained, "We have disposed of your earlier garments. You cannot be Brother Martin anymore. That man is dead. Only Herr Jorg can live."

"No one will take me for a knight," he objected.

"They will when your hair is grown in. Until then, you are to remain in this room. No one must know your former identity: not even my men here. I would trust them with my life in battle, but I would not trust their tongues once they've been at the drink."

The anxiety was building within Martin. It seemed they really did intend to kill him, but not by destroying his body. They were forbidding him to be a monk as surely as Staupitz once did: forcing him into a role he never sought, and why? *What good does it do the Elector to hide me away? But I cannot speak against the Elector.*

"I don't know what to say," Martin concluded quietly. "Am I to reside in this place forever?"

"That remains to be seen," the steward concluded. "I will leave you now."

For the next week, Martin remained alone in the chamber, receiving nothing but food and drink from his guards. It was a chilling experience: he was cut off from the world, robbed of information. Not only that, but he was robbed of human communion. Without books, paper, or pen—the few permanent residents of the castle were not of a scholarly bent, it seemed—he struggled to keep his mind calm as the walls seemed to close in around him.

The mornings were especially bad, and soon he was struck by torments of the bowels. Hour after hour, he crouched over the pot, praying for his shit to release. Sometimes it was hard as the rocks on which the castle stood, and sometimes it came forth in painful spurts, burning as it went. Day and night, the sound of boots pounding on floorboards seeped through the thin walls of his chamber. When finally, he was granted the gift of sleep, the noise of guards shouting to one another would call him back to the land of the living—if indeed it could be called such.

The days grew hot. With no shade to protect him, Martin seemed to bake, the air growing heavy. Suffocating! Intolerable! He began to sense a great darkness in the room, as if the devil himself were hovering over him. With every shit he struggled to pass, he felt himself torn open, his body the plaything of demonic forces. His mind was fraught—he was breaking down. The terror began to strike him regularly. He cowered in a corner, weeping in distress. He paced the room frantically, attempting to release what he felt inside. He lay prostrate upon the bed, wetting his pillow with his tears, drenched by successive waves of despair. Never had he felt so emptied of existence.

Even as Elijah confronted the prophets of Baal and then fled for his life into the wilderness, so he found himself: broken and alone, starving and exhausted, sick in body and spirit. Would God meet him there as he met Elijah, or had he come to be tempted by the devil? *That is the trouble with analogies,* he thought. *One never sees the end of the tale. Perhaps I am not Elijah at all, nor any kind of prophet. Perhaps what they say about me is true: I think myself wiser than all the Fathers, but I am a damned fool.* But how could he deny what he had seen and felt?

He longed for the certainty of Moses. "Even as he prayed, so I pray: Show me your glory!" But there was no reply. The God who hides himself would deny Martin Luther even the gentle breeze. "I would at least see your goodness," Martin pled quietly, overcome by the silence of the Almighty One.

Finally, he was given paper and ink. They had been forced to fetch it from the town. *Who doesn't keep such things on hand?!* He began scrawling out what he suffered, struggling to put it into words, throwing most of his drafts in the fire. As he sat writing by the light of a single candle, he felt a foul wind upon his neck—heard the biting whisper within his mind.

Fraud. You are a fraud.

"Be gone, devil!" he cried. "Leave me alone!"

But the voice continued to torture him. *You have come here to die. You will never get out. There is nothing left but death. You are a fraud!*

Again, the terror struck. Again, he was forced to talk to himself—to reason against his anxieties. And still his bowels were torn, his shit mingling with blood. He could hardly bring himself to eat. All was darkness. He thought often of death.

Who could understand the emptiness he felt? The world saw him as a colossus wielding the club of Scripture against the false gods of the Schoolmen—a man who would cast the whole of canon law into the flames without so much as blinking. They would read his attacks on the papacy and cheer. "Finally, a man willing to say it! A man brave enough to be free!" But they could not imagine the cost at which his freedom had come.

No one loved the Roman Church more than he did. No one followed its dictates more closely. He gave everything of himself to Rome! He traveled on foot to the Lateran and performed his obeisance on the Scala Sancta. The Church was his all. He was prepared to die for it! The only thing he was not prepared to do was stand idly by as it slid into damnable error, pulling countless souls into the depths of hell.

For this one thing—this thing that ought to have been applauded—he had been denounced, dismissed, excommunicated, and condemned to death. The Holy Father cast him out of his house as surely as Hans Ludher once did. Even Staupitz, to whom he had revealed his soul, forsook him in the end.

What he was certain no one could guess was how deeply this grieved him—he who never wanted to see a single division in Christ's Church. They spoke as if he had cast aside his vows on a whim, when the truth was that they were taken from him to save his life and Staupitz's reputation. They spoke as if he hated the Church when he loved it with all his heart. They spoke as if he rejoiced in this tragedy, but he doubted he would ever fully recover from the pain.

It would be so quick, promised the subtle voice, nefarious in its intent. *You could jump from the wall. You could take a blade to your throat. You could end it all, escape the pain, be free of the torment.* But there was another voice inside Martin Luther, and it spoke a better word. *Despair is not freedom, but annihilation: a darkness unending. I will cling to the light. I will choose to believe in its power. I will pursue Christ as long as I have breath.*

A month: he had been in the room a month. The terror would strike him by morning and the devil by night. He prayed through the Psalms, reciting from memory. He clung to any hint of joy he could find. He was stripped bare, laid open before the Almighty. He could almost smell the stench of the devil. Within the markings of the wood panels—the ripples and eyes—he thought he could make out faces twisted in hate, glaring at him with the force of hell. They were with him always. He could not escape. He could only fight them with the ink he continued to spread over page after page, writing relentlessly, hoping to find some comfort in the madness of words he released. One night, in a fit of anger, he pounded the wall with his fist, receiving a bruise but no relief.

Where are you, God?! he silently wailed. *Can't you see my suffering? Free me!*

He looked out the window and saw the ancient forest stretching endlessly over rocky hills, the sky above it perfectly blue save for a wisp of cloud here and there. The sun was streaming down upon the valley. The trees rejoiced in the shower, their leaves fully revealed, a sea of green on which the black birds played, resting momentarily on the high branches, then taking flight in groups, weaving and diving, circling and dancing upon the breeze.

Such goodness of life was present there, yet he felt the chill of death in his bones. In this frame of mind, the castle was not a fortress but a prison; the trees did not shelter but confine; the sun was not there to cheer him but to remind him that he would never know joy again; and the birds were not playful but murderous, waiting to devour flesh.

He pressed his right hand against the window frame—a sigh escaped his lungs. Such plaintive longing he had seldom known: a yearning for many things, but most of all for human love and the communion of fellow believers. He wondered if somewhere beyond the trees, another soul was staring back and yearning for the same thing, and perhaps by some miracle he would one day leave that place and find himself renewed in their fellowship. But it was only a passing thought, and he found himself alone once again: alone with his thoughts and the devil, with no one to comfort him in the world.

I would rather die than stay in this room forever, he thought.

Now, a slight change. Having succeeded in growing a sufficient beard, he was allowed to explore a few more rooms, so long as he kept the feathered cap on his head. He even joined the hunt one day, hoping that a foray into the woods might do him good. Yet, he felt out of place in the strange knight's garb, half his body encased in leather. It seemed obscene to be wearing a sword on one hip and a dagger on the other, with a crossbow upon his back. He had a poor seat on his beast, for he had spent the last fifteen years either walking or riding in a cart. He made no attempt to shoot the hares: shooting had been his brother's specialty, and his brother was dead.

About an hour into the hunt, they dismounted to follow their prey on foot. He happened to grab a hare running past his toes when no one else was looking. Hearing the ravenous cries of the dogs and seeing the terror in the black eyes of their prey, he took compassion on the poor thing. Instead of snapping its neck, he hid it under his cloak, cradling it against his chest.

He was halfway through congratulating himself on this act of mercy when one of the hounds caught the scent and lunged at him, biting clean through his cloak and into the hare's leg. "Get off! Get off!" he shouted, but even as he uttered this cry, he saw blood falling to the ground. The shock of it caused him to slacken his grip, and the tiny beast was shaken violently, pressed between piercing teeth, its brown fur stained dark red. *Even so would my enemies prey upon me,* he thought. *Even so does the devil treat Christ's flock.* He was shaken every bit as much as the hare. No creature could escape death's summons.

After he had been there about six weeks, he was allowed to visit another portion of the castle: the stone palace built for Ludwig the Springer, or perhaps St. Elisabeth. There for the first time since Worms, he saw himself in a mirror, only he did not recognize the face that stared back.

His tonsure was gone. Yes, he had known it by touch, but the sight of it still shocked him. His hair was short, but another few weeks and it would be fully grown. His face was covered in a beard: again, he had known this, but he had not realized it would contain some gray. *Have I grown so old? I suppose I must have.* The rest of his hair seemed less affected by this aging. He would not have believed the reflection belonged to him were he not just as thin as always, his clothes hanging upon him more than enveloping his form. But as he had given up mandatory fasting, that was likely to change as well. *If only the food agreed with me!*

"Who am I?" he whispered. "What have I become?"

It was only there—in that isolation, removed from the unfolding narrative, with little news to hear and few tasks to complete—that he could finally look inward and ask these questions. The fate he had expected to receive was denied him, and though he was glad to remain among the living, his sense of purpose was shaken. *I was meant to die.* As he looked at the strange image before him, he was painfully struck by an overwhelming absence not only of communion, but identity itself.

"Who am I?"

For his first twenty-one years, he had been a faithful son of Ludher. For the next sixteen, a faithful son of Rome. *Whose son am I now?* He was truly alone with none to claim him, and he felt so utterly empty that he ached and groaned. He had been cast into the wilderness, and there the devil would tempt him, stripped as he was not only of his former vestments but anything that might tie him to the world he had so long inhabited. Once he bore the name of Ludher, then Brother Martin, then Doktor Luther. "But what am I to God?" he wondered.

Then, as if they had descended from on high, he remembered the words of the prophet Isaiah:

> "For You are our Father, though Abraham does not know us
> And Israel does not recognize us.
> You, O Lord, are our Father,

Our Redeemer from of old is Your name."[20]

As he gazed at the hardened face in the mirror, weathered by years of want and worry, he saw tears descending his cheeks. There was no one about, so he closed his eyes and allowed it to happen. Great heaving wails exited his chest as the tension of years released, and when at last he caught his breath, he whispered, "I am a son of God."

From that moment, his anxiety lessened—he was strengthened against the devil's attacks. He would remember, when the old lies came, to cling to the promises of God. He rejected despair, but still had no idea why his life had been preserved. *I was meant to die. That was my task. Why was I brought to this place? Why must I strive?*

Finally, he received more news. The work of reform was continuing apace. Indeed, it was gaining ground. The Word was triumphing in spite of his absence: old superstitions were being cast off, and the gospel was being preached. Men and women alike were realizing the futility of their monastic vows. Some were even daring to marry. He could not help but laugh at the thought.

Good for them, but they won't get me a wife!

Longing to be of some help, he threw himself into his work. He wrote through the long days and into the nights, burning his candles down to nubs. He translated the New Testament into German, sending his work to Wittenberg, receiving Philipp's comments in return, and making corrections. He could practically feel the Spirit flowing through him, empowering him to bring the Word to every man, woman, and child. *They will all be taught of God,* he pledged. *They will all know him.* At last, he brought himself to write his treatise against monastic vows, dedicating it to his father and apologizing for the rash decision he had taken so many years earlier. He had loved the Order of Saint Augustine, under whose tutelage he came to know the meaning of grace. But he had moved beyond it—moved even beyond his mentor, Johann von Staupitz, whose betrayal still burned in his breast. *I must finish the work of translation, and then I can die,* he decided.

Then came a sudden change. The reports from Wittenberg were no longer good. Karlstadt had taken over preaching at St. Mary's Church and was pushing things beyond the breaking point. Strange

[20] Isaiah 63:16.

prophets had arrived, telling the people to cast off the Word and rely on new revelation. Martin heard things that filled his soul with terror. An imperial visitation would come to end their work. *My sheep!* He began to wonder how he could remain at the Wartburg while they were under attack. It was the height of dishonor. Whatever the threat, whatever the risks, he had to go back. He had to defend his own.

And so, when the time was right, he wrote to inform the Elector that he would be leaving the castle for good. The place that was nearly the death of him had forever changed his life. He departed no longer afraid of the Elector's censure, for he knew that light would triumph over darkness. He had been prepared to lay down his life for the sheep at Worms, but instead he would lay it down for them day by day, for however long God chose to spare him. He had survived his bouts with the devil. He would wrestle now with God and man.

On a cold March day in the town of Wittenberg, only days after his return, he ascended the steps of the pulpit, prepared to preach to a congregation that had suffered a year of tumult in his absence. He knew the scale of the task before him: he would draw upon everything he had suffered to save the work that was in danger of collapsing. He reached over and gripped his wrist, reminding himself, *I am a son of God.* Then he opened his mouth to speak, harnessing the fire within him to bring light to those in darkness. He granted them a truth for which they might not be ready, but which they needed to hear, nonetheless.

"The summons of death comes to us all, and no one can die for another. Each man must face his battle with death by himself—alone."

It seems like only yesterday, but it has been three years. The memories fill his spirit to the point of overflowing. Their power captures him and defines all he is: no longer Brother Martin the monk or even Herr Jorg the knight, but Doktor Luther the professor and pastor—the freed one. So powerful have his memories been, he is forced to remind himself of his present situation.

They are coming. They seek my life to kill me. Quickly, Martin! he urges himself. *To the lake and back. We must leave soon.*

He continues walking, passing the few shops and perhaps twenty homes, most little more than shacks of wattle and daub. His feet scrape along the gravel path, lending sound to the tension within. He thinks back over the course of his life: the many times he has already escaped the clawing hands of death. Always the devil has sought to smite him, and by no power of his own has he prevailed.

Long we have fought, you and I, and I will strike you again if I must, he pledges. *It was always the Lord who pushed me on, captured my heart, raised me to life.*

He has reached the edge of the water. The rushes are thick here, and the blue water glistens in the morning sunlight. A constant din of grasshoppers' legs—the cawing of distant crows. He picks a spot with a clear view of the water, sitting cross legged. He attempts to feel the pleasure of this place: the calm amid the growing storm. But still the specter of Müntzer—no, the specter of the devil—rises to seize all that is dear to him.

Suddenly, a question forms in his mind: *And what is dear to you, Martin?*

"The breeze on my face," he whispers. "The beauty of the water. The taste of food prepared with loving hands. The warmth of a friend's embrace."

On and on he goes, listing all the things that remind him of God's goodness: the wonders of creation laid out before him, ready for the taking. Once, he was persuaded to reject them. He believed the experience of earthly pleasure and the acknowledgment of his flesh could only lead him further from his Creator. He has come to see his error, but a host of self-appointed preachers rises to perpetuate it. Karlstadt with his rejection of the physical—even of human love! The radicals trampling the sacraments underfoot. The hearts of men grown cold as ice.

It is the old lie, he thinks. *The lie by which the devil kept me in chains.*

Even as he ponders these things, the question repeats: *And what is dear to you, Martin?*

"That is almost to say, 'Who are you, Martin?'" he reasons. "Well, who am I?"

He knows the answer: a son of God, a man, a creature certain to die yet raised to eternal life. No matter what anyone says, these things will always be true. He is a creature born of dust, part of a creation that proclaims the goodness of its maker. Day after day, the devil seeks to hide that goodness away—to keep men in chains. But God made man of the earth and declared him good.

"My body, this thing that will be food for maggots—yes, even my body is good," he declares to the grasshoppers.

The thoughts are flowing through him at a rapid pace. He is on the brink of something, but he cannot quite grasp it. This failure frustrates him. He continues to repeat the things he has learned through years of struggling with the Almighty, always gaining knowledge the hard way, always striving to prove himself only to have his inability revealed.

Then, as he looks on, a swan appears from behind the rushes, gliding upon the surface of the water, its form elegant, its bearing sure. A group of cygnets follows behind: creatures of gray fluff bobbing somewhat less gracefully. Finally, in the rear, another adult. This will be the mate of the other. Swans, he has been told, mate for life.

That is the way it should be, he thinks.

As he watches the family of birds swimming together, he feels the holy yearning within himself. These creatures are doing exactly what God designed them to do. He recalls the first thing—indeed, the only thing in the original creation—that God declared to be less than ideal: "It is not good for the man to be alone." And now he hears the voice of Käthe: "They lied to us."

He pinches his eyes shut, inflamed by the ache of the years: of all he has suffered and all that has brought him to this moment. He knows what he must do. It is written there before him in the book of creation. He has been fighting his own nature, refusing the goodness God intended. He has been the devil's fool, but he will be fooled no longer. Though the evil one comes for his life, he cannot steal the life that Christ has placed within Martin Luther. Yes, the path before him is clear, for there was one thing he left off the list of all things dear. In the stillness, he whispers, "Käthe."

He rises from his place on the damp grass and turns back toward the town, walking in the direction of the inn, crafting the letter in his mind. *What I have declared so boldly in print and taught from the pulpit, I will proclaim with my own life.* Rather than forbidding it, the possibility of death requires it. This is what he must do to die well—the final word he must leave. The closer he comes to the inn, the faster his mind whirls. He is preaching a sermon to himself.

When we erase good for fear of evil, when we attempt to destroy desire rather than redirecting it, when we spurn true beauty to avoid false worship, we place men under a second Law. We make them fear God but never love him, for though they acknowledge his holiness, they know nothing of his goodness. I see no righteousness in this denial of our humanity! It is the work of the devil that seeks to place us always in earthly chains rather than binding ourselves to the one who truly frees us. I have had enough of his lies. For too long I believed them, but no longer. I will spite him. I will spite the devil! I will not spurn the heavenly grace for fear to be a son of God. To every son he scourges, he gives bread and not a stone. He is goodness and he is grace: grace upon grace, which is not driven out by sin, but raises the sinner to life that he might sin no more.

He has come to the inn at last. Here is the door to his room: the last barrier between him and what he must do. He enters, takes up his parchment and pen, and continues the letter to his brother-in-law, speaking of the war that threatens them all and the danger to himself.

"This rebellion is an attack against me. I am well aware that the devil is angry, since up to now he has been unable to accomplish anything, either by fraud or by force. He wants me dead. He is set to get rid of me, even if he has to attempt the worst and confound the whole world altogether. I almost believe and think that it is because of me that the devil is making such a mess in the world, and God allows it in order to vex the world. Well, if I get home I shall prepare for death with God's help, and await my new lords, the murderers and robbers, who tell me they will not harm anyone."[21]

His spirit excited to the point of bleeding, he sets down his pen and bids himself be calm. *Softly. Breathe. Breathe.* He feels a peace come over him: a certainty as from on high. He raises the pen again—presses it to paper.

"If I can manage it, before I die I will still marry my Käthe to spite the devil—"

He stops mid-sentence, struck by the enormity of what he has just done. With two words—"my Käthe"—he has claimed Katharina von Bora for his own. But of equal significance, he has given himself

---

[21] The quotations from this letter are based upon the following source, with some changes for the sake of clarity: Martin Luther, "To John Rühel, Seeburgh, May 4, 1525" in *Luther's Works* (American edition), Vol. 49 - Letters II, 106-12.

to her in return. He belongs to her now as surely as she belongs to him, for he has said he will make her his wife, and to take a wife is to be taken. With these words, he feels his existence transformed, as if the heavens themselves had come crashing down. He can already hear his enemies' cries of indignation like a twisting of his gut. He is far more terrified than elated, but the die has been cast.

Home, he thinks. *I must get home. I must tell her.*

17 May 1525
Wittenberg, Electorate of Saxony

Philipp Melanchthon sits at the desk in his study, poring over the freshly printed pamphlet in front of him. He received it from a student just half an hour previous, and now he looks upon the latest words of Martin Luther: an admonition for the governors to take up arms *Against the Robbing and Murderous Hordes of Peasants.*

Having accompanied Martin on much of his recent preaching tour, Philipp is not greatly surprised that his colleague felt compelled to address this issue. He too saw the warning signs all around them—felt the aura of some foul presence possessing the towns of Germany. He sensed events were weighing on Martin, pulling him down into darkness. Often, it seemed Martin's body was present but his mind a world away. The less said about their embarrassing visit to the Ludher home, the better.

With a sigh, he presses the pamphlet down, laying its pages flat. He has reviewed it three times already, his concern ever increasing. Unlike Martin's earlier admonitions for peace, which conceded that some of the peasants' demands were valid, this is an unmistakable call to arms. Somewhere in their journey, Martin's mind was clearly changed: he speaks now as if the rebels were not merely peasants too long oppressed, but demons sprung from the depths of hell.

He must fear the princes will blame this all on our work of reform, Philipp realizes. *He is not wholly wrong to suspect that.*

Much of the pamphlet is reasonable enough, proclaiming the dangers of insurrection, the role of princes in enforcing justice, and the need to save simple persons from being taken in by lies. The plundering of churches and monasteries, the butchering of noble lords, the abandonment of law and order: these things are rightly condemned.

There is talk of the end of the world and plenty of blame cast upon the devil. But there are also a few paragraphs that in their intensity cause Philipp to cringe. *I would not have put it so harshly. The wrong people could take matters too far.* Thus, he reads once again the chief source of his concern.

> "For if a man is an open rebel every man is his judge and executioner, just as when a fire starts, the first to put it out is the best man. For rebellion is not simple murder, but is like a great fire, which attacks and lays waste a whole land. Thus, rebellion brings with it a land full of murder and bloodshed, makes widows and orphans, and turns everything upside down, like the greatest disaster. Therefore, let everyone who can, smite, slay and stab, secretly or openly, remembering that nothing can be more poisonous, hurtful or devilish than a rebel. It is just as when one must kill a mad dog; if you do not strike him, he will strike you, and a whole land with you."[22]

Simply reading it again stokes the tension within Philipp. *Could not a ruler take that as an excuse to butcher any of these poor souls on the spot, without bothering to investigate their true deeds?* For all the evils that the rebels have committed, he fears the reaction of the princes as much as the evils themselves: that in seeking to end the insurrection, they will cover Germany in blood. He remembers the terror he felt in his youth when his own town was besieged by the Swabian League. The very name now fills him with fear. *A war may be started for some righteous purpose, but it will not be waged in righteousness,* he thinks.

For as long as he has known Martin Luther, Philipp has urged him to rein in his anger—to still the waters that teem within him, breaking forth into bitter speech. At times, Philipp has witnessed signs of progress; at others, he has despaired that the man will ever change. For every admonition Philipp gives Martin to tame his tongue, there are others bidding him to strike harder. *They play upon his weakness,* Philipp thinks. *I wish he would listen to me. I wish my counsel was not in vain.*

Now, he hears the door shutting in the room just above him: his and Katharina's bed chamber. Little Philipp is wailing. Feet are

[22] E.G. Rupp and Benjamin Drewery, *Martin Luther: Documents of Modern History* (London: Edward Arnold, 1970), 121-6.

pounding on the steps. The door before him opens, and in strides his wife, looking positively harried. She shuts the door and leans her back against it, breathing deeply, eyes closed. The screams from above remain piercingly audible in this house with thin walls.

"I've just put him in the crib to sleep," she explains, opening her eyes. "Forgive me. I needed to escape."

"The crying still bothers you that much?" Philipp asks, pushing the pamphlet aside.

She nods sorrowfully, her expression one of utter dejection. "Yes. I wish it didn't, but it does. I can hardly think when I hear it."

"Then have a seat," he instructs, motioning to a single faldstool near the hearth to his left. "Wait him out."

Katharina sits reluctantly, hands clasped together, looking very tense indeed. Even with all the noise from above, he can hear her breath coming steadily. She looks as if she can bear it no longer: she is rising from the stool.

She blurts, "I must—"

"You must let him cry, Käthe," he tells her, finishing the sentence. "It was the same with Anna. I know how protective you are of him, but you must let him cry, at least for a few minutes."

Even as he speaks the words, a voice in his head warns, *But it is not the same as with Anna. Something could be very wrong with him. You know it in your bones.* He strives to press the feelings aside—the anxiety that eats at him day and night. But still, he sees tiny Philipp's blue eyes, forever appealing for help he cannot give. He does not even know what ails his son, let alone how to cure it.

Katharina returns to her seat, gazing sadly at the floor. She is leaning forward slightly, still ready to move at a moment's notice. Even in this state—with her emotions on a knife's edge, her eyes dark from lack of sleep, and her blonde curls a mess—he is struck by her beauty. Let others say what they want, but he knows his wife is the most handsome woman on earth. It pains him to see her still so weary and worn—stretched to the point of breaking. *I was wrong to leave in her hour of need.*

His shame gives way to spoken words. "I'm sorry I was away so long."

She looks up at him, brows bent in confusion. "You did the best you could to get back. We were alright."

"I thought about you every day. I longed to see your face." As he speaks the words, he senses a fierce burning within himself: the longing for union—for mutual comfort of the most precious kind.

Katharina looks over at the window behind him. She seems deep in thought. Her gaze has a certain distant quality to it. As the baby continues to cry, she asks, "Philipp, whose choice was it for you to go: yours or Doktor Luther's?"

He inhales abruptly, for she has hit a sore spot. Katharina's eyes are fastened on him, awaiting an answer he is hesitant to grant. *What does she wish to hear? That I cannot say no to Martin, or that I selfishly chose to go myself?* He sees no way to escape unharmed.

"You told me you were at peace with the idea," he finally replies.

"And so I was, but I don't think you were then, and I don't think you are now. You've been so restless of late. Tell me, husband: what is it that troubles you? Is it Doktor Luther?"

Philipp glances over at the pamphlet, tracing its edge with his fingertips. *She knows me too well.* He can hide nothing from her, nor does he desire to do so. If anything, he wants to hide it from himself, for declaring all he feels will require an admission that all is not well, and that might force him to take some painful action.

"As a matter of fact, yes," he answers, pointing at Martin's words with his index finger. "He released this pamphlet against the peasants. It was extreme, even for him."

"Did he consult you before publishing it?" she inquires, her tone indignant.

"No," he replies, but hastily adds, "He was under no obligation to do so. He may write what seems best to him, even as I do."

Katharina scoffs. "It is a matter that affects the whole work, no?"

"Yes, I suppose."

"And it bothers you."

He pauses, once again hesitant to admit how much the situation has affected him, for he fears the consequences. Finally, he answers, "Yes," his voice little more than a whisper.

"Has he even begun his reply to Erasmus?" she inquires, arms crossed in frustration.

"I don't know. I don't think so. Sometimes—" His voice trails off. He is afraid to continue—to speak his fear. But he reminds himself, *This is your wife, the flesh of your flesh and bone of your bone. You must be honest with her.* Marshaling his courage, he states, "Sometimes I feel he does not value my opinions: that he doesn't trust me as much as he does Jonas or Bugenhagen."

This admission robs him of breath. He realizes just how much he has come to fear the situation in Wittenberg. Camerarius is gone, and he was a key ally. *But do I truly need an ally? Am I engaged in a conflict here?* To his surprise, his wife immediately echoes the concern.

"Or Cranach, or Amsdorf, or—"

"Yes, exactly," he interrupts. "No need to repeat the list."

Good Lord! he thinks. *Is it really that bad? Have I been so unaware of my own feelings? It is as if they are all cutting me out: that Martin listens to everyone else before me. It did not always feel that way. Have I gone mad? Is the lack of sleep affecting my reasoning?*

"Forgive me, husband," his wife interjects, "for you know I love and respect you with everything I am, but if you have a weakness, it is that you sometimes fail to assert yourself as you ought."

He sighs deeply. "So I have often been told, but you must admit, I am surrounded by men far too keen to assert themselves most of the time."

"True," she agrees with a nod. "I should think that the greater weakness. But I know you, my Philipp. I know your brilliance and your worth. Do you feel that the others here in Wittenberg do? Your fellow professors?"

Here is a punch to his gut. True, some of his colleagues are fonder of him than others, but none are truly disrespectful. *They like me, don't they? Surely, they must!*

"I think they do," he concludes, "but perhaps you overstate my virtues."

"Why would you say that?"

"You have suggested on occasion that you might be fond of me. It could be clouding your vision." Here he winks at her playfully.

"That is true," she concedes with a smile, "but I believe I speak for many when I say you are brilliant. Is that not why Erasmus offered you the position?"

Nodding slowly, he stresses, "A position I cannot possibly take, and one he is not truly able to offer."

"Perhaps not, but he offered it all the same, and that shows his respect for you."

Again, her words astound him. *Has she been thinking about this for some time?* He had no idea it was occupying her mind, even as it does his, and unlike him, she seems willing to push the matter to its logical conclusion.

"What are you saying?" he asks tentatively. "You think Desiderius Erasmus values me more highly than Martin Luther?"

"No, you have said that yourself."

"Only because you implied it, dear."

She looks away for a moment, her eyes closed—whether overcome by emotion or exhaustion, he cannot say. "Perhaps you are right, Philipp."

"Really? I must treasure this moment forever!" he kids.

Rolling her eyes, she continues, "You are right that when it comes to you, I am entirely partisan, for I see your worth better than anyone. I may be a woman without fame or fortune or exceptional learning, but I take great pride in you, Philipp Melanchthon, and though I could never strike fear in the heart of any man, you will find I am prepared to defend you to the death. That is how a wife ought to feel—how she should behave."

He is suddenly aware of every beat of his heart: powerful, rhythmic, pumping blood to every corner of his body. Were he a cat, he would be purring, or perhaps roaring. After nearly five years of marriage and two children, she maintains the power to work this magic upon him: to make him swell with pride at the sound of her voice and pulse with desperate yearning when it declares her regard for him. But there is still the sad business to attend to—he must not set it aside.

"I am gratified by your love, dearest, but what would you have me do?"

"Be honest with Doktor Luther," she states confidently. "You must not hold these things inside. It will only make you bitter."

He swallows hard. "And if it should cause the heavens to fall?"

"Then we will build a new life together, perhaps in Basel, perhaps somewhere else. Where you go, I will go, and where you stay, I will stay."

"By God's grace, it will not come to that," he says quietly, "but my dear, please know how much it cheers me to hear those words. I love you."

As she beams with pleasure, he realizes her anxiety is gone. *Quiet. It's quiet!*

"Listen!" he bids her. "Philipp has stopped crying. Both of them are asleep."

"A miracle!" she declares. "What should we do?"

He gazes upon her face, thinking of how many days it has been—indeed, how many months—since they were joined together. "I can think of one thing in particular," he concludes.

"Yes, I feel tired as well," she says, mistaking his meaning entirely. "We can use the empty room so as not to wake them. We might enjoy an hour of sleep." Looking into the distance wistfully, she utters, "Blessed sleep!"

Though he feels guilty for suggesting any other activity, the desire within him is great. He must make himself perfectly clear. So, he walks over to where she is sitting and kneels before her. He places his hands on her knees—stares into her eyes.

"What is it?" she asks, face painted with confusion.

"I have missed you so much—so desperately."

There it is: recognition rippling across her features, channeling the breath from her lungs. She says nothing, and yet she is speaking. As her lips part and eyes glisten, he senses she has been struck by the same desire. She is beckoning him silently: willing him to act. He crosses the space between them—kisses her lips deeply. She reciprocates, her spirit fully awakened. Their hearts are in sync, beating as one, prepared for the union about to occur.

They stop for breath, and he asks her, "Are you healed?"

The birth of Philipp left its marks upon her flesh. This is the reason, as much as their exhaustion, that they have been parted so long.

She nods softly. "I think so. I am willing to find out."

He kisses her again, more fiercely this time, pulling her close to himself. For a woman utterly exhausted, she is responding with surprising enthusiasm.

Then, a disaster! Someone knocks on the door. Philipp attempts to ignore it, but the banging grows louder by the second, as insatiable as the desire within him. Katharina breaks away, no doubt terrified that the baby will wake. It is no good. He must address the visitor.

"Who is it?" Philipp asks, or rather groans.

"It's Veit," comes the young man's voice. "I have news."

Veit Winsheim is his pupil and one of their boarders. Philipp groans, head drooping, spirit utterly dejected.

Katharina pats him on the head. "It's alright, husband. We will find another time."

"Really?" he asks, looking into her perfect eyes. "When?"

She gathers his face in her hands and kisses his forehead—looks tenderly in his eyes. "Some other time."

Something like a growl escapes Philipp's throat. *If this is not an announcement of the second coming of our Lord, I will kill him.*

Heart still pounding, he moves to the door and pulls it open, instantly placing a finger against his lips to signal silence. A startled Winsheim nods in acknowledgment.

"Forgive me, Doktor," his pupil whispers urgently. "I didn't think of the children."

"Is someone dead?" he grunts, *Because if they aren't, you are about to be.*

Even as he asks the question, Philipp notices the strain on Winsheim's face: the eyes filled with a horror that cannot be due to his chiding.

"Yes," Winsheim replies. "Yes, I'm afraid someone is dead."

Katharina has joined them. "Won't you come in, Veit?" she asks.

"Yes," Philipp agrees, pulling the door fully open. "Yes, please come in. Forgive me."

Once the young man has entered and the door is shut behind him, they stand in a circle of sorts, Philipp and Katharina waiting upon Winsheim's words.

"The first thing you need to know is that our dear Elector, Friedrich the most magnanimous, has passed from this life," Winsheim informs them. "We now owe our allegiance to the Elector Johann. May he live and rule by the grace of God!"

"It is as expected then," says Philipp, "and yet, a great loss. Elector Friedrich was a gift of God to us."

"Even so, his brother will be, and perhaps a greater gift still," Winsheim concludes. "But I am afraid that is not the only death I have come to report."

"Is it not?" Katharina asks, her voice trembling with concern. "Has the rebellion spread? Did the princes meet with Müntzer and his followers?"

"Yes and yes," Winsheim replies quietly.

The young man takes a deep breath, evidently preparing himself for a long recitation. He closes his eyes, then opens them again—they are filled with visible lament.

"The rebels made their stand upon a hill near Frankenhausen. The Landgrave and Duke surrounded them, demanding they surrender Müntzer, but they refused. Then it began: the rain of fire. The cannons let forth their weights. The guns burst into blaze. It wasn't a battle, Doktor. It was a bloodbath. The rebels attempted to flee—to take refuge in the town—but the princes were too clever by far. Some say five thousand were killed, others ten thousand. It would have been easier to count the men left alive. Of those, the chief is Müntzer, who is in the possession of the princes and will soon meet a bloody end. I spoke with a man who lives nearby. He walked through the town after it all ended. Great rivers of blood, he said, like something out of the Apocalypse. He saw the piles of dead men, their limbs severed, entrails spilled out, eyes bulging from empty skulls, tongues hanging out of mouths like the dogs that licked up their blood.

The women of the town were ordered to put the survivors to death. The princes thought this would teach them not to support rebellion—a cruel demand. But they did not understand the wives of Frankenhausen, for no sooner had they given the order than the women grabbed whatever tools they could find and began beating the men savagely, releasing the blood, reducing their flesh to pulp. A savage day indeed when women would take pleasure in such business! This was the great wrath of the princes, and with it the rebellion of Müntzer is likely ended, but what an end it was! I reckon it will be a thousand years before any peasant thinks to attempt such a thing again. They found Müntzer hiding in an attic, unwilling to acknowledge his name or his part in the affair. Well, they saw through his deception and will have his head for it. No death was ever so deserved."

Philipp glances over at Katharina, who looks as if she might be sick. He takes her hand, intertwining their fingers, and says, "There you are wrong, Veit, for a man without bread has nothing to lose and will gladly risk his life in the hope of saving it. They will rise again, and again, and again."

Winsheim shakes his head bitterly. "How many widows were made at Frankenhausen?! What will happen to their children? Though I bear those rebels no love for their deeds, I cannot see any good in this. The princes will slaughter thousands more before they convince themselves that order is restored."

As he listens to Winsheim speak, Philipp thinks of the pamphlet he has so recently read. *Smite, slay, stab! Kill them like mad dogs!* His anger is building like a fall of rain on a summer's day, growing thunderous in its ferocity.

"Bitter are these words in my ears!" Philipp laments. "Would that Martin had said nothing at all!"

"Oh, you cannot blame Doktor Luther for this!" Winsheim urges him. "This happened two days ago. The princes will not have read a word of that pamphlet."

Philipp shakes his head, his thoughts bitter. "Even so, under the circumstances, the thing strikes me rather differently. He must get ahold of his temper! He must—" Words fail him. He looks over at his wife, whose eyes are wide. He knows that expression: she is begging him not to continue.

"Forgive me, Veit," Philipp says. "I should not speak of such things in your company."

Fortunately, Winsheim chooses not to dwell on it. "I am glad at least that the rebellion is at an end, or soon will be. Let us pray for our new Elector. He will need it."

"Yes, thank you, Veit," Philipp concludes.

A few breaths later, he and Katharina are alone again, but whatever Philipp was previously feeling is long gone. All he knows is the darkness that seems to pierce him at every point, flowing freely through his body, clouding his thoughts. He lets go of his wife's hand and strides toward the window, looking out over Colleges Street. There people go about their business, walking this way and that, carrying burdens both literal and figurative. He rests his hands on the windowsill, breathing deeply, attempting to suppress the terror within himself.

From behind comes a whisper—the gentle voice of his Käthe. "What do you see, Philipp?"

His breath comes haltingly. His spirit churns within him.

"I see an endless plain, dark and barren, full of cuts and fissures. I see the weapons of war stirring up the earth, the pounding of hooves and feet upon mud, the ripping of fire through every green thing. I see the forces of evil dispatching all in their path, breaking down the fortresses to which we cling, their banners veiling the light of the sun. I see the Prince of this world riding upon a foul beast, leading the mass of humanity behind him in chains. I see a fearsome woman drinking the blood of the saints, and beside her is the figure of Death himself, making her his whore. Every mile of the earth I see, from the mountain peaks to the abysses of the deep, fallen to the enemy, and nothing but the memory of goodness remains. For all our strivings are as nothing against the power of hate, and the Prince of this world will have dominion even to the ending of time."

Katharina takes her place beside Philipp, rubbing his back. She speaks no word but lends him the benefit of her presence. Her mere touch is a comfort: her head upon his shoulder the hope that he bears. At length, she addresses him.

"You are looking down, Philipp—only down. Look up! How can you see all of that? Because of this thing which I see. It is bright as the sun. Look, there: the breaking light! It was not the devil who rent the earth, but God himself. The Lord of Hosts is with us now: yes, he is here. Oh, Philipp! It is bigger and greater! I see the fortresses and hosts of heaven, brilliant as the midday sun, visible only through eyes of faith. I see the hands of God holding the waters—his feet treading the dry land. For the heavens have opened, and he has descended to take his stand upon the earth. He is Lord over all. The very stars are on his side! It is he who casts the thunderbolts. The marching of the evil ones is merely a retreat: a dying gasp. Oh, how I wish you could see what I see! But you do, Philipp—you do. It is that light which allows you to see the darkness for what it is. How bright then is the light in you! And the light will guide us, even in the valley of the shadow of death. For I know little, and I speak little, but this I believe: that the light shines in the darkness, and the darkness will not overcome it."

He looks at her with tears in his eyes, rendered mute by the power of her words. Within him, there is a teeming mix of fear and hope. The emotions are blending together, creating a thing of strange and glorious beauty, as brilliant as the woman who now stands before him, in her weakness far stronger than the Emperor Charles himself. He kisses her again with the force of the breaking waves, in his pain receiving the comfort of the love she offers. As they unite, he is struck by the promise of Scripture: "Perfect love casts out fear."[23]

25 May 1525
Basel, Swiss Confederation

There is a lightness to Desiderius Erasmus as he makes his way through the streets of Basel, each step coming easily, his spirit seeming to float upon the breeze. He whistles to himself softly, his lungs drinking deeply of the clear spring air, for today the world is renewed. True, it is still full of plagues, but one at least has spent itself: the insurrectionists are destroyed.

The news has been all over the city for days. It seems his fears were only a vapor now driven forth by the light of day. The world is not ending, or at least not until the Turks return. One day, the rebellion will rise again. Even in an uncertain world, Erasmus is certain of that. But the princes will be ready next time—they will no longer seek to appease. When men hold a knife to the Empire's neck, there is only one thing to be done: kill those men and repair whatever damage they have inflicted. Otherwise, they will come again, in larger numbers, demanding ever greater prizes. There is no negotiating with men who put knives to people's necks.

How sweet it is to be freed of the anxiety that tortured him! As he enters the yard behind the Froben house, Erasmus is filled with something less than hope, but a good deal more than despair. Then he glimpses a sight that immediately alters his frame of mind: the errand boy Sebastian standing with a smirk on his face and a bag slung over his shoulder, his hair a mess beneath his plain gray cap. It looks like he is attempting a beard such as the merchants tend to wear but failing miserably.

"Des-ee-deer-us Eras-mess!" the knave greets Erasmus.

"For God's sake, you are doing it on purpose now!" he gripes in response. "You know very well how to pronounce it!"

"Whatever," Sebastian mutters, reaching into the bag and retrieving a letter. He extends it to Erasmus and says, "For you—all the way from France!"

---

[23] 1 John 4:18.

"You speak as if the French king's lands were on the other side of the world, when in fact they are very close to us," Erasmus retorts, snatching the letter from Sebastian's hand with no pretense of gentility.

The young man cocks his head to the side. "I thought the French king was dead. Didn't the Emperor kill him?"

"Wrong and wrong. For a messenger, you are poorly informed. King Francis was captured in Italy and is now a prisoner in Spain, very much alive. I suggest you consult better sources."

"Don't care," Sebastian replies, extending his palm. "Pay me, and I'll leave."

I need not pay for such mistreatment! Erasmus thinks, but nevertheless reaches into his purse and makes a deposit in the young man's grimy hand—it is the only way to be rid of him. Without a word of farewell, Erasmus enters the house and makes his way up to his study, where he pours himself a glass of wine and sits in one of the plush chairs by the hearth, the letter still in his hand. He examines the address but cannot discern whose hand wrote it. It is from the Collège de Montaigu, the most prominent theological school in Paris, second only to Rome in the power of its theological pronouncements. There are few bishops north of the mountains who do not fall under its sway. Erasmus well remembers the time he spent there, feeding on bad eggs and molding bread, struggling to listen to hours upon hours of lectures about Scotus.

"A curse on you, Montaigu," he whispers.

To his dismay, the seal is broken. *How many people have read this already?* he wonders. Still muttering internally, he unfolds the pages. Even before he reads the name scribbled in ink, he knows it is from Nöel Béda, the head of the college and a violently devoted Franciscan monk. More importantly, Béda has friends in all the right places—or more accurately for Erasmus, in all the wrong places. A few months back, Erasmus' friend, Ludwig Baer, passed on a list of complaints Béda has about Erasmus' commentary on the Gospel of Luke. *Leave it to Paris to hate everything I write!* Béda's opinion carries far more weight than most, especially in the Roman curia. Erasmus had attempted to head off any potential attack by writing to Béda in the spirit of Christian brotherhood, but as he begins to read Béda's reply, he senses that effort was for naught.

"I must tell you that I have begun to feel some considerable anxiety for your soul," the Franciscan writes.[24]

Never a good sign, Erasmus observes.

"You are constantly exerting yourself," Béda continues, "for what you claim is the good of others, in writing an unending stream of new books which the churches do not need."[25]

Erasmus grunts in displeasure. *I'd like to see how many worthwhile books you have produced!*

"Make up your mind to stop publishing new books, so that you may find yourself again and prepare for the judgment of God, which, given our age, cannot be far away for you or for me."[26]

Well, I was not mistaken then. He truly believes my soul is in danger of hell and my books are things of the devil. Why else should he warn me of God's judgment? Erasmus laments.

The tension builds in his chest, stiffening his neck and flowing into his shoulders, for he knows the reverence in which the theologians of Paris are held by those in the Roman curia. There is a real danger in Béda's censure, not only for Erasmus' reputation, but for his body itself. Already, Erasmus can see himself burnt in a pile of his own books. A ghastly thought!

"You will not be on sure ground on theological matters until you unlearn many things," Béda writes, "humbling your spirit in the eyes of God, and trusting no more in your own judgment."[27]

Even as he reads these words, Erasmus wonders where Béda's reasoning might lead. *Does he mean to pursue an official judgment against me? Would they bring me up on charges of heresy?!* He is teetering on the edge of himself, his fear threatening to plunge him into the abyss. Nevertheless, he presses on with the letter.

"I tell you with all the passion I feel for the salvation of your soul that you have treated many matters in a manner which is dangerous and likely to cause grave scandal to Christ's people, matters such as

---

[24] "Epistle 1579: From Nöel Bèda" in *Collected Works of Erasmus: Letters 1535-1657*, trans. Alexander Dalzell (Toronto: University of Toronto Press, 1994), 117.

[25] Ibid., 120.

[26] Ibid., 121.

[27] Ibid.

the celibacy of the clergy, monastic vows, fasting and the interdiction against the eating of meat..."[28]

On and on, Béda lists Erasmus' faults, making him seem as foul as Beelzebub. It is a complete repudiation, not only of Erasmus' years of work, but of the New Learning itself. Béda has drawn the limits of heresy so widely that he has trapped at least half the scholars in Christendom within that fiery ring. The Holy Father would never throw so many in the flames, but Erasmus is well aware of how the world works. Even the pope is not a man apart: he feels the pressures of the hour—the great heaving of the earth—as keenly as any man alive. *If the mood in Rome swings too far in one direction...* But these thoughts are the product of anxiety, not reason.

Erasmus reads on, his damp palms struggling with the parchment, until he comes to the last page, where he finds Béda's account of a recent meeting of the theological faculty. Evidently, some of Erasmus' books were presented in their French translations, which had to be approved.

"The men appointed to this commission, following the usual practice of the faculty, read out from the actual translation anything which they had discovered to be unsound," Béda explained. "On hearing these, the whole assembly was dumbfounded—they certainly showed no sympathy with your views."[29]

This is grave, Erasmus concludes. He will have to make a full defense to the faculty. He might be forced to choose between forsaking his beliefs or perishing in flames. *Why is he coming after me when there are so many others writing things far worse?!*

He thinks back to his student days in Paris. He knew Béda only a little. They would pass occasionally in the street, but their times at the Collège du Montaigu did not properly overlap. *He was severe even then,* Erasmus recalls. *A real blot upon the name of theology.* They avoided one another for the most part. *Did I do something to offend him personally?* He would not have thought they talked enough for that. His disregard for the younger man was only a subject of private thoughts.

He reads Béda's salutation at the end of the letter, where the Franciscan again claims to be Erasmus' "friend." Erasmus focuses on the

---

[28] Ibid., 122.

[29] Ibid., 127.

letters one at a time. *B, è, d, a.* He reads them all together. *Béda!* Utterly common before, the name now seizes Erasmus. A memory is sharpening into focus. *Remember my name!* That was what Béda said to him.

He remembers the night so clearly. It was 1494, and he was most of three decades old. He had freed himself from the cult of ascetism at the Collège de Montaigu and found lodging closer to the Seine, in the home of a servant to the King of Scots who had two young men in need of tutoring: Thomas Grey and Robert Fisher. Fisher was unremarkable, but Grey had a mind as keen as they come and received Erasmus' guidance with relish, excelling himself in his studies with each passing day. What a pleasure to find another mind unsullied by the endless ramblings of the Scotists![30]

Grey's guardian noticed how close the two of them became, and it provoked the Scotsman's anger. *You take him to taverns, fill his head with nonsense, and then have the gall to demand payment!* the guardian would blurt. *What kind of monk are you, anyway?!* On such occasions, Erasmus might suggest that the Scotsman's newfound inability to understand Grey had more to do with the guardian's lack of education than anything else. This did nothing to improve the mood of the house.

Yet, it was not the Scotsman's railings that were chief of Erasmus' worries, but an old wound newly inflamed, for Grey reminded Erasmus very much of another young man he had once tutored: Servatius Rogerus, the one to whom he tried to give himself. There were important differences between the two, of course. Erasmus felt no fleshly attraction to Grey, nor had he found himself so attracted to any man since Servatius. Nevertheless, doubts that had been reduced to embers burst into violent flame as he was daily reminded of his previous failing.

I am no sodomite! Erasmus would tell himself. *It was a mistake—that's all. A dreadful mistake. I am a man like any man. I may read the ancient Romans, but I need not be like them.*[31]

---

[30] Scotists were followers of the medieval philosopher Duns Scotus, a member of the Fransciscan order. Erasmus tended to use the term during his time in Paris to refer to any tiresome, backward scholar of theology or philosophy. Despite the similarity of the words, Scotists should not be confused with natives of Scotland.

[31] It was common practice among the elite in ancient Rome to engage in sexual activity with people of both genders. They saw no contradiction between having a wife with whom one procreates and a slave or younger man with

But within himself, the cruel voice of doubt bellowed in the tones of Servatius, *You disgust me! You hear that? You disgust me!*

Rejected, forsaken, given over to putrid lusts: that was how Erasmus felt. Day and night, he was tortured by an idea of terrifying power. *God has chosen against me. That is why I am this way.* He cried out against his disgrace, yearning to be free of it. He grew desperate, and desperate men do strange things.

One day, as the sun began to dip in the western sky, Erasmus walked north upon St. Jacques Street, making for the other side of the river. Although he was not certain of the details, he had a general plan in mind: one he hoped would allow him to feel like a proper man and son of God. To accomplish it, he would need to cross into the realm of iniquity. *Well, why not? I am already immersed in sin,* he reasoned—and yet, he trembled.

He passed the Strand Square, where the Parisians regularly amused themselves with gruesome executions. A corpse was left hanging upon the gallows: a crow pecked at the soft tissues of its face. Erasmus gagged at the sight but continued on his way. Everything was filthy in that part of the city. The streets were turned to mud, the dirt having mixed with urine dumped from above. Everywhere he looked, there were dead-eyed children and wandering dogs, all covered with fleas, all sifting through the heaps of rubbish for scraps to eat. One of the children approached him and then five others, begging for coins.

"Get off me!" he sneered. "I do not want your diseases!"

"Moine maléfique!"[32] one of the boys cried, but Erasmus pushed him aside, unwilling to accept the judgment of a witless child.

He passed the Church of St. Gervais, then under construction, and walked onto St. Antoine Road, uncertain of where he was going, for he had not made a habit of frequenting that part of the city. The narrow houses with their exposed timbers rose four stories high, like sentinels looking down on him, already condemning him for the act he intended to commit.

---

whom one has dalliances, so long as the family patriarch was always in a dominant position. Such relationships between older and younger men continued to be tolerated in parts of Europe up until the modern age, a holdover from pre-Christian cultural ideals.

[32] "Evil monk!"

I must do this, he told himself. *I must know.*

At last, he found a house that was exactly what he sought. A pair of women stood outside, their brightly colored hair hanging loose, their simple chemises hugging their curves. They were calling to passersby in French, and while he could not understand everything they said, he surmised their intent, for each had a gold cord tied around her waist.[33]

I must choose one, he thought, but had no idea which was more appealing or might be more expensive.

As he stood there in his monk's cowl, the taller woman looked at him and asked, "Can I help you?"

Erasmus approached her, his heart beating twice for every step. For a thin woman, she was oddly well endowed. Her dark eyes seemed a poor match for her reddish hair, and as he came close, he realized she was wearing a wig of animal hair dyed an unnatural color of crimson. *What else about her is fake?* he wondered.

"Do you want to come in, love?" she inquired.

Erasmus squinted his eyes, striving to convince himself that he found the woman attractive, though he thought her skin lacked something of the color it ought to have. *What if she is carrying something?* He knew the houses were full of disease, but if he was willing to risk his immortal soul, he might as well risk his mortal body.

"I can pay you," Erasmus assured her, drawing upon his partial knowledge of her language.

With a smile that seemed rather tired, she beckoned him into the house and up three flights of uneven stairs. They passed one room in which he saw a couple locked in the throes of something like passion, and another where a woman sat on the floor holding a babe to her breast. He was led still higher: to a tiny chamber with a single straw pallet on the wood floor. The only window was covered with black cloth, and there were no ornaments on the walls or anywhere else. An oil lamp on the floor was the only source of light, and a poor one at that. It lent an unnatural orange glow to everything he saw, as if he had stumbled into a world not quite real. He was tensed from the soles of his feet to the crown of his bald head. The perversity of what

[33] The French king Louis IX outlined the portions of the city where prostitutes were allowed to work and required them to wear golden cords.

he was about to do was striking him in the gut. *I will break my vows. I will summon the wrath from on high.*

The woman turned to face him, speaking both loud and slow as one tends to do with foreigners. "How old are you, love?"

"Eight and twenty," he replied softly, the words sticking in his dry mouth.

She smiled. "Over here, we call that twenty-eight. But you don't look it, do you? Skin and bones, you are, with the face of a babe."

A rush of anger lashed his insides. "I am a man!" he insisted.

The woman chuckled softly. "Yes, you've come here to prove it, haven't you?"

"How dare you?!" he cried, unwilling to accept her rebuke. "You know nothing about me!"

"Easy, love!" she pleaded, lowering her hands to signal calm. "We get all kinds here: brutes and weepers, both." She made a quick study of his face and concluded, "But you're not one of them."

"Do you want my money or not?" he asked, tiring of her analysis.

She moved close to him, running her fingers up and down his left arm. "Am I the first woman you've ever been with?"

He exhaled sharply. "I ask you again: do you want my money or not?"

The woman dropped her hand and took a step back, crossing her arms. Through the open door, Erasmus could hear the couple in ecstasy below: the floor shook with their efforts. But he was focused entirely on the woman before him as she announced her judgment.

"If you want to leave, then leave. No one's stopping you. But you don't want to leave, do you? You need to be here: I can see it in your eyes. You haven't come on impulse. I get plenty of men who do, but not you. Whatever it is you need, I can do it with you, but you must shush yourself, love. You must let it happen."

Erasmus breathed deeply, attempting to do as she suggested: to allow what was natural within him to rise. He stared at her exposed cleavage, her lips, her eyes. He was beginning to feel something, or maybe it was just the anxiety. He risked a moment of vulnerability.

"You are the first: the first woman I've been with—perhaps the last I'll ever be with."

She moved close to him—wrapped him in a tight embrace. "Then we had best make it worth your coin," she whispered.

With these words, she kissed him brazenly, practically swallowing his tongue. Her years of experience were clear, even as he felt utterly lost. But despite his ignorance, Erasmus was filled with delight, for he felt the effects of this act upon his body. What was meant to happen was happening.

She pulled back and asked, "Did that make you feel anything, love?"

"Yes," he whispered, gasping for breath. "Yes, it did."

He pressed his lips awkwardly onto hers. He could sense he was doing it all wrong, so he stopped and gazed at her face again, and there he noticed something incredible. For the space of a breath, he saw in her eyes a fire not of his making: a remnant of the very moment of her creation. It was a flame he suspected had been long suppressed—withheld to the point of near oblivion. Yet, he saw it in that dark room, and in a moment of abandon, he whispered, "You're beautiful."

"There's no need for that," she insisted, shaking her head.

He nodded. "There is for me."

Erasmus left that house having eaten from the tree of knowledge. He walked along the right bank of the Seine, body still tingling from the experience. *I have done it. I have united myself with a woman, flesh with flesh.* Yet, it was not quite what he expected. He had learned that he could lie with a woman exactly as nature intended. That, at least, was a great relief. But there was another reason he had entered the house.

For those whom the Lord loves he disciplines, and he scourges every son whom he receives.[34]

Those words echoed in Erasmus' mind as he paced along the gravel path, the river rats scurrying beside his feet.

God deals with you as with sons, for what son is there whom his father does not discipline? But if you are without discipline, of which all have become partakers, then you are illegitimate children and not sons.[35]

As he set foot upon the City Isle and made the turn to the left, down a narrow street where the gables on either side jutted out so far they nearly touched, he searched within himself for the shame he

[34] Hebrews 12:6.

[35] Hebrews 12:7-8.

ought to feel, for he had surely disobeyed his father. Ever since that night when he placed his lips upon Servatius', and perhaps even long before it, Erasmus had felt himself spiritually illegitimate: deprived of divine communion. When he prayed, there was no comforting presence to be found. His world seemed utterly devoid of whatever celestial spark had set the heavens in motion. So, if he could not provoke God's love, perhaps he could provoke his anger. It was a plan very much lacking in specifics, but a plan, nonetheless.

He came before the great doors of the Cathedral of Our Lady, its twin towers looming against a darkening sky without the faintest hint of stars. Above the central portal was a depiction of the Last Judgment with Christ seated upon his throne and the rising bodies of the dead below, hastening to their appointed hour. The very thought of that day of wrath caused Erasmus to convulse in horror: the sun turned to darkness, the moon to blood. The towers seemed to him great giants—watchmen calling a rebellious people to task. He gripped his arms with his hands, bidding himself be still. *I must do this. I have no choice.*

Having neglected to confess his transgression nor even clean himself from the act, he entered that sacred temple—the holiest ground in the city—in fear and trembling. Before him, twin rows of rounded columns stretched along either side of the nave, drawing his eyes to the high altar beyond. Although there was no light streaming through the colored windows, thousands of candles illumined the space, creating a flickering patchwork of light and shadows. But there was something false about it—an almost sinister appearance. The glory of God was meant to be displayed in pigments of red and blue splashed across the rough stone, but he could not see it. The gray shadows and yellow-orange light of the candles transformed all they touched, robbing the scene of color and definition. It was as if his very mind had conjured the chamber in which he would now be tormented.

Breathing deeply, his pulse racing, Erasmus walked up the northern side of the nave, his feet shuffling over the burial places of departed saints. He felt the devil upon his back like a wild animal clinging and biting. Too afraid to approach the altar itself, he ducked into the Chapel of St. Clotilde, his head and back bowed. There were few candles there: the light was just enough to make out a massive vertical slab of rock. Here again, a scene of resurrection was depicted, but whereas the Christ on the exterior of the church was smiling, this Christ gripped a rod of iron in his mouth, prepared to smite the earth with his very breath. Erasmus approached hesitantly, attempting to make out the inscription faded by years of weathering. It was evidently the burial place of a canon—a former servant of the cathedral.

Here, where no one can see me, he decided. *It must be here.*

He knelt upon the painted tiles, extending his empty hands, palms facing upward. His body protested the effort, driving his pulse faster, as if to say, *Flee, you fool!* Yet, his will held fast. He ought to have pounded his chest in contrition, but instead he stared at the face of Christ before him with its piercing eyes of wrath and whispered words to God that nearly split him with the effort.

"I come before you steeped in sin to beg the discipline of a son."

He focused on the image before him with an overwhelming intensity, face shaking, breath pulsing. As the tears flowed from Erasmus' eyes, he begged, "Smite me, O God! Smite me here and now!"

There he waited, desperately longing to be scourged: to receive the acknowledgment of his spirit at the price of his flesh. His soul yearned to be smitten like a babe crying out for its mother. As the moments continued to pass without a response, he wished to strip the flesh from his own bones. If you had asked him in that moment why he was doing such a thing, he could not have told you, and yet it was an urge so powerful, he was utterly overwhelmed, transfixed before the specter of the Judge.

For an hour, he remained there, his tensed muscles longing for relief. Dreadful silence! There was no answer from heaven—not the slightest sensation of anything, whether good or ill. The shadows grew deeper and longer. There would be no relief for Desiderius Erasmus. All was silence. All was darkness.

So, Erasmus rose to his feet, his knees and back aching. He made his way to the exit as disconsolate as any man on earth. Then he paused for a moment and looked back down the nave. He could feel the despair taking him: dragging him down, down, down.

He denies me the light of his countenance. He denies me even the strange consolation of Job. He will not come in the whirlwind.

Yes, the despair was total. He was in danger of annihilation. So, in that moment, Erasmus reached a conclusion that would carry him through many long years: *If he will not speak to me, then I must learn to live in the silence.* Why should he beat his fists against the air or kick against the goads? He had been offered the possibility of a life in scholarship: an existence far better than most men receive. *I must live in the tension,* he concluded. *I must accept the uncertainty, for every truth the world gives, it snatches away, and hope is often disappointed.*

As he departed the cathedral and entered the cold of night, he made a pledge: *I will not abandon hope completely, but I will place it in the right thing. I will not pursue what God has withheld, pressing past the point where the Holy One has said, "Here you may come, but no further."*

He had almost submitted himself to this proposition, but the silence of God seemed a deafening roar more offensive than any speech. He was only a hair's breadth from the abyss. *What can I do? I must attempt to live, for that is what men have always done: they have accepted the silence, or else gone mad.*

So intent was he upon these thoughts, he nearly collided with a young man in a Franciscan habit who stood with his hands clasped in prayer.

"Watch yourself!" Erasmus grumbled.

"It is you who should watch yourself," the Franciscan responded darkly.

Erasmus strained to make out the man's features in the dim light. "What do you mean?"

The Franciscan moved closer, his brown hood raised, his hands still pressed together. "I saw you come from the right bank, walking the walk of shame. Did you find your forgiveness in the church?"

Acknowledge nothing! Erasmus urged himself. *He does not know you.*

"It would be better to ask why you spend your time spying on others," Erasmus sneered. "But in any case, you are wrong: I was gone to see the work on St. Gervais, and then I wished to pray. That is no crime."

"Erasmus of Rotterdam, isn't it?" the Franciscan asked. "I've seen you about. They say you made a poor showing at Montaigu."

"I don't have to answer to you!" he retorted. "And I don't care that you know my name."

As Erasmus departed, he heard the Franciscan call after him, "Béda: that's what they call me. Remember my name! Remember it, Erasmus!"

The memory rushes over Erasmus like a violent wind. Until this moment, he had not realized that his association with Béda went back so far, nor that it was connected with one of the most miserable nights of his life.

He knows, Erasmus realizes. *He remembers my name, and I did not remember his. It is a slight he will not forgive.*

Whatever peace Erasmus gained from the defeat of the rebels has flown with the birds of summer. Once again, he exists within the vice grip of fear.

Summer

12 June 1525
Wittenberg, Electorate of Saxony

Martin Luther sits at one of the long tables in the Cloister refectory, a bowl of stew before him. He stares into its depths, the last of the season's cabbage swimming in a bland broth. Wolf has assured him the fruits of summer will soon arrive, but it is hard to have faith after the endless months of sodden leaves. Even the salt has now run low, the last consolation they were afforded. Seated on the bench opposite is Eberhard Brisger, sipping from his own bowl, but Martin cannot find it in himself to sup, even if the bowl were filled with venison.

Since he returned to Wittenberg, a great many changes have taken place. First, and most importantly, the threat from the rebels has decreased after their defeat at Frankenhausen. While there are still pockets of insurrection scattered across the Empire, the immediate danger to his person seems to have lessened, and anxiety is no longer the first thing he feels upon waking. Second, there is a new Elector who thoroughly desires reform in the Church. That is a great consolation at a time when they mourn the loss of the late Elector Friedrich, who had proven himself in the end to be a truly great man.

I suppose I will have to respond to Erasmus after all, he realizes. *In sparing me that, death may have been kinder than life.*

The crisis has passed, at least for the moment, but Martin has no peace, for there is a task still before him. He very much intends to make good on his decision: he will ask Katharina von Bora to be his wife. So intent was he to carry out this pledge—so utterly emboldened by his sudden burst of clarity—that he spoke to Doktor Hieronymous

Schurff almost immediately upon his return, hoping for counsel from a professor of the law. He sought out his colleague after the day's work had ended and found Schurff standing in his small office full of thick legal tomes. The room was dark save for a single candle which Schurff held in one hand, using it to illumine the volume laid open in the other.

Upon sighting Martin, Schuff glanced over the spectacles perched on the rim of his nose and inquired, "What could bring Doktor Luther here at such a time?"

Martin made no effort to engage in pleasantries, but answered directly, "I require your advice, friend."

Schurff slammed the book shut, placing it on the shelf next to its fellows. He then held the candle aloft, examining Martin's features. "It must be serious if you need my help. I do hope you're not about to be bound in chains."

"Nothing like that," Martin assured him. "At least, not in the way you are thinking."

Schurff frowned, clearly unamused. Martin had been generally inclined to forgive his colleague's overly grave manner, for Schurff was a man both stalwart and brilliant, with the bravery to stand beside him at Worms. But upon this occasion, his colleague's poor humor set Martin ill at ease, creating a tightness in his throat.

"Well, what is it then?" Schurff barked. "Speak quickly."

Martin breathed deeply, preparing himself for an extraordinary statement. "I suppose I'll just come right out and say it: I plan to enter the married estate, and while I am thoroughly convinced it is no violation of the law of God, I wish to know if there will be any difficulties with the Saxon code. It is important to me that my wife should have all the legal benefits of that estate."

Here Martin ceased his speech, for his colleague's eyes had bulged in concern. After a moment's silence, Schurff asked, "Is this a general request, or do you have a specific woman in mind?"

"I am to marry Fräulein Katharina von Bora, provided she will have me," Martin explained. "I have not formally asked for her hand. I was waiting to speak with you first."

His colleague's brows sharpened, pressed by the folds in his muscles. "Von Bora the former consecrated sister?"

"That's correct."

"I see," Schurff said rather deliberately. "Just tell me one thing, friend, if you would."

"Certainly."

Suddenly, Schurff's whole expression caught fire. "Have you gone mad?! How could you even think of doing this thing?!"

Martin had anticipated some level of concern, but the strength of Schurff's objection caught him off guard. Shuffling his feet nervously, he inquired, "Why not? Why shouldn't I?"

His colleague scoffed. "It would be a black enough mark upon your work if you married anyone, but for a monk to marry a nun—"

"We are neither of us in that state," Martin insisted. "I was released from my vows, and she was forced into hers under obscene circumstances." This distinction was, to Martin, highly important, for in all the years he belonged to the Order of St. Augustine, there was no man who took his vows more seriously.

"That doesn't matter!" Schurff declared, practically seething. "By the powers, you must not do this thing! It will bring disrepute on us all. Why can you not continue as you are?"

Easy for you to say! Martin thought. *You have not walked in my shoes or felt what I have felt. Do you know what it took to bring me here?!* But hoping not to inflame Schurff further, he answered, "Because the Lord has called me to wed."

"I doubt that very much. What is more, I doubt he would tell you to marry that woman," Schurff snarled.

The heat within Martin reached the boiling point and threatened to spew forth. "'That woman,' as you call her, is the one God intends for me. It could not be any clearer. We have labored under the same weight, and now we must cast it off together."

Schurff stepped closer, the candlelight reflected in his spectacles, transforming his irises into beacons of fire. "If you do this thing, the devil will rejoice, and everything you have built will be destroyed. Christendom will not countenance the union of spiritual siblings, Doktor. They will say it is incest!"

Somewhat to his own surprise, Martin chuckled softly. "Oh, Schurff. That is where you are wrong: it is the angels who will laugh for joy. The devil will weep! He will weep because I have cast off the chains with which he bound me and so many others! Saint Paul wrote that in the last days, men would forbid marriage. What further proof do I need that the end is upon us than to hear you, a man I greatly respect, attempting to draw me away from the purpose set out by God?! Well, get behind me, you devil! Let my enemies exult. They condemn everything I do, or else they make up things I haven't done and condemn those. Attempting to please them is folly. I seek only the approval of God."

Schurff did not take kindly to this diatribe, but Martin found he did not care. He had gone to the man for advice and found himself accused of incest. No doubt, it is a preview of things to come, but he did not think to endure such vitriol from a fellow professor. Rather than granting him pause, the exchange has strengthened Martin's resolve to do what he must do. However, in the days since that meeting, he is now convinced that it will do no good to seek further counsel or inform anyone else of his plans. Only those who must know will know. Anything more would lead to vile gossip. Such things must come, but he would rather endure them after the wedding. *I will not allow the devil to frighten me!*

Bold thoughts, to be sure, but there was one thing he had not considered: namely, that Katharina's desires might have altered. *She was willing to marry me a few weeks ago. Might she have changed her mind?* This alone has caused him to hesitate.

He wished to seek her hand on Saturday, but his stomach was not in agreement. Then on Sunday, he meant to do it but found himself too busy with pastoral tasks. Now most of Monday has passed—yet another day without seeing her, without asking her, without achieving his desired end. As he sits across the table from Brisger, staring at a bowl of stew he cannot bring himself to eat, he finds once again that he cannot escape the thought of her. *I will have no peace until this is settled—until I hear her voice.* Yes, he feels in every ounce of his flesh that the time has come. Without a word, he rises to his feet and steps over the bench, making for the exit.

Brisger calls after him, "Martin, where are you going?"

"To the Cranach house," he answers, too intent on his purpose to turn around.

Then realization strikes him: what he is about to do will affect Brisger as well as himself. Perhaps his housemate should have a chance to voice an opinion, even if others do not. Therefore, Martin turns and says to his former prior, "I am going to see Fräulein von Bora. I will ask her to marry me."

He would have expected this announcement to provoke a strong response, but to his surprise, Brisger nods and says, "Very well, then. Remember to lock the door when you return."

So extraordinary does Martin find this reaction, he wonders if his friend has misheard him. "I am going to ask her to be my wife," he stresses.

"Of course, you are," Brisger asserts with a smile. "I was wondering when you'd get around to it. Have no fear! I'm taking a pastorate and will soon have a wife of my own, so you won't have to care for old Eberhard."

Now Martin feels the shock that seems to have eluded Brisger. A hundred questions flood his mind, demanding to be asked—*How did you know I felt this way? Whom are you planning to marry? You're planning to marry?!*—but he remembers his objective. There must be no further delays. With a simple nod of the head and offer of, "Thank you, brother," he moves again toward the exit. However, three steps later, he has further thoughts.

Do I look alright? How should a man look when he asks a woman to marry him?

He is wearing the same attire as always: his scholar's robes and cap. He turns back to Brisger, and feeling extremely awkward, asks, "Do I look alright?"

Brisger scrunches his brows. "Look alright how?"

"I don't know," Martin admits. "Am I covered in dirt? Should my hair be different somehow?"

For a moment, Brisger looks him up and down, then concludes, "Well, you've got far less dirt on you than the average man, and as for your hair, I have no idea what you could do with it, but at your age, she should just be glad you have some."

This is a sensible answer. With a nod of appreciation, Martin declares, "I'm really going this time," then departs not only the room, but the entire Black Cloister, walking boldly down Colleges Street. No, not boldly: that is a lie. He does, at least, walk with a purpose.

How many times has he traversed this stretch of road? A mere five-minute stroll, but it seems an eternal distance from what he once was to what he is swiftly becoming. He passes the Wittenbergers working at their trades, drinking their beer, throwing out their slop, yet there is nothing in his thoughts but the task ahead. For twenty years, he believed this moment would never come, but it is here now, imposing its urgency upon his being.

In the great scheme of history, it is a small thing. Even in his own life, this is not the most important moment. But with each step he is drawn closer to his destination, he feels in his soul that it is a very big thing indeed: far bigger than it must be for other men. He is long past the point when couples are typically matched. Perhaps it is youth that allows them to meet the moment with anything like confidence. Is it the fact that every person in Christendom will have an opinion about his decision that causes him to tremble, or is it those eyes of Katharina that make his gut lurch whenever they lock onto his? *Give me the words, Lord,* he prays. *I have no idea what I'm doing.* He is utterly helpless, flailing against the surf, longing to be swept into a safe harbor.

At last, he comes to the yellow door and knocks. He is seized by questions that surge within his being. *Will she be happy when she hears my proposal? Or am I fooling myself after all?* He attempts to beat them down. His mind is made up, and he cannot change it by any power he possesses. Once again, he feels a deep longing to hide. There is something buried deep inside him, like a smoldering fire in his breast, and if he allows it to break free—might it destroy him? But Barbara Cranach is opening the door. These thoughts must cease.

"Herr Doktor!" she greets him. "How may I help you?"

He swallows hard. "I must speak with Fräulein von Bora."

"Very well," Barbara agrees. "Shall we all sit in the hall again?"

"Actually, I was hoping to speak with her alone," Martin explains, for though he knows little about such things, he senses this is one occasion when privacy is expected.

Fortunately, Barbara accepts his request with a nod of the head. "Käthe is tending the garden. Let us walk around the back."

She joins him outside, closing the door behind her, and leads the way to the rear of the Cranach complex. Here by the city wall, there is a sizable garden plot with beds of herbs, strawberries, squashes, melons, and lettuces growing in neat rows. "This is mostly Käthe's doing," Barbara informs him as they step between the carefully tended plants.

Martin's gaze moves to the far end of the plot, where Katharina is bent down on her knees, plucking weeds from a patch of turnips. She is clothed in a cream-colored chemise beneath a brown dress, with a white apron over top. Her hair is covered by a simple white cloth that allows some of her braids to show. Wearing a pair of gloves to protect her hands, she digs in the rich earth, searching out the roots. He has seen women doing this thousands of times, yet they never caused his pulse to speed.

"Käthe!" Barbara calls. "Doktor Luther is here again."

Instantly, Katharina looks in their direction and stands at attention. *Does she seem happy to see me?* he wonders. She appears more shocked than anything. Still breathing heavily from her work, she views him with softening eyes, her being somehow resonating—pulsing with a strange energy. The early evening light, resplendent with a thousand hues, illuminates the stray tresses that gently brush her face. She bows her head, and he observes how graceful is her neck as she does this: how very much like a swan's. Then, for the first time in weeks, he hears her voice.

"Always a pleasure to see Doktor Luther," she says.

He notes the blush in her cheeks. *What accounts for it? Her work or my presence? Might my own face be similarly affected?* He cannot decide. Indeed, he can hardly tell up from down. Nothing is as he thought it would be. The whole world seems changed.

"He has requested to speak with you alone," Barbara explains. "I will return to the house."

Martin watches as Barbara departs, his eyes clinging to the last thing he will see before he must begin the nerve-wracking conversation. Now, Barbara has turned the corner: there is nothing left to do but look at Katharina, which he does with all the bravery he can muster. She has moved a few paces closer to him and removed her leather gloves, holding them in one hand. There is a smile on her face, and though her apron is covered in dirt and her forehead is damp with sweat, he sees in the fading light of day the woman he saw in his dream, and his heart races with fear.

"Good evening, Fräulein," he manages to say.

"Good evening, Herr Doktor."

How to begin? he wonders. *The usual questions. Yes, the familiar questions.*

"Are you well?" Martin inquires.

"Fairly well," she replies, still granting him a smile. "And you?"

"Yes," he responds automatically, then realizing he has failed to match the nature of her query—*Already a mistake!*—he adds, "That is, I am well." He asks another question to distract from his error. "What are you doing?"

"Tending the herbs," she explains, rather obviously, as it now occurs to him. "Forgive me. If I had known you were coming, I would not have appeared in such a state."

He reckons she is a good bit more put together than himself, what with all his nervous sweat. "Have no fear. I am the one interrupting you. How is it going?"

"The gardening?"

"Yes," he replies, feeling incredibly awkward.

"Pretty well, I think. The weeds don't pull themselves, sadly."

"So I've heard."

There is a moment of silence, which Katharina moves to fill. "I see a weed, and I have to pull it! I'm afraid it's a bit of a compulsion," she explains with a laugh, but when he does not respond in kind, she adds, "I'm sure you aren't here to discuss weeds. You can have only one purpose in coming like this—speaking to me alone."

"Oh?" he mutters, feeling more nervous by the second. "And how do you interpret my actions?"

"Your actions I might dare to interpret, but I cannot account for your manner. You speak to me alone because it is a subject which might lead to embarrassment, and it is likely one and the same as that subject you always raise with me. So, tell me then: Who is to have the misfortune of being my husband this time? Student, pastor, professor?"

As she follows this line of inquiry, Martin is sliced by the sharp edge of fear. *She does not desire me, but someone else!* Bidding himself remain calm, he states, "I'm afraid you misinterpret."

"Do I? A tradesman then? Surely not a lawyer!" she concludes, chuckling softly at her own joke, but again her smile fades in response to his silence. "You are not laughing. Forgive me! I will be silent."

He stares at the ground, shifting his feet. Why is this thing that so many men do easily proving so difficult for him? *You must do it, Martin,* he bids himself. *Delay will solve nothing.*

So, he looks her in the eye and says, "Fräulein von Bora, you once stated that you would be willing to marry me. I come here to ask if that is still your opinion or if you are of a different mind."

What a change comes over her countenance! Her eyes widen—her whole expression is utterly opened. She seems to flutter like a pair of wings. He can sense that her heart is beating with as much force as his own.

"I—" she stutters, mouth agape. Then recovering herself, she speaks to him softly. "Yes. Yes, it is still my opinion, though I understand if you—" Her voice trails off as her eyes search him out, darting across his features.

"If I what?" he prompts her with an unsteady voice, for he is unnerved by the power of her gaze.

"Are you saying—that is, have you changed your mind?" she inquires.

He sighs and nods his head, averting his eyes toward the dirt below, for he must remain in control. "I have been thinking a great deal since we last spoke."

"You have been through a great deal," she says, granting him her compassion, entering into his pain.

"Yes," he agrees, daring to look up again. "There are moments when a man is faced with difficulties that reveal to him what truly matters, or who he truly is. I have been teaching the virtues of Christian marriage for years now, but I never thought that God was calling me to that blessed estate. But since the last time we've spoken—let's just say I fear my time is short."

Now, there is fear in Katharina's eyes. Stepping closer, she asks breathlessly, "Are you in danger, Doktor?"

"Not as much as I was a month ago, but I still feel a sense of urgency," he explains, gratified by her concern for his welfare. He moves to draw upon that strength. "The devil is pressing on me—pressing hard. He is trying to keep me from doing the work God has for me, just as always."

He pauses and stares at this woman who, against all odds, has transformed his life in the space of two months. *How did it begin? What was it that set me on this path?* He thinks back to the time he heard her story, receiving the words she offered to him as shining gems: precious pieces of herself forged under heat and pressure. That gift, offered so wholeheartedly and without expectation, is the reason he stands before her today. Her words have transformed him.

"I thought a lot about what you told me," he explains. "When you said, 'They lied to us'—They did lie to us. They told us righteousness came through poverty, chastity, and obedience. They ought to have told us we could never be righteous, no matter how hard we tried. I had always thought that the oddities of my life—my host of enemies, the probability of my death—meant that I ought not take a wife, but now I think it the other way around. It is precisely because of my situation that I must make good on my claims. I must give the lie to these damnable doctrines by which the devil keeps so many in chains. And yet, I cannot do it alone. I need another who has felt what I have felt—who feels what I feel."

As he speaks these words, he thinks, *We are tied together, you and me. You must know this. You knew it before I did.* It is a thought so powerful, it terrifies him: that she might, in some sense, know him better than he knows himself. *But she does not know everything.* That is a thought equally terrifying.

"Are you saying what I think you are saying?" she asks, eyes expectant.

Of course, I am. But he cannot continue—indeed, it would be dishonorable to do so—without revealing exactly what marriage to Martin Luther would mean for her. This is the part that causes him greatest fear, for were he to reveal all, he cannot imagine that any sane woman would accept him. He wants her to say "yes"—far more than he dares admit, so much that he will be crushed to a pulp if she refuses—so he will not attempt to scare her off, but he must be honest as becomes a man.

"There are a few things I must make perfectly clear before we proceed any further," he states. "First, I have very little money and next to no possessions. Second, I do not own property, and the house I live in could be taken from me at any moment. Third, I am under the ban of excommunication with an imperial edict calling for my arrest and execution. Just because it has not been enforced does not mean that it won't be enforced. I will not cease to proclaim the gospel, nor will I hide in a cave like some coward, so there will always be danger. Fourth, I am old, and my health is poor on account of the great harm I did my body over many years attempting to earn what cannot be earned. Fifth, I do not have much in the way of practical skills and am only useful for lecturing, writing, and preaching. A reasonable woman might object to any of these points, and I do believe you are a reasonable woman."

Here he ceases his disclaimers, a bit out of breath. He is keenly aware of his own failings: the fragility of his situation is a building whine suffusing his mind, lending doubt to every hope within him. *Does she care about me enough to suffer all this?* His heart aches.

Katharina looks at him steadily, her eyes pooling with fierce intensity, and passing over his warnings, inquires, "Herr Doktor, are you asking me to be your wife?"

This is it, he thinks. *This is the moment.*

For the space of a breath, he kindles the fire within him, drawing energy from its heat. "We do not know each other that well, but I can tell you are a woman of character. After I heard your story, I might have pitied you, but I didn't: I respected you. Pity would be too slight a thing for me to give to you. I do not pretend I am a great lover or can speak that language well. This is the first time in my life I have ever had a conversation like this, and I'm sure I've done it all wrong, but in short, Fräulein von Bora, I offer myself to you as your husband for as long as we both live, however long or short that may be, along with whatever meager possessions I have or am likely to have. I will be faithful to you alone. I will do everything in my power to provide for you. I wish I could offer you far more than that—more than just my name. God knows you would deserve it. But I think you understand what it is I offer. Whatever days we have are likely to be difficult, but I will strive to do right by you. I am talking too much. Do you have any reply?"

How does she look?! What is she thinking?! He sees that her eyes are filled with tears. She wipes them with her free hand, inhaling deeply. He thinks—indeed, he prays—that they are tears of happiness. *What will she say?!* At the sound of her voice, his pulse increases.

"I am deeply honored by your proposal—more than I can possibly express in words. But tell me, Herr Doktor: you are not doing this out of obligation, are you? For as I said before, I am perfectly content to—"

"I assure you, I do not act out of obligation, charity, or pity," he insists, speaking the truth. It would be far safer to attribute his decision to such things, but he must not do so, even if he struggles to lend voice to the totality of what he feels. At the very least, he must not give a false impression.

"And is this what you truly desire: for me to be your wife and not another?" she asks.

Yes, that is what I desire, he thinks. *That is what I desire with all my being.* But he has long since passed the point of his comfort. He opts again for the reply that is simplest—safest.

"It is," he assures her, thinking for a moment how odd it would be for him to have this conversation with someone else. He doubts very much that any other woman on earth could have brought him to this point.

"Because if marriage alone is your desire, I am certain there are other women—"

"No," he says firmly, his will absolutely set. "I am asking you. Do you need time to consider?"

His heart beats once, twice, three times. Then she seems to trust his assurances—the muscles in her face relax. She is caught in a breathless smile, shaking her head in wonder. "One moment, please," she begs, dropping the gloves to the ground, removing her apron, and brushing off her skirt. He begins to worry, but she requests, "Ask me again if you don't mind—directly, clearly."

He nods and takes a final breath, then inquires, "Fräulein Katharina von Bora, will you marry me?"

"Yes," she instantly replies.

This single word, poured forth from her lips, is like a rushing water within him, filling him from top to bottom, quenching a thirst he barely knew he had. *Thank God! Oh, thank God!*

"Yes?" he repeats, feeling an intense need for confirmation.

She nods, the joy written upon her features for him to read. "Yes, I will."

He breathes in sharply, his eyes moist. "Well, good. I am glad to hear it." Quite overcome by the moment, he repeats, "Very good. Yes, very good," attempting to steady his form, which feels as if it might race in a hundred different directions. Then another thought seizes him. *What next? What must I do?* He was so focused on receiving the right answer, he never considered the next steps. *Plans: we must make plans.* He inquires, "Should we have the betrothal tomorrow then?"

"Tomorrow?!" she cries, eyes bulging.

Oh dear. I've made another mistake! he worries, the waters within him breaking upon the rocks.

"Is that too soon?" he asks desperately.

She chuckles, granting him a smile that lessens his anxiety. "You must admit, Doktor, it is rather soon."

"I just remember how long that scoundrel kept you waiting," he replies, the sting of that betrayal still pulsing in his breast. "I don't want to be like that. And the longer we wait, the more people will gossip. We will have the public homecoming later, of course. There will be time to prepare."

She nods her head. "I suppose that makes sense. Tomorrow, then?"

"Yes, tomorrow evening."

"Where?"

"At the Cloister, unless you have some objection."

"No, no objection," she utters softly. "And what should I wear?"

"Pardon?" he asks, thrown off by her question.

"I only have this dress and one other," she explains, lifting her skirt slightly.

Evidently, this is the sort of thing that matters to women but had never occurred to Martin. Not wishing her to feel ill at ease about her humble situation, he assures her, "It doesn't matter what you wear."

"I see," she mutters, looking slightly downcast.

Quick, Martin! he bids himself. *Come up with something!* Ah, but to delve deeply is a thing fraught with risk! He thinks of her that night when he came to respect her so thoroughly. He remembers how he felt—the heat within him.

"Wear the dress you were wearing last time I saw you: the newer one," he concludes, then feeling utterly self-conscious, he shifts to more mundane matters. "I will speak to Doktor Pomeranus. Apel can witness the signing—Schurff would not approve. The Cranachs, Jonas, but no others. I will take care of it all."

"Very well," she agrees. "You know best about these things."

"Shall we go in and tell them, then?" he asks, realizing this is the next logical thing.

"Yes, I suppose we should," she agrees.

Collecting her gloves and apron, she walks toward him, and he turns to lead her back to the house. Then to his surprise, she places a hand on his arm. It is a rush moving upward—lodging within his chest. He spins round and looks into her hazel eyes, which reverberate with her regard for him.

"Herr Doktor—" she whispers, dropping her hand.

"Yes?" he asks desperately.

"Thank you. I did not think you would ask me, but I'm so glad you did."

For a moment, he wonders if he ought to say or do something more. After all, they have just agreed to marry. *Ought I to speak of my affection for her?* But that is something he hardly understands, an immensity in which he could easily lose himself. It was not outward beauty that drew him to her, but the strength of her character. He esteems her more than any woman he has ever known. He would lay down his life for her if asked, as any husband should. *Could there be any higher love than that?* And yet, it is not the fullness of what he feels. There is something hidden in the depths of his soul: a thing of fearsome power far beyond his control.

Should I take her hand? He does not think he could do it. *What if she were to pull away from me—to shun my touch?* No, he had better not. *Should I kiss her cheek?* The very idea induces panic. So, he attempts no show of affection but simply concludes, "I should be thanking you."

They tarry for just a moment—a chance to reconsider his silence. A part of him longs to cross the space between them, while another part recoils at the thought of it. He looks into her eyes and feels himself suddenly brave. But the moment is gone. She is striding past him—making for the house. The burst of strength ebbs from him, but he assures himself, *There will be time. You need not achieve it all at once.*

And so, stepping quickly, he follows Katharina into the house, where she receives an embrace from Barbara, and he a firm pat on the back from Lucas. It is a momentous achievement for a man who not so long ago believed he would never take a wife. What a comfort to see that there are some who will rejoice in their union! But even this happy moment is, in its own way, unsettling for him. *Why should it be so?*

He feels a change in the air as he returns to the Black Cloister—a chill in his bones as he locks the door. His hand still on the latch, he asks himself, *What are you afraid of?* Alone in the dark, he allows himself to go to the place where his fears reside, and there he is struck by a startling thought: tomorrow evening, they will plight their troth before God himself, and then they will be laid out on the bed before a witness. There will be nowhere to hide. He feels his sinews tighten—his arms and legs stiffen. *I can do it,* he thinks. *By God's grace, I will do it.*

And yet, he doubts.

13 June 1525
Basel, Swiss Confederation

Desiderius Erasmus stands in the yard behind the Froben house, pulling at his shirt and releasing it in turn, attempting to send his sweat to flight. It is the Ides of June, and Basel is sweltering, the air thick with water. Only now, when the sun has dipped low, has he dared to venture out of doors, and still the heat offends. But he must go out, for he has been summoned along with the entire Froben family to the home of Adam Petri, their main competitor in the printing business.

Everyone in Basel knows Petri and Froben loath one another, and it is precisely for this reason that they must make the journey crosstown to enjoy the hospitality of the enemy, putting on a show of mutual respect. No doubt, Froben will be forced to return the favor in time. *We know it is fake, they know it is fake, but we all pretend it isn't fake,* Erasmus grumbles. No sooner has he thought it, than he hears shoes brushing over gravel and turns to find Margarethe approaching from the house.

"Margarita!" he greets her. "Are you to blame for this infernal weather?"

She plants her hands upon a broad pair of hips. "Care to take my place in the kitchen, Your Excellency? It's twice as hot in there!"

"Do I pay you to bake my bread or complain?" he quips. When she merely scowls at him, he begs, "Don't hate me, Margarita. The heat has worked its sorcery upon my mind. It is a great evil!"

"You want to know what's evil? That fat mouse has been scurrying about again, getting into my stores!"

"I thought Froben got you a mouser."

"He did, but your godson went and scared it away with his pranks!" she snarls, her nose wrinkling with the effort.

Erasmus sighs deeply. He has seen Johann Erasmus torturing the poor feline: dropping it in a barrel full of water or springing from behind a door to watch the beast's hair stand on end. Boys will have their amusements, surely, but Erasmus must have a talk with the young man if they are to keep disease out of the house. *Hopefully he still has ears for the ancient.*

"I'll see to it that he behaves," Erasmus assures her.

"I don't have to work here, you know," Margarethe states, clearly unconvinced by his assurances. "I could return to Leuven!"[1]

A step too far, he broods. *She says it to provoke me. She'll have it back and then some!*

"Ha!" Erasmus cries. "And who would have you?"

Margarethe crosses her arms and raises her chin proudly. "Meneer Bouts, that's who! He swore he would have me to his person."

Erasmus' jaw drops slightly as he attempts to make sense of this revelation. *Bouts? The physician? That Bouts?!* He used to call the good doktor to his house at least once a week to attend to his ailments. *The best such man I have ever employed, without a doubt.* Never did Bouts arrive without a smile on his face—ever attentive, ever punctual. Indeed, Erasmus used to marvel that Bouts could make it to the house so quickly. Now, perhaps, the mystery is solved. *But of course! He hid in the drying shed with Margarethe. That's why he was always on hand.* What favors she gave the physician, Erasmus can only imagine. She must have to receive such an offer! Erasmus never imagined a man would seek Margarethe for his wife, unless he had no regard for his ears. *Come to think of it, Bouts was slightly deaf. I suppose it does make sense!*

"It must have been ten years since he made that offer to you, back when God was still painting your hair that color and not those potions you wield," he states, pointing at her exposed tresses.

"Oh, he was soft on me and no mistake!" Margarethe declares. "Treated me far better than you ever have. So, why not? Why shouldn't I? He must have a Guilder or two, and he'd do right by my bosom, he would."

---

[1] Leuven is the Dutch name of the city also called Louvain, which boasted one of Europe's great universities at this time and had been one of Erasmus' previous residences.

Erasmus turns his head slightly, as if another angle might make sense of his confusion. *Could she be serious?* For years, he has teased her to the point of bleeding, but he never imagined she might take it to heart. *You fool! You have failed to properly express your gratitude, and now she heads for greener pastures. Who else could cook your food the way you like? Who could endure your jibes?* There is an ache in his chest. *Am I really going to lose my Margarethe?!*

"Are you serious?" he asks softly. "Margarita, you must know—surely, you must know how I value you. You wouldn't abandon your Erasmus, would you?"

Now, she positively bursts with laughter, her shoulders heaving with the effort.

"What's so funny?!" he demands to know. "Has this all been a trick? You know how I feel about tricks!"

"You should have seen the look on your face!" she cries, eyes twinkling and cheeks pink. "Looked as if you'd seen the devil, you did!"

"Maybe I did see a devil," he growls. *And to think I paid you extra last month!*

Before he can properly sink his teeth into her, the men of the house—Johann Froben, his sons Hieronymous and Johann Erasmus, and their guest Łaski—stream out of the house, all looking displeased. The patriarch is scowling, his sons walk with sunken shoulders, and their Polish companion clasps his hands in prayer, eyes searching out the heavens for deliverance. Froben's wife and daughter are nowhere to be seen.

"Kýrie eléison!" Łaski cries as they draw near. "Christe eléison!"

"What on earth is wrong?" Erasmus asks them all.

"It will be Fräulein Justina," Margarethe surmises. "Still at her tricks, Herr Froben?" she inquires.

Froben grunts, staring off into the distance, but Johann Erasmus is willing to report, "She ruined her hair! Dyed it some foul yellow to fetch a man. Mother insists she must hide it away. 'Only the Italians do such things!'" the boy whines in a passable imitation of the woman who bore him.

"Your mother is correct. Such a thing would never happen in our kingdom!" Łaski declares, crossing himself solemnly.

There are many things that would never happen in your kingdom, Erasmus thinks.

Now, the queen bee and her rival come striding out of the house, clothed in their best silk gowns, the fabric purchased from a merchant of Genoa. Her head wrapped in more cloth than a Turk's, Justina is unleashing the full force of her petite lungs. "I spent all week bleaching it! What's so wrong with letting people see it?"

Gertrude rolls her eyes with such strain that Erasmus is amazed they do not lodge in her brain. "How many times, Justina?! How many times have we been over this?! You have no idea what men are like!"

"How could I when you never let me see anyone?!" Justina objects.

"They're creatures of filth, that's what they are!" Gertrude concludes, ignoring her daughter's objection. Then looking at Froben, Łaski, and Erasmus in turn, Gertrude assures them, "Present company excluded, naturally."

Given how weary they all are of Justina's moods, Erasmus is disinclined to take offense at this desperate judgment, and he suspects the others are equally forgiving.

Froben places a hand on Justina's arm, but she jerks it away, so her father grasps both her shoulders and yells, "I've had enough of this! You hear me? Shut your mouth, or you won't see the sun for a month!"

The young lady is seething, her nostrils flaring with the force of her breath. Erasmus half expects her to spit fire. Nevertheless, Froben's threat seems to achieve its aim. Within seconds, they are all walking south along Nadelberg on their way to the Petri house, with Justina bringing up the rear, muttering curses too soft for her parents to hear. Erasmus slows his pace until they walk side by side, then whispers to Justina, "It is your very resistance that brings you low. Were you to temper your behavior, your forebears would expect no ill from you, and the world would be yours to command."

Their steps slow as they begin the descent to the Birsig. She glares at him, her green eyes digging into his person. "If I had wanted your help, I would have asked for it!"

"Peace! It was kindly meant," he protests, raising his hands in surrender.

Justina looks to see if the others are listening, then declares, "They may all adore you, but I don't have to!"

He cannot help but laugh. "Oh, what a world it would be for Erasmus if everyone was forced to adore him!"

"I can do as I wish," Justina declares. "I am a free person!"

She has seized the breath from him: surely, she has! Why else does he suddenly feel this way? With her forked tongue, she has spoken the words he has so often uttered himself: *I am a free person!* Coming from her lips, they seem utterly robbed of power. She is fifteen years of age and under the authority of her father until such time as she must labor under the authority of a husband. *What does she imagine she is free to do?* And yet, he wonders if the words are any truer when he speaks them. It is an unsettling thought. Rather than dwell upon it, he leaves her to sulk and moves forward to rejoin the others, his pace quickening down the slope.

They have made the turn onto Heuberg and are passing the monastery of Saint Leonard: no longer a home to monks, or at least none of the traditional variety. Like so many others of their kind, these brothers have cast off the cowl and their vows of celibacy, but they have had the audacity to remain in their lodging at the expense of the Church. He pities whatever wives they manage to snare, for a man who cannot control himself while in holy orders cannot be expected to control himself once he is bound in wedlock.

Łaski seems to guess his thoughts, for he muses loudly, "Herr Erasmus, you and I may be the only celibates left in Christendom!"

Erasmus merely grunts in response. He cannot confirm Łaski's statement—not completely. For there was the time in Paris: the time he dared to cross the bounds. Now, the one man who knows what he did is threatening him. With each day, Béda moves closer to his goal. His assessment of Erasmus' character was set in stone decades earlier, and the Franciscan will surely pursue the charges of heresy to the very seat of power. It is only a matter of time before Béda appeals to His Holiness in Rome. *Will this be the last year I am alive on earth?* Erasmus wonders, the fear trickling down his neck. *Well, if they are going to kill me, let them do it soon and spare me another bout of the stone!*

They have come to the Birsig: he cannot yet see the waters of the stream, but he can smell the refuse within it. Here the tanners engage in their trade, dumping the excess into the water. For some reason known only to God, Adam Petri has chosen to place his home nearby.

He must lack a sense of smell. They have turned down the correct road. He can see Petri's home on the left, a four-story dwelling with exposed timber frames and a roof of slate tiles.

Good God! Why are we here? he wonders. *Why must we do these things to ourselves?*

Froben takes the brass knocker in hand and pounds it thrice. The door is answered by Frau Anna Petri, a genteel woman of modest stature, like her husband well into her eighth decade. She is clothed in a black, laced bodice with a green jacket overtop, and her braids are contained in gold netting decorated with pearls.

"Herr Froben, come in!" she insists, beckoning with a wrinkled hand. "Frau Froben, Herr Łaski, Herr Erasmus! Children! All of you, come in!"

One by one, they follow her orders, entering a foyer with a black and white tiled floor and wood panel walls and ceiling. As he makes his way through the portal, Erasmus wonders, *How did it go so wrong?*

Johann Petri, father of Adam, was a partner to both Froben and Amerbach. They slaved away together in the print shops, debating fonts and devices, scrutinizing paper quality, pulling the levers with their own hands. But Johann Petri is now long dead, and his son has proved to be a rather different beast. Although he has never formally parted with Rome, everyone knows Adam Petri is a Lutheran sympathizer. He prints everything sent from Wittenberg, building up a large fortune, and sends gifts of books to the Carthusian monastery across the river—books that have a definite reforming character. No doubt, Petri hopes the Carthusians will go the way of the monks at St. Leonard's, but Erasmus has heard from young Bonifacius Amerbach, who lives next door: the Carthusians are wise to Petri's schemes, and though they place the books in the library, they do so after adding a prominent warning on the front page.

Money, Erasmus thinks. *That is how it went wrong: because Petri thought it no robbery to sell out the Church of Christ for his own gain.* While Froben never puts out a book he does not believe in, Erasmus suspects Petri would publish any piece of libel if it might turn a profit. *Why are we here? Why must we put on this act?*

They are led into the dining hall on the left, a room with high ceilings and a massive marble hearth in which a pair of carved angels hold the mantle aloft. The long table is set with brass plates, surely fashioned in Nuremberg; glass beakers painted with the Petri device, the like of which he saw everywhere in Venice; and silver cutlery with jasper handles. At least a dozen dishes of food are laid out for the taking, and in the middle is an enormous display of flowers bursting into brilliant color, illumined by the gold chandelier above. It is Petri who has laid this table, but Erasmus knows most assuredly that it is Martin Luther who is responsible for it.

The owner of the house approaches in his thick, ermine-lined coat, a gray beard tucked within its folds. "Herr Froben, my friend!" he cries, embracing his fellow printer as if they were brothers. "How I have longed to welcome you back to my table!" Here Petri slaps Froben on the back with such force that it prompts the younger man to cough.

Standing just beside them, Erasmus comments dryly, "It is kind of you, Herr Petri, to undertake the work of reconciliation."

Petri turns his attention to Erasmus, a smile growing on his face. "How right you are, Herr Erasmus! In my heart burns a fierce desire for reconciliation: to put aside the petty disputes of our time and enter a noble brotherhood in which all men may share the same table!"

"And would you have me at your table?" Erasmus asks softly.

"I would, friend, I would!" Petri exclaims. "Why, there is a seat for you in the honored place!"

He motions toward the far end of the table, well past the flowers and a world away from where Petri and Froben will be sitting. Erasmus seethes internally, struggling to remember the last time he was sent to the foot rather than the head. Normally, whoever invites him to sup wishes to have him close, the better to engage in witty conversation. But Petri's opinion is clear: he wants Erasmus as far away as possible. *The scoundrel! What kind of man humiliates a guest?!* Erasmus shoots a pained look at Froben and Łaski, both of whom appear equally perturbed, but there is nothing for it. He must simply obey the wishes of his host.

"Come, friend!" Petri says, placing a hand on Erasmus' back and motioning with the other. "Your honored place awaits."

Erasmus makes the long walk to the far end of the table, muttering every curse he knows in four different languages, for he learned the English ones at Cambridge. It is only when he passes the large floral display that he realizes there has been another person standing there the whole time, remaining silent throughout their discussion. A blow seems to strike Erasmus' chest as he realizes he will be sitting next to Johannes Œcolampadius. *What is he doing here?! No one said he was coming! The devil curse you, Petri!*

Œcolampadius smiles and extends a hand, but Erasmus snaps, "Is this some kind of ambush?"

"Hardly!" Œcolampadius swears, though Erasmus doubts him entirely. "Surely you knew I was coming?"

Erasmus lets out a low growl. "Don't play coy with me! How stupid do you think I am?"

Raising his hands in surrender, Œcolampadius begs, "Please, friend—"

"A friend would not ambush me!" Erasmus insists.

With a deep sigh, Œcolampadius says, "If you would allow me to finish, I only accepted Herr Petri's invitation because he expressly pledged that he had explained the situation to someone in the Froben household."

The possibility of a traitor in his house rankles Erasmus exceedingly. "Who was it?" he demands to know.

"You would have to ask Petri," Œcolampadius concludes, taking his seat and placing a cloth over his shoulder.

As the rest of the table's occupants have taken their places, it becomes incumbent upon Erasmus to follow suit, but he does so very much under protest. A prayer is said, the venison is carved, and wine is poured, but none of it relieves the tension he feels inside. With one hand he raises his beaker to his lips, but with the other he presses into the table, his thoughts frothing into a violent rage.

When everyone else is caught up in their own conversations, Œcolampadius says to him quietly, "I was sorry to hear about your trouble with Béda."

"I do not wish to discuss it," Erasmus insists, ripping the chunk of meat before him.

"It is shameful, truly shameful," the younger man continues, pressing on despite his warning, "but do not fear, Erasmus. You have friends here in Basel. The council would never allow for your extradition."

"How kind of them," he responds, voice dripping with sarcasm. "As long as I have no wish to see the rest of Christendom again, I need not worry! Oh, but who would not love this blessed city which teems with maniacal preachers and threatens every day to burst into conflagration? I could not think of a better place to pass one's autumn years, save perhaps a leper hospital."

"You speak as if it were hell on earth when nearly every man in town reveres you," Œcolampadius remarks, shaking his head in wonder.

Erasmus bends close to his former colleague, bringing his face within half an arm's length of Œcolampadius' nose. "You know nothing of hell."

Œcolampadius's gaze softens considerably. "I beg you, friend," he whispers, "let go your burden. Let us heal this rift between us, and between all the men of the New Learning. What could we not do together if we set these hatreds aside?"

Erasmus leans back, taking a piece of meat in hand and shoving it in his mouth. "I used to think like that, many years ago, before the world was changed."

"Our dream has not died!" Œcolampadius insists with real feeling.

Perhaps it should, Erasmus thinks. He was ready to say his final farewell to Œcolampadius long ago—certainly, by the time of the Farel debacle there was no friendship remaining—but now he has annoyingly been forced to listen to his entreaties once again. *Ignore him: I must simply ignore him,* he decides, accepting a piece of bread that is handed to him. He uses it to sop up the juices on his plate, even as Œcolampadius does the same. They manage a minute or two of silence: a blessed thing. Then the younger man forcibly grasps Erasmus' attention.

"Have you heard from Melanchthon recently?"

Erasmus struggles to quickly swallow. "No. Have you?"

"No," Œcolampadius says sadly. "Listen, Herr Erasmus: I know you wish him to come to Basel."

Why is it so impossible to keep a secret in this town?! Erasmus fumes, for he made a point to reveal this fact to as few persons as possible.

"Who told you? Camerarius?" Erasmus asks, already cursing the man for breaking his promise.

"No one told me," Œcolampadius claims. "I can see your regard for him—that is all."

Somewhat dubious, Erasmus responds, "And I suppose you are going to tell me off for attempting to pilfer the prize of Wittenberg."

"No such thing! I would love to have him here."

Erasmus groans. "Oh, of course, you would! You would distract him from his studies—force him to join you in some doomed exploit of valor."

"It is his friendship I covet," Œcolampadius responds, brow furrowed. "Why must you always be so suspicious?"

"Because I have lived long enough to know it is the only sensible course."

Œcolampadius leans in slightly, fixing on Erasmus' eyes with his own. "You will not have your peace, Erasmus, until you allow yourself to be captured by the love of God."

Erasmus snorts. "I should have known I would receive another of your evangelical nothings."

"It's true," the younger man says quietly, "even if you refuse to accept it."

With that, Œcolampadius turns his attention to the food in front of him, and Erasmus is left to marinate in his own thoughts, which darken by the second. He could not let Œcolampadius win the point—that would have been intolerable in addition to everything else—but even as he casually dismissed the man's words, he finds them slowly penetrating his being, moving closer to the critical point.

God loves you, Erasmus! God loves you!

Those words of Brother Ansfrid, offered to him so many years ago, continue to echo despite his efforts to suppress them. They speak to a younger age: a time when faith was simple and ready for the taking, or perhaps he was ready to be taken. But by the time he received them, he was already as ancient as the earth. Perhaps when he was still a young boy, before doubt had laid its claim upon every inch of his existence—perhaps he might have found it in himself to surrender to the message of Œcolampadius. But he has been rejected by his father, slapped across the face by one he loved, left to scream into the void of the house of God where he ought to have felt the divine presence. He has found the world a terrible darkness: an unending torment of doubt and pain. Whatever the answer is, it cannot possibly be that simple.

An hour later, he is mercifully returning to the Froben household along with the rest of its occupants. The dinner has not agreed with him: he suspects the night ahead will be most unpleasant. He trudges back up the hill, the ache biting now at his hips, his knees, his ankles. He thinks of Béda and Œcolampadius—of controversies great and small—and he thinks of Martin Luther sitting in his cloister in Wittenberg. *What is he doing this very moment?* he wonders. *Will he ever respond to what I wrote?* At first, he feared the hammer blow, but so much time has passed that Erasmus begins to hope Luther might not respond at all. It would be beneath the honor of a gentleman—an insult to Erasmus' standing as a scholar—but he would breathe a sigh of relief.

Suddenly, he finds himself joined, very much to his surprise, by Justina, who he was certain loathed his company.

"How did you like the supper?" she inquires, meeting him stride for stride.

"I didn't," Erasmus responds. "I was forced to converse with a man I would have preferred to avoid."

"About that—" she begins quietly, then summoning either courage or cheek, explains, "I only remembered in the middle of the meal: someone from the Petri house came by a few days ago. He mentioned something about an Onkelam—"

"Œcolampadius!" Erasmus cries, enraged to discover that this message was entrusted to the one person in the Froben household who could not possibly be relied upon to deliver information correctly.

"There's no need to yell," Justina argues, and in the light of the lanterns he can see her glaring at him, a most unfair reaction given that she is in the wrong.

"Do you realize what you cost me by failing in your charge?! Is there anything in your head but jewels and silk?! You know that poison you force upon your tresses is likely to ruin them and you!"

"I was trying to be nice. I apologized," she argues, then concludes, "I don't know why everyone grovels before you when you're so tiresome."

He growls as she moves forward to join the others. Hands clasped behind his back, Erasmus treads the streets of Basel, brooding over the evening's occurrences.

I have remained in this city too long! he fumes. *There is no salvation to be found here: not even a moment's peace.*

14 June 1525
Wittenberg, Electorate of Saxony

Martin Luther awakes in the same bed as always—the same ceiling above him, the same plain white walls. Yet, it is a new reality: a strange world, a fierce existence, a realm of endless possibilities both promising and terrible.

Who am I? What am I?

He realizes he is alone, which would not be odd at all, except he distinctly remembers he was not alone last night. She was here in his room—in his bed! He took her as his wife, but now she has vanished. *Could it all have been a dream?*

He lifts his hand and sees without question a ring gifted him the previous day. The gold band glints in the early morning sunlight seeping through the window behind him. Another ring, he knows, resides on the finger of Katharina. It wasn't a dream: he is bound to her, and she to him. They are now one flesh.

Who am I?

The enormity of his decision has struck him in waves as relentless as the shifting surf. One by one, they have broken upon him—kneeling, taking her hand, reciting. It was as if he was acting out a scene from someone else's life. He saw the light of the candles reflected in her tear-filled eyes. The way those eyes looked at him: *What was she feeling?* There was something there he could not understand, and it troubled him.

The marital night was another wave. He had thought about it as little as possible beforehand. Some might conclude he was frightened, but he doesn't think so—not of the act itself. Despite his years in monastic life, he understood the concept well enough. He remembers struggling to sleep as a boy due to sounds from the next room: grunting, banging, scraping of wood on wood. Hans Ludher was never quiet about anything, and that least of all. He remembers his student days in Erfurt. More than once, he came upon a fellow student doing the deed. Life has made him familiar with this common human activity, but theory and practice are two different matters. There are many ways of knowing something, and he has much still to learn.

He had not counted on Jonas's presence. Yes, he knew someone must witness the act—the very law requires it—but he failed to consider the effect it would have. Katharina, who had spent years hiding herself from men, was clearly frightened. He wanted to comfort her but was uncertain of the best way to do it. At one particularly critical moment, he could hear Jonas crying, which would be enough to frustrate any man in his position. Few experiences in his life had left him feeling more incapable. But he discovered a trick: he was able to block off his mind and carry on with the business, cutting out the awkwardness, refusing to overthink it.

Thus, the thing was accomplished, and they were joined in the eyes of the law. He thinks it went, for the most part, as it was supposed to, though it was not the transporting existence the poets claim. How could it be under such circumstances? As for what his wife thinks, he has no idea. He is far too afraid to ask. Perhaps her absence from his bed is proof enough of how she feels.

Now, as he stares at the ring on his finger, he is struck by a third wave. *I've done it: I've made the final breach.* If there was any chance of him being restored to the Roman priesthood, it cannot happen now. As much as his burning of the bull and testimony before the Emperor, this is a severing of the cord—a final renunciation of his former identity. Not only has he married, but he has married a former nun. The enormity of it overwhelms him. Any last vestige of devotion to Rome—any final hope of reconciliation is dead. Though fully certain of the righteousness of his decision, he can feel the terror growing within him.

I must get up. I cannot stay here.

The tension is surging through him as he strains to brace the floodgates of his soul. He grasps the doorknob with trembling fingers and turns it to the left, pushing forward. Stepping into the outer chamber, he glances through the open doors all the way into the far lecture hall but sees no one. He breathes deeply—attempts to release his anxiety. Then, as if he had dreamed it, he hears a sound rising from the kitchen below him, filtering through a grate and echoing in his ears.

It is Katharina's voice. She must have woken early and started on the meal for last night's participants. He has heard her speak of grand plans for some sort of cake. Now, she is singing to herself—he cannot quite make out the words. It is the first time he has truly heard her sing. She has some real skill, no doubt gained through her years of chanting the Psalms. The music so sweet to his ears, the tones she shapes like a potter at the wheel—it kindles a panic within him, even as it awakens longing. He feels the tightening of his bowels: the irresistible urge to flee.

An activity, he thinks. *I must set my mind to a task. It will relieve the tension.*

So, he does not move to join his wife below but enters his study to the right. He ducks beneath the lines hung with drying papers; steps around the piles of books, discarded bits of food, and empty beakers; and comes at last to his chair, collapsing into it under the weight of the world. Upon the desk before him is a stack of parchment leaves, a pen, and an inkwell. *There are so many people I must tell.* Of course, the whole world will know soon enough—a tale like this cannot help but spread—but there are a few persons whom he must inform directly, in his own words. The first is the most important: indeed, it will be one of the most consequential things he has ever written in his life, though the world will not view it as such. He dips the nib, presses it to parchment, and writes.

> To my dear father, Hans Ludher, burgher of Mansfeld. Grace and peace! I write to inform you that, in accordance with your will, I have taken Fräulein Katharina von Bora as my wife, or Frau Katharina Luther as she must now be called. We will have the church service and homecoming in two weeks' time. Do come, if you can, and share in our joy. Give my love to mother, and Jakob, and all the other relations.
>
> Your devoted son,
>
> Martin Luther

He sets down the pen and stares at the words he has just written. A terrible thought passes through his mind: *That will give his heart the shock it needs!* But it is only a jest, and one far beneath the genuine affection he still holds for the man who made him what he is as surely as any other. So many years of struggle, twisting and turning in one another's grasps, shaking the earth with the force of their collision! Perhaps now that he has finally done the thing his father desired, he will know the warmth of communion he ought to have enjoyed from the start. The thought overwhelms him. In his present state, it does not relieve, but sharpens his anxiety. His eyes wander to the corner of the desk, where he notices a sealed letter that must have been placed there by Brisger.

I will read it, he decides, rushing to the next activity to avoid the grasping fingers of terror. *Please, Lord, let it have nothing to do with the eel of Basel. That's the last thing I need.*

He reaches into the drawer to retrieve his knife. He is getting through it: keeping the fear at bay, holding his muscles in check, refusing to succumb. Every fiber in his body seems transformed into a thing of metal as cold as ice. The anxiety grates upon him—back and forth, up and down, inside and out—but he refuses to yield. *I am a married man. I ought to be joyful. I will be joyful,* he tells himself. But at the back of his mind, burrowing through the recesses of his brain, is another thought. *She will find out who you really are, and when she does, she will hate you. You cannot protect her from yourself.*

He struggles to put these thoughts to death. Then he hears a noise which jolts him from top to bottom and back again: someone is pounding on the door as if they mean to break it down. Martin's insides clench. His heart rushes blood to every extremity, readying him for the conflict he fully expects but does not yet understand. Now comes a voice like a thunderbolt.

"Martin! Martin, I must speak with you—now!"

It is Philipp Melanchthon. Never has Martin heard his voice shaped thus: turned into a dragon of fury prepared to consume. He senses—yes, deep within himself he knows that every fear he has had about Philipp's state of mind is about to come down upon him, tumbling from the heights and crashing over his head. Much as he hates to do so, he summons the courage to reply, "Come in."

Philipp thrusts the door open and strides boldly into the room, slamming the thing behind him. He is breathing heavily—almost shaking with rage. His pupils seem to pulse with the force of it. The muscles in his face are strained nearly to the point of tearing. Martin feels himself caught up in the whirlwind, but he will not be transported to heaven. He is plummeting in the opposite direction.

"How could you?!" Philipp bellows.

14 June 1525
Wittenberg, Electorate of Saxony

Philipp Melanchthon had woken that morning on the floor of his study. Having worked the previous night until the candles were spent, he chose not to risk waking the members of his household, but curled up on the floor like a dog, legs and arms tucked in. He passed a few hours in fitful dreams before finding himself still on the floor. He then determined by the soft light filtering through the windows that it must be almost dawn.

Yawning and rubbing his eyes, he felt a sudden crease of pain cutting down the right side of his neck, snaking beneath his shoulder blade, and depositing near his hip. "Curse it," he muttered, rising cautiously to his feet. He made his way down to the ground floor, thinking as he did so of his son Philipp, now four months out of the womb. His wife, Katharina, had noticed that other children young Philipp's age were rolling over or pulling themselves across the floor, while their son was not.

"Something's wrong with him. I know it is!" she had declared only the previous day. "We must have the physician examine him."

What more the physician could discover than he had the previous week, or the week before that, Philipp could only guess. Ever since his son's painful entrance into the world, there had been a permanent knot in Philipp's stomach and a constant weight upon his thoughts. Few things in his life had torn him to this extent.

What if he never walks? What if he never talks? What will become of my son? My son!

The war had surely done nothing to improve the situation: the images of twisted bodies cleaved in two by halberds or trampled underfoot by horses were often on his mind. The prospect of being seized and put on trial for his beliefs, the potential breach with Erasmus, the lack of communication between himself and Martin—all these thoughts were spinning, whipping themselves into a whirlwind that threatened to pull Philipp off his foundations.

As he made it to the bottom of the stairs, one hand massaging his inflamed neck, he was met by their faithful assistant, Famulus Koch, who held a metal bucket in his hand.

"Back from milking the goat?" Philipp asked.

"Yes, she gave quite a bit," Koch replied, displaying the sloshing liquid for Philipp to inspect. "I was out of feed for the hens, so I went over to the cloister to fetch a bit from Wolf."

"Ah," muttered Philipp, not truly interested. "And how is he?"

"Ha!" Koch scoffs. "He's in a right state. The new mistress is already rearranging the kitchen."

So exhausted was Philipp, his attention had wandered to a point on the opposite wall, which he stared at without intent, his vision growing blurry. He sensed that something about Koch's statement was odd, but he could not quite grasp the words. Looking back at his assistant, Philipp grunted, "What?"

"The wedding!" Koch responded, shaking his head. "Honestly, Master Philipp, I wish you had told me it was going to happen! I must have looked a great fool standing there with my mouth hanging open."

Philipp aligned his stance with Koch's, a tension gripping his bones. "I have no idea what you're talking about."

"You mean they didn't tell you either?" Koch laughed. "Well, it will be all over town soon enough: Doktor Luther is married. Wed the Bora girl last night."

A blow—yes, a lance penetrating deep into Philipp's chest! He turned to hide his reaction from Koch. *Married?! He married without telling me?!* Philipp took several harsh breaths, his lungs expanding and contracting like a giant bellows. His blood pulsed with a rattling hum. The thoughts and memories within him were heated to the point of flame. And then, in the space of a single breath, it all broke free: everything he had suppressed for years—everything that had ever troubled him about his colleague. He could feel it releasing, rushing through his extremities, singing all it touched.

He hid it from me. He lied to me! Well, maybe not a lie, but he clearly doesn't trust me!

So great had his anger become, it took on a logic of its own, bestowing upon him a fierce sense of purpose. He remembered the words of his wife: *Be honest with Doktor Luther. You must not hold these things inside.* He thought over the past seven years of his life—all the sacrifices he had made for the sake of his work with Martin Luther. *Reuchlin! It is because of him that I was torn from Reuchlin!* His soul had been twisted and tortured for months upon months, and at last, it had broken. His very skin seemed to burn.

Perhaps he was shaking with the rage, for Koch inquired, "Master Philipp, are you well? I didn't mean to upset you."

Philipp turned slowly to address his assistant and spoke with words far calmer than he felt. "Famulus, if anyone asks after me, I have gone to the Black Cloister."

"Very good," Koch concluded simply, displaying a remarkable lack of curiosity.

Within seconds, Philipp was walking in a fury down Colleges Street, cursing his stupidity. *Why did I ever think he cared about me?! I was only ever a tool in his hand to be used one day and discarded the next. Well, not anymore: it ends today!* Having devoted every ounce of his strength to defending Martin against the criticism of the entire world, he was ready to defend himself.

He stormed through the gate and approached the Black Cloister with a will, preparing a series of barbs in his mind, ready to plunge them into Martin's flesh. When he came to the main door, he found it standing open—likely for deliveries, as there was a pile of foodstuffs sitting in the foyer. He could hear voices within the nearby refectory. Under normal circumstances he would have made his presence known, but these were not normal circumstances. Philipp raced up the spiral steps, taking them two at a time. So quick was his pace, he had to urge himself to regain his breath so he would have some left to blast at Martin.

The indignity, the fear, the pain: it ends now!

It was in this mood that Philipp Melanchthon arrived at Martin Luther's study and banged his fist on the door. Hearing a muffled reply, he threw the door open and strode through, taking his stand with fists clenched. And that is where he remains, still breathing heavily from his effort, staring at the man he thought he knew. Once, he saw the fire of the Spirit in those eyes, but what does he see now? *Fear,* Philipp thinks. *He is afraid. He should be.* Martin sets aside the letter and pen knife as Philipp takes a deep breath and releases the first volley.

"How could you?!"

Martin inhales, the look on his face pained. "You refer to my marriage, or something else?"

"I could refer to a hundred different things, but yes, it is your recent marriage that has brought me here now: a plan you neglected to mention to me though we were many days in each other's company!"

"If you mean when we were in Mansfeld, there was no plan then. It has been a recent decision."

Philipp shakes his head in disbelief. "You say that as if it makes it better! To join yourself with this woman while the fields are still wet with blood, when you know full well the damage it will do to our work—the number of allies we will lose! How could you, Martin?! I thought we were friends!"

"I hope we still are," Martin replies softly.

How can we be when you have so deliberately wounded me?! Philipp wonders. He has known this fight was coming for a long time, yet he can scarcely believe it is happening.

"I cannot think what possessed you," Philipp says, "or how you could have been induced to act so foolishly."

Martin sighs deeply, a reaction Philipp finds entirely unwarranted. "No one induced me. This was a perfectly rational choice. People get married every day."

How can you treat this as if it were a trifling matter?! Philipp rages inside. *How can you be so willfully obtuse?!* He clasps his hands behind his back and begins pacing the floor, weaving around the piles of books. "You have allowed your pity to tempt you to rashness, or else—"

He cannot finish. He is thinking of their journey in April: the many times Martin seemed utterly distracted. *Was he lovelorn? Was that what it was all about? He was imagining her—longing, desiring? It must be so. Yes, it explains everything!*

"Or else what?" Martin demands to know. "You started boldly, now finish it!"

His anger long past the boiling point, Philipp plants his feet and lobs another charge. "Or else you are burning with lust—driven wild by passion!"

Now, Martin seems to boil as well. He slams his right hand on the desk and declares, "That is not the reason! You may ask Bugenhagen or Jonas: they will confirm it!"

"Yes, you open your soul to everyone but me," Philipp snaps. Usually as composed as any man on earth, he is quickly losing control. Out of frustration, he blurts, "It was a stupid thing to do!"

"Ah, yes! How stupid of me to make good on everything I have been preaching these past eight years!" Martin cries, shaking his head. "You speak as if we should stop living life in times of war. I say we should live for what matters most! This is not the hour for deliberation, but action!"

"You did this thing without informing anyone—without asking anyone's advice. I knew you could be rash, but I never thought you capable of this."

"I think you will find I did inform more than one person: several, in fact."

"Cranach? He was probably just hoping to be rid of her."

Martin clicks his tongue disapprovingly. "That is unkind, Philipp, which is not like you. Katharina is perfectly lovely and a hard worker. She was no burden on them."

"Well, how would I know, since I have barely met the woman?" he asks, overcome by the ache he feels inside. "How could you not tell me, Martin?! Do you think that because I am young—because I am not a lord on earth that my opinion has no value? Do you dismiss me so?"

"Of course not! You know I value your opinion."

"Yet you cut me out," Philipp laments, tears forming in his eyes. "You keep me in the dark! That is not the mark of a friend. After all we have been through, after everything I have done for you, you treat me like a stranger!"

They both stop to breathe. Philipp is uncertain how the conversation can possibly end in a positive manner. It has so far done nothing to allay his fears: Martin is as intransigent as ever.

"Have you ever stopped to ask yourself, Philipp, why you feel a need to be loved by anyone and everyone?" Martin inquires.

Philipp scoffs. "Not by everyone, but I would have your respect, yes!"

"What does it matter what I think?" Martin asks. "What am I to you?"

Philipp shakes his head, scarcely able to process the words he is hearing. "What do you mean?! My whole life is built upon our work together!"

"Why are you such a respecter of persons?" Martin presses again.

Philipp's thoughts are spinning madly. *How has this become a reckoning upon my character and not yours?!*

"You betrayed my trust!" Philipp cries.

Martin breathes deeply, as if bracing himself for a harsh blow. "Now, Philipp, listen to me: I am not your father."

This statement crushes Philipp. *Not my father? Not my father?!* He curses Martin internally. That his father's memory should be invoked—that he should be compared to Martin in such a way—enrages Philipp, working his insides into a frenzy. It is a deep wound delivered, he suspects, without the slightest consideration. "How dare you!" he bellows.

"Philipp—"

"I know perfectly well that I am not your son!" Philipp cries, his tears flowing freely. "Honestly, how can you say such a thing?! My father was a great man—a godly saint who was never less than kind. I stood by his bed as he suffered and died. He spoke a word of promise over me. He speaks to me still. No man could replace him, and certainly not you! But that is your arrogance: you think yourself the center of the world, and everything is about you—even me! I am denied your respect. Do you know how much that hurts?!"

Martin shakes his head. "Philipp, if you were not given over to your own compulsions, you would see that you have my respect. I rely on you utterly to carry out this work—our work—God's work! If I had not thought of you as highly as I do, would I have fought so hard to keep you in Wittenberg? Why am I fighting now for the Elector to double your salary?! No, Philipp, it is you who are focused only on self," he charges, pointing squarely at Philipp's chest. "I take a wife—yes, I alone take a wife—and your first thought is not to congratulate me but reprimand me for not seeking your permission! That is not friendship. That is making the issue about yourself."

"Even if this action of yours compromises everything we have achieved?!" Philipp bellows, unwilling to concede the point. Already, he can hear the insults from the Romanists—can see the scurrilous pamphlets they will produce. He feels their allies shrinking from them, ashamed to be associated with scandal.

"You turn things around!" Martin responds, striking the desk again with his palm. "A man who needs the approval of others is a bottomless cup that can never be filled. Find yourself in Christ, brother, and then come to me with talk of friendship. The point cuts both ways. I tell you, I have fought with the devil, and I have seen the breaking light. This action of mine was ordained by God. I hope in time you will see that."

Philipp wipes his tears with his hands, attempting to regain his composure. He closes his eyes and breathes deeply, and in that brief pause, he thinks of the field of blood: the great pile of bodies. He thinks of how he felt when he read Martin's attacks on the peasants. Every action taken without proper thought—every word spoken in anger blends together, and he now sees his colleague not as Elijah confronting the prophets of Baal, but a bully swinging his club wildly, not caring whom he hurts.

"You are no god, Martin," Philipp begins, his voice soft. "There are many who wage war against the devil—who walk in the shadow of death and feel its sting. This work of reform doesn't belong to you alone. It belongs to me, to my children, to my students and the peasants in the fields, to princes and burghers, to people yet unborn!" He gains strength, his voice sounding loud and clear. "When you act without taking counsel, you risk everything we have achieved. Yes, we, Martin! You place it at risk not only for yourself and your reputation, but also for my dear Anna. Could you look her in the eye and tell her you are without sin, or could you say it to those who were cut down at Frankenhausen? They too wanted a better world and were not as fortunate in their knowledge as you and me. Do you feel no compassion for your fellow man?! You fear the end of our work, but it is as likely to come from your own misdeeds as those of the peasants. When you act without thinking, you make those of us who have followed you into fools, and what is far worse, you make the gospel appear foolish as well!"

Philipp stands there, eyes still leaking, breath coming steadily. *I have said so many things. So many things!* He wonders if there is any coming back from this, or if the breach is final. He looks into the eyes of Martin Luther, and no longer sees fear there, but hurt: deep, abiding hurt. Philipp had sought to wound him—to make Martin feel a fraction of the pain he has endured. What he sees now is that his colleague does hurt, perhaps more deeply than Philipp will ever understand. *It is not my fault,* he thinks. *He brought it on himself. He doesn't care about me—not really. Right?*

"Is that all?" Martin asks quietly when enough silence has passed.

"For the moment," Philipp says, wiping his eyes and sniffing. "Let it be enough."

He turns and takes a step toward the exit, then realizes he must make the gravity of the situation clear. Turning to face Martin again, Philipp tells him, "I don't know if I can stay here—stay in Wittenberg."

Even as he speaks the words, Philipp finds himself hanging upon Martin's response. Perhaps, despite everything that has passed between them, there is hope for reconciliation. After all, even as he spoke the words, Philipp felt a great part of himself that wanted to stay. *Please,* Philipp silently begs. *Please, tell me you want me to stay!*

But there is no visible reaction on Martin's face. "You are as free to go as you were to come," he responds without hint of emotion.

Why did I hope? Philipp wonders. *Why did I allow myself to be hurt again?* "And to think that you offer such a reply," he says. "I take my leave of you."

He then attempts to make an authoritative exit, moving boldly toward the door, but as he does, he stubs his toe on an object he failed to notice. When the initial pain passes and he has ceased cursing under his breath, Philipp leans down and lifts the object in question: a bent silver crucifix as one would place on an altar, with the figure of Christ entirely smashed.

"What is this?" Philipp asks.

"From the church in Kahla," Martin says, his voice scarcely above a whisper. "I've been meaning to have it repaired."

"I suppose you will get to it right after you reply to Erasmus," Philipp cannot help but retort, shooting a glare back at Martin.

"First, I was too hasty. Now, I am slothful," Martin complains, but there is no force behind his voice. It is robbed of strength, trailing off into the void. "If it bothers you, take it and repair it yourself."

"Very well," Philipp concludes.

With that, he departs the study—makes his way back through both lecture halls and the long passage robbed of its saints. He descends the stairs with nothing like the energy of his ascension, the hard metal of the cross bitter against his skin. He cannot remember the last time he felt so low. It is worse than when he thought Martin was dead, for then he at least maintained his love. As he moves to exit the building, he nearly collides with a stunned Katharina, whose face is heavily flushed in surprise.

"Herr Doktor," she says, bowing her head. "I did not know we would have the pleasure of welcoming you. Is there anything I can do for you—anything you would like?"

"There is nothing you can do for me," he responds, "for I am no longer welcome in this house."

As Katharina looks at him in horror, Philipp marches out the door, no longer able to contain his emotion. He weeps openly, his shoulders shaking with the effort. Hoping to avoid his fellow Wittenbergers, he takes the back way to his house. When he arrives in the yard, he falls to his knees by the animal pens, allowing the crucifix to drop. He knows he must cry to God, but he cannot find the power within himself. Then his wife—the great love of his life—emerges from the house, holding young Philipp in her arms. She asks no questions nor offers any advice, but drops to her knees beside him, clutching him to herself, allowing him to weep. In years to come, Philipp will not remember how long they stayed there, clinging to each other while the world spun wildly around them. All he will know is that she was the only reason he ever found the strength to rise again.

14 June 1525
Wittenberg, Electorate of Saxony

Martin Luther sits in his study, his whole being in turmoil, staring at the door Philipp Melanchthon has so recently slammed shut.

He's gone. He's gone, and he's never coming back.

Every fear within him has been confirmed. He knew it from the moment Philipp burst through the door. The tension that had built since Martin first woke ascended to a ruinous climax as the verbal blows rained down on him one after another, ceaselessly reproaching, stripping his defenses, exposing his flaws and failures. He did his best to respond—to channel and direct Philipp's anger—but it was a thing far beyond his control.

What will I do without him? How can I go on? How can any of this go on?!

The panic is singeing him from head to toe, burning a great hole in his chest. His pulse speeds with wild abandon—his breath comes short and cruel. Unable to gain mastery over his own form, he slumps to the floor and lies transfixed, his muscles twitching anxiously, the accusing voice seizing command.

You fool! You've ruined everything! He sees through you. They will all see through you.

He reaches over to grasp his wrist, but his grip feels weak. He tries to remember the words: the promises to which he is meant to cling. But everything is a chaos, spinning and twisting, dragging him down into the caverns of the deep. Someone else bangs on the door.

"Martin! Martin, are you in there?"

It is his colleague and confessor, Johannes Bugenhagen: the very man who conducted the marriage the previous night, come for the celebratory meal Katharina is preparing. *Katharina!* The very thought of her fills Martin with shame, hot and surging. *Why did I think I could do this? What have I done?!* He longs to disappear into himself. *I cannot protect her—not from this.*

"Martin, I'm coming in," Bugenhagen informs him.

I must get up! Martin realizes, but his strength is utterly sapped. *Pathetic! You are utterly pathetic!* He is powerless against the accusations—impotent in his moment of greatest need.

The door opens slowly and Bugenhagen walks in, dressed in his black robe and matching cap. Upon seeing Martin sprawled on the floor, his eyes bulge with concern. He rushes to Martin's side and bends over him, frantically searching for signs of injury.

"Are you hurt?! What's wrong?!" Bugenhagen urgently inquires.

As he looks into his friend's desperate eyes, Martin knows he can hide no longer. For years, he has attempted to conceal this side of himself, even as he has hinted about it on many occasions. He has spoken of battles with the devil, but not of the full extent of his weakness.

"The terror," he confesses with trembling lips. "I am having the terror."

"What do you mean?" Bugenhagen asks, his brow furrowed. "Is it the devil?"

"I think so," says Martin, working to pull himself up. "It strikes me from time to time. I go rigid: my heart and lungs struggle." Even as he says this, he works to catch his breath, striving against the air.

When Martin is sitting upright, Bugenhagen seizes his shoulders and asks, "Brother, what are you thinking? Are your thoughts accusing you?"

Martin nods, too frightened to speak the horrible curses passing through his mind.

"I heard that Melanchthon was here," Bugenhagen says. "Your wife said he was most upset."

"My wife," Martin whispers, the words infinitely strange.

"I will go get her. She can attend to you."

"No!" Martin cries in desperation. "No, please, I beg you!" For if she comes now, she will see the worst of all he is: hideous, weak, impotent. *She will hate me.*

Bugenhagen looks at him oddly—perhaps even judgmentally. "You do not wish to see her?"

"I do not want her to see me like this," Martin explains.

His colleague sighs. "Let's get you up. Can you stand?"

"Yes, I think so."

His heartrate slowing and breath growing steady, Martin stands upon legs that are stronger than he imagined. The worst of the panic is fading, though he is still gripped by uncertainty and grief.

"He was so angry with me, Johannes," Martin laments. "I have never seen him so angry. The things I said—I'm afraid I only made it worse. I should have told him about my intentions with Katharina. I can see that now. How was I so blind?"

"Maybe you just wanted to get married, and you were tired of people criticizing you," Bugenhagen reasons.

Martin nods. "Yes, I suppose that is what happened. Everything has been so difficult these past few months. He said he might leave, Johannes! What will we do without him?!"

Bugenhagen places an arm around Martin's shoulders. "I want him to stay as much as you do, but he is in God's hands. If the Lord calls him to go, he must go."

"It is not the Lord calling him to go, but my stupidity driving him away," says Martin, shaking his head in disgust. "He will make for Basel and the house of Erasmus. How I have feared it! Now, it has come to pass. All is lost."

"There is still time. Tell him how much he means to you," Bugenhagen urges.

Martin pinches his eyes shut, attempting to hold back a new rush of tears. "He does not want to speak with me. He made that quite clear."

"Sit down," his friend instructs, helping Martin back into his chair. When he fully settles, Bugenhagen states, "At the present, I am more concerned about the situation with your wife."

"What situation?" Martin asks incredulously, although he knows precisely what his friend means.

Bugenhagen moves to face him directly, staring him down. "You cannot hide from her forever. You must be honest about how you feel—allow her to share in your struggles."

"I would have to hate her quite a bit to do that," Martin retorts. "No one on earth would want to share in my struggles." As he speaks the words, he feels the pang in his heart: the holy yearning for a form of communion that seems utterly impossible.

"But that is what a wife does, and what a husband does," Bugenhagen insists. "God has brought this woman into your life and your home. If you are going to be wed, then you must be truly wed. You must take it seriously."

"I am taking it seriously!" he objects, his shame giving way to anger.

"Sometime soon, you must find a way to do it," Bugenhagen concludes. "You must not hold her at arm's length."

The fear is growing within Martin again. *Philipp saw through you. She will too. She will be sorry she ever married you.* The thoughts torture him, sending his joy to flight. He sits in silence, uncertain how to respond—uncertain of so many things.

"Now, if you are well, I will leave you to whatever you were doing," says Bugenhagen.

"I had a letter," he mutters.

"Then get to it!" his colleague concludes. "I will check and see if they need help below."

With that, Bugenhagen departs the room. Martin takes up the knife and slices through the seal, brooding over the many things Philipp yelled at him: *You are burning with lust—driven wild by passion!* What damage such a charge could do if repeated abroad! No one must think that he wed Katharina merely to bed her. He has unfolded the letter and takes in the opening lines.

"God's grace and peace! Reverend Doktor, this is my request: that you forgive me everything."[2]

It is in the hand of Andreas Bodenstein von Karlstadt. *Of all the people in the world who could have written to me today!* He groans, cursing his ill fate. Still, he hears the cries of Karlstadt's parishioners last summer. "You are damned to hell, Luther! Damned to hell!" He hears Karlstadt's whisper in his ear when they met in Jena. "You mean nothing to me." There is a white-hot burning in Martin's breast. He breathes deeply, willing the memory out of his body. But the pain of betrayal is written in his flesh. He prays, *Lord in heaven, show me how to forgive.* Then, summoning the deepest powers that reside in his gut, he continues reading.

"Take pity on my poor wife and child, and pledge that they can join you there!"

Your family?! Here?! After everything that has passed between us—after you condemned me as a heretic—you seek my hospitality?!

"There is turmoil from here to France. I am everywhere considered a hateful enemy, and I can neither trust anyone, nor do they trust me!"

Can you blame them?

"I understand the rules of this world now: if you find something in my books that is too close to the bone or uncomfortable, then punish me—make me pay! I have decided not to write, preach, or teach anything more in the future."

We shall see how long that lasts.

"Act as a Christian brother and friend, and commend myself, my wife, and child to our most gracious Elector, so that we will no longer be in disfavor."

Martin drops the letter on the desk and buries his face in his hands. His relationship with Melanchthon is on the brink of ruin, his relationship with his wife is not what it should be, and now a relationship from which he has longed to break free is pulling him in once again.

How can we welcome them here after everything he has said and done? How can I welcome anyone into this house when I need time to

---

[2] This quote and those that follow are based upon a letter Karlstadt wrote to Luther dated 12 June 1524. They are not an exact translation but capture most of Karlstadt's intent.

settle into married life? It is his own fault that everyone hates him! He reaps only that which he has sown. And after everything I have done to convince the Court of Karlstadt's errors, how can I now write to the Elector and beg for him to be readmitted?

He places his head on the desk, remembering that just below him, a feast is being prepared for what is meant to be a celebratory day. He took a leap of faith in proceeding with the marriage. *Was it really God's will, or am I suffering under some illusion?* No, surely, it was God's will. He has rarely felt so strongly about anything. Yet, everything is going wrong: there is great doubt within him. *I must place Karlstadt aside. It is Philipp who needs my attention. Karlstadt does not deserve it!* Even as he thinks this, he knows such things have a way of coming back to demand attention at the worst possible moment. Nevertheless, he must risk forgetfulness if he is to have any peace.

He looks out the window in front of him. The sky is resplendent with light. All creation seems to celebrate, but he alone cannot.

Please, Lord, he prays. *Please, let me see your face.*

16 June 1525
Wittenberg, Electorate of Saxony

Philipp Melanchthon sits at the desk in his study with a blank piece of parchment in front of him, his spirit in utter turmoil. It has been two days since his fight with Martin: two days of wretched uncertainty in which he has avoided conversation as much as possible, wallowing in his own company. *Must I say farewell to my beloved students? To the Krapp family, as dear to me as my own?* He has turned the situation over in his mind, kneading it like a great pile of dough, but despite all his efforts, he cannot find his peace. He has barely eaten—his slumber comes only in rough spurts. How could any man reach a momentous decision under such conditions? In desperation, he has decided to do what he ought to have done at the first: seek the counsel of his good friend, Joachim Camerarius. He has only an hour to compose the letter before his afternoon lectures.

How should I begin? Philipp wonders. *I suppose it is best to be straightforward.* He writes a single word of greeting, then proceeds to the issue at hand. "On June 13, Luther unexpectedly and without informing any of his friends what he was doing in advance, married Katharina von Bora."[3]

Philipp has had two full days to adjust to this news, and still, it defies comprehension. After that dreadful period of chaos in Wittenberg, when Karlstadt was enacting sweeping changes and Philipp felt himself utterly lost, Martin preached the value of patience. "Wait until the people are ready, don't do things that will upset consciences, maintain a sense of order, etc." *He is hardly practicing what he preached,* Philipp thinks. *Has he too been inflamed by the strange fires sweeping the land?*

So troubled are Philipp's thoughts, he finds it impossible to write. *When we all need his counsel, when everything is falling to pieces, he goes off and does this, not caring whom he hurts!* There are tears forming in his eyes, hot and stinging. *I thought I had found a home: a place where I could love and be loved. I thought I had found a mentor I could trust, as if the very Spirit of God had led me here. Well, what sort of spirit is this but the spirit of chaos that caused the insurrection?!*

These bitter thoughts are interrupted by loud footsteps outside, banging up the stairs as if they were meant to bring the house down—and that would not take much, given the poor construction. Philipp yells over his shoulder and through the closed door, "Be quiet! I'm at work!" Anna's laughter filters into the study. In any other circumstance, he would count it among the most blessed sounds on earth, rising and falling in delightful bursts of exuberance, but in his agitated state, it grates. He cries again, "Be quiet! Papa is working!"

There is no reply, which he takes to be a positive sign given his request. His head aching, he places one hand on his temple to help relieve the pressure and writes with the other, his frustration releasing onto the page.

---

[3] This quote and those that follow are based upon the following translation: "Letter 692 – Melanchthon to Joachim Camerarius" *in Luther's Correspondence and Other Contemporary Letters*, Volume II, trans. and ed. Preserved Smith and Charles M. Jacobs (Philadelphia: The Lutheran Publication Society, 1918), 325-6. There are two surviving versions of the letter, one dated 16 June and the other 24 June, with the most important differences occurring in a single paragraph. It seems likely that the first reflects Melanchthon's initial thoughts, while the second was the one he sent to Camerarius.

"The man is certainly pliable, and the nuns have used their arts against him most successfully; his companionship with the nuns has likely softened or even inflamed this noble and high-spirited man. In this way, he seems to have fallen into this untimely change of life."

As he gazes down at the words, Philipp frowns. *Perhaps that is a bit unfair.* His pen dangles in the air as he is caught between affection and frustration. *I have every right to criticize this man! He hasn't even bothered to contact me since our dispute. Is that not proof enough of his disdain?* Yet, the bond of love is not so easily broken. Philipp feels himself longing for answers—anything that might explain how things went so terribly wrong. He wants to see Martin absolved. *But he will not listen to anyone. If I fail to hold him to account, then who is to stop him from doing whatever seems best at any moment? Our work will be ruined!* Does he seek Martin's absolution, or his own? Is there any difference between those two things when Philipp has given all of himself to their work together at the expense of his reputation and his family's welfare? *God only knows...*

Uncertain how to continue, he is spared the effort by an interruption. Someone is knocking on the front door below: perhaps a pupil who has misplaced the paper he was meant to hand over in a few minutes' time. Koch and the boarders have all left the house, and Katharina is busy with the children, so Philipp rises and walks out into the passage, descending the stairs to the ground floor. There he nearly collides with Katharina, who is exiting the kitchen with young Philipp in her arms, her face strained and breath labored.

"Have you seen Anna?!" she inquires desperately. "I left them both in the parlor for a moment, but now I can't find her!"

There is another bang on the front door as Philipp strokes his wife's hair and assures her, "She's upstairs. I just heard her a moment ago. She's probably hiding."

Katharina sighs in relief. "I saw the back door was open. I was worried she had gone out."

Philipp looks down the passage to his right: the rear door is still ajar, swinging in the breeze. He moves to close it, but Katharina instructs, "See who has come to call. I'll take care of this."

He kisses his wife and son in turn, then rushes to the front door, which is being subjected to someone's fist for the third time.

"Just a moment!" he calls, releasing the lock and swinging the door open to find Frau Katharina Luther standing there in a simple brown dress, her hair now contained in the black netting reserved for doktor's wives and those of the upper class. The sight of the woman who has caused so much convulsion in his life lends a sharpness to Philipp's gut, and he finds himself lost for words. Fortunately, his visitor takes the initiative.

"Good day, Herr Doktor," she greets him. "Do you have a moment to talk?"

"Yes," he replies automatically, then wonders, *Do I truly have a moment to talk? Do I want to talk to her?* But it is too late: she is already moving toward him, and he has stepped aside to grant her entrance.

"You are most kind to receive me in this fashion," Frau Luther says, bowing her head.

"Would you like to—" he begins but is silenced mid-phrase by screaming from above.

"No, no! Bad! Get out of here!" his wife cries.

What on earth?! he wonders, his heart shocked into rhythm. Looking into his visitor's concerned eyes, Philipp begs, "Excuse me," and gallops up the stairs, his wife's exclamations ringing harshly in his ears—"Give that to me! Stop! Bad, bad, bad!"—even as their son weeps.

When Philipp reaches the landing, he is alarmed to find young Philipp lying flat on his back on the floor, limbs flailing in the air, his tiny face scrunched with the force of his vocalizations.

"Oh, my son!" he cries in alarm, scooping the boy up and moving toward the study, from which his wife's panicked voice emanates.

Pushing the door open in fear and trembling, he finds something truly horrifying, though not in the way he expected. His wife is running around the room wildly, chasing after their goat, who is chewing some of Philipp's correspondence. Books have been knocked off the shelves, and there are shredded bits of paper scattered about. Meanwhile, young Anna is standing near the hearth, giggling uproariously.

"Philipp, help me!" Katharina pleads, grasping the goat by its hips and attempting to snatch the papers from its mouth. The animal's hooves slide across the floorboards in a desperate attempt to break free. Finally understanding why his son was set on the floor, Philipp does likewise, placing him gently next to Anna. He then springs toward the goat, grasping her by the neck and ripping the papers from her teeth. Placing the damp remnants of his correspondence on the table, he lifts the goat by her front legs, angling her body to avoid being kicked. He looks at his wife, who is bent over and gasping for breath, then turns toward Anna, who is crouched on the floor, patting her baby brother's head.

"Anna, did you let the goat into the house?" Philipp asks.

"She was lonely, Papa," his daughter replies earnestly, her blue eyes round and full, longing for his approval.

Anger is pulsing through Philipp. He looks at the mess strewn over the floor, wondering how many books have been destroyed and letters lost forever. He wants to release what he feels, but as he gazes upon Anna's precious face, he is filled with compassion. *She didn't know. She is only a child.* He is her father, and she must not doubt his love, so he chooses the path of grace: he remains silent rather than cause her to tremble. However, the girl's mother reacts swiftly.

"Very bad!" Katharina cries, swatting their daughter's hand. "You know you are never to let the animals into the house."

"But she was lonely!" Anna protests.

Katharina looks up at Philipp, as exasperated as he has ever seen her. Taking a few breaths to steady himself, the goat now limp in his grip, he says, "It's alright, dear. She meant no harm. Now, if you can deal with the children, I'll return the goat to the pen."

Katharina nods and asks, "Who was at the door?"

"Frau Luther," he replies, remembering that he must quickly adjust to a conversation he is not eager to have.

His wife's features wrinkle in concern. "She is here—now?! I haven't cleaned! There's a goat inside! She's going to think we run a mad house!"

"I doubt she will be concerned about any of it," Philipp concludes, departing the study with the bleating goat in his hands.

They move down the stairs with some difficulty, the wall and bannisters receiving several kicks in turn. When he reaches the main floor again, Philipp finds Frau Luther standing exactly where he left her, hands folded and face expectant. Her eyes focus on the goat and grow large.

"Please, forgive us for the interruption," Philipp begs. "You may have a seat in the parlor."

With that, he turns down the passage and exits the house, depositing the goat where she belongs. Aching from the effort, he enters his home again, securing the door behind him. He is met by his wife and children coming down the stairs to receive their guest. Philipp takes the baby in his arms and pats his back gently, even as Anna runs ahead to play with her dolls. Before they enter the parlor, his wife tugs on his robe and whispers, "Have you had any further thoughts about whether we are staying or going?"

"Nothing yet," he replies softly.

"Then we had best proceed with caution," she concludes.

Philipp nods in agreement, and at last the entire family joins Frau Luther in the parlor, Philipp and his wife taking the two chairs across from the couch where their unexpected visitor has made herself comfortable, her hands clasped in her lap, her eyes taking in every detail of the room. As Philipp sets the baby down to play with his sister in the corner, he has a few seconds to prepare himself for their conversation.

Lord, grant me the right words, he prays, dreading the task before him. He is seated upright again—the moment has come.

"Frau Luther, welcome to our home," he begins. "It is an honor to meet you properly."

"The honor is mine," their visitor replies. "Forgive me: this is a bit awkward, but I would not recommend letting your goat roam indoors, even if it seems tame. I was raised with them, you see, and I assure you, they will eat anything."

Philipp looks over at his wife, whose smile is highly strained. He can tell that she is livid. The tension is palpable up and down his spine. She shoots him a look as if to say, *I told you so. Didn't I tell you so?!* Breaking away from her glare, Philipp attempts to diffuse the situation with a joke.

"If only you had given that speech to my daughter a few minutes ago! I assure you, we do not allow the goat indoors. It was unintentional."

"Perhaps you need a better pen," their guest concludes, looking from one of them to the other. "Do you wish me to have a look? I might be able to suggest something."

"No, thank you, we have the matter in hand," Frau Melanchthon replies, her voice ice cold, the muscles in her face taut.

Philipp is far less upset by the turn of events than his wife, so he urges her, "Dear, why don't you take the children outside to play? The weather is lovely."

After shooting one more glance at the woman across from her, Katharina Melanchthon rises and takes her children in hand, leading them down the passage to the yard. *Not a good beginning,* Philipp laments, returning his gaze to Katharina Luther and forcing a smile.

"Now, why did you come?" Philipp asks. "You wished to discuss something with me."

Katharina shuffles in her seat, the look on her face pained. "It is about your conversation with my husband the other day. He has been in a terrible mood ever since: locking himself in his study, refusing to come out. It seems his whole world has turned to gloom. I do not know all that passed between you, but I take it he had not informed you we were to be married."

Why are you here and not him? Philipp wonders, the frustration building in his gut. For the moment, he sets the question aside and offers a terse reply. "No, he did not."

Katharina nods sadly. "I am sorry, Herr Doktor. I do not believe he meant to deceive you. It all happened so fast. Even I only had one day's notice! I humbly request your forgiveness." Here she bows her head respectfully, the apology seemingly sincere.

Philipp's emotions rush like a brook in spring. He feels as if he is reliving his argument with Martin—the torment to his being is equally acute. His colleague's voice is ringing in his mind: *I am not your father.* He pushes it aside.

"Fräulein—that is, Frau Luther," Philipp begins, correcting himself, "I mean no disrespect to you, but your new husband and I have a relationship of fairly long standing, and it has—" He pauses momentarily, mouth slightly agape, searching for the right word. "I suppose I would say it has its complications. Perhaps this is a matter for the Doktor and I to discuss privately, for it does not directly concern you."

"But you said you do not feel welcome in my house," she replies softly, her shoulders slumped. "That concerns me greatly."

Philipp looks into her eyes, which seem to him the color of rain. He takes in the contours of her nose, the sharp cheekbones, the hands clasped in expectation. *Why of all women on offer did Martin choose this one?* he wonders. *Why not someone who had never taken vows? What is so special about her, or is anything special about her? Did he simply decide to marry and snatch the first woman he saw? And what does she see in him?*

At last, he asks the chief question on his mind. "Did he send you here on his behalf?"

"No!" she responds quickly, as if pained by the suggestion. "He has said nothing about it. I am not yet in his confidence: not to that extent. But I can tell it is weighing on him." She bends forward slightly, addressing him as if the whole world depended on it. "If I am the cause of your rift, then I must strive to promote reconciliation. You are so important to his work, Doktor: to everything that happens here in Wittenberg."

That is rather bold of you, he thinks. But to her he says, "Perhaps you should tell him that."

"He believes it! I am certain he does."

"But I am not in his confidence either."

Katharina looks at him firmly, determined to prove her point. "He has every confidence in you, Doktor. He told very few people of his plans because he did not wish to subject me to gossip. That seems to me an honorable thing."

"Or he thought I would disapprove of his decision," Philipp comments, risking impropriety.

Katharina leans back, as if struck by his suggestion. "And do you?" she asks pointedly, matching his nerve.

Philipp stammers, uncertain how to answer without causing offense. "It is not that I do not like you or find you unsuitable as a person. I'm sure he would not have been interested in you if he did not think you a woman of character, though—"

No, I dare not continue, he thinks. *I have said too much already.*

"What is it, Herr Doktor?" Katharina inquires.

So sincere is her gaze, he is persuaded to continue. "It all happened quickly, at a time when he was very emotional. Perhaps he was driven to pity by your situation."

"Pity?" she mutters, her brow furrowed.

Philipp rubs his face with his hands, longing for some release from the situation. "Look, it is hard to explain without sounding insulting, but you must understand—there are many things at play here." He is losing her by the second: the fire in her eyes is bursting into flame. "We must think about how things will appear to people who do not know him as well as you and I. They will think that you took advantage of his compassion to secure a famous husband."

"They will think that, or you will?" The words fly from her lips like daggers aimed to kill.

"No, I didn't mean—"

"Whatever you may think, Doktor Melanchthon, I did not lure him under false pretenses. I swear it! I was quite ready to live out my days alone and impoverished. I told him as much. The fact that I am now speaking to you as Frau Luther was entirely his choice, and he came to it by reason. He did not marry me out of lust, nor I think even out of compassion, but because the war made him realize what was most important, and believing his time on earth to be short, he wished to take his stand upon the principles he has so boldly proclaimed."

Philipp nods swiftly, longing to restore calm. "Frau Luther, please—I never suspected you of seducing him or playing upon his compassion for gain. His compassion flows out of who he is. You would not have to manipulate him to draw it out." As the heat of her glare has lessened somewhat, he dares to inquire, "But if you don't mind me asking, why did you agree to marry him? You know he is a condemned man."

She inhales deeply, sitting up straight. *She's going to blast me,* he thinks, recoiling internally. But her mood seems to settle—she speaks in complete control.

"Herr Doktor, I assure you that while it fills me with great concern to know there are evil men who wish to put my husband to death, I feel no shame whatsoever. I am proud to be his wife and will do everything in my power to support him as long as we both live. I know the risks. I am terribly afraid, such that I spend both my days and nights in prayer for him and the work of reform. But I am also determined, Doktor, and you will find I can be stubborn as well. Sometimes stubbornness is a good thing. I don't know what the future will bring. If I did, it would strike me with terror. But I will cling to my Doktor, and I will cling to Christ."

Philipp cannot help but admire her for these words. *She is more impressive than I first imagined.* At the very least, she is brave, and she will need plenty of courage if she is to live with Martin Luther.

"You support his work. That is admirable," he acknowledges.

Katharina's gaze softens. She breathes deeply, preparing herself for a great statement. "It's more than that, Herr Doktor. You ask why I agreed to marry him. Because I adore him—that's why." She shakes her head in wonder. "Is that not strange? I love him far more than I have dared to say before this moment: more than I ever thought I could love a man, given everything I've been through. Whether he feels the same way, I don't know, but I am happy enough that he treats me well. He esteems me, cares for me, shows me Christian kindness. That is far more than I could expect from most men, and I am grateful."

As the words flow out of her, Philipp senses they are genuine: she truly loves her husband as her own flesh. *Does he not have a right to that, even as I do? Should he not have a wife who adores him, even as I do?* His frustration is easing a bit, though his broader concerns remain.

"You may not believe me, but it warms my heart to hear you speak thus," Philipp explains. "I was not certain about his decision to marry, true enough, but I am glad he has found a companion prepared to support him for all his days, and one who loves him truly. I hope in time, you two will come to enjoy the same affection that I share with my own Katharina. However, none of this changes the fact that your husband and I have real disagreements."

"Of course," she replies, nodding her head. "That is only natural with two great minds such as yourselves."

She has earned enough of his respect for him to speak to her plainly. "Martin is my senior colleague, and as such he is entitled to my deference. He must lead our work of reform, but I must know that he is on my side even as I am on his—that he values my opinions, and our friendship is built on mutual trust. I have felt that fracturing of late: our communion is diminished. Once, we would feast together at the great table of theology, feeding upon one another's discoveries. But since he left—since that dreadful, abominable year—I no longer feel the same connection."

Katharina leans forward—speaks to him tenderly. "You know he does not fault you for what happened, and you should not fault yourself."

Philipp swallows hard. *She barely knows me, and yet she has located the precise point of my pain and attempted to apply a poultice to it.* When he feels able to speak, he replies, "That is kind of you, but I fear if another moment comes when he is pulled away, he will be less confident in my abilities, and I could hardly blame him."

Again, she breathes deeply, as if preparing for something great. He feels ready to receive, for she has set him at ease.

"Doktor Melanchthon, you and I have both been placed in the orbit of a rather singular person: a man of great strengths, but with all the weaknesses common to his kind. God brought you here because the Doktor needs you. It is his strength that he realized that need from the beginning, and it is his weakness that he has not always made it sufficiently clear. But if even I can see his regard for you—I who know him far less than I desire—then you can be certain of it. I don't know everything that brought you to this point, but I beg you, do not tear down what you have built by the power of the Spirit. He needs you. We all need you, Doktor, for the Lord has given you immense gifts to serve his Church. Please, for all that you have meant to each other, and all that you have left to do together, forgive him. Or if you cannot yet forgive him, at least grant him a chance to explain. For if I were to guess, I would say that you need him too, and if you were to walk away now, you would end up regretting it."

Philipp is deeply moved by her words, so much so that he inhales swiftly to hold back the tears. He reaches a conclusion.

"I am willing to meet with him, but I do not know if the outcome will be exactly what you desire."

A smile breaks over Katharina's face. "I have faith, Doktor: faith in the two of you and faith in Christ. So, I will tell him what you have said, and perhaps he will let you know a time to meet and discuss this. Now, I have taken up too much of your valuable time. I will be on my way."

As she rises from her seat and moves to depart, Philipp says, "I hope he values the service you have performed for him today."

She looks at him earnestly and pledges, "I would do far more for the sake of my husband, and for you, Herr Doktor."

A few minutes later, Philipp is sitting on the couch with his own Katharina, watching Anna play on the floor with young Philipp. He puts his arm around his wife, still attempting to process everything that has transpired.

"I can't believe it," he says. "That is, I can believe it, and yet it confounds me."

"What's that, my love?" Katharina asks.

"He stumbled blindly, grasped with hardly a thought, and still managed to snare the perfect woman."

Katharina pulls away from him, her gaze biting. "Perfect woman?"

"No, I don't mean—" Philipp sighs, reaching desperately for the right words. "The perfect woman for him."

This at least puts his wife's glare to flight, but Katharina is still frowning, her lips slightly pursed.

"What?" he asks. "What is that look for?"

"You will say I am terrible," she replies hesitantly.

"I grant you pardon before the fact," he offers, making the sign of blessing with his fingers.

"Very well," she agrees, nodding softly. "Didn't she seem a bit bossy?"

"Bossy?"

"You know—pushy."

Philipp chuckles. "Because she made the comment about the goat?"

This is evidently the wrong reaction, for his wife's glare returns, her very eyes accusing him.

"She came over here without being invited," Katharina says sharply.

"My students do that all the time. You've never complained." As Katharina's brows rise and her eyes catch fire, Philipp corrects himself. "You've rarely complained."

"But you already know them well. It is less of a presumption."

He shrugs. "I don't see the problem with it."

"It's not a problem exactly, but—well, I would never go to one of your colleague's houses unannounced, by myself, to discuss some personal issue."

"No, they would bore you to death."

With a pronounced roll of the eyes, she asserts, "I'm sorry I said anything."

As Katharina rises from the couch, Philipp places a hand on her arm and explains, "I said she was perfect for him because I can tell she has it in her to stand up to him. If she is bold enough to approach us on her own, she may be bold enough to handle his moods and temper him a bit, which would be a great happiness for everyone."

Katharina grants her husband a knowing look. "Or make him even bolder."

Philipp cringes reflexively as he tries to imagine a bolder Martin Luther. *That would be a fearsome thing to behold!* He attempts to shake off the feeling.

"Well, perhaps you will be proven right, and if that happens, I do not doubt that you will remind me of the fact often," he concludes.

"I hope I am wrong," she says quietly, bending down to attend to the children.

Philipp watches Katharina place their young son in her lap and help Anna arrange the dolls, seeing to their children's every need with gentleness and love. He always finds his wife so beautiful when she does things like this, her depth of compassion on display. Over the past few days, he has been reminded in numerous ways of just how blessed he is to have her through all the difficulties of life. *You are the perfect woman,* he thinks. *The perfect woman for me.* And yet, his perfect woman does not seem to have gotten off to a good start with Martin's perfect woman. Sensing he knows what is truly bothering her, Philipp asks Katharina, "You're not jealous, are you?"

"Jealous?!" she cries, whipping her head around.

Any trace of gentleness is drained from Katharina's features: she looks as if she might punch him in the throat. Nevertheless, he dares to continue.

"I hope you are not concerned that she is more learned than you, because if you do feel that, dear, please know I consider you the perfect woman for me. I would not want you to feel insufficient in any way."

Katharina scoffs loudly. "The very idea! You make her sound as if she were the Queen of Sheba, but she is only a runaway nun. I promise you, I'm not jealous."

So vociferous is her reaction, Philipp guesses he has hit very near the mark, but he will grant her the point. He knows where his happiness lies.

"I am glad to hear it, because you need not be," he assures her. "You have nothing to fear."

"Oh, my love," she replies, shaking her head. "There is always something to fear."

17 June 1525
Basel, Swiss Confederation

Erasmus of Rotterdam exits the Froben house and walks north along Nadelberg, muttering under his breath. He is headed for the bookshop, there to retrieve a volume he has been less than eagerly anticipating. No classic work of the ancient world awaits him, nor even the response from Luther that he now doubts will materialize. It is a diatribe first released in the spring but only now come to Basel: an examination of Erasmus' views on confession by one Godefridus Ruysius Taxander—only, he is assured by his spies that no such man exists. A mystery, then, and one he rues.

He comes to the small building no more than fifteen feet across and two stories high. The owner, Dietrich, sells his goods on the lower level and makes his bed above it. As Erasmus stares at the shop with its swaying wood sign displaying a quill and ink pot, he observes that the whole edifice leans slightly to the left. It has a thatched roof and gables, and the front door stands open, ready to receive customers. Though it is not much to look at, this shop has one key benefit: it stocks plenty of Erasmus' books and none of Luther's.

Only in this part of the city could Dietrich get away with that, he thinks. *He'd be out of business down by the merchants' houses.*

With a sigh, Erasmus enters the shop, ducking to avoid the lintel. He is immediately struck by the unmistakable smell of parchment and vellum. He closes his eyes—breathes deeply.

"Ah," he whispers ecstatically. "The scent divine."

Opening his eyes again, he uses them to absorb the fullness of the room. All four walls are covered from floor to ceiling with shelves of books, along with glass jars full of quills, vials of ink, pen knifes of various sizes, bundles of fresh parchment, balls of string, and rolls of vellum. In the corner, Dietrich sits at a desk little bigger than a lectern, his form balanced upon a three-legged stool as he writes in his ledger book. He is a man nearly equal in age to Erasmus, with more hair on his face than his head and a pair of round spectacles seated upon his pointed nose.

"Dietrich!" Erasmus calls loudly, for the shopkeeper is half deaf.

The man in question looks up, removing his spectacles with a shaky hand. "Herr Erasmus! I was wondering when you would come for your book. I've had it two days now."

"Well, is it any wonder I did not race over when it contains such vile slanders?" he retorts.

Dietrich smiles knowingly and stoops down to the lowest shelf to retrieve a thin volume so poorly bound, it seems to be already coming apart. He rises with a soft groan, rubbing at the small of his back.

"I'll have you know I would never stock such rubbish in the normal course of events," the shopkeeper insists, "but for you, Herr Erasmus, I would fetch Jove himself from Mount Olympus."

"Ha! Have you read anything of the ancient Greeks? The gods are angry, friend."

With a smile, Dietrich extends the volume and Erasmus takes it gingerly in hand, wondering how it survived the journey to Basel in such poor condition. He reads the title printed on the front page: *An Apology for Erasmus of Rotterdam's Book on Confession.*[4]

"It took a good bit of work to track down a copy," Dietrich notes. "The name Taxander is not well known."

"That's because he doesn't exist," Erasmus notes firmly. "It is a product of my old institution, the University of Louvain, though who penned it I have yet to confirm."

Dietrich places his spectacles back on his nose. "You suspect someone. I can see it in your eyes. I see something else there too if I am not mistaken: the fear of Béda."

"If you see all that in my eyes, those spectacles must have demonic powers," he jests. "Of course, you are right. First, Paris pursued me, and now Louvain. I will be lucky to survive the year."

---

[4] The title is a bit misleading to our modern ears: the author intends to criticize Erasmus' book.

It is an exaggeration for effect. Even if charges of heresy were pursued, they would be unlikely to reach their conclusion in such a short span of time. Yet, Erasmus feels the pull of these words upon his joints and sinews. His brain tells him that the danger is minimal, but his bowels declare the opposite. Béda is a menace like no other he has faced.

Dietrich scoffs. "No need to be so grim! You are quite safe here, and you know I would never stock anything by a heretic. So, since I sell your books, you must be pure as the snow upon the mountains!"

"I doubt that logic would hold up before the faculty of Paris," Erasmus notes, then after a moment of thought, corrects himself. "What am I saying? You could get anything past them as long as you claimed it was written by Scotus."

Dietrich sits upon his stool again, taking his quill in hand. As Erasmus turns to leave, the shopkeeper asks him one more question.

"When will there be a reply from Luther?"

Erasmus glares at him, growling internally. "I had thought this would be the one place I could escape that name."

"Fair enough," Dietrich responds, adjusting his spectacles. "I'll know he's replied when the other bookshops are full of customers."

This line was meant as a harmless joke, but it tightens the fibers of Erasmus' stomach. *Luther, Béda, and now whoever wrote this—I have too many fires to smother!* he laments.

Volume in hand, he departs the shop and begins the short walk back to the Froben house, brooding all the way. The machinations of Louvain are bad enough, and any reply from Luther would be thoroughly unpleasant, but it is Béda who causes his heart to burn. He has just completed a letter—no, an entire pamphlet—and sent it to Paris for his accuser's perusal. In it, he addressed at length every one of Béda's complaints, repeating the long tale of all the persons he consulted when producing his theological works: the countless revisions to ensure doctrinal accuracy, seeking out theologians from varying perspectives to ensure no stone was left unturned. But none of this touches Erasmus' primary fear, for he knows that Béda knows. *My iniquity has been revealed.* Why else would Béda press on and on about the danger to his eternal soul? The implication was clear: *You are a transgressor of the worst sort, and you are destined for hell.* So, he has written to Béda, attempting to set his mind at ease.

"I am touched by your kindness and your deep concern for the salvation of my soul. But at least on moral questions and on matters of faith, I have no misgivings about my writings, for I still see nothing in them which is improper or irreverent or seditious."[5]

As for the possibility of the theologians of Paris ruling against him, Erasmus has reminded Béda that judgment is not always blind, or not in the way a person would prefer.

"Moreover, I am aware of the insults and venomous attacks which certain members of your fraternity have been aiming at me for some time now," he wrote. "Can you expect a fair verdict from men who are totally dominated by a blinding prejudice?"[6]

But there was one paragraph in particular that touched the core of Erasmus' fear: one thing he absolutely had to set straight. His accuser is likely to skim over it, but to Erasmus it seems a thing of critical importance.

> "For years now, I have worked with heart and soul to clear my conscience before Christ my judge, and I am preparing myself, as best I can, for that day which my age and health tell me cannot be far off. I believe that through Christ's mercy, which I never cease to ask for in my prayers, I have made some progress. For I await that day with a mind which is more and more at peace, and no talk is more welcome to me than that which fosters or excites such feelings in my heart."[7]

Now, as Erasmus enters the yard behind the Froben house, he thinks to himself, *Peace? What peace do you imagine you have? You are dying—already one foot in the grave—and can you claim that you have felt that mercy of which you so boldly write?* He stops in his tracks for a moment, releasing a painful sigh, for he has never known the mercy of man, and it is only the faintest of hopes that leads him to believe God might be any different. But is the judgment of the holy one likely to be kinder?

I cannot dwell on it, he decides. *It will drive me mad. I need a distraction!*

---

[5] "Epistle 1581 – To Noël Béda," in *Collected Works of Erasmus*, Vol. 11, trans. Alexander Dalzell (Toronto: University of Toronto Press, 1994), 150.

[6] Ibid., 147.

[7] Ibid., 134.

So, he decides then and there to visit his horse Thomas—yes, he has named it after his great friend More—to see how the beast fares. *I will offer him some oats, and somehow that will make me forget the hail of misery about to fall!* He enters the stables—stepping carefully upon the straw-covered dirt, ducking below a low-hanging beam—and rounds the corner toward Thomas' pen. There he is struck by an image like a withering blast: Justina Froben pressed against one of the wood posts, the errand boy Sebastian attacking her face with his own. Yes, attacking is the appropriate word, for he appears to be forcing his tongue down her throat. With one hand, he grasps Justina's rear, and with the other, he explores her breasts.

A fire of thunderous intensity is lit within Erasmus. With the fury of Jove, he releases his voice like a lightning bolt. "Get your hands off her, boy!"

Sebastian spasms at the sound of Erasmus' voice, his body instantly disengaging. Both he and Justina are thoroughly out of breath. Erasmus lunges toward the object of his rage, gripping him by the shoulders and pressing him against the opposite fence. The book has fallen to the ground, but it is the least of Erasmus' concerns. He moves his face close enough to Sebastian's to feel his breath in all its foul glory.

"How dare you?!" Erasmus bellows, so angry he is tempted to spit in Sebastian's face. "I should have you arrested!"

Then, to his surprise, he hears the voice of Justina behind him crying, "Let him go!"

Without relaxing his grip one iota, Erasmus turns his head to view Justina, who is frantically adjusting her gown and head covering even as she stares at him plaintively, her eyes wet and inflamed. Behind her, Thomas the horse is munching softly on a mouthful of feed, unmoved by the drama unfolding before him.

"You need not defend him," Erasmus assures Justina. "I've been watching this knave for some time. He's spawned of Beelzebub, but I never thought he would attempt this!"

Sebastian now draws upon a previously hidden strength, pushing Erasmus backward and crying, "Get your hands off me, old man!"

Erasmus takes a moment to catch his breath and adjust his robe, then grabs Sebastian's arm, ready to pummel him verbally if not physically. "You think it permissible to violate any woman, let alone one of this esteemed house?!" he demands to know, his sense of honor deeply offended.

Sebastian's face twists into a scowl as he exclaims, "Violate?! Mother of God! You monks really don't know anything about the world, do you?"

"Ha!" Erasmus scoffs. "I know far more about the world than you do, boy."

Justina tugs upon Erasmus' robe, demanding his full attention. He grants her his gaze in time for her to say, "Please, he didn't violate me! It's not what you think."

Erasmus relaxes his grip ever so slightly, looking from one young person to the other. Sebastian's eyes are bold and angry, his pupils digging into Erasmus' face, whereas Justina's are soft and pleading, their brown depths appealing to his compassion. For his part, Thomas is still chewing, utterly uninterested in it all.

"Do you mean to tell me that you wanted this scoundrel to do this to you?" Erasmus inquires of her.

"Seriously, get out of your cloister and join the rest of us!" Sebastian yelled.

But Erasmus is not bowed. He asks again, "Justina?"

"We're in love," she says softly, nodding her head. "I love him."

Oh, for the love of Christ! he thinks, marveling at the girl's stupidity. *How could such noble sires have given birth to you, child?!* But once the shock is past, he focuses on her eyes: those eyes which have burned with anger every time her parents have thought to command her. *This is an act of rebellion. She thinks by doing this thing, she will break free of it all.* She could not be more wrong, but nothing will be gained by continuing to fight. He therefore bows to fate, letting go of Sebastian's arm. Looking at him with eyes to kill, Erasmus states, "If I witness anything like this again, I will report you, regardless of what she says. Have no doubt about that. Now, go!" Here he points firmly in the direction of the exit.

"Leck mich am Arsch, Teufel!"[8] Sebastian cries in his native tongue.

"Pleur op!"[9] Erasmus responds.

---

[8] "Lick my ass, devil!"

[9] "Get tuberculosis!"

With a final crude gesture, Sebastian makes his departure from the stables, petting the nose of one of the other horses as he goes. Erasmus lowers his brows and lets out a growl. "It is you who stink of the devil, boy." He then turns to Justina, who is now infected with Sebastian's glare. "Fräulein, we must discuss what has just occurred."

"Are you going to tell father?" she inquires.

"I ought to," he concludes with a nod of the head, noting that she seems far more concerned with this possibility than the risk of disease. "Tell me—were you intending to do the full deed with him?"

"Oh, God in heaven!" Justina cries, rolling her eyes and covering her face with her hands. "This is a nightmare."

"Young lady, that man is taking advantage of you, and if you do not put a stop to it and quickly, it could have devastating results for the rest of your life, not to mention your family name!"

She drops her hands at her sides, shrugging her slumped shoulders. "We were just having fun."

"Everyone always is. Much harm can come of such fun."

"You don't understand!" she cries, painfully animated. "He wants to marry me!"

Now, it is Erasmus who rolls his eyes and sighs, "Godverdomme," smacking his palm into his forehead.

"What's that?" she demands to know, her arms crossed and nose scrunched.

He looks at her wearily, shaking his head in disbelief. *You long for freedom but would throw yourself into a slavery even more degrading.* "Of course, he wants to marry you!" Erasmus cries. "You belong to a wealthy family! You will receive many such offers over the next few years if you are not stupid enough to take the first one that comes to you from a random person on the street!"

"It's not like that!" she protests, her tone growing so shrill that it provokes a whinny from Thomas. "I know him. He's the one—the one I'm meant to be with."

He cannot help it: he laughs. "No, he's not. Trust me."

Nostrils flaring and fists clenched, Justina nearly ascends into the rafters as she shrieks, "Oh, why?! Because you're God Almighty and everyone worships you?!"

Her whole manner is so excited that he feels a need to calm her before she explodes. So, he points his finger at her forehead, pressing the tip against her ivory skin. This action confuses her: she goes cross-eyed attempting to make sense of it. "What are you doing?" she inquires, pulling back.

When she is breathing normally again, Erasmus says, "Here is why you should listen to me: because I am older, wiser, and not blinded by infatuation. Truly, Fräulein, he is not worthy of you. He is not worthy of the greatness of this house."

She huffs loudly. "All I ever hear about is 'this house,' but no one in this house understands me or cares what I have to say."

Suddenly, Erasmus feels within himself the pull of compassion: an understanding built upon mutual experience. He makes an appeal to her spirit.

"It is possible that I comprehend something of your situation. I was young once myself."

"I doubt that!"

"Doubt it or not, it was so."

"What do you know about love?!" she objects, growing excited again. "You're a monk, aren't you? A monk!"

A sting ripples through his body—the tinge of memory colors his thoughts. Bidding himself not to give way to regret, he addresses her again.

"If you cannot take my word as truth, then at least consider this: if I catch you with him again, I will tell your father, and you will feel the heat of his wrath. As this is a youthful indiscretion, I would spare you that wrath for the present time. But an hour may come when I must save you from your own folly."

"Why do you care so much?" she asks incredulously, her brown eyes surging with frustration.

Because I was you once, he thinks. *Because I am still you.* But it will do no good to say that. He is not about to entrust himself to one who has shown herself false. So, he reaches for something else that will pacify her.

"Because I am a Christian man who loves his neighbor."

"Oh, don't make me laugh!"

"Very well," he agrees, realizing only savagery will do. "Because your father is my publisher, and the news that his daughter has made herself a whore would hurt my book sales. Do you at least believe that?"

Justina screws up her face until it is fully red, then blurts, "Fine! I won't see him. Happy?!"

"Not really, but I've long since given up on that." he concludes, retrieving his book from the dirt and leaving her to sulk with only the horses for company.

As he walks toward the house, he cannot decide whether to be disgusted by what has just occurred, or to laugh uproariously at the ridiculousness of it all. Or should he, in fact, be sorrowful that he has never enjoyed such a moment of iniquity with one he truly loved? *But such things are truly enjoyed for one moment only,* he concludes, *and then they plague the rest of one's days.* The years have taught him what she has yet to learn: there is no true freedom to be had on earth. He pauses his steps for a moment. *Have I really become such a cynic? I who once proclaimed the breaking of a golden age?* The possibility disturbs him.

He passes a few hours in troubled thoughts—attempting to read his correspondence, attempting to negotiate a pay dispute with Margarethe, but all the while his thoughts speeding chaotically like a bee flitting from bloom to bloom. When at last the sun bows its proud head below the horizon, Erasmus sits with Johannes Froben in the house's great library, the pair of them in identical high back chairs, sipping from beakers of wine. His host was mostly quiet throughout supper and is now positively mute. Erasmus attempts to engage him.

"I know who wrote the pamphlet: Vicentius Theoderici—the Dominican ignoramus himself. No one else could have produced such a dull and stupid book. So, the Dominicans skewered Reuchlin, and now they set their sights on me. Truly, I know that passionate love is blind, but hate all the more!"

This speech does nothing to break Froben out of his melancholy. He stares at the empty hearth, drink in hand, looking as depressed as any man on earth.

"What is it, friend?" Erasmus inquires. "I have never seen you so low."

"It's my daughter," he grunts more than speaks. "Always the daughter."

"Oh?" Erasmus mutters, wondering if he is truly losing his mind, for he does not remember mentioning anything of Justina's misbehavior. *I suppose her general rudeness is enough to produce this reaction,* he reasons.

Froben shakes his head sadly. “I’ve tried with her. You must believe me. I’ve tried.”

“I believe it,” Erasmus assures him. “You cannot control her, Johann. She will attempt to fly free, for better or for worse.”

“I fear very much it will be for the worse,” Froben says bitterly, his teeth clenched. “Her head is full of dreams that cannot take shape in this world. If you knew the kind of things she has done, your respect for me would diminish. I dare not speak of them.”

Erasmus reaches out—places a hand on Froben’s. He attempts to imagine what it would be like if Justina were his own daughter: a truly ghastly thought. He draws upon the farthest reaches of those imaginings to produce words of comfort.

“She is still young. She has not yet learned how much she is bound: by expectation, by nature, by the strange chances of this life. In time, she will come to see. I only hope it is sooner rather than later, for your sake as much as hers. But believe me, friend, nothing you could tell me would diminish my respect for you.”

Froben places his free hand on top of Erasmus’, patting it firmly. “Erasmus of Rotterdam, you are not only the scholar of scholars, but also the friend of friends. How you need the comfort of a friend yourself! But I have been negligent. Always busy—always distracted.”

“I have others to lean on,” Erasmus assures him. “Łaski, Amerbach, Baer—”

“But it is not enough,” Froben asserts. “Not enough for you to rest content, and I am at fault for that, for I promised you a home. You have not found your peace here, and now you cannot leave.”

There is an elongated silence as Erasmus struggles for the right thing to say. He does not fault Froben for his situation, but it is true that he feels no peace, either within or without. *But what hope is there of peace on earth?*

“Have no fear,” he assures his friend. “Soon, I will be dead, and Justina will be the responsibility of some poor lad who has no idea what is about to hit him.”

For a single moment in time, they laugh together—not the laughter of the young, full and carefree, but that of the aged, who laugh so they do not weep. It is a moment's freedom from fear, and for Desiderius Erasmus, that is a thing of gold.

18 June 1525
Wittenberg, Electorate of Saxony

Philipp Melanchthon stands before the western entrance of the Castle Church watching the final worshippers trickle out from evening Mass. He has been summoned here to the home of the All Saints' Foundation for a meeting of tremendous importance to himself and the work of reformation. This moment seems to him as enormous as the sky itself—an hour of yearning and a thirst that all the seas on earth would fail to quench. Yet, it is infinitely small: two colleagues, two friends, two brothers, speaking together apart from prying eyes, their spirits converging—or perhaps colliding.

He walks hesitantly through the open door and finds himself in a space he knows as well as his own mind: a nave crowned with fan vaulting and covered on every side with niches of stone, wood, and brass in which the Elector's collection of relics was once kept. It has been two years since the relics were displayed, and the Elector himself sleeps with his fathers, but the mark of the late Friedrich of Saxony remains unmistakable, etched upon every inch of the church. The greatest artists in Germany have adorned this space—Burgkmair, Dürer, Cranach, Elsner, Wolgemut, Vischer—and there is hardly a surface not painted with some color. A feast for the eyes, and yet Philipp has seldom felt more starved in the depths of his being.

Even without the gold and silver reliquaries to reflect the light of the stained-glass windows, the whole place seems to shimmer, a marvel of human craftsmanship at the service of divine worship. Glistening chandeliers hang from the ceiling high above, their flames shifting slightly with the currents of the air. What an expense of precious stone and metal! The whole place is a living monument to the passion and ambition of a ruler whom Duke Johann will now strive to match in skill and grace. But Philipp feels himself somewhere else entirely: a river dark and cool at twilight, beside which a single man stands waiting.

He moves forward, each step like the beating of the drum or the sounding of a bell, summoning him to battle. A single row of wooden faldstools crosses the nave not far from the altar, the central aisle cutting a path between them. In one of the chairs on the right, just below the immense pulpit, sits Martin Luther, bent forward as if in prayer. The sight of him presses against the ache in Philipp's chest. *I loved you—I still love you. Have I lost your love?*

They have come here to attempt a reconciliation, but there is much yet to be determined: a horrific rush of uncertainty that floods Philipp's veins to the point of bursting. Not wishing to disturb his colleague, he takes one of the seats on the left and folds his hands in his lap, waiting to be addressed.

He remains there in silence, fighting the urge to look over and glimpse the expression on Martin's face. *It is not my fault we are here. It is Martin's choices that have led us to this point. He must go first.* But the silence is interminable—far worse than any speech he could possibly make. Finally, he gives in and turns his head, only to find Martin staring back at him. As they lock eyes, he sees the sorrow written upon Martin's face—his drooping cheeks, his darkened eyes. Were Philipp to guess, he would say his colleague is deeply weary in body and spirit. *Is that my fault?* His insides wrench with guilt, but he reminds himself, *It is not your fault. He made these choices. Be strong!*

Martin's lips part—he speaks softly. "I wasn't sure if you would come."

Philipp draws upon deep resources of breath, attempting to still the chaos within himself. "Then you don't know me at all."

"There is much I thought I knew," Martin utters, his voice trembling slightly, "but you have shaken it from me."

Again, Philipp is seized by guilt, but he remembers, *It was you who shook me first. You shook the world entire.*

Taking in their surroundings—the altarpiece depicting the Virgin and child, the brass candlesticks as tall as a man, the lectern carved with the eagle of Saint John—Philipp asks, "Why did you choose this place?"

Martin's gaze wanders about the room. "Because this is where it started for us. This is where we entered the university, where we first met, where we came to fully appreciate the evils of superstition: the powerful hold of idolatry upon the minds of men. Much has been emptied from this temple—much has been overturned. But there is a great work left to do. That is why we are meeting here."

"I suppose that makes sense," Philipp concedes. Attempting to quiet his spirit, he thinks back over all that has occurred since that morning he stormed into Martin's study. He did not know then if they would ever have a meeting like this one: the actions of Frau Luther have made it possible. Therefore, he stresses, "It was kind of your wife to visit us."

"I didn't send her," Martin says so quickly, it leaves Philipp confused.

"You should have. She did you a good turn. I was too hasty to condemn your union—I freely admit it." This is the extent of what Philipp is prepared to surrender, and now he makes the turn: "But you should not have kept it a secret."

Martin stares down at his hands, fumbling with the new ring on his finger. "In my mind, at the time, it seemed the right thing to do, but had I known it would cause you such distress—"

"How could you have imagined it would have done otherwise?!" Philipp blurts, his anger getting the better of him. He then raises a hand and begs, "Forgive me. I should let you speak."

If Martin is annoyed by the interruption, he does not let it show but proceeds upon another line of thought. "Philipp, what you said to me that day—your frustrations with me, your anger at my words and actions—am I correct in suspecting you had felt that way for a long time?"

Philipp is caught up—his spirit stirred to a froth. He looks upon Martin with moist eyes and whispers, "Yes."

"And yet, you said nothing."

"I said many things, but you did not hear them."

Martin frowns, his mouth scrunching even as his brows sharpen. "Perhaps you skirted around the issue. You must come right out and say what you mean. Call the thing what it is!"

"So you are always telling me," Philipp begins, repressing the urge to roll his eyes, "but you must admit, we are here today because of what you chose to withhold. You have entrusted yourself to others rather than me, and it has created a distance between us."

Martin straightens up in his seat, pulling his shoulders back. "I am sure you believe that to be true."

"It is true. That is why I believe it."

Philipp can see that Martin is unconvinced. His colleague seems to scoff at the comment. "And you have never withheld anything from me? Anything substantial that affects our work?"

It is a leading question—one that cuts Philipp to the quick. Rushing headlong, he replies immediately, "No, of course not! I have too much respect for you."

"Are you certain?" Martin asks, pronouncing each word deliberately.

Philipp begins to doubt himself. "Clearly, you feel I shouldn't be."

Then comes a question that nearly stops Philipp's heart, so close does it cut to the bone.

"Tell me, Philipp, when were you planning to inform me of Erasmus' offer?"

A wound, deep and biting! Philipp stares at his colleague as if for the first time, his heart pulsing like the rippling heat on a summer's day. He is seized by fear, sadness, and most of all, guilt: the deep shame of a man who has been found out. *But why should I feel ashamed?* He is too overwhelmed to arrive at a proper answer.

"What?" he blurts, praying he might have misunderstood.

"The offer he made for you to join him in Basel," Martin replies calmly. "When were you planning to tell me about it?"

How does he know?! How long has he known?! Again and again, Philipp is struck by the questions, each pulling him further into a ferocious whirlpool of self-doubt. Of course, there was nothing nefarious in his silence. He was honoring his pledge of discretion. It would only have angered Martin to reveal the truth. *But how did he discover it? Surely not Camerarius!*

"Who told you?" Philipp demands to know, his breath coming quick and shallow.

"No one. I figured it out on my own."

Philipp shakes his head in desperation. "I fail to see how you could have simply figured it out."

He is obsessing over the wrong question. *What is done is done. I must simply repair the damage—if I can.* But Philipp finds himself distracted, unable to take in the immensity of it. He has been pulled into the depths, wrapped in the tentacles of some foul beast, slowly choking, without hope of escape. Martin addresses him again.

"You didn't tell me about it, which means you did not reject the offer out of hand. You have sat on it for a year, saving it just in case, at a time when he attacks me in print. How do you think that makes me feel?"

The words slice into Philipp, separating bone from marrow. He is starting to panic. He must right the ship. *It is not the same as what he did! I had no choice but to keep it a secret!* But it is not enough: Philipp feels himself undone by shame. He wonders how many of their conversations over the past year have been colored by this information—the countless times he has begged Martin to respond to Erasmus, and always Martin seemed unwilling to engage.

"If you have been angry all this time, why didn't you say something?" Philipp asks.

Again, he glimpses the sorrow in Martin's eyes. Philipp had entered believing himself almost totally free of guilt, but now he wonders if the situation is reversed. *He still should have said something! He withheld as much as I did!* He wishes he could be more convinced by these arguments.

"I said nothing because I was striving to trust you," Martin explains, "and I respect you enough to let you make your own decisions."

No, Philipp thinks. *No, you have gone too far! You are not blameless.* Unable to help himself, he mutters, "Only sometimes."

Martin inhales deeply. "Well, can you blame me? How can I continue this work without you?!" There is a fire in his eyes now. They radiate with holy longing.

Philipp wants to believe Martin's words—to know that they are still bound in communion, and he is respected by the man who holds his respect. But a shadow of doubt passes over Philipp's mind like the image of a cloud. He finds himself saying, "You have plenty of others to assist you."

"They are not on your level, Philipp, and you know it," Martin insists, hands planted on his knees, leaning in to make the point. "But in any case, it is not your skills alone that I need, but your character. I am the one who comes in rough and breaks up the soil. You are the one who follows behind softly and plants the seeds. We were meant to be partners, Philipp. I knew it from the first lecture you gave upon your arrival. Now tell me, why do you want to throw that away?"

In an instant, Philipp feels it all coming back: the fear he experienced upon coming to Wittenberg and the uncertainty as he addressed his colleagues for the first time, knowing how many of them had opposed his appointment. And then, at a stroke, he gained the admiration of all! Martin placed his hands on Philipp's shoulders and proclaimed, "Thank God, you are here! How I have needed you!" The casting out of fear—the full acceptance of brotherhood! He remembers it, even as he longs for it.

Philipp shakes his head, his eyes filled with tears. "I desire no such thing. I have never wanted to leave Wittenberg."

"Then what is this about?!" Martin cries, his voice fraught. "As God is my witness, I would rather lose my right arm than you, but you seem always turned in on yourself, unable to release whatever it is you hold inside. Now, out with it, man! Whatever it is, let me have it!"

Philipp plumbs the depths of his emotions. *What are you afraid of?* He thinks of the day Martin set out for the Diet of Worms. The party was already loaded into the cart, but Philipp ran up to it, unwilling to let Martin go—fearing he would never see him again. Martin reached down and pulled him into an embrace as they both wept. Then Martin held Philipp's face in his hands and spoke the words that would haunt the younger man ever after: *I will not be a great loss, provided you remain.* How those words sting now, so desperately bitter to the taste! Philipp slams his eyes shut, shaking his head in distress. Then he opens them again, breaching the floodgates and allowing the waters to spill forth. He speaks from the depths of his soul.

"I failed, Martin! You entrusted it to me, and I failed."

The words move upon the air, crossing the space between them, entering Martin's ears and transforming his expression. He sets his face like flint, releasing the breath from his lungs. "No, you didn't."

It is a word of authority meant to drive away doubt, but the wound is too deep: it has festered for three years and is now a gangrenous mass mere inches from Philipp's heart, threatening to quench the fire within him.

"Then what would you call what happened?" Philipp asks softly. "Our work was nearly destroyed because of me. Everything happened so quickly. I could not control things, no matter how much I tried. We were nearly shut down! I strove by all my powers to keep the ship afloat—to lead the people in the way of truth—but I could not steer between Scylla and Charybdis, the desires of the Elector and those of the strange prophets. I was as weak as I was young."

Again, Martin seeks to calm his fears. "Do not be so prideful as to take the blame that belongs to Karlstadt! I have never faulted you for what happened. Please know that."

"Then why do we lack the same closeness we had before you went away?" he inquires, the tears running into his beard. "I would rather have died than been separated from you! Even now, I long for the communion we once enjoyed." And as he stares into Martin's eyes, he begs, *Tell me you are my friend. Tell me that you love me, even as I love you.*

Martin nods in acknowledgment, his eyes filled with compassion. "I long for that too. Things have changed—we have changed. You married. The nature of our work shifted. It was always going to be different, but I still consider you my chief partner and the best asset the university has. I could never do what you do, Philipp, nor could anyone else, and your friendship is one of the greatest of my life. If you were no more than a common peasant, I would still fear to lose you on account of that friendship. Truly, I thought you knew that! I never meant to leave you in doubt."

Philipp inhales abruptly, as if he were a drowning man finally surfaced, gasping for air in the land of the living. How he has longed for those words! How he has prayed for them night after night! As they wash over his spirit, he feels brave enough to voice even the worst of his fears.

"Some nights I tremble so fiercely," he admits.

"A man who does not tremble is a man who has never met the God of Jacob," Martin replies.

"I wish I could say it is the ancient one who haunts me, or even that I have been visited by the devil," Philipp explains, "but in this you are correct: I do fear man, for I have seen what evil men can do. Why do you think I am so concerned about education? It is not simply to build a moral society, Martin. It is because I know a day is coming—perhaps very soon—when our time will run out. The Emperor will come. The armies of the Pope will come, and we will be helpless to resist them."

As he says this, Philipp can already see the Emperor Charles upon his white horse, marching through the city gate, the host of

Christendom at his back with banners unfurled. There will be nowhere to hide on that day of wrath when the heavens and the earth are moved.

"We have princes to protect us," Martin reminds him.

"Will that be enough? Will it be enough if the Turks should come? Listen to me, Martin! Every day, I live in fear of what will happen when they tell us we cannot preach the gospel anymore. When that happens, it will not be men like us who will preserve it. We will be the first cut down. It will be the pastors we have trained. I think about that every day when I teach. They can kill some of us, but they will not be able to kill us all. That is why we do it. For I know the Word of God will never return void, but it could be silenced in our lifetimes: it could be silenced in this place forever. I cannot bear to think of it after all we have sacrificed."

Martin nods sadly. "I hear your concern, and I share it. We must train ministers of the Word. But we need more than that, Philipp. The common people must be taught! If the average man does not know the gospel, does not have the Scriptures, and cannot read them, he will not resist when they come for us. But if he has had the Word preached to him, has his own Bible that he can read, and has been taught in the doctrines of the faith, he will not be so easily tricked by whatever false prophets they send our way."

"That is a long work, Martin, and a much harder one," he responds.

"Then let us pray that the Lord gives us enough time, and he will, Philipp—he will."

Philipp struggles to withhold his tears as he whispers, "I don't know how you do it, Martin. When I think of what it would be like to stand before the emperor, to have the hopes of so many resting upon me—I would crumble. I know it."

"No, you wouldn't," Martin insists. "You would survive it even as I did: by the power of one greater than myself."

Philipp sighs, a thousand scenes passing before his mind's eye. He thinks of the work of the university: his colleagues old and new. He thinks of his good friend, Joachim Camerarius, who is closer to him than a brother, and he thinks of Justus Jonas, whose respect he certainly owns. Then he thinks of Nikolaus von Amsdorf at his pastorate in Magdeburg, still managing to cast an eye of judgment upon Philipp despite the distance. Never openly hostile, they have nevertheless found themselves at odds on multiple occasions—and there are many others who take Amsdorf's part.

"Sometimes I fear they will come for me," he whispers.

"The Romanists?" Martin asks in confusion.

"No," Philipp replies pointedly. "People here."

Martin breathes in deeply, the look on his face stern. "Then they will have me to answer to, and I will speak for you, Philipp."

"You may not always be here to speak for me," he whispers.

Silence falls. Philipp lifts his eyes heavenward, staring at the flames suspended in midair. The Scriptures say that flames descended on the saints of old, but he has always struggled to see fire as anything but dangerous and deadly. To serve a God of consuming fire is a fearsome thing, and over the past few years, he has been scorched—burnt beyond the point of recognition. *You revealed your goodness to Moses,* he prays. *Oh, that you would reveal it to me! I have seen your glory from afar, but your nearness would be my good.* He thinks of the night all hope was lost: when he first held his son in his arms, the boy's tiny body straining against the matter of the world, desperately struggling for breath. *Breathe! Live!* Philipp looks back at Martin and speaks with the tenderness of a father.

"My son is not well. We do not know how much he will ever be able to do. It breaks my heart. I think it always will."

Martin speaks softly. "I am sorry, Philipp. I have not always been thinking about that. So much has happened this year—these years. I do not know what will become of us, and I do not know what will become of little Philipp, but I know that the gospel will prevail. I believe it with everything I am." Then with fierce conviction, he proclaims, "For what I have done wrong and what I have failed to do, forgive me. I beg you: do not make me walk the fearsome path alone."

"I would walk that path with you into the very depths of the hell," Philipp pledges, "but will you allow me to beg something in turn?"

"We are all beggars, Philipp," Martin replies, smiling sadly. "We hold nothing in our grasp. Only when we cling to Christ are we secure, and then not because we cling, but because we are held."

Philipp nods. "Then allow me to beg this of you, though I know I cannot hold it for any length of time: listen to what I say and heed my counsel, for it is not offered idly. You say you long to walk in company, but you often stride ahead, and I fear that I have lost you. You take decisions suddenly. If we are to walk together, then you must remember that each step I take is shorter, and you will have to be patient with me."

"A fair request, and one I hope to fulfill," Martin responds. "But try as I might, Philipp, there will always be times when I cause you discomfort. And though you claim it is only flesh and blood with which you wrestle, you must remember that there is one who condescended to take our flesh upon himself. Are you quite certain that all this time, it is I whom you have longed to control and not the one who kills and makes alive? For he does whatever he pleases."

Even as Martin speaks, Philipp recalls the words of the Lord: *You cannot see My face, for no man can see Me and live!*[10] How then did Jacob look upon God face to face? How can any man live before the face of the Almighty? Philipp sighs deeply, his heart churning within him, his mind unable to grasp the infinite strangeness that is the Ancient of Days.

"If it is the Lord with whom I wrestle, then I wish he would grant me the same mercy as Jacob and allow himself to be overcome in a single night," Philipp concludes. "As it is, I have wept through nights unending, seeking the joy that comes with morning, but finding it denied. Perhaps even joy is something different than I thought. I fear I know nothing anymore."

Martin takes a breath, his aquiline eyes fixing on their target. Out of his mouth comes the flame from on high.

"Oh, Philipp. Do you think you can harness the wind, or would you hold the very waters in the hollow of your hand? So quickly they would slip, first as drops in a bucket, then as the deluge that came upon men in the days of Noah to change and remake—to create and destroy. And you cannot contain it nor direct it by your will, but only be swept up in the torrent, groping and feeling for the one solid thing in all this earth: the eternal rock to which a man may hold fast, if indeed he is held.

"Even if you could end disease, your body would be subject to decay. Even if you could change the weather and halt the shifting sand, the land would still be broken by war. And there is nothing over which

[10] Exodus 33:20.

you have less control than the evil within yourself unless the Spirit of God should empower you. In him is the very essence of power, but there is none in yourself save that which you are given, and only in surrendering yourself to the flow may you arrive in the harbor safely. Only in clinging to the immovable rock may you hope to stand."

There it is, thinks Philipp. *There is what captured me at the beginning.*

With a loud voice, Philipp declares, "The chariots of Israel and its horsemen! As the Lord lives, and as you yourself live, I will not leave you. Wherever you are, there I will be, right beside you, where I belong."

Martin nods at him, his eyes welling up. "And I would have you there if it cost me everything, for you are the gift that God has sent, not only to me, but to us all."

27 June 1525
Wittenberg, Electorate of Saxony

Martin Luther stands in the foyer of the Black Cloister, clothed in his scholar's regalia. A thing he never imagined possible is about to occur: he will walk hand-in-hand with Katharina to the parish church of St. Mary, the street lined with well-wishers and pipers urging them forward. They will stand before the western portal of the church and exchange vows before God and the congregation, then embark upon a day of revelry to celebrate their union. The whole university will share in their joy. Distant friends have made the journey, and most importantly, his own family. Their marriage already legitimated in private, it will now be made fully public.

Not for the first time, he shakes his head in disbelief, amazed that the thing is happening. He feels a tension in his chest, as if a thousand bees were buzzing nervously, swarming here and there in a wave of commotion. Already, he can hear the crowd gathering outside, ready to cheer them at the cloister gate.

Your ways are certainly higher than my ways, Lord, he thinks, *for I can make no sense of this thing.*

A succession of giggles sounds forth in the spiral staircase to his right, bouncing off the walls in a flourish of unbridled joy. It is his six-year-old goddaughter Anna Cranach, clothed in a white gown with a blue satin sash around her waist, holding a bundle of dandelions with one hand and the edge of her skirt with the other. Her abundance of brown curls, sprinkled here and there with yellow blooms, bounces happily with each step. She is beaming—yes, positively radiating enthusiasm for the day's events. As she reaches the bottom and skips toward him, she proclaims, "Herr Luther! Herr Luther! I told you!"

He chuckles. "That you did, dear one."

Anna sways on the spot, whipping her skirt this way and that, her shoulders pinched toward her neck. "Oh, I knew you would get married! I just knew it!" She bounces lightly on tip toe, her gap-toothed grin warming his heart.

"I am a man of my word," he notes, pointing to the flowers. "Are you prepared to carry out your task?"

"Yes! Yes, yes, yes!" she assures him, for it is Anna who will lead them in procession down Colleges Street. It may not be quite in line with tradition, but the girl made it abundantly clear she would do no other. She moves close to him and whispers, "Mama is just finishing with Käthe. She is so pretty!"

"You look quite pretty yourself," he whispers in turn.

"You like her! I can tell."

"Ah, really?" he asks, feeling somewhat uncomfortable. "What gave me away?"

Anna chuckles uproariously, snorting in her effort. "You do! You like her! She likes you too: she told me so."

The child's complete lack of discretion sends a shock through him, catching in his chest, quickening his breath. Although he knows he ought not pry, he cannot help but ask, "What did she say?"

Smiling from ear to ear, Anna shakes her head, then skips out the door to join the others, leaving him alone with his questions.

What did Katharina say to her? Or did she say nothing of consequence and the girl is just hearing what she wants to hear? He considers for a moment, then decides, *Nothing. It means nothing. She is just a child.* But there is a yearning deep within him—and a faint hint of terror.

Now the girl's mother, Barbara Cranach, makes her descent, her right arm threaded through the handle of a basket, the contents of which are a mystery to his male mind.

"She's all finished!" Barbara declares, a bit out of breath. Pointing toward the door, she says, "I'll join the others."

He nods in recognition as Barbara passes him, but as she is about to cross the threshold, she places her free hand on the jam and looks back at him.

"I hope you have been storing up your breath, Herr Doktor, so you have plenty to give her when she takes it away."

With this mischievous comment, Barbara departs, leaving Martin standing alone in the foyer, his heart pounding.

He stares at the spiral staircase, his whole being bent upon it. His hands are clasped together—the tension ripples through his arms and legs. As one minute goes by and then another, he is struck by an irrational fear: she has decided she does not wish to marry him after all. *But we are already married,* he assures himself. And yet, there is something welling in the cavities of his soul—a longing that can only be satisfied when she is revealed. Unable to endure the tension of the moment, he looks away, inhaling sharply. Then he hears a soft voice call to him, "Doktor—husband." He turns swiftly and finds himself captured by a sight that is instantly impressed on the width and breadth of his memory.

It is certainly Katharina, but not as he has ever seen her in life. She floats down the stairs like a bird upon the wind, the folds of her skirt lightly brushing each step. Over her ivory chemise, she wears a light green dress gathered at the elbows and wrists. The layers of fabric cling tightly to her chest and waist as if holding them in a loving embrace, then billow at the hips, creating the folds that sway with every graceful movement of her body. As it is her wedding day, her tresses hang loose, falling hypnotically down her neck and stopping a few inches past her shoulders. Her head is crowned with a ring of blooms: periwinkle cornflowers, marigolds in shades of orange and red, white chamomile with golden centers, and a few others he cannot identify except to declare them beautiful. A sheer white veil is attached to the floral crown and trails down her back, swishing with every movement. She clutches a bouquet in her hands—a stunning burst of color drawn from the very hill of the gods. Around her delicate neck hangs a string of pearls lent to her by Barbara Cranach, and on her left hand she wears the golden ring gifted to her when they first exchanged vows.

Swallowing hard, he dares to glimpse the details of her face—her blushing lips, high cheekbones, and irises the color of rain. He could almost swear she is emitting a heavenly glow, but perhaps it is a reflection from the window. She is approaching him now: smiling broadly, delighted to be in his presence on this day of rejoicing.

Say something, fool! he urges himself. *Don't just stand there!* But he lacks the power to convey what he feels in his pulsing chest, his heart that expands and contracts ferociously. He ought to declare everything he is experiencing in this moment, but there is a fundamental discomfort within him, a haunting whisper that holds him back. *She doesn't know you—not really.*

Chiding himself for his cowardice, he asks, "Are you ready?"

"I think so," she replies, nodding her head softly. "I keep fearing I've forgotten something: that the flowers are crooked, or my face smudged, or God only knows what else. My mother superior would say it is vanity, and perhaps it is, but I just hate to disappoint anyone."

A word breaks from his lips unbidden. "Impossible."

She stares at him with wide eyes, desperately searching the nooks and crannies of his features. Making a great effort to hold his fear at bay, he extends his hand and inquires, "Shall we go, then?"

With a smile of infinite sweetness, she grants him her hand in turn, interlacing her fingers with his. There is an immediate heat within him: the same rush of life that pulses through his veins whenever they touch. He is reminded of the words of Scripture. *For this reason a man shall leave his father and his mother, and be joined to his wife, and they shall become one flesh.* As he leads Katharina out the door into the bright sunlight of a summer morning, he remembers also what comes next: *And the man and his wife were both naked and were not ashamed.*[11] He wonders if he will ever achieve that level of openness.

The ceremony itself is a triumph. He cannot remember a time the town was so jubilant. Their hands are joined before the door of the church with an enormous crowd looking on, and in the front row of the crowd, Martin sees his father and mother, who have made the journey to Wittenberg with the rest of the Ludher kin. His mother's eyes are filled with tears of joy, while his father looks on serenely, his lower lip quivering ever so slightly.

---

[11] Genesis 2:24-25.

When the business is completed, they all process to the green yard in front of the Black Cloister, where two rows of tables are set up, all decorated with bunches of wildflowers Katharina retrieved from a glen near the city. There is venison provided by the Elector, a barrel of beer each from the rival brewing centers of Einbeck and Torgau, whole platters of fruit and vegetables contributed by the farmers among the congregation, twenty loafs of bread from the baker Scholl, and from the kitchens of the Cranach household, piles of sweets and a four-tier cake of such magnificence it seems more appropriate for a royal wedding than his own—not that Martin is complaining.

During one of Martin's trips to the barrel, he is met by his brother Jakob, who wraps him in a firm embrace, clapping him on the back and causing some of the liquid to escape Martin's mug.

"Jakob! How I have longed to see you again! And what a joy it is to meet little Fabian!" he exclaims, referring to his youngest nephew.

Releasing him, Jakob looks over at Katharina. Instinctively, Martin does the same. His wife is seated next to their mother, nodding and smiling as the older woman goes on and on about the best way to roast a hare. The sunlight catches Katharina's red locks as they are softly tossed by the wind. Her eyes are sparkling—her laugh a melodious sound that awakens all he is. Without truly realizing what he is doing, he smiles.

"Well, we finally have the answer to my question," Jakob concludes.

Martin looks back at his brother, who is shaking his head and grinning mischievously. "What's that?"

Jakob chuckles. "She's not hideous."

Martin represses the urge to roll his eyes and immediately changes the subject. "If you have any suggestions for how I can survive married life without completely ruining everything, do feel free to voice them."

Again, Jakob laughs. "Oh, you're woven into her plaits now, brother: make no mistake! A few weeks on the pillow would do you both good."

"You haven't seen the state of my pillow," he mutters, embarrassed at how poor he had allowed his living situation to become—not that he had much time or money to do otherwise.

"Need a new one already, do you?" Jakob teases, punching him lightly on the arm.

Immediately and against his will, Martin's mind is overcome with sensations: the glow of candles in the dark of night, the way the light shone upon the skin of her back, the smell of rose water when he held her close, and all the while, the terror of knowing himself so near his desires and yet impossibly distant.

"No, that's not what I—never mind," he mutters. "I should have known better than to ask my little brother for advice."

"God bless you, Martin!" Jakob concludes, patting him on the back. "And God bless the woman the Lord has brought into your home."

Martin turns with his mug in hand and walks to the far end of the table, where his former colleague Nikolaus von Amsdorf is seated. Taking his place on the bench next to Amsdorf, Martin says, "Thank you for making the journey. It's good to see you, Nikolaus."

Consuming the final bite of cake lying on the table before him, Amsdorf responds with a full mouth, "You didn't think I would miss this, did you? It's not often I get to watch a man so thoroughly devour his own words."

"You should be content enough in your victory without boasting," Martin chides him.

"My victory?! Ha! Only the Lord could have done this. I hear men say that miracles are a thing of the past, but I beg to differ. This happy occurrence is far past the abilities of man and nature."

Martin thinks back to the day Amsdorf met him with news that Katharina had refused to marry Glatz. How he had sworn up and down he would never make a bride of Katharina von Bora! Some part of him sensed even then that he was beating his wings against the wind in vain. Remembering that stern refusal, he feared after taking Katharina as his wife that Amsdorf would think it the action of a man possessed by lust. After all, plenty of other people have reached that conclusion. Therefore, when he wrote to Amsdorf to invite him to the wedding, he assured him, "I feel neither passionate love nor burning for my spouse, but I cherish her."[12]

---

[12] Martin Luther, *Luther's Works*, v. 49 – Letters II, American edition, ed. and trans. Gottfried G. Krodel (Philadelphia: Fortress Press, 1972), 117.

Now, as Martin thinks back over all that has transpired, he says to his friend, "If I may speak in earnest—thank you, Nikolaus, for passing along her message. It was the Lord's will that I should make this statement of my faith."

Amsdorf bows his head. "Even if I accomplish nothing else, mine will have been a life worth living."

As he makes this heartfelt sentiment, Amsdorf's gaze fastens on something behind Martin, who turns to find his father, Hans, standing with a mug in one hand and a bun in the other. Hans motions to the side with his head, indicating his desire for a private audience, which Martin nervously grants. They walk side-by-side around the dormitory, away from prying eyes, then Hans turns on the spot, having ingested the last of his morsel.

Does he mean to lecture me? Martin wonders, bidding himself remain calm. *I have done what he desired today. He cannot possibly be angry with me—can he?*

Hans eyes him up and down, taking a swig of his beer, then wiping the drips from his chin.

Twenty years of this! Always wondering where I really stand with him, Martin thinks. *If there is ever a day to end it, it is today.* He braces himself, feet fastened to the ground beneath him, his spirit drawing upon everything he has experienced over the past few months to lend him strength.

"Dear Father," Martin utters, his insides clenched.

"Yes, son."

"Do you remember that night when I came home from university? When I told you God was calling me to be a priest?"

Hans gives him a pointed look. "How could I forget it?"

"You said something to me then—You said, 'If you do this thing, don't you dare call yourself my son!'" Even recalling the event fills Martin with sorrow, but he presses on, unwilling to give way to the pain—to let this precious moment slip away. "The years have passed, and much has changed, but what I want to know more than anything is, do you accept me as your son?"

It is the question etched upon his soul. As Martin voices it, he feels himself caught upon the waves, tumbling and crashing, beaten against the rocks. But his father's eyes are not angry: Hans sets the earthenware mug upon the ground and moves closer to Martin, evidently preparing himself for a great declaration. Martin looks at him with moist eyes, seeking to find in those wrinkled features a trace of the love he longs to receive.

"We've had our rows, you and me, always beating on each other, always saying things we both regret. I know what it is I detest in you. I'm not as thick as you suppose!" Hans asserts.

Martin's breath catches. He is only seconds away from the blow.

Then something happens which catches Martin completely off guard. His father's gaze softens as he says, "I detest myself. I see myself in you—in your worst moments—and I detest it, because I gave it to you. So don't say your old man never admits anything!" Hans shakes his head, exhaling sharply. "Here I stand, ancient as the earth, losing my piss every five minutes, and I finally know what it is I am and what it is you are. But you still don't know me, boy. You don't know me if you think what I was doing that night was refusing to accept you as my son," he insists, pointing a finger at Martin's chest. "I was angry. Furious! And terrified—Terrified of what we would do without you there. Terrified that all that was good in our lives was being snatched away. But when I said what I said, I meant that you were choosing not to accept me."

Hans takes a step back, breaking into tears. The distant chatter of the wedding guests flits upon the breeze, but Martin is deaf to the sound of all but one thing: his father's voice, speaking to him, overturning everything he thought he knew.

"When you did what you did, when you disobeyed me and left us all to rot, when you declared that you didn't need the wisdom of my years, you were refusing to accept me!" Hans states emphatically. "That is why I said, 'Don't call yourself my son.' Because you were rejecting me as your father, and it hurt, son. It hurt like the devil's brand!" He pounds his chest with his palm, his spirit seemingly breaking beneath the impact of the words. "It took me a long time to get over it. But I see you now, son. I see that you have truly found God: that it has all worked out the way it was probably meant to work out. The devil torments us, but the Lord laughs at us—that's what I always say. And so, though I am an old son of the mine, and I wouldn't know a nicety if it bit me in the ass, today is your wedding day, and you are my son, and—"

His voice breaks. He takes Martin's face in his hands and solemnly declares, " I may be a fool, but I would never be fool enough to refuse you as my son. I am proud of you."

Martin stares into those ancient eyes the same color as his own, and he feels himself overcome—yes, utterly overcome by joy. He falls upon his father, melting into his embrace. They are both weeping, the sound of it loud enough to carry back to the assembled guests, but Martin does not care. He shakes and cries again and again, "Father! Father!" And he is held there—made firm by a love granted by heaven itself.

Hans grasps Martin's face again with his calloused fingers and says through the tears, "If I was harsh, son, it was always for your good. I always sought your good."

"I know, Father," Martin replies, nodding quickly. "I know. And I would seek your good always."

"I'm sorry I mocked you. I was just angry."

"I know, Father," he assures him. "At last, I know you."

It is a blessed moment: a feeling so powerful that Martin nearly floats through the rest of the day's activities, his spirit light enough to dance upon the breeze. The celebration proceeds to the new town hall for a time, then those who still have the energy walk in the dark of evening with Martin and Katharina back to the gate of the Black Cloister, singing hymns and folk songs, wishing them happy and healthy for all their days. By this point, his students are struggling to remain upright. As Martin moves to bid them farewell one by one, he comes upon Philipp Melanchthon, who in line with their reconciliation has shown himself most enthusiastic upon this day. Caught up in a swell of positive emotion, Martin assures his colleague, "I will respond to Erasmus: you have my word. I will begin it as soon as I can, and it will be respectful. You need not fear."

"Thank you—But be sure to spend some time with your wife as well!" Philipp instructs him.

Martin then wishes Johannes Bugenhagen a very good night, making sure to thank him for performing the ceremony. Bugenhagen draws Martin close, the look on his face serious—almost stern.

"What is it?" Martin asks, feeling suddenly alarmed.

"Do not hide from her," Bugenhagen instructs. "You know what I mean. This is the hour. Let her in."

The confidence brimming within Martin quickly dissipates. He longs to do what his friend and confessor urges, but it seems a thing far too high for him. Once again, he asks himself, *What are you afraid of?* Like a thunderbolt, the answer comes: *I am a man like other men.* Before, this fact was a comfort. Now, it is utterly terrifying, for Katharina has great affection for Doktor Luther, but what on earth will she think of plain Martin when she really gets to know him—when she discovers he is a sinner as much as he is just? How will she curse her choice when she finds him balled up on the floor in sorrow, terror, or some combination of both? Yes, she has seen him stripped of his clothes, but not stripped down to his soul. If he longs to hide the imperfections of his body, how much more does he wish to conceal the putrid desires of his flesh and the weakness that infects every fiber of his being? How can he possibly protect her from the demons upon his back?

Martin walks with Katharina into the Black Cloister, the distant shouts of well-wishers ringing in their ears. They enter the foyer, and he shuts the door behind them, keenly aware that as he does so, he is cutting himself off from everything in the world: everything but her. Brisger has already moved out, and Wolf knew well enough to find lodging elsewhere. "A man should be alone with his wife on their wedding night," Wolf had said with a mischievous grin.

Martin turns to look at Katharina and finds she is staring back at him, her gaze keen, her features softly illumined by the flame burning in the sconce—and yet, he suspects it is no external illumination: that she is lit by a fire within, which burns with fierce intensity as she stares into his eyes.

"How are you feeling?" he asks, mouth terribly dry, spirit quivering in expectation.

"Exhausted," she replies with a smile, removing the ring of flowers from her head and setting it on the steps. "You?"

"The same, though it is a good kind of exhaustion."

"Yes, of course. It's been a wonderful day. Your family was so kind to me."

He removes his cap and leans down to set it on the same step, then rises again and assures her, "You're the answer to their prayers—years and years of prayers."

"I would hate to let them down," she whispers, her expression suddenly solemn.

He moves a step closer to her. "There's no chance of that. If anything goes wrong, they will blame me."

Katharina chuckles, her smile returning—a truly beautiful smile. "I loved meeting the children especially. The new baby—"

"Yes, he was adorable," Martin agrees, stepping closer once again. "I wish I was able to see them more. Every time I do, it is a balm for the soul."

"Perhaps this time next year we will have our own child."

The thought of it grips him mightily, like the coming of some heavenly apparition. "Perhaps," he says softly.

He is very near her now—so close that he must look down to gaze into her eyes and watch the flames dancing in unison. He can hear the voice of Bugenhagen in his head: *Let her in.* Oh, how he wants to, even as he yearns to be received into everything she is! *But I am only a man.* The taunting voice resounds in his head. *You are a fraud. She will find out. She will hate you for what you've done—for what you are!* Nevertheless, he dares to speak.

"Tell me, Katharina," he inquires, his words coming hesitantly, "are you happy?"

"Of course!" she replies, her face alight. "A bride is always happy on her wedding day."

No, she has not understood what I mean—not quite, he thinks, but he has lost his nerve. "If only that were true," he mumbles.

"I am very happy, I assure you. Are you happy, Herr Doktor?"

He nods swiftly. "Yes."

Katharina inhales deeply and draws nearer, her face within inches of his. With great firmness of conviction, she asks, "Do you know how proud I am to be your wife?"

Her words run into his ears like honey, so infinitely sweet. But their full effect is muted, for there is another question in his mind: *Is she saying this to me or to the Luther whose writings she devours? Is she speaking to a sinner or a saint?*

So, he attempts to laugh it off. "Clearly, you haven't been reading the pamphlets they print about me!"

Katharina brushes his comment away like a stray hair. She moves toward him boldly and rubs her nose against his, pressing back and forth. He closes his eyes, overcome by the feeling. She lets her lips brush gently upon the stubble of his cheeks, then pulls away. He lifts his lids, searching her out desperately. *Why did she stop?!* Her complexion is flushed—her eyes full of desire. Before he can say a word, she speaks into the depths of his soul.

"Don't be afraid."

Then, for the very first time, she kisses him mouth to mouth, seizing the breath within him, exchanging it with her own. Instinctively, he takes her in his arms, feeling the warmth of her body, treasuring her corporal existence. With everything he is, he longs to believe her words: to know there is truly nothing to fear. They part if only to catch their breath.

It is time, he thinks. *I must tell her everything.* His desire is utterly fixed upon her. There is nothing he would not surrender to be united with her not only in body, but spirit. His every intent is to declare, *I need you desperately!* His lips part, but he hears something that stops him in his tracks: the cries of a baby growing louder by the second.

No, that's impossible, he thinks. *She might be pregnant, but I know well enough it takes nine months to give birth, and what's more, I would have remembered the event!*

"Is it my imagination or is there a child wailing?" he asks, looking around in confusion.

"I hear it too," Katharina assures him. "You are not losing your mind husband—not yet." Here she winks at him playfully.

The plaintive cries are deafening now. He can hear footsteps and lowered voices just outside.

"Probably a beggar seeking some leftover food," Martin concludes. "I will get the door."

"No, I should get it. I am the keeper of the house," she insists. Patting him on the arm, she says, "You rest, husband. You've been working so hard."

"If you insist," he agrees.

As Katharina moves toward the door, Martin sits on the steps and places his head in his hands. *Can a man not have some peace on his wedding night?! After everything I do day after day after day—it never stops!* Then he chides himself. *You are just sore because you were about to break through with Käthe. Be patient. You can try again.*

His wife says, "Good evening. How may I help you?"

Then he hears something all too familiar—a voice he knows as well as his own. Rising immediately, he moves to join her at the door and sees the very thing he fears: Andreas Bodenstein von Karlstadt standing in tattered clothes, looking very much as if he could use both a shave and a bath. Beside Karlstadt stands his absurdly young wife, Anna, who looks upon Martin with eyes full of fear. In her arms she holds their weeping babe, frantically bouncing him in a vain effort to calm the storm of tears, and beside her stands a boy no more than two years old.

"Good God in heaven," Martin mutters.

Karlstadt steps up to the threshold, perhaps attempting to assert his physical authority—but he is a shadow of his former self, gaunt and bent. The sight of him in such condition strikes Martin to the core.

"Doktor, you must have mercy," Karlstadt begs. "We have nowhere else to go!"

In this moment, Martin thinks of their meeting at the Black Bear, when Karlstadt told him, *You mean nothing to me.* He thinks of his visit to Orlamünde, when Karlstadt's parishioners greeted him with a hail of stones. He thinks of the wild ramblings, apocalyptic visions, and constant denial of the gifts of God. He thinks of the endless attempts by himself and others to help their colleague back to the truth. He thinks of the indignities against the Elector, and most of all, he thinks of the many times Karlstadt supported Müntzer in word and deed: Müntzer whose head is still planted upon a pike, being picked at by the birds. How many thousands of deaths have been blamed upon Martin, when all the while, it was Karlstadt who gave comfort to the insurrectionists!

As he examines Karlstadt's sunken eyes, now ringed with dark circles and looking suspiciously pink, Martin's fury bursts forth in a single word: "No!"

"Good husband," Katharina begs, placing a hand on his arm, "does not the Lord command us to take in the destitute and treat them as our own?"

"You know nothing of what he's done—what he still intends to do!" Martin cries. Yet, even as he shouts these words, he feels a rush of guilt.

"I cannot leave them out on the street," she whispers desperately, her eyes urging him to compassion. "Can you?"

These words offered quietly, appealing to his sense of honor, convince him to yield. He has no intention of forsaking his principles, but he will give his adversary a final chance.

Turning back to Karlstadt, Martin says, "I will grant you refuge on one condition: that you retract your pernicious doctrines, apologize to everyone you have wronged, and go live a quiet life and trouble us no more, even as you have pledged. That is your price of passage into this house. Do you consent?"

For a moment, the two men simply stare at one another. Less than a year earlier, it would have been unthinkable for Karlstadt to accede to these demands, but Martin suspects something of the strength Karlstadt once possessed has been wrested from the man forever. He can sense it in the deep fatigue of his opponent's eyes, the slump of his shoulders, the slight wheezing of his breath, the tears in his clothes that suggest a struggle of epic proportions just to arrive in Wittenberg.

Therefore, it is perhaps less surprising than it otherwise might have been that Karlstadt replies, "I do," his voice frail and tired.

Martins nods in assent and steps to the side, allowing the Karlstadts to enter. The babe begins wailing again, disturbed by the new surroundings. Anna shushes him, thumping the child's back with her petite hand. Martin can tell from her desperate manner—for she seems very much on the brink of tears—that she and her children have suffered a horrific journey, no doubt made worse by her husband's frenzied ramblings. When Katharina holds out her hands and offers, "Let me take the baby," Anna doesn't put up a fight, even for show. She immediately sets the child in Katharina's steady arms. Then Martin watches in amazement as Katharina gives the babe her finger and allows him to chew on it, which seems to instantly improve his mood.

"He is getting his teeth, right?" Katharina asks.

Anna nods silently, and Martin cannot help but observe in this moment how very different his own wife is from Karlstadt's. His colleague married a girl, but he has clearly married a woman.

"Do you all sleep together?" Katharina inquires.

"Yes, mistress," Anna responds. "Any bed will suit us."

Katharina nods. "There is a room made ready upstairs. Follow me."

With that, the women ascend the spiral staircase, the older Karlstadt boy trailing behind. Martin watches them go, very much fearing he has lost his chance with Katharina, and not only for the evening. There is a fierce churning in his gut: he knows there will be no peace until the Karlstadts depart. *Then we must be rid of them quickly,* he thinks.

Stepping forward to meet Martin's eye line, Karlstadt says, "I will not forget this kindness."

He looks back at Karlstadt knowingly, his whole being weary. "Nor will I."

1 July 1525
Basel, Swiss Confederation

Desiderius Erasmus winds his way through the streets of Basel with Jan Łaski at his side. Their journey began with a declaration from the Pole: "Herring! I need herring!" When it became clear that Margarethe was in no position to sate him—the phrase, "Get your own damn herring!" escaped her ample lips—Łaski practically dragged Erasmus out into the street, crying, "Walk with me, man! The air will do you good!"

What good the summer heat could do for his aging frame, Erasmus cannot imagine. He passed the previous night in misery, turning this way and that upon his bed, reversing position in search of a cooler clime. Who could sleep with beads of sweat upon his back? The very devil's breath seemed to form them. If ever he found himself comfortable, his thoughts oppressed him, gnawing upon his membranes, denying him rest. The decay of his mortal frame has been hastened by the torture of his immortal soul.

Now, his leather soles brush over the dirt road, its moisture driven off by the summer heat. Dust rises to infect his nostrils. Great heaving coughs escape his lungs—hacking, biting, rattling as they go. Łaski pats him firmly on the back, eyes filled with concern, but Erasmus waves him off.

"There's nothing for it! Leave me be!"

"You should see a physician, friend," the Pole insists. "You are most unwell."

"I am dying, Łaski!" he retorts. "There is no cure for that."

The words echo within his mind, bouncing off the corners of his brain. *I am dying. I will soon be dead.* His bowels tighten—his breath catches in his throat. Is it the burden of age that weighs upon him, or merely the sense of foreboding? He has already consulted every physician in Basel, or at least every physician worth consulting. No one has a cure for the heaviness in his bones. "You could live another decade, if the plague does not take you," they assured him, but he struggles to believe it. He hears the bells of St. Andreas ring and wonders when they will sound for him. They pass a stall where a woman is dyeing cloth. The stench of the chemicals assaults his nose. He remembers the smell that rose from the abyss: heat, sulfur, overpowering blackness. *I do not have long.*

"Any news from Paris?" Łaski asks as they turn onto Saddle Alley, where leather from the tanner's shops is fashioned into proper seats for exalted bottoms.

"Nothing," Erasmus replies, his pulse increasing as he thinks of Béda and his pack of wolves circling ever nearer, the saliva seeping from their jaws. "Perhaps it is too soon."

"Or perhaps they do not intend to strike you, but only to make you fear," Łaski offers, sidestepping to avoid a boy chasing a pigeon.

As if that would not be punishment enough, he groans internally. When they walk again side by side, he assures his friend, "Oh, they will strike me, sure enough—strike my name upon a shard and send me off into the wilderness!"[13]

"The wilderness is becoming rather crowded with all the people they've sent off, so much so I think we may call it a city!" Łaski jests, amusing himself so greatly that he fails to notice a rut and stumbles forward, his feathered hat falling to the ground.

As the Pole reaches down to reclaim the cap and his dignity, Erasmus mutters, "Not a city I wish to inhabit."

They are passing the merchants' houses now, each three or four stories tall. The noise from the square filters down the alleyway. Łaski steps in front of him, halting their progress.

---

[13] The ancient Athenians would at times hold a vote over which of two citizens to banish. Voters would place the name of their selected person on an *óstrakon*, the Greek word for a shard of pottery. This is the source of our modern English word "ostracize."

"Oh, Erasmus!" the Pole cries in amusement, smiling broadly. "All day long, I hear, 'Paris! Luther! Louvain! Paris! Luther! Louvain!' Always your foes' names upon your lips!" He places one hand on Erasmus' shoulder and the other on his own chest. "Look, I am a Pole."

"You've mentioned it once or twice," Erasmus notes wryly.

"Everyone in my kingdom loves you! Come: live among us! We will treat you like the god you are."

It is a kind offer—sincere in the extreme. But as much as Erasmus hates the smells of this city and the constant chatter assaulting his ears, he has no choice but to remain in Basel. If he did not leave for Italy, France, or England when he had the chance, he is not about to attempt a journey to the far reaches of Christendom, where he is certain the strange food will hasten his demise.

"You are further from the center, friend," Erasmus explains. "And in any case, I can no longer travel. I am half-dead. The next stone will be the end of me."

Łaski drops his hand and shakes his head, thoroughly exasperated. "Always moaning. Always unhappy. Poor Erasmus!"

"You, on the other hand, are annoyingly exuberant these days," Erasmus notes, his eyes narrowing as he searches out his companion's face. "What's happened to you?"

Oh, how Łaski's expression changes! He is instantly lighter, happier, freer. "I found something: something I was always looking for."

Erasmus cannot help but snort. "Many answers to this riddle occur to me, each more evil than the next."

"God!" Łaski bellows, face beaming. "I found God, Erasmus!"

"Oh, by the powers!" he mutters, placing a hand on his forehead. "I should have known."

Immediately, Erasmus resumes his progress toward the market square, having no desire to hear further details. He remembers when Łaski arrived in Basel: a man boisterous but sensible, unwilling to depart from the old ways, whether religious or diplomatic. Then the letters began arriving from reformers and radicals alike. Łaski started disappearing at odd times. He asked to borrow Erasmus' copy of Melanchthon's *Common Topics.*

I knew he was headed this way. I could sense it in my bones, Erasmus thinks, *and yet I was not prepared for the blow.*

"Do you want to know the best thing about it?" Łaski calls after him, rushing to keep up.

Erasmus groans softly. "You will tell me whether I wish it or not."

Łaski reaches his side, laughing merrily. "It was he who found me! Only, God doesn't have to look for me. He knows where I am always. And I suppose I always knew where he was—in theory, at least. So, maybe no one was looking for anyone. Am I making sense?"

Erasmus looks into his friend's kind eyes and assures him, "Not remotely."

They have entered the square bursting with life, its cobbles covered in stalls selling every product imaginable—or at least, everything imaginable north of the mountains and far from the sea. Merchants, knights, cooks, and clerks all race to and fro, making their way from one part of the city to the next, hoping to grab some turnips or ale along the way. On the opposite side of the square, the towers of the town hall rise against the blue sky, their faces painted in brilliant hues of yellow, red, and green.

"No matter," Łaski decides, his gaze redirecting. "Here is young Bonifacius!"

Sure enough, Bonifacius Amerbach is racing to meet them. He is dressed in a doublet of red damask, a black velvet cap on his head and a smile on his face.

Here is a sight for sore eyes, Erasmus thinks. *I will hear only good sense from him.*

"Master Amberbach!" he cries, opening his arms to receive the younger man.

Amerbach runs into his embrace, exclaiming, "My lord! My teacher!" Then pulling back he proclaims, "And Herr Łaski—always a pleasure!" gripping the man's hand in his own.

But Łaski is distracted: a faint smell has drawn his nose and eyes to the fish stall some twenty yards away, its red and white striped canopy marking it out clearly. "I must buy the herring," the Pole asserts, breaking away to pursue his main objective.

The two of them watch Łaski go, his skirt kicking up with the effort. There is something unavoidably humorous about it.

"Does he always rush off like that?" Amerbach asks, turning back to Erasmus.

"Only when herring is involved," he quips.

"Right," Amerbach concludes, eyes suddenly filled with light. He clasps his hands together, producing a popping noise. "Have you heard the news?"

Erasmus tilts his head slightly. "What news?"

"Why, the news that has shaken the world! The news that has the saints turning in their graves!"

"Not nearly specific enough," he insists. After all, the world has been shaking without relent for the past eight years. It will take something truly remarkable to affect his person.

Amerbach steps closer, hands now held behind his back. His gaze seems to penetrate Erasmus' eyes. The older man feels a twitch in his stomach.

"Luther has married," Amerbach announces. "Not only that—he's married a nun. A nun, Erasmus! Probably bedding her as we speak."

Erasmus may have doubted Amerbach's ability to shock him, but the younger man has done his job and then some. *Luther married?!* The force of it vibrates through his bones, racing across his nerves, provoking the tremors of the deep. For some reason, he had not thought Luther the marrying type—a foolish notion, he now realizes. After all, celibacy is currently being rejected at the rate of last week's meat. Why wouldn't Luther marry? *But he is a dead man as much as I! Perhaps that is why I always assumed it could not happen.* As the news is absorbed into his fibers, Erasmus surveys his own emotions. *How do I feel about this?* He realizes he needs more information.

"What, did he break into a consecrated house and tear off her habit?" he asks.

"No," Amerbach replies, stretching the word out to the point of breaking, "but in a manner of speaking, yes."

He shakes his head in frustration. "Pray, speak Latin. You make no sense."

"Her name is Katharina von Bora," Amerbach explains, "a Cistercian sister from somewhere in Duke Georg's territory. She absconded two years hence, and now they are wed—not that a monk and a nun can wed. It is an abomination in the eyes of God! The Lord does not acknowledge such things, and neither should we. Isn't that what everyone is always saying? A monk and a nun will give birth to the Antichrist."

In this moment, Erasmus thinks of his own parents: a priest and a whore, as he so often heard them titled. His mother was no whore, and neither of his parents belonged to a monastic order, but he knows what it means to be the product of a union contrary to divine command. He has felt that pain every moment of his God forsaken life. There is no insult, no biting jest that has not passed into his ears, burning as it went. Perhaps that is why he immediately responds, "Come now, Amerbach! You're too clever for that by far. If it were true, we would have hundreds of Antichrists running about!"

The younger man scoffs. "Who's to say that we don't? The days are evil. But why are you laughing? I expected you to be incensed."

He is not properly laughing—only chuckling softly as he watches Amerbach's face twist in semi-righteous indignation. The longer the news of Luther's marriage resides in his thoughts, the more Erasmus finds himself giving way to pleasure. *The audacity! The utter deliciousness of it! It will offend all the right people.*

"You ought to be incensed!" Amerbach repeats, hands planted on hips. "Aren't you incensed?!"

"Hardly!" he replies. "This news has delighted me exceedingly."

"How can you say such a thing?!"

Erasmus sighs, placing a hand on the younger man's shoulder. "My dear Bonifacius, we've been living through a bloody tragedy for years now. I have spent every day in fear of how it would end, but now I see I need not have wasted my energy, for like all the good comedies, it has ended with a marriage!"

Amerbach backs away, eyeing Erasmus warily. "Sometimes I cannot tell if you are in earnest or jest."

"Entirely in earnest, I assure you."

"I did not think you were one to approve of fornication!" Amerbach complains, exhibiting a degree of anger that Erasmus previously thought contrary to his makeup.

"Well, I would most certainly disapprove if such a thing had taken place, but that is not what you told me," Erasmus reminds him. "You said they were wed, nothing more."

"Ha!" Amerbach shouts, drawing concerned glances from the shoppers nearby. "Did you think a man like Luther could behave honorably?! They had no choice but to marry. She was about to give birth, and indeed she has done so now, about a week after the blessed event, not that there is anything blessed about it."

Erasmus suddenly feels rather ill. His mood is utterly transformed—his joviality hurled upon the rocks. *He is not what I thought. He is something else entirely.*

"Do you mean to say he had taken her as a concubine?" he asks, realization washing over him.

"Concubine, whore—who knows? But she has borne his child, and it seems hard to believe that even a man with such divine powers as Luther could bring a babe to term in less than a month."

Erasmus stares at the ground, shaking his head in disbelief. *I thought him at least an honorable man, or honorable enough not to misuse a woman.* But Luther, it seems, is very much like Erasmus' own father Gerard: happy to present one face to the world and another to those he claims to love.

"What now, Erasmus?" Amerbach asks. "You were happy when you ought to have been outraged, and now you look outraged when you ought to feel vindicated."

Slowly, he raises his gaze, meeting Amerbach's eyes. "I cannot account for it."

The younger man is clearly perturbed—he scoffs loudly. "Can you not? Is it not exactly what one would expect from a man as iniquitous as Luther? A man who, I should remind you, has sent all his demons to attack you—who has destroyed so much of what you hold dear!"

Erasmus struggles to hold back a tear. *Why is this bothering me so much?* He replies softly, "I acknowledge that some of his doctrines are erroneous, and he would do better to keep his dogs in check, but I had not thought him a liar. And that is what he is, if indeed he fornicated with her."

Amerbach nods, his expression softening. He places a comforting hand on Erasmus' arm. "She was lured by his words, even as so many have been. She gave herself up to him as if in a trance. He is a liar of old, and now he has stolen the virginity of one who was sworn to a better husband. She looked to him for guidance, and he took advantage of her. That ought to offend you."

"It does offend me," Erasmus assures him, yet even as the words escape his lips, he doubts. "But are you very sure all this information is correct?"

"We have it from Duke Georg himself, along with a host of others," Amerbach replies, his brow furrowed. "I would not spout half-truths to you! All the townspeople passing the house can hear the baby wail and see that so-called nun cherishing it."

Erasmus nods, conceding the point, but he finds himself tired: utterly weary of the world. He has less appetite for their conversation than he did for Łaski's herring.

"Very well," he concludes, his voice fading like the late summer blooms. "Thank you for informing me."

With that, he takes his leave, wandering through the rows of stalls alone, searching for nothing in particular. Painful thoughts consume him, pulling him down in the undertow. Any final shred of faith he had in Martin Luther—his ability to right the ship and bring positive change to Christendom—has utterly died. *He is just like the others. There was never any point in trying.* And he thinks of Philipp Melanchthon, laboring under the tutelage of such a man. *What must he think of all this? If he will not forsake Luther now, he will never forsake him.*

He finds himself before the façade of the town hall, staring up at the great clock that counts down the minutes of his life. *So few—so few are left to me!* Will he meet the end with any of his faith intact? Is God looking for him at all? He has long since ceased hoping to find God. And yet, in the middle of that commotion, he finds himself praying.

Kýrie eleison. Christe eléison.

27 July 1525
Wittenberg, Electorate of Saxony

Martin Luther kneels in the small chapel on the second story of the Black Cloister, his knees resting upon a straw-filled cushion. This room with dark walls tucked beside the spiral stair grants the only privacy on offer. Here the incessant cries of the Karlstadt babe are muted, and he can barely hear the team of men whitewashing the walls, something Katharina insisted on soon after the Elector announced he was gifting them the Black Cloister as a wedding present. It is a mixed blessing: a home of their own, but one in desperate need of repairs. The floors are being cleaned—the cobwebs have been banished. In the kitchen below, Wolf is hard at work scouring the pots and pans. Not a single surface has escaped the great change. The noise—the smell! His senses are under assault.

Hands clasped anxiously, mind struggling to focus, he stares blankly at the contents of the room: the barest of wood tables, the crucifix mounted on the wall, the iron candelabra standing to his right, its tapers burning low. For a month now, his frustration has been building—first a faint whisper in one ear, then a cacophony literal and figurative draining him of joy. When he married, he had a great plan: he would cancel his summer lectures, make his response to Erasmus, and work on building a relationship with his wife. But always the noise! Always the distractions! He has made little progress in his reply—indeed, he has made little progress in anything.

Having entered wedlock with a great sense of purpose, he now feels himself drifting helplessly, struggling to regain what he felt at the first. Every conversation he has with Katharina involves some sort of project around the house. Worse yet, many of them are about money—a necessary topic, but one that has never set his heart aflame. His sleep is constantly interrupted, either by the wails of the youngest Karlstadt, or by Katharina's tendency to wake long before it is decent to do so. Whenever his frame of mind improves for an hour or two, he finds himself locked in discussion with Karlstadt, and his mood plummets like a pebble heaved into the abyss.

He pinches his eyes shut, attempting to block out the world. *Our Father in heaven*—The sound of some object crashing in the distance breaks his flow, pressing into his skull, redirecting his thoughts to the problems at hand.

Perhaps most troubling of all, he and Katharina are not physically uniting, or if they do so, it is difficult. How could it be otherwise when they are both utterly exhausted, struggling to find a single moment alone? The situation has brought the most grating aspects of Katharina's personality to the fore: the incessant commenting, always thinking she knows best, always attempting to improve things—to improve him. He is certain it has brought out his worst characteristics as well.

If we can just get rid of Karlstadt, if we can just put an end to these constant improvements, then we will have peace! he thinks. Concerned friends show him scurrilous pamphlets making the Black Cloister out to be some sort of pleasure palace where he beds Katharina day and night, each of them bending the other to their will. *If only they knew the truth,* he thinks, then mutters ruefully, "I do not burn."

With a sigh, he rises to his feet, crosses himself, and departs the chapel. *If I cannot find comfort in prayer, at least a beer may do me good.* He descends the steps, his thoughts black, his nose scrunching from the heavy smell of lime. *Beer! I need beer!* As he reaches the foyer, he nearly collides with young Anna Karlstadt, who uses one arm to hold the crying babe Andreas and the other to grip the hand of the thoroughly muddied Hans, her two-year-old. The poor babe is sobbing—thrashing in his mother's embrace. Great tears run down his red cheeks as he releases wails sharp and twisted, which burrow into Martin's head, causing his brain to throb.

"Forgive us, Doktor!" Anna begs, scurrying around him and practically dragging her elder son up the stairs.

Martin places a hand on his temple, closing his eyes, attempting to block out the ache. *Beer! I must have beer!*

He restarts his progress to the refectory, passing through one door and then another to his left. Descending the stairs to the refectory floor, he rubs his eyes with both hands, then massages the skin of his forehead, attempting to release the pain. He only ceases these efforts when he takes a seat upon one of the long benches. By that point it is too late, for as he drops his hands and his vision focuses, he sees Andreas Bodenstein von Karlstadt sitting beside him, cherishing a pewter mug. *For the love of all that is holy! This is not what I need!* Since his arrival in Wittenberg, Karlstadt has visited the barber and looks somewhat less like the wild man who showed up at Luther's door in the dark of night, but the fire remains in his eyes.

"I did not think to see you here at midday, Doktor," Karlstadt comments, taking a sip of his beer.

Martin stares out the window at the garden plot, where the seeds Katharina planted are beginning to bear fruit. He allows his vision to blur, indulging his desire for rest, then after a few seconds, he focuses again.

"The noise—it's unbearable," he mutters.

"Stay seated," Karlstadt instructs. "I'll get you a drink."

Before Martin can respond, his former colleague is exiting the room on his way to the kitchen. Crossing his arms on the table, Martin lays his head down in exhaustion, blocking out the light. He attempts to corner the pain in his head and extricate it by sheer effort of will. Suddenly, he thinks of a day one month ago when he received a kiss that nearly banished his fears. It seems a thousand years ago: he could not have been the same man then. *I must return to that moment. Somehow, I must return.* But it seems a thing far beyond his ability.

Karlstadt returns with a mug in each hand and slides one down the table to Martin, who lifts it to his lips and begins to drink the water of life. Then comes a sound so loud he nearly spits out the beer: metal crashing upon metal in shrill bursts and deafening booms. "Sorry! I dropped the pans!" Wolf cries from the kitchen. Again, Martin's skull is pierced, and he winces.

"Are you unwell, Doktor?" Karlstadt asks.

Martin says nothing, sipping quietly, allowing Karlstadt's question to hang in the air. This has a clear dampening effect on his former colleague. Karlstadt's gaze drops, and he traces the rim of his mug with his finger one, two, three times.

I never wanted him here. He shouldn't be here! Martin thinks, but in truth, Karlstadt has been somewhat more bearable than usual. To regain the Elector's good favor, he has pledged to adopt a quieter life and keep his more controversial opinions to himself. *My days as a prophet are over,* he has promised. *God will raise up others in my place.* Martin found this comment both self-important and menacing, but it was a kind of admission of defeat.

So, despite the pain in his head and the strain of the last few weeks upon his spirit, Martin decides to make a small attempt at conversation, the better to promote harmony. Reaching for a topic he hopes will be thoroughly benign, he remarks, "It must have been difficult for you and your wife, traveling with two little ones."

Karlstadt's countenance lifts—he is fully engaged. "We have always had others to help us. It makes the burden lighter."

Martin nods. The Karlstadts have been somewhat coy about the details of their recent travels: where they went, whom they met, how they managed to survive. When Karlstadt was still in Thuringia, Martin received continual updates about his dealings, but for a period of about six months—a period in which Karlstadt evidently endured a lifetime's worth of troubles—Martin heard nothing, and he feels as if the man before him is somewhat of an enigma.

"Who are young Andreas' godparents?" Martin asks, afraid to know the answer.

"He doesn't have godparents," Karlstadt replies quickly, taking a swig of his beer.

Brows scrunched, Martin inquires, "Doesn't have them? Why not? Did no one stand with you at the baptism?"

Karlstadt sets down his mug with a thud that vibrates through the table, disturbing the liquid in Martin's own receptacle. Wiping the foam from his lips, Karlstadt stares into Martin's eyes, smiling wearily. "You shouldn't ask questions if you don't want to know the answer, Doktor."

Martin inhales sharply, feeling very much as if he has been punched in the gut. Of course, he heard tales of Karlstadt's time in Orlamünde. Some said they had abandoned the sacraments entirely, but it was a thing too monstrous to accept without hard evidence. Even if the congregation had abandoned them, surely Karlstadt would not deny the grace of God to his own son—would he?

"Andreas," Martin begins, an edge to his voice, "is it possible that your son has not been baptized?"

Karlstadt sighs deeply. "I told you not to ask."

Something fierce is awoken in Martin. *The monstrosity of it! The utter contempt for God's Word!* The fire rushes forth, scorching as it goes. "Dear God, it's true! I didn't want to believe it. You must allow us to baptize him!"

Karlstadt scoffs. "You didn't think I would practice what I preach? Why should my wife and I do such a thing when it goes against our firmly held beliefs?"

"You mean your beliefs," he replies, glaring forcefully. "Do not blame poor Anna."

Karlstadt merely smiles at him, taking another drink of his beer. *I must make him see,* Martin thinks. *I must help his son if he will not.*

"Who exactly do you think that child belongs to?" Martin demands to know. "Clearly not God, or you would have brought him to be baptized. Are you suffering under the impression that he belongs to you, or are you so deluded as to think he belongs to himself?"

"Are you so deluded, Doktor, as to believe that he belongs to the Elector?" Karlstadt asks, leaning close enough for Martin to smell the beer on his breath. "Because that is what you are arguing."

Martin shakes his head, thoroughly exasperated. "That does not follow at all, and it demonstrates the sedition to which your thoughts tend." *As if baptism were merely a matter for the state and not the very goodness of God given for man!* he grouses internally.

Karlstadt leans back again, crossing his arms and sitting up straight. "Conscience for me, but not for thee—is that the way of it?"

"When I speak of conscience, I do not mean that every man should do what is right in his own eyes," Martin insists. "I mean that every man must do what the Word of God commands. If you have any fatherly love for that child, bring him to the font now!" And though he does not say it, he thinks, *Why do I care more about your child, whom I barely know, than you do as his father?!*

Karlstadt's fist comes crashing down upon the table, the force of the blow momentarily levitating both mugs. "You are in error because you are still in thrall to the doktors of Rome!"

A ludicrous charge, Martin thinks. The fire is burning in his breast, consuming his innards. He abandons civility entirely.

"There was enough shit in that sentence to spread over a field! It is unforgivable—utterly unforgivable what you are doing! You are denying your child the washing of regeneration! You are denying him the promise of redemption!"

Again, Karlstadt scoffs, a terrible guttural sound. "Washing with water alone avails for nothing but the removal of dirt from skin, but those who are baptized with the Spirit are sons of God. It is they who should receive the sacrament."

"You turn things around! We bring nothing to God. He gives everything to us."

"So you say, yet you would despair for my child because of the choice of his parents. That shows what you truly believe: not in the Spirit, but the letter of the Law."

Martin stares into Karlstadt's eyes, shaking his head in disgust. *How sad to live in the world where you reside,* he muses, *where God remains far away, and we are left to struggle alone!* His fever has reached the boiling point, provoking an explosion. "Honestly, I hate this Christ you preach! A Christ who refuses to unite himself with man: who disdains human flesh and denies his goodness to the sinner!"

"I would hate that too, but it is not what I preach," his opponent insists. "You should give my works a proper read."

Martin rolls his eyes. "I have, many times over, and each worse than the last."

"Rage all you want, Doktor, but you know which way the wind is blowing. The old superstitions are dying! Already, they are rejected in Strasbourg, Basel, Zürich. They would be rejected here if men were free to choose."

The implication of this statement is not lost on Martin: *You are a bully who does not allow men to choose.* All because he has taught what the Church has always taught—what the apostles most assuredly taught.

"It is no superstition to say that Christ gives himself to us in the sacraments," he states, unwilling to yield.

Karlstadt presses on, ignoring his words. "Again, I say, you may beat your chest and bellow at the clouds, but the thing is out of your control. The Spirit has awakened men to the truth: men who are not afraid to do what must be done. Look at me!" he demands, pounding his chest with his right palm. "I have no prince to support me as you do, and yet I am a free man, beholden to no one. It is your very safety that prevents you from risking the plunge. Thank God there are others not bound to earthly power!"

Again, the wicked implication: *You are more concerned with earthly power than the truth of God.*

"I will not accept this defamation of my character, as if I were not convinced of these things by the Word of God!" Martin asserts. "We do not hold these positions because the Elector commands it or because I have bullied anyone into it, but because they are true: the very Word of God given to us. It is not our job to question that which is above us. If we could grasp it ourselves, there would have been no need for him to send his Word down. We have received that Word gratefully as the assurance of our salvation, but you would cast men out of the nave of comfort into a great sea of doubt!"

Karlstadt makes no immediate reply. He seems to be having a very great think, his eyes squinting, his breath deep. Then his lips curl into a sly smile.

"I wonder," he whispers, his voice fading.

"You wonder what?" Martin asks, dreading the answer.

Then Karlstadt reaches in his metaphorical pocket and pulls out a knife which he will twist into Martin's belly. "I wonder what Melanchthon would say if he were here. He has been kind to me since my return—but he was always so kind, so gracious. During that period when we were often in each other's company, he would sit listening to me, and when brothers visited who held different views, he would not spout some nonsense about how it was wrong to ask questions, or that we shouldn't try to understand the things of God. He knew a man can never escape the questions. The two of us were of the same mind, but then you came swooping in like a raptor to the kill, and it was I who was left to hang alone. I wonder, Doktor—are you very sure that your boy agrees with you on all of this? Are you even sure he is your boy? Because it seems to me, he has a mind of his own."

Karlstadt has hit the sore spot—the point of greatest vulnerability—and the pain is acute. It was no cut made at random, but the skillful work of a surgeon who knows his patient inside and out.

"You only say these things to frighten me," Martin insists, his rage barely suppressed.

Karlstadt presses down on the table with one hand, leaning forward, delivering his words with relish. "But you don't need me to frighten you, do you, Doktor? You have been frightened since the beginning."

The fire within Martin is white hot—the pressure upon his skull unbearable. He can stand it no longer. With a parting shot of, "Baptize your child!" he rises to his feet and abandons their conversation, passing into the kitchen.

Draining his mug, he tosses the empty vessel in the wash basin and steps around Wolf, who is scrubbing a large pan with the full force of his body, as if he wishes it to surrender information. Martin then steps left to avoid a stack of pots on the floor, and as he does so, he feels a rush moving through his bowels, burning as it goes. *Oh no!* He hurries toward the lower entrance to the tower, where he will have access to the old abbot's privy. Slamming the door behind him, he moves to sit on the wooden bench suspended over a stinking hole. Here he has spent many an hour pondering theological truths while in excruciating pain.

He releases the contents of his bowels with a tormented cry, wincing and gritting his teeth, possessed by angst. It passes quickly—a small mercy, but it likely means there are further torments to come. Suddenly, he hears footsteps upon the floor overhead. *Someone is in my study!* He is seized with panic, cold and cruel, as he realizes not only that his private realm has been invaded, but someone has just heard him taking a shit.

Cursing under his breath, he finishes the business and races up the winding iron stair that passes through the opening in the study floor, his head still throbbing. There he sees, to his horror, that the mess on the floor is completely gone, and he hears a broom scraping across the wooden floorboards. Ducking under the hanging pages that block his view, he finds Katharina standing near his desk, sweeping the dust into a pile. As she becomes alert to his presence and stares into his eyes, he is struck to the core by a piercing arrow of shame, for she surely heard what just took place: the gruesome noises that escaped from him as he fought against his flesh. Not only that—she has gone through his things! She has seen the state in which he lives, the floor covered with dust and dirt, the windows utterly filthy, the remnants of food scattered about. His whole life is on display for her here, and in this moment, Martin Luther feels more exposed than he ever has in their bed chamber.

"What are you doing?!" he bellows, his voice as strong as a thundering herd, his spirit as weak as the falling leaves.

Katharina looks upon him with wide eyes. After a moment's hesitation, she replies, "Cleaning the floor."

"You should not be in here!" he insists.

His mind churns desperately, anger meshing with embarrassment. *Where did the stacks of books go?!* He looks to his right and sees that they have been placed back on the shelves. He rushes over, running his fingers over them, searching for any form of organization. What pleasure it has given him to arrange them just so! How it has aided him in his efforts! But there is no longer any form of organization he can discern.

"Look—you've put all my books out of order!" he complains. Then he turns to examine his desk, where the loose papers have been gathered in a neat pile. Pointing angrily, he cries, "And those papers—those are private correspondence! You have no business handling them! They could be from congregants seeking counsel."

Katharina's eyes are desperate. "Herr Doktor, I—"

"Do you not see what a breach of trust this is?!" he yells, every part of him longing to be alone—to shut out the entire world. His head is pounding. He yearns for release.

Now, Katharina breathes deeply, as if attempting to strengthen herself. "I didn't read them!" she declares. "I swear, I didn't!"

He steps toward her abruptly. "I never gave you permission to enter this room! The public rooms—those are yours. If you insist on tearing them apart, fine. I will hold my tongue. But this crosses a line!" As the torrent of shame sears him inside and out, he bellows, "You are not to interfere with my work! You are not to meddle in things I have forbidden! Do you understand?!"

She sniffs, her face contorting to hold back the tears she is unwilling to surrender. "I was just trying to help you. Please, see that!"

"I don't need your help!" he insists. "Truly, I don't. Now, leave!"

With these words, Katharina's resolve cracks. She moves backward, seeming to shrink into herself. The muscles in her chin momentarily twitch—her lips quiver and her nose scrunches. Then the waters are released from her eyes like the bursting of a dam. She gasps and drops the broom on the floor, placing both hands on her belly. She is not merely crying: her whole body is heaving, her spirit utterly destroyed. The sight of it shocks him, for he had never thought such a thing within her nature. Turning on the spot, she flees from him, rushing desperately to the door. Throwing it open, she stumbles across the threshold, not bothering to shut the thing behind her. One of the men working in the outer room steps into Martin's view, looking first at the distraught Katharina running through the sequence of open doors, then back at Martin. Perhaps sensing that silence would be safest, the man shuts the door, leaving Martin as he has longed to be: alone.

Feeling himself in something of a trance, Martin takes a seat at the desk and begins the arduous task of sorting through the papers, attempting to create some form of order with which he can work. The experiences of the past few minutes sting from head to toe. Again, he puts a hand to his temple, attempting to relieve the pressure. He sits there breathing heavily, shaken to the core. *I must move on. I must get to work,* he thinks, turning back to the stack of papers, attempting to make sense of it.

But after a moment or two of shuffling them back and forth, he realizes he is not paying attention. The cries of lament that escaped his wife's lips, the way she looked at him with fear in her eyes—his attempts to escape them are entirely in vain.

You hurt her, Martin. You hurt her deeply. What have you done?!

Giving up on his task, he instead takes a blank sheet of parchment from the drawer and prepares his pen to write. *It was her fault. She should not have been in here!* He hacks at the quill with his pen knife, utterly failing to shape it to his desires. *Was I really angry at her, or was I angry at Karlstadt, or was I angry at the whole world?* The questions come fast and furious. His efforts to repress the shame—to justify his own actions—are failing miserably. *I was angry at myself.* He places a trembling finger on the thing that terrifies him: *I repulse her.*

The pen appears ready for work. He dips it in the well, then holds it motionless in midair, the nib hovering over the page, a single drop of ink falling softly. He cannot bring himself to write. His insides are screaming—the wells of his eyes filled to overflowing. His skull pulses with the pain. *Käthe! Käthe!* He drops the pen and holds his face in his hands, overwhelmed by sorrow. How many times has Bugenhagen told him? *You must get control of your temper, Martin.* Too late—much too late!

He has struck the one he swore to defend—wounded her deeply. The pressure built until he exploded, and now he is left with the shattered remnants of his hopes. *I must talk to her. I must make things right.* But the accusing voice speaks to him: *She does not want to talk to you. She is afraid of you—and she should be. Who could ever love a creature as disgusting as you?*

"Shut up!" he cries. "Shut up, damn it!"

But he is helpless to stem the tide. He gives way to tears, the frustration of the past month seeping from his eyes. And in this moment, finally hidden from the world, he burns.

Autumn

1 September 1525
Basel, Swiss Confederation

Dusk has fallen over Basel and the mills have ceased their daily work as Erasmus of Rotterdam crosses the lone bridge spanning the Rhine. He makes for the home of Bonifacius Amerbach nestled beside the Carthusian monastery, there to attend a supper held in his honor. The newer portion of the city—"Little Basel" as it is often called—was not a location previously sought out by the city's rich and powerful, but the relentless turning of time's wheel has brought the most daring to the one place within the walls where they are likely to find room to breathe. Little Basel may now be the most desired patch of ground on either side of the river, but there is nothing there to tempt Erasmus, save for the prospect of a supper free of the machinations of the radicals.

"Come, Erasmus! I will grant you an eve of peace: an eve such as you used to have every eve," Amerbach had pledged, desperate to entice him.

"To which portion of my life do you refer?" he retorted. "When I was dreadful sick in England, when I was hounded by wolves in Louvain, or when I was scrounging for coin in Venice?"

"There will be no need to fear," Amerbach assured him. "I will invite the best sort of people: men who have not succumbed to the excesses of Wittenberg or Paris. You will be allowed to speak freely."

He snorted loudly. "It will be a small party, then."

Having made his way to the far side of the river, Erasmus walks for a short spell past a high wall covered in draping vines, behind which the roofs of the Carthusian buildings are only just visible in the fading light. Reaching the square, he turns left and finds a house three stories high, its walls the typical cream color of so many in Basel, its shutters painted a brilliant green. A double door stands ready to receive him into the home of Bonifacius Amerbach, its oak panels painted with the family's device: a basilisk clutching the shield of Basel in its beak. He strives mightily to convince himself that he wishes to enter, for his young friend means well enough, but not all that means well ends well.

Just do it. There is nothing for it, he urges himself.

Before he can knock, the door is opened to him, and Amerbach pops his head round, motioning for Erasmus to enter. A blast of pungent air wafts from the house, infusing Erasmus's nostrils with the scent of garlic. His stomach lurches.

"What on earth are you cooking in there?" he inquires of his host.

"An Italian recipe!" Amerbach proclaims, smiling broadly. "I had hoped the smell might draw you inside."

"It is having the opposite effect," Erasmus grouses, covering his nose with his hand.

"Oh—pity," the younger man mutters, his mouth drooping. "I'm afraid my long absence has led me to forget one or two of your proclivities."

"Do you possess the fruit of Burgundy?" Erasmus asks hopefully.

"Of course! That I did remember, friend. We are well stocked."

"Good," he declares, finally crossing the threshold. "I need not eat. Just place the pitcher as close to me as possible."

Erasmus is led into a dining room about twenty feet square, the walls covered in linenfold paneling and the white plaster ceiling molded with images of grapevines twisted into a wide oval. There is a fire in the tiled hearth—the table is laid with burning tapers and vases full of the season's last roses. At the head sits Bishop Christof von Utenheim, recently returned from his summer residence. Seated on the far side of the table are Ludwig Baer, professor of theology at the university and Erasmus' chief counselor on all matters divine, along with Nicolaus Episcopius, a graduate of the university now working as a proofreader for Froben. Seated next to the bishop on the other side of the table is Hans Lützelburger, a craftsman of some renown who produces the best woodcuts in the city, often in collaboration with Erasmus' friend, Hans Holbein.

"The man of the hour is here!" Amerbach declares, placing a hand on Erasmus' shoulder. "Let's show him that a pleasant evening in Basel is still possible."

All four of the seated men smile, nod, or otherwise indicate their appreciation for the sentiment as Amerbach takes his place at the foot of the table. Erasmus sits in the lone empty chair, lowering his aching frame onto a velvet cushion. He places a hand on his belly, commanding it, *Be still!* The host then yells through the open door behind him, "Bring out the food!"

There will be no need for the beautifully painted plate in front of Erasmus, nor the silver fork which he guesses has been laid out in line with the evening's Italian theme. There is only one thing to cancel out the overpowering odor—a single remedy for the churning of his bowels.

"Burgundy," he whispers, lifting the metal pitcher and pouring wine into the glass beaker before him. "Do your work."

The first glass provides little relief. The guests are all conversing on various topics—the work being done at the town hall, the clogging of the Birsig with refuse, the tendency of students at the university to neglect their assigned reading—but Erasmus remains decidedly taciturn, waiting for the second glass to perform its magic. Slowly, he feels his balance returning, whether due to the wine or Amerbach's order for the windows to be opened, he cannot say.

While filling his beaker for the third time, he addresses the man seated on his left. "How goes your business?"

Lützelburger is somewhere between thirty and forty years of age, his face clean shaven and his hair black as ink. Looking up from his plate, he turns his smallish eyes upon Erasmus and speaks from a pair of thin lips. "It could be better. Holbein was my best artist, but now he's gone to England, as you are more than aware."

"Ah," mutters Erasmus, feeling a bit awkward, as he was the one who encouraged Holbein to seek out commissions across the Channel. "I am sorry to hear it. Your work together was superb."

"Now I am left trying to find someone to help me complete the Dance of Death!" Lützelburger moans.

As Erasmus takes a long drink from his beaker, he observes what an odd statement this would seem to an ignorant listener, for Lützelburger refers not to his own passing into the underworld, but a series of prints he has produced depicting scenes from the city's famous mural.

"Nothing sells in this city like the dance," the woodcutter laments. "Death may be bad for humanity, but it is good for business!"

"Perhaps very soon, I will be able to relate my own experience of the dance, though I will need a necromancer to accomplish it," Erasmus notes ruefully. "More and more, the decay sets in. Do not be surprised to hear of my passing."

"Is it the theologians who have brought you low?" Lützelburger asks, his brow furrowed.

Again, the questions about theology! *Good Lord! Why do I talk to people?* Erasmus asks himself for what seems the thousandth time. *More wine. I need more wine.*

By the end of the fourth glass, his whole body feels lighter. The pain in his joints melts—his tongue loosens. Soon, he is regaling them all with sayings of the ancient Greeks and Romans, anecdotes from his time in Italy, and mockery of the fools in the Roman curia. The laughter flows from his fellows as easily as the wine from the pitcher. It seems that Amerbach was right: there is still pleasure to be found in Basel if one is among friends. Then Baer asks a question that is somewhat less to his liking.

"Does Luther intend to reply to you? It would be a shame if all that work came to nothing."

Always, the theology—always! I will need another drink before answering that question, Erasmus decides, filling his beaker yet again. A few seconds later, he replies, "I think not. Luther is far too busy with his own amusements."

He remembers the sad tale of his opponent's misbehavior: the many months Luther was living in sin, casting scorn upon Erasmus while flouting God's laws himself. Erasmus thinks of his own parents, who were never allowed to marry—the pain, the ignominy. *Damn him.*

"He will reply to you," Episcopius insists. "Surely, he will! You are too great a scholar to go unanswered."

Erasmus releases a rather unseemly snort. "I assure you Luther has no regard for my skills as a theologian. He insults me in all his letters. I've seen them, you know."

"And to think that he would judge you, as if he were some great theologian!" Amerbach cries, utterly indignant. "No one would have cared about him were it not for that idiot preacher. What was his name again?"

Lützelburger is the first to answer. "Tetzel—a Dominican."[1]

"The Dominicans!" Erasmus exclaims, his every fiber offended. "Now, there's a plague upon Christendom! Do you know the story of Saint Dominic's birth? His mother received a vision in which a dog sprang from her loins, gripping a torch in its jaws. The beast ran wildly about the earth, setting all creation aflame. Naturally, she thought it the fire of the Spirit, but it has been a fire of destruction and no mistake. I've never met a Dominican who didn't wish to burn all humanity!"

As he says the words, he thinks of the torment inflicted upon Reuchlin in his autumn years—of the centuries of Dominicans who have insisted upon adherence to the principles of Aquinas,[2] forcing students to wallow in the mire of scholastic disputation, never once setting foot in the real world.

"That's a rather harsh judgment, friend," says the aged bishop, his wrinkled face morphing in disapproval.

"Not half as harsh as the Dominicans," Erasmus insists, suppressing a burp.

"I still say Luther should reply to you," Episcopius declares, striking the table with his palm. "If he is a man of honor, he will."

Like a dragon filled with flame, Erasmus fumes and spits. *Luther, Luther, Luther! When will I escape that name?! Always he haunts me! Always he steals my joy!* In an instant, he channels the fire within him and bellows without a hint of decorum.

"He is no such man, Nicolaus! That was my error. I treated him kindly when I should have gone for the throat! How can he live in

---

[1] Luther's work *The Ninety-Five Theses*, also known as the *Dispute on the Power and Efficacy of Indulgences*, was the thing that first made him famous internationally. It was written in response to the actions of the Dominican friar and indulgence seller Johann Tetzel, which Luther felt must be in violation of the Pope's wishes. However, it led Luther on a path that ended with his excommunication.

[2] Thomas Aquinas (Tommaso d'Aquino) was a Dominican friar and priest who lived in the 13th century and came to be regarded as one of the greatest theologians in the Church's history. His ideas were often defended by the Dominicans against those of John Duns Scotus and William of Ockham, both of whom belonged to the Order of St. Francis.

open violation of God's laws and pretend to act as a judge over others? Who doesn't know that he was bedding that Bora girl the whole time, battering her to the point of bleeding?! And now that they have a child so suddenly after the wedding, I suppose he has no time to respond to poor Erasmus. Well, damn him! Damn him to hell! I will not take him as my judge."

He pounds his empty beaker on the table, practically seething. The pressure of the past eight years and the heat of constant battle have produced an explosion.

Amerbach is the first to offer support. "Nor should you! The man is a hypocrite through and through, and that wife of his is a whore!"

Bishop Christof shakes his head sadly. "I pity the young lady, whether she was willing or not. She will have a lifetime of troubles."

"Yes, and mostly of his making," Erasmus argues.

Despite his anger, Erasmus is exceedingly gratified to be sitting at a table where he need not hide his true feelings—to know that there are others who see what he sees. The rest of the supper proceeds without incident. The talk is mostly of inconsequential subjects: the collection of rags for the mills, the pleasantly cool weather for such a time of year, the latest projects of the Froben print house, Amerbach's dealings with the monks next door. When the supper is complete and they have all risen from their places, Baer pulls Erasmus aside, begging his attention. As they huddle in a corner near the hearth, the others still caught up in their own discussions, Baer addresses him, speaking softly.

"Erasmus, you should be more discrete," the professor warns.

He wrinkles his nose. "How so?"

"It is unwise for you to speak thus about Luther in present company." Here Baer tilts his head toward the others.

"Why?" Erasmus demands to know, feeling rather perturbed. "Everyone here is of the old faith."

Baer breathes deeply—shuffles his feet. "Did you notice how quickly Lützelburger arrived at the name of Luther's Dominican opponent?"

Erasmus' mind flails, grasping for the moment in question. He sorts through the memories of the past two hours, most of which seem to him a great blur. "What of it?"

"Perhaps you have forgotten his other employer, but I have not," Baer explains, his face painted with concern. "He does not only make cuts for Froben. He works for Faber, and Faber is a Lutheran through and through."

Leaning his weary frame against the wall, Erasmus scowls at his fellow. "Again I ask, what of it? Holbein works for Faber as well, but he would never go in for that nonsense!"

Baer sighs, a reaction that Erasmus finds unwarranted. *I am speaking perfect sense! Why does he act as if he were speaking to a naughty child?!*

"Look, perhaps you are right," Baer concedes. "Perhaps this Lützelburger keeps an icon of the Holy Father by his bedside. But the fact remains, you must take care what you say, even around men you think are safe. If the Wittenbergers were to discover what was spoken tonight, it would be open war and no mistake."

"As if they haven't already declared war on me!" he cries, rather too loudly. "I tell you, Ludwig, I don't give a damn what they think! I yield to no man!"

Baer's nose scrunches. "You've had too much to drink."

"Don't lecture me! Leave me be!" Erasmus yells, abandoning Baer's company.

He offers a prompt farewell to the rest of the guests and their eminent host, then departs the house in a fury, his thoughts spewing forth hot and moist.

Who is he to lecture me?! I am no drunk! I am no fool!

With each step he takes, some far stabler than others, he is driven into a heat not unlike the flaming furnace of Babylon.

Always they hate me! Always they pursue me! Damn them!

He stumbles over a loose cobble and falls to the ground, scraping his hands and ripping a hole in his tunic. Now, he begins cursing wildly, releasing a string of coarsest Latin, Greek, and Dutch. Perhaps there are even a few French words included—he has little sense of what he is saying. He manages to rise to his feet and begins the walk across the bridge, but when he reaches the halfway point, he is suddenly taken ill. Pressed against the stone rail, he retches uncontrollably, but there is no release. He remains stuffed with the fruit of Burgundy.

"Good God, it hurts!" he wails, tears filling his eyes.

He stares down at the waters of the Rhine weaving their way softly around the pillars. In the light of the moon, the river is a ghostly thing, the faintest shimmer playing upon its surface, but the depths below as dark as the pit of hell.

"Cold," he whispers.

Even as he speaks the word, he can feel it seizing his body: the same sensation he experienced all those years ago. Naked, trembling, overwhelmed with despair! He had taken his final breath—he was prepared to face his going under. Then that feeble voice made strong by depth of feeling: *God loves you!* The faintest hope that maybe, somehow, God was good, and his goodness would be granted to Desiderius Erasmus.

He closes his eyes, pinching back the tears. He is still in that river—still shivering in the cold.

"Herr Erasmus!" someone calls. "Are you looking for something?"

His spirit awakened by the familiar voice, he glances toward its source: Bishop Christof walking toward him, lantern held aloft. *He will be making for his own residence across the water.* Realizing he must appear respectable, Erasmus repeats the bishop's question in his mind: *Are you looking for something?* It is a query open to multiple interpretations. The only response he can muster is to admit, "I don't know."

Christof chuckles, nearing his position. "Well, if you don't know, then I certainly don't know."

The simplicity of the old man's words and his kindly demeanor break the spell of Erasmus' anger. Now, the rush of shame comes quickly, striking him in the gut.

"I was having a memory—that's all," he says quietly, feeling thoroughly embarrassed. *He knows I am drunk. He saw how much I had. He heard what I said.*

"A pleasant memory, I hope," Christof says with a smile, placing his lantern on the rail.

Erasmus stares down into the unending black—the waters performing their icy dance. His memories could not be more unpleasant, and he carries them with him always.

"What is it, friend?" the bishops asks, regaining his attention. "You are not yourself."

Erasmus frowns. "Whatever do you mean by that? How could I be anything other than myself?"

"You seem downtrodden."

"But that is exactly me. Painfully so!"

Christof does not take kindly to the jest. His expression is stern—his gaze intense.

"Will you tell me what is wrong?" he inquires, very much implying that Erasmus ought to tell him.

No, Erasmus thinks. *It is not safe. That is the lesson of this evening: I must never say anything to anyone. I relaxed my guard unwisely. I will not do it again.*

So, he replies, "Christof, I know you mean well, but you must believe me, there is no cure for what ails me."

"Is it your body or your spirit?" the bishop asks, his brow wrinkled in confusion.

Erasmus ponders the question, then answers, "Yes."

"I see," says Christof, resting his hand on the rail. "Well, since you insist upon reticence, I can only give you a general word of comfort from the Scriptures: 'The Lord is near to the brokenhearted and saves those who are crushed in spirit.'"[3]

As Erasmus stares into his friend's eyes, he thinks of that day when he was most brokenhearted: when he read from the Scriptures with his spirit in agony, receiving not a blessing, but a curse of divine judgment.

"Tell me, Christof," he says, an edge to his voice, "is it not the case that every person in the Scriptures who encountered the Almighty was struck with terror? The angels ministered to the Son of God, but to men they seemed to float upon winds of divine judgment, which fed them like burning flames. If the Lord draws near to a man, it is not always to provide comfort."

Even as Erasmus speaks the words, he is filled with sadness. For years, he has proclaimed a God of mercy who lends grace to sinners. He has longed to believe that that grace might be lavished upon him. But always in his heart, a doubt of terrible intensity! When he has knelt to pray, he has done so in fear and trembling. That peace which men say is felt by the saints—he has never known it. His deepest fear resounds in his head: *He has rejected me.*

---

[3] Psalm 34:18.

Christof responds emphatically. "Then why did the Psalmist write that the nearness of God was his good?[4] Truly, he comes to comfort you, Erasmus! There is nothing he does not touch! The heavens and the earth are filled with his glory!"

"And yet no man may see his glory and live," he laments. "I tell you, there is nothing you can do for me! Rest is what I need: eternal rest, where I may be freed from the convulsions of this present age." He speaks the words boldly, but in his heart, he remembers what it felt like to be wrapped in the clutches of the beast, and he knows there is no escape—no place of safety to which he can flee, whether in living or dying.

"So, that's it, then?" Christof asks grumpily, crossing his arms. "You are resigned to death?"

He shakes his head despondently. "Death will come for me whether I welcome it or not. It is in its nature. There is nothing over which a man has less control than the length of his own earthly existence." Always he is crushed upon the wheel of Fate!

Christof exhales heavily, retrieving his lantern. "Very well. I will leave you to your thoughts, but mark my words: there is angst at your very core. My aged eyes can see what youths cannot. Whatever it is that torments you, do not take it to the grave! When you are ready, you know where to find me. I will be waiting, prepared to listen."

With that, the bishop departs, leaving Erasmus with no one for company—at least, no other humans. There is a dark presence lurking around him: he can feel it in his bones. Whether the very demons of hell or some spectral manifestation of his fears, Erasmus knows most assuredly that it trails him always, clinging to his form.

"I will be free of you," he whispers. "I am free, or I am nothing."

15 September 1525
Wittenberg, Electorate of Saxony

Martin Luther stands alone in the kitchen of the Black Cloister, sipping from a glass of wine. It is nearly evening: his work for the day is miraculously complete. He has ensured as much, for he has long purposed to spend time alone with his wife, though the idea of it

---

[4] Psalm 73:28.

makes him uneasy. The Karlstadts have finally gone, Andreas having published a recantation of his former views and thereby secured the Elector's permission to settle within the bounds of Electoral Saxony. This change is surely for the best, although Katharina had come to treasure the children by the end of their stay, and Anna was exceedingly grateful for another helper. So, it is only Doktor and Frau Luther in the old dormitory, along with their trusty Wolf, who keeps to himself as often as not.

Martin leans back against the wood table used for preparation, its surface now covered in flowers laid out to dry before being crushed into dye. His thoughts whir at a rapid pace. Through the window above the wash basin, he sees the garden plot Katharina has been cultivating all summer. Once a sad reminder of the Cloister's neglect, it is now bursting with life, the squashes nearing harvest time. In the distance, he sees Katharina bent over a row of lettuces, pulling the weeds that spring up between them. There is a twinge in his stomach as he thinks of all that has passed between them since they wed—most of all one specific occasion when, overcome by frustration, he treated her as she never ought to be treated.

Of course, he apologized soon after he lost his temper, admitting himself entirely at fault. She immediately forgave him: indeed, her forgiveness was so swift, so absent of negative feeling that he felt a new rush of shame. He could see in her eyes that things were not the same as they had been. Yes, she had forgiven him, but it felt very much as if there was a wall between them, and that he was the one who had caused it to be built. In the weeks since, he has often sought an opportunity to address her again—to somehow restore their communion. But try as he might, he cannot conquer his fear of rejection. She is not pregnant yet, but that is hardly surprising. They both fall into bed exhausted, speaking only those words most necessary to the functioning of the house.

As he continues watching her, waiting for her work to end so they might have a chance to converse free of distractions, he is struck by the depth of his loneliness: a yearning that consumes him from the inside out. *Lord, show me the way to her,* he prays. *How can I ever make things right?*

Suddenly, he hears footsteps in the refectory—now moving up the wooden stairs. He turns to his left and sees his colleague Justus

Jonas enter the room, cap in hand. *Wolf must have let him in,* Martin thinks. The look on Jonas' face is intensely serious: his brow wrinkled, his lips firmly set. *This can't be good.*

"Martin, do you have a moment?" Jonas asks.

He looks out the window again and sees that Katharina is still fighting with the tangled vines. "It would seem so."

Jonas looks squarely at the floor, shuffling his feet and fumbling with his cap. "I have debated whether to tell you this, but I think I cannot reasonably hold it back." Looking Martin in the eye, he explains, "I have received a letter from our ally, Johannes Œcolampadius."

Martin feels an ache in his bones, for Œcolampadius is now clearly denying the real presence of Christ in the Sacrament.[5] It is a terrible blow, for Martin had always thought well of the man, knowing him to be a good friend of Melanchthon, among other things.

"Is he an ally?" Martin inquires, feeling more sorrowful than angry. "I become less certain by the day."

"Some of his views we may question, but the man's character is unimpeachable, and he has nothing but good will toward us here," Jonas insists, leading Martin to nod in grudging agreement. "In any case, I received a letter from him earlier today, in which he relates a story told to him by Jakob Faber, the Basel printer."

"Yes, of course. I know him well."

"Faber has a woodcutter who serves him often: Lützelburger is his name. This man was recently invited to sup at the home of Bonifacius Amerbach, and Erasmus was there. Lützelburger heard things of such a character that he thought it imperative to inform his employer."

At the mention of the name Erasmus, Martin feels very much as if he were sinking—plummeting into the watery depths. Yet, he knows rumors are only that. "What kind of things did he hear? Be specific."

Jonas nods. "They spoke of you, of course. There were some who said you are no theologian and mocked you openly."

Well, that is no surprise, he reasons. *All my opponents think that.* He seeks clarification. "And was Erasmus among them?"

[5] When capitalized, this word indicates the Sacrament of the Altar, also known as the Lord's Supper, the Eucharist, or Communion.

"That he did not say, but of greater concern were some comments Erasmus made about you and Katharina."

Now Martin is sinking no longer, but positively drowning, unable to escape the crushing of his lungs, the splintering of his bones.

"Käthe?" he whispers, horrified by the thought.

"I'm afraid so," Jonas replies, his expression pained. "He said— Now, remember, Martin: I am only the messenger."

He cannot abide delay—not when it concerns his wife. "Out with it, man!"

Jonas looks deep into his eyes as friend to friend more than colleague to colleague, beseeching without words. Then he opens his mouth to speak and releases a stream of lament.

"He claimed you had committed fornication with her over many months prior to your marriage, that this resulted in a pregnancy, and that it was the reason you were forced to wed: to hide your sin. He then cursed you in the foulest terms. Lützelburger also heard your wife referred to as—"

Jonas seemingly cannot continue. He inhales swiftly, eyes moist, his whole countenance relating his sorrow. Martin, on the other hand, is burning from head to toe, his spirit worked into a frenzy, the fury barely contained within his skin and bones.

"Honestly, whatever you say cannot be worse than my suspicions," he says, attempting to prod Jonas into speech.

Taking a deep breath, Jonas responds with leaking eyes. "They called her a whore and mocked her. I am so sorry, Martin. As I said, I wasn't sure if I should tell you, but I thought you had a right to know."

Whore?! The terrible word consumes Martin, melting him like wax. His thoughts are blackened. *I have never known hate until this moment—not like this.* No charge on earth could be less just. His sense of honor is not merely offended: it is positively inflamed, a red-hot sword in his hand ready to smite the monster who would attack the woman he loves—the one he has sworn to defend with his very life.

He looks out the window again and sees Katharina gathering leeks in a basket. She had told him she would make a soup for supper. Always, she thinks of his needs. Always, she puts others before herself. *Perfection: she is absolute perfection.* He turns back to Jonas, who is wiping his cheeks.

"Well, this settles it," Martin concludes, his words a billow of smoke. "I'm going to be executed. Not for heresy though—for murder!"

Jonas' eyes widen. "Must I remind you that the Elector has forbidden you to set foot outside his territory?"

"Of course, I am not serious, although God knows he would deserve it!" Martin cries. "It is bad enough that he slanders me to everyone he meets, but now he comes after my wife, who has never caused hurt in her entire life! She is an infinitely better person than me. Only a creature of hell could speak of her thus! He treads the very angels underfoot when he slanders my wife!"

In his mind, Martin is already devising the written arrows he will fire. He longs to shred Erasmus to a pulp, transforming him into a bloody pile of skin and organs. Jonas seems to read his thoughts.

"Martin, I know you are writing your reply to him. I must beg you not to allow this to poison your rhetoric. You know in what esteem he is held by all who follow the New Learning. We cannot be seen to mistreat him. It would be disastrous."

Easy for you to say! he thinks. *It is not your wife!* He inhales and releases a blast. "Always, I am told to hold my tongue, but my enemies labor under no such constraint!"

Jonas reaches out to him—places a hand on his arm. He speaks with great conviction. "That is as it should be, for you are the better man, Martin. You must prove it to him."

"Why did you tell me all this if you didn't want me to do anything about it?" Martin inquires, uncertain how he could ever escape the anger in his breast.

"Because you are my dear friend," Jonas says softly, "and I thought it unfair to withhold the truth."

Martin looks down at the floor, exhaling loudly. *He is right. Of course, he is right.* He gazes out the window at Katharina, who has moved on to harvesting garlic. There is something fierce inside him as he watches her: a feeling so powerful, it defies comprehension.

"How can I tell her, Justus?" he whispers.

"Do you have to tell her at all?" Jonas asks. "It might not be wise."

Might not be wise?! His head snaps back—he looks upon Jonas with piercing eyes. "You have just explained that you felt compelled to tell me because of our friendship! Now, how much more ought I to share the troubles of my heart with my wife, who is dearer to me than anything on this earth?!"

Jonas swallows hard. His powerful voice is reduced to a whisper as he says, "You must love her a great deal."

These words strike Martin anew, for he senses the enormous gap—the infinite distance between the love he feels and the love he has demonstrated. *How far I am from the perfection of God!*

He shakes his head, eyes welling with tears. "That is the trouble: I do love her, Justus, but I have made a mess of everything." He hesitates, then feels compelled to emphasize the point. "I'm an utter failure as a husband."

"I'm sure that's not true!" Jonas spouts automatically.

"It is far truer than I care to admit," he insists. So troubled is his spirit, he dares to open himself up to his friend: to reveal his chief fear. "I am terrified that when she finds out who I really am—what I'm really like—she will want nothing to do with me."

"And you think she doesn't already know what you are really like?" Jonas asks, tilting his head.

Martin shakes his head, lost for answers. "I must find a way through to her if it is the last thing I do. I cannot live like this anymore."

As he speaks these words, he realizes just how much the thing has sapped him over the past few months: how the deepest recesses of his soul have been disturbed as he has tried, unsuccessfully, to overcome the fear that keeps him from his Katharina.

Jonas seems to experience a change of heart. Dropping his hand and standing up straight, he says, "Then you should tell her, but do so gently. I would hate to see her brought low."

"Pray for me, Justus," he begs, knowing his own strength will fail.

"I will," Jonas assures him, nodding. "I do."

With that, Martin's colleague departs, leaving him to consider all that has transpired. Alone in the kitchen, he closes his eyes and breathes deeply. He senses a part of himself still holding back: attempting to protect him from the full force of his emotions. *Let it go,* he bids himself. *Release it.* He begins to give way. Yes, he can feel the change in his person. It is happening now: it is all happening!

Love is flowing through him with such force that he feels robbed of breath. He has experienced at times the tightening of some muscle in his back, immovable for days, then released in a single moment in which the fluids are suddenly freed. That is how he feels in this instant: as if he has been clenching his fists for months and finally let go his grip. As he thinks of his wife, he is overwhelmed by desire—to protect her, to know her, to be one with her. He longs to shower his love upon her, filling her to the point of overflowing, until she will never have cause to doubt him or anything else again.

Are these feelings separate from the anger or one and the same with it? He can hardly tell where one starts and the other stops, for it is his immense love for his wife that causes him to despise Desiderius Erasmus with every ounce of his flesh, but it is his anger that reveals the full extent of his love for Katharina—the flesh of his flesh and bone of his bone. Her life has been nothing but one man after another letting her down, exposing her to ruin, treating her as less than a person. *And I have become the latest.* The thought of it tortures him.

She is not to blame. She has held nothing back. From the moment she gave him her hand, she has given him her all. And how has he repaid her? He has barricaded himself off for fear of her, and not without good cause, for she holds the power to destroy him. That penetrating gaze—the way it searches him out. Until this moment, he could not admit to himself just how much he belongs to her.

She must have not only the public Martin whom everyone loves or hates, but the hidden Martin that disgusts even himself—the Martin only God can abide. She must have his fears and failings. She must have him body and soul! *Will she want that?* He cannot be certain, and that is the risk. Whatever game he has been playing the past few months is over, for he must place all he is on the altar and hope and pray that he receives it back. He longs for her acceptance like a man who has wandered forty years in the desert and finally glimpses water.

In his mind, a single plea: *Do you love me as I am?*

Then, in an instant, a change comes. His heart is racing, but not with romantic passion. Every muscle within him tenses—his lungs begin to ache. *No! Lord Jesus, no!* He grips his wrist tightly. *I am a child of God. I am flesh of his flesh, joined with him in baptism, raised to new life.* He feels the panic setting in, overtaking all his senses. *Away from me, devil! Get behind me!* It is not working.

He runs into the refectory, then out the door toward the foyer, galloping up the spiral staircase, taking the steps two at a time. His heart is pounding—he can hear his pulse like a beating drum. Through the Aula he goes and the smaller lecture rooms, then veers to the right and enters his bed chamber. The voice is screaming at him: *She will hate you! God hates you, you worthless piece of shit!* The pain in his chest frightens him—he cannot escape the angst. He moves to the far corner of the room and thrusts his back against the wall, the force of it rippling through his members. Then he sinks slowly until he is crouched on the floor, head held between his legs, rocking back and forth, praying for the attack to pass.

Why did I think I could do this? he asks himself. *I cannot do this!*

Then he hears the creaking of floorboards outside. The door is pushed further ajar, and Katharina strides into the room, heading straight for the wash basin. She is unaware of his presence, and he is silenced by the fear within him—unable to call out for her. He watches as she removes her dirty apron and then her gown, setting them both on the floor. Only her chemise now provides a covering for her form. She looks in the mirror, frowning at her own reflection—leans in to examine a black smudge on her chin. Filling the basin with water, she throws some on her face, scrubbing her skin vigorously. He hears her muttering something but cannot quite make it out.

Then she removes her head covering, revealing the hair knotted tightly against her head. One by one, she removes the pins holding her tresses in place until they cascade down her back. She takes the ivory comb sitting on the basin's ledge and runs it through her hair, working out a few knots, still blissfully unaware of his presence.

He pinches his eyes shut, attempting to calm his heart. *Now—I must do it now!* With the minimal strength available to him, he prays, *Lord, who made the mute to speak, grant me the words!* He gathers what he can of his shortening breath and manages to say, "Käthe."

At the sound of his voice, she jerks slightly and turns on the spot. Her eyes focus on him, and he watches the realization spread across her face, sharpening her features, causing her to gasp.

"What's wrong?!" she cries, rushing over to him, crouching down to his level. "Are you unwell?"

"Käthe," he breathes, chanting her name like a holy spell. "I need your help."

"Of course," she agrees, nodding her head. "What's wrong?"

"I am having—" he begins, but a new rush of pain causes him to halt. He grits his teeth, attempting to work through it. "I call it the terror. I have them sometimes. I can't—" Again, he is overcome.

"That's alright. You don't have to speak," she assures him, rubbing his arms. "Is it in your chest? Your limbs?"

He nods his head and wonders, *How did she know?*

"Your thoughts are filled with fear? With shame?" she inquires.

Again, he nods. He looks on her in awe, as if seeing her for the first time. Her eyes are filled with compassion.

"I know this," she concludes. "I have seen it before."

"You have?" he asks weakly.

"Yes, some of the sisters used to have them. Just breathe, my love. It will be alright."

What did she say? He repeats the words in his head. *'My love': She has never called me that before.* A rush of hope cuts through his despair. "Käthe," he whispers again, finding comfort in the repetition of her name.

"I will do for you what I would do for them," she offers.

He expects her to fetch some remedy and force it down his throat, or perhaps drag him through a long exercise of prayer and meditation for which his scattered thoughts will be entirely useless. Instead, she wraps her arms around him, drawing him close, swaddling him in her embrace. As she holds him, she breathes deeply—in and out, in and out. He finds himself automatically doing the same, his breath slowing, his muscles relaxing. The warmth of her body penetrates his chest, bidding his racing heart be still. The tension is lifting from his neck, his legs, his chest. He is utterly overwhelmed by the goodness of her embrace, which seems to him a safety beyond all others on earth. He tightens his arms around her, clinging to her form, and as he does so, he feels the wall within him—the barrier he constructed in fear—cracking and crumbling, like a city at the end of a year-long siege.

"Come," she whispers. "Let's get you up."

He calls upon the muscles in his legs, which fire with newfound ability. Placing his hands on Katharina's shoulders for balance, he rises to his feet, taking a moment to steady himself. She pulls his left arm around her for support. He doesn't truly need it, but neither does he mind. Together, they walk the two steps to the bed, and he sits on the edge, breathing deeply, staring into her eyes as she kneels before him. She resumes rubbing his legs, attempting to aid the blood that flows through him.

"How do you feel now?" she asks.

"Better, thank you," he replies honestly. "How did you know what was happening?"

"I told you: I've seen it before. We had many sisters who suffered from melancholy. How could they not, living in such a place? Often, they would come to me, filled with anxiety, longing for relief. It seemed the very devil of hell was tormenting them." She pauses for a moment, desperately searching his face. "Then the first time I met you, Herr Doktor, I sensed the same shadow hanging over you. My heart hurt to think of what you must have suffered. It was clear you had been to hell and back."

There is a new stiffening of his muscles as he realizes she has known all along. All those times he was made uncomfortable by her gaze, the many occasions when she aggravated him with the accuracy of her judgment—On some level, he always knew that she knew, or that she was very close to discovering all the flaws in his person.

"And did you think me weak then?" he inquires, afraid to know the answer. "Did you think me less than a man?" For in this moment, that is how he feels at his core.

Her brow furrows—she takes his hands in her own. "Of course not! You are the bravest man I know! I think no less of you for what you have suffered—for all that the devil has inflicted on you. It is because you are such a threat to him that he torments you so! But when did they first begin: these terrors?"

Her words grant him confidence. He feels able to share as he has not done before.

"When I was still a boy," he responds. "They would only come very rarely, but they scared me to death, and my father—he did not understand. He would taunt me. Then, when I entered the monastery, they became more frequent. I thought at one point I had overcome them. I went several years without one, although my bowels began attacking me after I received the bull. Then, when I was forced to appear before the Emperor Charles, I had the worst terror of my life. I thought I was dying right there before all the princes! The shame that I felt—the agony! People speak of it as if I were a conquering hero: a very Caesar riding in triumph. But it was only by grace that I survived. And then the Wartburg—" He chokes up, overpowered by memory. "Let us simply say it was a darkness I hope never to know again. Now these terrors come from time to time, particularly when something is troubling me."

She has witnessed his confession with tears in her eyes, leaning toward him, placing a hand on his knee. At last, she inquires, "And what is it that troubles you now, husband?"

As he sits enveloped in her compassion, he remembers his conversation with Jonas just a few minutes earlier: the blistering anger, the scorching torrent of shame.

"Oh, Käthe! Forgive me!" he begs, shaking his head in distress.

"Whatever for?" she asks.

He releases the words with great pain, shaking beneath their weight. "I have failed to protect you. Because of me, you have been subjected not only to my own ill humor, but the ridicule of the forces of evil, and you will be made to suffer that for as long as you live. How can I ever forgive myself?!"

"But I knew the world would scorn our union," she insists, placing a hand on his. "You warned me how difficult it would be."

"Yes, but I never thought it would come to this!" he cries.

"Come to what?" she inquires, pulling back.

"Erasmus of Rotterdam, the great scholar in Basel—"

Her brows scrunch. "The one who wrote that terrible book?"

"Don't tell me you read it."

"Ha!" she cries. "Even if my Latin were good enough, I would know better than to waste my time on him!"

This comment catches him entirely by surprise, filling him with intense pleasure. *It would not be possible for me to be any more in love with her,* he thinks, and he finds that his heart is racing again, only this time for a different reason.

"We have heard from a friend in Basel," he explains. "Erasmus has been spreading lies about us, claiming you were pregnant when we wed. I cannot tell you how angry this makes me! To think that he would say a word against you! He is no man, but a fiend—a very eel of the devil!"

She pats his hand gently. "You need not be angry on my account, husband."

"I am absolutely furious on your account!"

Katharina shakes her head. "This Erasmus does not care about me. What am I to him? It is you, Doktor! You are the one he attacks with these slanders!"

"That is bad enough, but that he should bring you into it—how it eats at my soul!" he cries.

Katharina considers the matter for a moment, her expression thoughtful. She reaches a conclusion. "Well, it is clear what you must do."

"Will you tell me to turn the other cheek like Jonas did?" he asks weakly. It would be very like her to make such a gracious reply, but in his heart, he longs to know that she sees things as he does—that they are united in spirit and purpose.

Then, suddenly, she releases a cry of indignation: "Certainly not!"

"No?" he asks, utterly bewildered.

Katharina crosses her arms, exhaling in annoyance. "When our Lord commanded turning the cheek, he was not speaking of men who habitually assault servants of God. If you do nothing, it will only encourage him! He spreads these lies because he believes you are weak. He has no respect for you as a theologian or a man. Otherwise, he would never risk it. That is not your fault, Herr Doktor. You ought to have earned his respect many times over with everything you have done. But since he is fool enough to slander you, there is only one solution: you must make him fear you. You must respond to him so thoroughly, so perfectly, so unflinchingly that it puts the fear of God in him! You must take his argument and pound it into the ground under the sheer weight of the truth. That is the only way to deal with such a man. By the time you are done with him, he must be so completely humbled that he will never dare cross you again. Make him fear you, husband. It is the only way."

Well, I was wrong, he decides. *It was possible for me to be more in love with her.* He shakes his head in amazement as he realizes that everything about her—her experiences, her knowledge, her personality—seems to have been miraculously designed to complement him. *It could only be the Lord's doing,* he thinks. *Surely, this is a gift of God.*

"You think it can be accomplished?" he asks, leaning closer to her.

"Well, I certainly couldn't do it, nor I think could most scholars, but you can do it, husband. I know you can! You have written things far greater than this: words that set my heart aflame."

He thinks, *Why on earth have I not talked to her like this before? Why ever did I cut myself off from this?* The wall within him gives way like the fortress of Jericho, and he is captured—yes, absolutely compelled to speak. So, he does, placing his faith in the demonstration of her character and the declaration of her affection for him.

"Käthe, I am not just the man who wrote those words, and stood before the emperor, and defied the pope, and debated with giants, and become a byword to princes. I am also something else: something terrible. I am a man who can't take a shit without immense pain—who is frightened of the dark and tormented by devils. I am a man who stood before an emperor, felt the hand of death upon him, and froze, unable to speak, long before he uttered a word. I am a man who can't look at himself in a glass without loathing himself—who dwells in stink without hint of civility. I am a man of flaws and failings, more so than even my foes would claim. And always the storm rages within, and some part of me is still back in that place: flat on my back, staring up at the heavens in terror, fearing the wrath of the Almighty.

"This is the man few see, and if they did, they would never have taken me as a leader or teacher of anything, nor I fear would you have suffered to bind yourself to me until I perish in flame or my flesh gives way to corruption. And of all the unforgivable things I have done, it is this last that torments me now, for you are the very fount of human goodness, and you seem to me the fairest thing on God's earth. I cast myself daily upon the mercy of God with nothing to offer, and I come before you now with empty hands and beg you to forgive this wretch of a man."

He ends this speech somewhat out of breath, his whole being hanging upon her response. He is caught in the undertow, waiting to be pulled to the surface: to receive from her lips the breath of life.

But her eyes are sad. She responds quietly. "Herr Doktor, you ought not speak this way."

He is seized again by fear but tells himself to trust in what he has seen and heard. "It is not fitting that a man should withhold the truth at the crucial moment," he whispers.

She takes a deep breath, even as he sits like a man waiting upon the sentence of judgment. Then she says, "Do you think I was ignorant of these things when I took your hand? I didn't join myself to you for your fame, nor would I have been frightened by this report of your struggles. For you are another man as well: a man who showed me kindness when I faced the world's scorn—who risked his reputation to help me and my sisters. You gave me a home when I had none. You listened to me when others only laughed. You are an angel of heaven to me, Martin Luther, even if you be tormented by devils, and for all the good you have done me, and for everything good that you are, I will love you as long as I live. And when we have passed through the gate of death and find ourselves in that great assembly of the saints, I will rejoice to see you freed of your burdens, and I will love you then as well. That is the man you are to me: the one who showed me the grace of God, not only in word, but in deed—the man who captivates me daily with both his mind and his heart."

How blessed are these words! Infinitely pleasant is the outpouring of her heart!

"You are too good—far too good for me," he replies, completely besotted. "It frightens me, yet I desire this gift with all my being."

She holds his face in her hands, his skin burning beneath her touch.

"That is the grace of God," she tells him. "I delight to be yours. I love you truly—wholly."

"And I you. Forgive me, my Käthe. I should have told you from the beginning."

She runs her fingers through his hair, stroking it gently. He feels the sensation trickle down his neck, cascading along his spine. It is a bellows upon the fire within him that burns for her unceasingly.

"Be still," she whispers, pressing her soft lips against his forehead. "Quiet your spirit."

"No," he replies, staring desperately into her eyes. "I have been quieting it for far too long. It is filled with a righteous flame. Do you know of what I speak?"

She drops her hands. To his immense delight, she is blushing deeply. "Yes," she breathes. "I feel it too."

He places his right hand behind her head, drawing her face close. Her pupils widen and her breath catches as he declares, "I love you, my beautiful one."

With these words, he kisses her with complete abandon. Immediately, he feels it is different than before: a meeting of persons in full acceptance and without fear. He caresses her lips, drinking in her sweetness. As much as he gives, he takes, and as much as he takes, he gives, for they are exploring each other's mouths, finding mutual enjoyment in every inch of flesh, uniting body and soul. Her breath comes hard and fast, even as his own: there is a music to the exchange. Their lips part, and he stares in wonder upon her face. *I am my beloved's, and my beloved is mine.* With one finger, he traces the outline of her chin—tucks a lock of hair behind her ear. She closes her eyes and exhales. He kisses her neck, her cheeks, her mouth. He has long since forgotten what day it is, or indeed if there was ever another day of his life, for it seems he is born anew.

Then she takes hold of his fingers, calloused and stained with ink, and kisses them one by one as if they were holy relics, treasuring and cherishing them. She stares into his eyes with her irises of hazel which would lay him bare, but he is no longer afraid, for he sees within them the same fire that resides in himself. Then together—so wonderfully together—they pass a night which he will treasure all his days.

When he awakes the next morning, it is fully dawn. *Could I have slept so long?* He hears a dove cooing, perched just outside his window. *Has it always done that at this hour?* He has never stopped to listen, always too busy lecturing or preaching. Truly, a sacred hour!

I have slept a sleep fit for angels, he muses.

He turns on his side and glimpses the source of his delight: this amazing gift of God. She is still asleep, breathing softly. Her shoulder can just be seen above the sheet. She is curled up slightly as she tends to be in slumber, contracting by instinct against the cold of the air. *What a strange wonder it is to wake next to such a creature!*

He chooses in this moment to do something he has never done before. Instead of rising to begin the work of the day—work that will take him to a thousand worthy places, but never with her—he remains where he is, residing in the bliss. He allows, for one moment, the world to go about its business of writing and printing and grumbling and disputing. He moves over and embraces his wife, shielding her from the cold, breathing as one with her, rejoicing just to be alive together.

Directly in front of his eyes is her hair. So absurd is the idea of Brother Martin waking up next to this sight that he struggles to stifle a laugh, only to be seized with his next breath—utterly seized by the memory of her words. *I watched as my hair fell to the floor. I was weeping—shaking violently. I looked at myself in the mirror and didn't recognize what I had become. I was no longer a woman.*

As her words run through his mind, he sees not merely hair but a glorious fall of red. No, not exactly red: deep brown that glows red in the light of day, as the golden trees of autumn in all their perfection. It is a thing of beauty created by God. He feels a sudden urge to bury his face in it and smell it, as if by doing so he could absorb all she is. *She is so utterly a woman—so completely the image of Eve.* And she is his, the pride of his heart, and he is hers to have and to hold, in living and dying and everything in between. She stirs slightly—breathes in deeply. As she turns toward him, he sees her lovely face, and it smiles at him.

"Good morning, Herr Doktor."

"Good morning, my lord Käthe."

"Lord Käthe?" she responds, her smile morphing into a smirk.

"That's right. You have conquered me thoroughly."

She laughs. "So, this is to be my new title then?"

"If you are on your best behavior."

"Ha!" she exclaims but refuses to be drawn. "'My lord Käthe.' I like it. No, I love it!" Then her expression becomes more serious. She whispers, "But most of all, I love being your Käthe."

"That is the best of it," he replies, kissing her softly.

She nestles her head against his chest, and placing her hand in his, begins to sing, the music of her voice sweet beyond even the cooing of the dove. The words are his, written in a darker hour, but the music itself is God's. He joins his voice to hers, and they begin to harmonize, the notes weaving back and forth around each other, crafting a beauty never achievable alone. The words pour forth like the summer rain to replenish and revive. It is the tale of Christ and his Bride.

> "To me He spoke: Hold fast to Me,
> I am your rock and castle;
> Your ransom I Myself will be,
> For you I strive and wrestle;
> For I am with you, I am yours,
> And evermore you shall be Mine;
> The foe shall not divide us."[6]

16 October 1525
Wittenberg, Electorate of Saxony

Philipp Melanchthon departs the New College building of the Leucorea, a bag slung over his aching shoulder. In frustration, he moves it to the other side. This grants little relief, for the slant of that shoulder has never been ideal for the purpose. He must raise it continually, tensing his muscles, tightening the flesh against his spine. His nerves and sinews cry out in objection. *Perhaps I will drop the bag at home before my walk,* he muses, for this has become his habit of late: in the late afternoon, he departs the city gates and strolls along the Elbe, attempting to locate some hidden wisdom in its waters.

As he nears Colleges Street, he comes upon his colleague, Justus Jonas, like him departing the university buildings for the day. *I must speak with him,* Philipp realizes. For the past few weeks, Martin has been furiously writing his reply to Erasmus' diatribe *On Free Will,* and as Martin's usual translator, Jonas might have a tale or two to tell.

"Justus!" Philipp calls. "Have you seen Martin's latest draft—the one for Erasmus?"

Jonas halts, examining him with weary eyes. "He's making good progress now. He sends me pages faster than I can translate them."

---

[6] Martin Luther, "*Nun freut euch, lieben Christen g'mein,*" Trans. Richard Massle, public domain. https://hymnary.org/text/dear_christians_one_and_all_rejoice_with.

"And how do you find it, Jonas?" he asks, working to steady his voice, for he must not reveal the desperation behind his inquiry.

"I find it to be an excellent reply that cuts to the heart of the matter," Jonas replies curtly, making to depart.

"I would like to read it before it is published," Philipp adds. "Perhaps I could offer some suggestions."

Jonas turns on the spot, his frown bordering on a scowl. "Is this your reply or Martin's?"

"He promised me he would be respectful," Philipp explains, unable to account for his colleague's annoyance.

"Then what are you afraid of?"

"Erasmus was perfectly reasonable in his argument—entirely civil," he asserts, bidding himself remain calm. "We ought to respond in kind, even if we disagree with his conclusions."

His colleague sighs and rubs his forehead. "There are more things in this world than even you know, Philipp Melanchthon." With this, Jonas forsakes his company.

Philipp stands in place for a moment, thoroughly befuddled by their interaction. *What on earth was that about? What did he mean—'There are things you don't know'?* The students are coming and going, passing him as if nothing is amiss, but something is very wrong in Philipp Melanchthon's world. *My request wasn't unreasonable. Why would he respond so?* Having felt a degree of confidence since his reconciliation with Martin back in June, Philipp now wonders if he has understood the situation correctly.

Feeling very much off kilter, he makes his way into the street and drops his bag at the house, continuing east toward the Elster Gate. This is not the most direct route to the river, but it is the quickest path out of the city walls—the swiftest freedom from the rage of the theologians. As he passes through the gate, paying his respects to the guard, Philipp's thoughts cascade into darkness. Try as he might, he cannot escape the feeling that he is on the outside looking in: that he is not strong enough for the task ahead, and the whole world is, in some way, set against him.

While Karlstadt was residing in the Black Cloister, Philipp did all he could to avoid him. Every time he happened to see Karlstadt in the street or at Sunday services, it awakened the old pains. His failures, the rejections, the disappointments—it felt as fresh as the first day, as if he were still living in that time when Wittenberg was a spinning chaos. What fear it provoked in his bones! So, Philipp welcomed his former colleague's departure, but he has still been forced to write a denunciation of Karlstadt's views on the Sacrament, a task he has accepted without relish. *Will I ever be free of the past?* he wonders.

He comes to the break in the road. Walking right would bring him to the river: his usual path. To the left is the Sacred Fire, which is to say, the slaughter ground and fire pit. It was on that cursed ground that they burned Pope Leo's bull, but it is not the sort of place where one would wish to spend much time: not if one has a nose and eyes. It is hard to imagine a site where the primary purpose—indeed the very appearance—is further removed from its sentimental value.

He squints, focusing on the distant smoke that rises to meet blue sky above. There could be nothing to draw him that way—nothing warranting a trip into hell on earth. And yet, he finds himself turning toward it, as if driven by some primordial force.

Why am I doing this? he asks himself. *Could it be Fate...God... the devil?* He cannot say, but he senses he must proceed.

Moving swiftly, he comes to the land of bare dirt stretching for several acres. There is nothing of life here, save for the animals trapped in their wooden pens, waiting for their blood to be spilt. Avoiding them, Philipp moves in the direction of the pit: a burning expanse about twenty yards across filled with remnants of Wittenberg life. Here, old rags are turned into ash and broken boxes into flaming embers. Darkest black is that pit, save for the orange flames that move in channels across the pile, carving their way through wood and dung, consuming all in their path. Gray smoke rises in curling streams. The cracking, the sparks, the noxious odor filling his nostrils! *The very scent of Beelzebub.* Philipp covers his nose with the sleeve of his robe—strives to breathe in this place of the dead.

Here is a vision of hell.

The smoke parts for a moment, and Philipp sees on the far side of the pit a man with a cloth pulled over his mouth and nose. He prods at the embers with a long iron poker, shifting the rubbish this way and that, his apron and gloves covered in soot. The man's name is Matthias: he and his family are scavengers who live in a hut about half a mile outside the walls. Long ago, they were set the task of collecting Wittenberg's rubbish and dragging it to this location, there to set it alight. On account of their profession, they are outcasts who mostly keep to themselves, though Matthias has been lured to the church on occasion to hear Martin preach. Bugenhagen makes efforts to incorporate the family into the life of the congregation, but he struggles to undo the hostility and disdain built up over multiple generations.

Perhaps the Lord wishes me to speak with him, Philipp reasons.

He makes his way round the pit, coughing as he goes, until he is close to Matthias' position. The scavenger looks up from his work and exposes the bottom half of his face, which is notably lighter in color.

"What on earth are you doing here, Professor?" Matthias asks.

Philipp shrugs, the irritation building in his throat. "Walking aids my thoughts."

"You don't have enough of those already?" Matthias jokes, causing himself to chuckle. It is a harsh sound, rasping and straining.

"Good point," Philipp admits. When Matthias recovers from the coughing fit, Philipp says, "We'd like to see you in town more. You are missed."

"Now, don't lie!" Matthias cries, shaking his head in amusement. "No one wants to see this face, Professor. It looks just like my pa's face, and they didn't want to see that one neither. Give them the creeps, we do! Because we're the burners, we are! They send us what they don't want—what they can't bear to see, you see?" Here he chuckles again. "People want to forget. 'Burn it!' they say. Well, I've burnt a lot of things, Professor—a lot of things. They say one day the whole world will be burned!" He points at Philipp with a gloved hand, his eyes growing large. "You're one of those theological types. You must know about that. All I know is, burning can't destroy memories. Take it from an old burner! Maybe the eternal fire can do that, but not any flame of this earth."

With this, Matthias restores the cloth to its place and resumes prodding the fire, digging deep into the blackened layers, sending the sparks flying. Philipp is filled with memory—he speaks from the outpouring of his soul.

"In ancient Jerusalem, there was a valley called Gehenna. They would burn the refuse there—the remnants of the animals. It is said that sometimes they even burned their children. Always, the smoke would rise—always the smell. The worm never died. The fire was never quenched." He ends this speech with moist eyes, the thought of it tearing at his soul.

Matthias ceases his work, looking at Philipp oddly. "Are you making some sort of point, Professor? Because I'm pretty thick. You'll have to pound it in." Here he taps his head for effect.

"If I have a point, I've yet to find it," Philipp admits.

"I remember when you all came out here to burn the pope's letter. Oh, that must have put him in a right state!" Here Matthias giggles, wheezing with the effort. "I think it gave you a lot of trouble."

"Yes, it turns out you are right," Philipp admits, staring back into the flames. "Even fire can't destroy certain things, much as we may wish it."

Matthias resumes his work, moving the trash this way and that, his lungs heaving with the effort. "You have to prod it, see," he instructs. "That's the key. Keep everything burning nice and even."

"I know," Philipp whispers, the words carrying far more meaning than Matthias could possibly comprehend.

Philipp stares into the fiery pit, his spirit trembling, the memories pressing upon the bounds of his brain.

Where on earth have you been?!

The image before him blurs, giving way to a scene from his past: a day that is branded upon the sinews of his consciousness. He was eight years old, and the town of Bretten had only recently emerged from the siege of the Swabian League. The people and buildings alike had been broken—it would be years before they were properly remade. His father, Georg, was suffering the effects of poisoning, his bowels scorched and bleeding, his groans echoing through the old house as he endured his catharsis. Perhaps it was because of these things that no one seemed to notice what was happening to Philipp.

They thought nothing when he kept to himself, becoming suddenly taciturn. He appeared no more sorrowful than most of the townspeople. Yet, in his silence, he was screaming, the victim of ongoing torture, for every time he left the safe confines of his home, he would run into them: the boys who made his life a living hell.

Always they taunted him, mocking his appearance, demeaning him to his face. And for every word they shouted, he knew there were others the boys would whisper in the dark, imagining the tricks they would play on him—the pleasure they would take in his pain.

Philipp never told his mother, for how could he add to her burden? He sought merely to endure. Yes, always to endure. Then came the day he broke.

As he made his way home from the baker's stall, a loaf tucked under his arm, he encountered the three boys in an alley. They had hidden in wait for his appearance, then leapt into view just in time, their larger frames towering above like the fearsome pillars of the deep. They were a year or two older than him, and thus they thought themselves wise.

"What's wrong, Crookback?" the first one asked, grinning savagely.

"Yeah, Crookback!" a second yelled, kicking Philipp in the shin.

"Did your ma drop you when you were a babe?" the third inquired in the tone one would use with an infant, his lips pressed into a pout.

Philipp clutched the bread tightly. "Sssss—sssss—" he stuttered.

"What's that?" the first boy asked, placing a hand to his ear. "I can't hear you, Crookback."

"Stop it!" Philipp managed to yell.

"Did he say he wants us to kick him again?" the third boy asked.

"That's what I heard," confirmed the second boy.

"No!" Philipp cried desperately. "Sssss—"

The second boy began assaulting Philipp with his foot, striking his knees and belly, causing him to drop the loaf. "Fight back, Crookback!" the boy taunted. "Fight back!"

"Too afraid to fight? Little baby Crookback!" the third boy mocked, laughing cruelly.

The barrage of kicks momentarily ceased, and Philipp stooped to recover the bread. Rising again to his full height, he proclaimed, "I'm not afraid!" But even to him, the words seemed weak. He could hardly raise his volume above a whisper.

"Really?" the first boy asked incredulously. "Because you look afraid, or is your face just messed up like that?" Here he pointed squarely at Philipp's nose, crinkling his own features in disgust.

"His face was always messed up!" the second boy claimed. "Too many punches."

"Yeah, what happened to your nose?" the third demanded to know.

The first boy bent down in mockery of Philipp's height. "Maybe all dwarves have ugly noses."

Now the other two boys also stooped, and the three of them began lumbering in a circle, singing, "Little bitty scared Crookback! Crookback! Crookback!"

So great was Philipp's shame, he felt sick to his stomach. *Something—I must do something!*

And so, very much against his better judgment, he cried, "I told you: I'm not afraid! I can prove it to you!"

The boys ended their taunting dance and stared at him so forcefully, it caused Philipp to shiver.

"I think you're going to have to," the first boy said devilishly.

Oh, no. What have I done? Philipp thought, gulping hard.

"You think you're as brave as us?" the third boy demanded to know, stepping closer.

"Yes," Philipp whispered.

The first boy crossed his arms and declared, "Alright. If you're so brave, meet us in the square at midday tomorrow. We'll see what you're really made of."

As he spoke the words, his fellows both looked at him knowingly, breaking into mischievous smiles. Philipp noted it, but so desperate was he to demonstrate his courage—to be accepted by his peers—that he instantly agreed to their proposition.

"I'll prove it," Philipp assured them. "You'll see!"

"Midday tomorrow!" the second boy cried as the group turned to leave.

"If you don't show up, we'll know you're a coward!" the third yelled over his shoulder.

Philipp passed that night in uneasy slumber. He knew whatever challenge his tormenters intended to place before him was likely to be humiliating, but he felt he had no choice. *I can't keep living like this. I must do something to get them off my back!*

So, the following day just before noon, he put on his shoes and cap and made to leave the house. He was about to cross the threshold when his mother asked, "Philipp, where are you going?"

A ripple of fear surged through his body. *I can't tell her the truth,* he reasoned. *She'll forbid me to go. They'll call me a coward!* Ever the honest boy, he lied to his mother. "I want to see the neighbor's new dog."

"I told you: no one goes out today," she replied firmly.

She had commanded it, sure enough, but Philipp had forgotten in his eagerness to prove his worth. *Why doesn't she want me to go out?* He could not recall a reason being mentioned.

"I'll be back really quick!" he insisted, unable to make sense of the prohibition.

"No exceptions!" she cried, eyes wide, voice strained. "You are to stay here, and that's final."

But Barbara Schwarzerdt was not God Almighty—she lacked his power of sight.[7] Within minutes, she was detained, tending once again to the needs of her husband. Philipp stood in the foyer of their home, staring at the door through which a bleeding Landsknecht had stumbled only a few months earlier.[8] A part of him recoiled, unwilling to cross into the realm of iniquity. Yet, he also knew the consequences of failing to appear: he would only ever be known as Crookback the Stutterer. He placed his hand on the latch—pulled the door open with anxious fingers. Then he stepped onto the cobbles beyond, sensing as he did so that it was a momentous thing. When he returned to the house, he would not be the same.

As he began walking toward the market square, Philipp was joined by many of his fellow townspeople, all moving in the same direction, as if some unnatural force were drawing them hence. The cold of late autumn licked at Philipp's neck—he grasped his arms to still the trembling. The closer he came to the square, the thicker the crowd became, but the people were oddly silent, speaking only in hushed voices. *Something is wrong. Maybe I should go back,* he reasoned, but he feared a pummeling from his tormentors more than a scolding from his mother.

He arrived in a square packed with people from edge to edge. Some were clearly farmers come in from the fields, while others were dressed rather grandly—perhaps officials from the court in Heidelberg. As Philipp's eyes searched desperately for the group of three boys, one of them grabbed his shoulder from behind and spun

---

[7] Schwarzerdt is Philipp Melanchthon's original family surname, Melanchthon being a Greek translation of the same.

[8] A Landsknecht was a German mercenary fighter common during this period.

him round. Looking up slowly, Philipp found a pair of dark eyes glaring at him with the force of cannon balls.

"There you are!" the boy cried. "You certainly took your time in coming! Feeling scared, are we?"

"No!" Philipp insisted. "I came, just like you asked. Now, what must I do?"

All three boys grinned broadly, flashing their crooked teeth.

"Just enjoy the show," the second boy told him. "Go up to the front so you get a good view."

"A good view of what?" Philipp asked, his pulse racing.

The boy snickered. "You'll see."

With that, Philipp made his way forward timidly, threading his way between bodies, becoming one with the stinking mass of humanity. When he had moved several yards, he looked behind him, where he assumed he would see the three boys—except they had not followed him. *Maybe I need go no further,* he reasoned.

But now, a sudden change. The low buzz of conversation became a deafening roar, and all at once the crowd pressed forward as a single body, pushing Philipp ever further. He began to panic: his lungs strove with the air, desperately gasping for more. Then with a great thud, he collided with a wall of wood—well, not a wall, as it turned out, but a scaffold hastily erected in front of the town hall. *Oh, no!* Philipp's eyes grew larger than ripe apples as he was crushed beneath an avalanche of realization. Two stakes were set up on the scaffold, and as he looked to the right, he saw a massive pile of wood. The crowd pressed in on all sides of the platform, eager to get the best view.

Immediately, Philipp turned to flee, pressing against the plump bellies of the men behind him. But there were more people behind them, and still others behind those. One of the men cried, "Watch it, you little shit!" and the other struck Philipp over the head, at which point he surrendered to his fate. No sooner had he given up, than the crowd parted in the middle and a procession of dignitaries began passing. Some were lawyers carrying books—others were churchmen with their heads bent in prayer. Last of all came a man in magnificent robes with a shining crucifix round his neck and a great pointed hat on his head. *A bishop!* People reached out to touch the holy man, begging for his intercession. While the rest of the important men had moved off to the left, out of Philipp's line of sight, the bishop ascended the steps to the scaffold and turned to face the crowd with his hands folded.

Then drums began sounding in rhythm, their owners beating them to a pulp. Blood rushed through Philipp's veins with a tremulous force. The crowd let out a deafening roar as a new procession, less glorious than the first, began.

They were women—or at least Philipp thought so on account of their petite size—but their heads were roughly shaven, a few tufts of hair clinging on in places and blood seeping from their scalps. Each wore only a tattered undergarment—their bodies were covered in bruises, scrapes, and dirt. The sight of them was like a shot of molten ore through Philipp's innards. One woman lacked the use of her feet, so she was dragged across the ground by two soldiers who gripped her beneath the arms. The others were prodded forward at the end of spears, their eyes shot with blood, their heads bowed as people threw all manner of food scraps at them: moldy bread, wilted lettuce, meat gone rancid and filled with maggots.

Are these the same people I see every day? Philipp wondered as he witnessed the hatred of the crowd. *The ones who kneel so peacefully in church, whispering their prayers?*

As he looked into the eyes of the helpless women, he could not believe that they were guilty of any heinous crime. There were five in all, and four were weeping: crying out for mercy from a crowd prepared to give them none. So hoarse were their voices and so loud the curses from the crowd, Philipp could barely make out their pleas. One of the women met his gaze, her eyes pooling with desperation. "Have mercy!" she called. "I am no witch!" And Philipp felt a pity such as he had never known, overwhelming his senses, the dread fulminating within him.

The fifth woman was bolder that the others, returning curse for curse. When a man dared to reach for her breasts, she clutched his hand and bit down hard, provoking a shriek of pain. This earned the woman a few pokes from the soldiers, who yelled, "Move along, witch! You'll work your sorcery no more!"

For just a moment, Philipp stared up at the sky above. So distant it was, yet perfectly blue—a purity of color without hint of blemish. How he wished to fly there! To escape what his eyes were seeing upon the earth: the evils performed under the sun.

Once all five women were herded up the steps, the crowd swiftly collapsed on itself, pushing Philipp back against the scaffold. One by one, the soldiers stripped the women of their measly garments, exposing their flesh to the unkind air. It was the first time Philipp had seen a grown woman naked, save for his near relatives, and it filled him with fear, as if he were at fault for looking upon their forms, though he had not chosen to do so and took no pleasure in it. The women were chained by the wrists—three on one stake and two on the other—with their arms held high above their heads. Then they were wrapped about with chains so tight they cried in pain. Last of all, the wood was brought forth and piled up to their torsos. All this Philipp was forced to watch, feeling very much as if he had swallowed a consuming worm, so great was the distress in his bowels.

The bishop strode forward with a leaf of vellum in his hands, which turned out to be the official sentence of death. In a loud voice, he proclaimed, "Thus says the Lord: 'You shall not allow a sorceress to live.'[9] These women have been convicted of the most heinous crime of witchcraft! When they ought to have loved their neighbors, they cursed them! When they ought to have offered themselves body and soul to God, they surrendered themselves instead to the devil! Only at our peril would we allow such women to live among us. We will do as the Lord commands. Those who kindle strange fire will themselves be kindled!"

Philipp's spirit sunk at this pronouncement. *Aren't men of the Church meant to show mercy?* Nothing seemed as it should be. The people were cheering when they ought to have been weeping. They clapped and hooted as the bishop rolled up the decree and clutched it in one hand. He then began a new speech in which he said to the crowd, "I beseech you not to pray for these witches, for most assuredly their souls belong to the devil whom they served in life, and it is the Lord's will that they should go down—"

"Suck my taint, you bastard!" one of the women cried.

The crowd gasped in unison as the bishop spun around, his vestments whipping like a whirlwind. He glared at the woman who had made the remark: the same who had so recently bitten a man.

---

[9] Ezekiel 22:18.

"Since your tongue is useful only for cursing," he cried, "it must be cut out!"

This provoked the biggest roar yet, with several of the men loudly shouting their approval. One of the soldiers stepped forward, his knife drawn. Philipp pinched his eyes shut, unwilling to look upon such a horrific act, but he could still hear it: a howl of pain escaped the woman's throat as her flesh was rent, and it seemed in its agony to be as sharp as any blade. This brought immense delight to those assembled, though Philipp could not imagine why. He had never witnessed such cruelty, even in the dark days of the siege. *These are my neighbors—the people I live with every day. I never knew they were like this!* When he finally dared to open his eyes, the soldier was displaying the severed flesh for the crowd. The woman, for her part, could only gurgle, the blood flowing down her chin. The bishop raised his crucifix high, displaying it for each woman to see.

"In the name of Christ, begone!" he cried as the women wept. "There is none who will speak for you now!"

With this, the bishop moved out of sight, and two men emerged with flames born at the end of great sticks of iron. As the piles were set alight, those at the front of the crowd pounded the scaffold with glee. "Burn! Burn! Burn!" The men continued to prod the flames with pokers, stoking them to the point of conflagration. Slowly, the fire sprang fully to life, consuming all in its path, creeping further up the pile. Philipp wanted so badly to believe it was all a nightmare—that this could not be the life he was living nor the earth which God had created. And yet, the fire burned, the flames licking higher, the smoke rising to the sky. Before Philipp truly realized what was happening, he was weeping, his whole body shaking. No one could hear his howls of sorrow: no one could see that he was there, too small to be recognized, too unimportant to have any say in what was occurring.

One of the condemned women cried, "Have mercy on me! Lord Jesus, have mercy on me!" The other women joined her to the extent that they could, seeming to draw strength from one another. In time, their prayers were overtaken by something else: terrible noises issuing from the deepest chasms of their soul. The fire had reached their feet, and they were wailing with the pain. It was a ghastly, sickening sound, like nothing Philipp had heard before—beyond the ability of human language to relate. For there is a pain that knows no language of men but can only be spoken in groans of the underworld: the tortured vernacular of those who reside in the depths.

Then Philipp smelled something rather like burning meat, and he realized to his horror that it was the scent of human flesh surrendering to the flames. Pulverized by terror and disgust in equal measure, he looked away just in time to spew the contents of his stomach on the man directly behind him. This accomplished what his cries could not: it caused the man to move backward, which in turn forced others to shift, and still others beyond them. *This is it—my only chance!* Philipp burst through the brief opening, claiming each yard of progress with a Herculean effort.

When he reached a point where he could go no further, he dropped to the ground, crawling forward on his belly, moving between the legs of several astounded men. It was a miserable task, groping and shifting, dragging his body through piss and slop, the grooves of the cobbles pressing against his ribs. His muscles were stiff with fear, but somehow, he pressed forward, praying, "Ave Maria!", again and again. When at last he cleared the final set of legs and was able to stand to his full height, he took off running as fast as he could, cutting down an alleyway, refusing to look back.

When he reached the end of the alley and turned the corner, he nearly collided with an old man, who upon witnessing his great hurry, reached out and held him by the shirt. Unable in his frightened state to interpret this as anything but an attack, Philipp screamed with all his might, completely given over to terror. The man began shushing him, placing one hand on each of Philipp's shoulders.

"What is it, lad?" he asked. "What's got you spooked?"

Philipp looked into the man's cataract-infested eyes. His wrinkled brow seemed somehow menacing—his missing teeth almost demonic. Philipp shrieked again, breaking free of the man's grasp, rushing for his home in desperation. There he entered without announcing himself and slammed the door behind him, only to be greeted immediately by his mother, who exclaimed, "Philipp! Where on earth have you been?!"

Far too terrified to speak, he clung to his mother, burying his face in her chest as he wept uncontrollably, the trauma releasing itself as a river of lament. So intense was his sorrow, his mother put off scolding him and urged him, "Breathe, Philipp! Breathe!" She stroked his hair gently, struggling to assuage his grief, but it was no good. In the end, she was forced to drag Philipp over to the couch and lie there with him for several minutes, wrapping her body around him, waiting for the storm to pass. "Breathe, Philipp. Just breathe." Finally, he regained enough of his composure to sit up—though as he did so, he felt the terror filling him again, threatening to retake control.

"Philipp," his mother said softly, massaging his back, "did you go to the market just now?"

So terribly hot was his shame! He closed his eyes, a new flow of tears releasing as he nodded his head in the affirmative.

"Why did you go out when I told you not to?" his mother asked. "Don't you know I only say these things for your good?"

"Yes, mother," he whispered, still unable to look her in the eye.

"You aren't ready to see things like that—in fact, no one is."

Slowly, Philipp met her gaze and asked the question that was on his heart. "Then why do they do it? Why do they burn people?"

His mother sighed knowingly, brushing the damp hair from his forehead. "Because the world is not what it should be, son: not anywhere close to what it should be. But why did you go? This is so unlike you!"

Philipp flinched at the sound of her rebuke. His eyes focused on the floor.

"Because I wanted people to know I'm bbbb—that I'm brave," he answered, his voice halting.

"What people?"

"Just people."

Philipp's mother took hold of his face, directing it toward herself. "It's not those boys who torment you, is it?"

He could do nothing but nod in acknowledgment.

"Oh, Philipp! Those boys are not your friends!" his mother insisted. "They're the worst sort of brutes! Pay them no heed."

"Easy for you to say," he mumbled.

"What was that?" his mother asked pointedly, crossing her arms.

"It's easy for you to say that: you're all grown up. You can—" His voice caught—he stammered for a few seconds.

"Take your time, love," his mother encouraged him.

He nodded and tried again. "You can ignore people if you want to, but I doooo—I don't have a choice. I have to see them all the time!"

His mother inhaled deeply, placing an arm around his shoulders. "Philipp, you do not have to prove your bravery to anyone, and especially not those boys. Do you understand me?" When he did not reply, she repeated, "Philipp, do you understand me?"

"But I'm not brave," he argued. "I'm not strong like the other boys."

"There are many forms of bravery, son."

"Like what?"

"Like refusing to do something you know is wrong just to win approval from others," she said, a fierce determination in her voice. "Refusing to seek the approval of those who do not mean well! Do you know how your father got his burns?"

Philipp thought of the awful marks upon his father's hands and arms. They had been there as long as he could remember. He had never questioned their existence. After all, many people in the town had burns, and his father worked with hot metal. But now his mother told him something that shocked him to the core.

"He was just beginning as an armorer, but he was the brightest of them all. The other apprentices were jealous of his talent. One day, out of spite, they pushed him forward into the pot of boiling liquid." Here his mother's voice caught—her tears began to flow. "He was scalded so badly, they nearly despaired of his life, but the Lord sustained him. He went on to become a great man: the bravest man I know."

Philipp's heart ached to think of what his father suffered. *He was bullied too! They hated him before me!* Yet, the contrast between his father and himself could not be clearer. His father had never sought the approval of brutes, but that was exactly what Philipp had done. *I am a coward.*

"So, you don't think I'm brave either," he concluded sadly.

"No, I didn't mean—" Here his mother stopped to sigh, her eyes searching the room as if it might surrender an answer. "Philipp, do you remember your first day at the school? There was another little boy who was scared. You went up to him and made him feel welcome. Do you remember that?"

"That's not brave," he asserted, his spirit still trembling. "Anyone can do that."

"But no one else did. You were the only one who saw him and felt compassion for him—who was willing to take the risk and speak to a stranger. You associated with him without thought of the cost. Then here at home, when your sisters fight, you help them make peace with each other. Do you know how extraordinary it is that you would do that at your age? You are such an extraordinary boy!"

Philipp hung his head. "Only you and papa think that."

"No, that's not true! Many people value you. They know you're the smartest boy in town and kind to everyone you meet."

"They think I'm weird," Philipp moaned, the pain of judgment searing him internally. "They laugh at me! They make fun of me because I'm small and my back and nose are crooked."

"Only someone with a cruel heart would make fun of those things," his mother assured him.

"When we play ball in the street, none of the other boys want me on their team. They think I'm not tough enough."

"What they think is their business. Just make sure you don't believe it."

"And they make fun of me when I stammer! I try so hard not to, but—I don't know."

His mother drew him close to herself, holding his head against her chest so he could hear the beating of her heart. "It will get better, son. When you are older, you will go away to school, and there you will find people like you: people who value your gifts."

"What gifts?" he asked, thoroughly unconvinced.

His mother held his face in her hands and spoke to him with the certainty of a prophet of old.

"Your intelligence, your wisdom beyond your years, your kind and patient heart. You were born in the wrong place, Philipp. People in Bretten don't care much about books, so they don't understand what a gift you are to them and what a gift you will be to the world. The very gifts the world needs most are the ones it tends to refuse. Trust in the Lord, my son, and he will direct your path. And next time those boys attempt to strike at you, run the other way. There is no shame in that! When all is said and done, they will be forgotten, but you will remain, my son. You will remain."

The words resound in the adult Philipp's mind as he takes his leave of the fire pit, for Matthias was right: there are some things even flames cannot destroy. For years, he strove to believe what his mother told him. He searched for a place where he could find acceptance—where his gifts would be valued. He did not seek to gain approval at the expense of his own dignity, nor did he cower in the face of persecution. Then, when his moment came—when Luther was gone and everything depended on him—he was given cause to doubt. As he treads through the dirt and grime, he wonders if the ultimate truth was not in his mother's words, but the horrors he witnessed in the marketplace. Humanity is a burning chaos held in check only by the Almighty, and if given the chance, it would chart a course of destruction to the ends of the earth, banishing all that is good and fair. Why should it be so?

All my life I prayed, 'On earth as it is in heaven,' he thinks. *Once, I thought I had an answer.*

The old questions are stirred up within him as surely as the ashes in the pit, for when he stood before the stakes that day, he doubted not only the goodness of man, but the goodness of God. Now, as he takes his place on a favorite hill overlooking the Elbe, the grass beneath his feet already half brown, he wonders if the silence will ever be broken again: if the Spirit is with them despite it all. For he has striven to see the light, but all about him seems dark.

He whispers, "On earth as it is in hell."

21 October 1525
Wittenberg, Electorate of Saxony

Martin Luther sits at the desk in his study, scratching out sentence after sentence, paragraph after paragraph, page after page. His reply to Erasmus is nearly complete: he has been working on it every night. With each word, he strikes a blow, declaring his firm belief in the sovereign power of God.

How different his labor for this book has been! Following Erasmus' example, he is using an old method of scholarly argumentation: one that has served him well throughout his years as a student and professor. Old though it may be, he has striven to breathe new life into it, and now he is reaping the rewards. He first set about dismantling Erasmus' argument, and true to his pledge, he has done so thoroughly. Only now, after weeks of work, is he finally defending his own position. The effect, he hopes, will be utterly confounding to anyone who would stand against him.

The other reason this book is different is that it is the first thing of length he has written since his marriage, which is to say it has been a rather more pleasant business. Having very much learnt his lesson, he is now taking his wife's advice—getting a proper sleep each night, eating two good meals a day, and taking a walk in the Cloister garden whenever weather permits, always with Käthe by his side.

It is not simply her company he covets. She has helped him work through his thoughts in a way he has never previously enjoyed. Often during their afternoon stroll, he will describe the point he hopes to make that evening. Sometimes she will simply listen. At others, she offers a thought or two—not the exalted arguments of a scholar, but the practical concerns of a Christian. That is of great interest to him, for he can think of no issue more pertinent to the Christian life than whether man can achieve his own salvation.

Having thoroughly repented of his previous overreaction, he has welcomed Käthe into his tower domain under certain conditions: if he is at work, she remains as silent as possible, and if she must move things, she attempts to put them back in the same order. She has learned his system of organization, waiting until he is busy lecturing to clean up the previous night's mess. She always knocks before entering with food or drink, and she always embraces him before departing.

So anxious is he to have her near that she sometimes sits on the floor of the study knitting, peeling vegetables, or simply perusing a book. He encourages her to read as many of the volumes as she can, and she is devouring them as one would expect for a person so long starved. More than once, she has fallen asleep on the floor waiting for him to finish. When he finally blows out the candles, he takes her in his arms and moves her to their bed, where he lies beside her, kissing her gently and whispering, "Good night, my Käthe."

Now, as he sits alone in his study, eagerly awaiting a supper he has been smelling for the previous hour—the scent of garlic, onions, and rosemary is captivating—he marvels at how much these changes have aided his work. His thoughts seem more ordered than usual. The clean floors have somehow cleansed his brain. Occasionally, he does find himself distracted, thinking of what he intends to do with Katharina once the day's work is complete, but then he reminds himself there will be no time for such endeavors if he does not make progress, and his pen begins scratching again.

He dips the quill in ink and grants Erasmus a sentence more straightforward in character than anything the Dutchman has produced: "For my own part, I frankly confess that even if it were possible, I should not wish to have free choice given to me, or to have anything left in my own hands by which I might strive toward salvation."[10] He smiles as he writes it, thinking of how deeply it will annoy its recipient. *If only you could experience what I have experienced,* he thinks, *but you never will, for you are a fool indeed, whereas I am a fool redeemed.*

There is a light rain falling: each drop makes a tinkling sound as it collides with the thick glass window before him. *Many years I have sat here pondering the truths of Scripture. So much the Lord has shown me in this place!* It was grace that found him in those hours of darkness and grace that brought him out of his grave. Even this year, he has experienced the grace of God in the form of a woman. There are still uncertainties. If they cannot have a child, it will confirm the doubts many have about their union. Of course, if they do have a child, the same people will claim the babe is the Antichrist—a demon spawn heralding the end of the world. The danger is real, but he trusts in the grace that has brought him this far. Again, he sets his pen to parchment, arguing for the superiority of grace over any work of man.

> "For whatever work might be accomplished, there would always remain an anxious doubt whether it pleased God or whether he required something more, as the experience of all self-justifiers proves, and as I myself learned to my bitter cost through so many years. But now, since God has taken my salvation out of my hands into his, making it depend on his choice and not mine, and has promised to save me, not by my own work or exertion but by his grace and mercy, I am assured and certain both that he is faithful and will not lie to me, and also that he is too great and powerful for any demons or any adversities to be able to break him or to snatch me from him."[11]

---

[10] Martin Luther, *De Servo Arbitrio* (On Bound Will), trans. and ed. Philip S. Watson in *Luther and Erasmus: Free Will and Salvation*, ed. E. Gordon Rupp and Philip S. Watson (Philadelphia: The Westminster Press, 1969), 328.

[11] Ibid., 329.

He is interrupted by a knock at the door and a request in his wife's voice. "Herr Doktor, may I come in?"

He chuckles softly, for though he has told her she need not use his title every time, she objects that she has always used it, and to change now would seem a dishonorable thing. He therefore chooses to respond in kind.

"Yes, Frau Doktorin," he replies with particular eagerness, for she has come to tell him that supper is ready, and his stomach has been pulsing for the past half hour.

She enters the room clothed in her plain work dress with a white apron and matching head scarf. In the waning light, he can just see a trace of flour on her cheek.

"Husband," she says matter-of-factly, "if you are granting me this title so easily, without attending a single lecture, then I must conclude that the standards at the Leucorea are slipping."

"On the contrary, you receive far more lectures from me each week than any of my students," he concludes with a grin.

She seems to consider for a moment, then stands a bit straighter, her mouth breaking into a brilliant smile. "You're right. I do deserve it."

She laughs merrily, then her eyes grow large as she observes the number of pages hung from the lines—so many, in fact, that Martin has begun laying the new ones out on the floor.

"Oh, husband," she breathes, "look what you've done!"

His heart swells with pride—there is a warmth in his chest, filtering through his arms. *Am I proud of what I have done, or proud that she appreciates it?* He isn't sure, but it feels very good in any case.

She steps gingerly around the rows of parchment, staring down at them in wonder, then reaches for those hanging above and allows her fingers to pass over them lightly, as if she were a child grasping at leaves. Turning, she notices a stack of pages piled on the desk, just to his left.

"Is that all for the book as well?" she asks in amazement.

"Yes, the ones that Jonas has returned," he says, placing his palm on top of the pile. "I'm afraid it will be far longer than Erasmus' little pamphlet, but I'll remind you, you did tell me to pound it into him without relent."

"That I did," she acknowledges, stepping toward him with a smile on her face. "Do you mind if I look at them?"

He motions for her to proceed, and she begins lifting the pages one by one with her left hand, even as she rubs his back with her right, releasing the tension from hours of bending forward.

"I wish my knowledge of Latin was better," she laments. "It has been many years since I received any proper training. They didn't think we would need to read theology."

"Jonas will make an excellent translation," he assures her, placing his arm around her waist. "He's better at that sort of thing than me."

She reaches a page that causes her some confusion: her brow wrinkles. "You've made a mistake, husband."

"What? Where?" he asks.

She points with one finger while holding the previous pages in the others. "Just here: You've accidentally written a sentence in German. 'That is too much.' You wrote that in our language."

"Ah," he responds, grinning. "That wasn't a mistake."

Katharina looks at him pointedly. "Does he speak German?"

"He claims he doesn't," Martin responds, taking the pages from her hand and placing them back on top of the pile, "and yet he has been living in the German lands for years, and he manages to read anything in our language he wishes to know. It is only when he seeks to deny that he makes the claim of ignorance."

With this, he pulls her into his arms, sitting her on his lap. It is so natural, as if she has always belonged there.

"Might he take objection to it?" she asks, her mind still preoccupied.

"I'll be honest with you, dear," he whispers close to her ear. "I don't care."

Her face breaks into a mischievous smile as he kisses her on the cheek. Then, for some reason he cannot discern, Katharina breaks away, suddenly restless. She begins pacing back and forth, staring up at the drying pages.

"I can see how much this means to you," she concludes, turning to face him. "It is everything you've been preaching."

There is a deep pang within him as he nods in agreement. "It is the center, the heart, the critical point: the difference between a man forever enslaved to anxiety and a man set free to live for righteousness. Käthe, you know me well enough now. If there is anything—yes, anything at all—that I must do to obtain the grace of God, then I am lost! The eternal condemnation of the Law awaits me: the fires of hell are my desert. Not only that, but I am damned even on this earth to live forever as a beast that eats itself, constantly waging war in my spirit—devoured by shame, driven into darkness, never knowing the love of God." He breathes deeply, overcome by the powerful memory of his many years of despair. "And I fear that is where Erasmus is, caught forever upon his own sword, bent upon self-destruction. Why else would he say the things he does, as if none of this matters?"

The words begin to burst from his lungs, fired by the eternal flame that burns within him. "Of course, it matters! It is the difference between life and death! He strives and strives, but to no end, for he refuses to strive with God. The man who refuses to wrestle with God will never rest in his embrace."

Katharina speaks softly, her eyes moist. "I pity him. How sad his life must be!"

"I would pity him more were he not seeking to make more sons of hell," Martin concludes, shaking his head in disgust. "Were he merely ignorant, I would pity him, but he is a very adversary of Christ who opposes the gospel at every turn. I thought I hated God once, but he hates him to the end, for he cannot fathom the love of God. He has never been captured by it."

His wife remains silent, nodding her head softly. He takes the most recent page he has finished and walks toward her, reaching over her head to attach it to the only empty space on the line. She turns her face away from him, staring at the fruits of his efforts. He embraces her from behind, nuzzling her softly, kissing the back of her neck.

"What are you doing, Herr Doktor?" she asks, giggling softly.

He breathes deeply—her scent fills his nostrils. "I'm rejoicing in the wife of my youth."

She turns around, looking at him skeptically. "Your youth?"

He breaks into a smile. "If you refer to the difference in age between us—"

"You are a good bit aged, dear husband."

"—then I would kindly remind you that the Lord works all things in his own timing, according to his will. Had I married you when I was a young man, you would have been only a child. Even Karlstadt might have objected."

Congratulating himself on this quip, he leans in to kiss her, but she places a hand on his chest to stop him.

"Yes, it was good of the Lord to delay our meeting until you had sufficient time to mature," she retorts.

"I would object to your statement were it not so obviously true."

"You know I only tease," she replies with a wink.

He sighs a sigh of deep contentment. "Pester me if you must, but you will not put me off. I am determined, as the poet writes, to drink deeply from my own cistern."

He looks into her eyes in love, his heart pumping with expectation. Again, he leans forward to kiss her—but again, she stops him.

"Oh really? And what else does the poet say?" she inquires, grinning a bit too broadly.

You know exactly what you are doing, you vixen! he thinks. *Well, you are going to pay!*

He leans forward and whispers into her ear the words of the ancient rhyme:

"'As a loving hind and a graceful doe,
Let her breasts satisfy you at all times;
Be exhilarated always with her love.'"[12]

He pulls back to judge her reaction. To his disappointment, she is not smiling. She looks at him seriously, her lips slightly parted, as if attempting to produce words that simply will not come.

"I thought that might provoke a response," he comments, beginning to feel worried.

Katharina gasps softly. There are tears forming in her eyes.

"Good husband!" she says, her spirit worked into a froth.

Her tone strikes him in the gut. "What is it?" he inquires desperately. "Are you alright?"

She nods softly—breathes in deeply. "It has happened. I have missed my time."

It takes him a moment to comprehend what she has just told him. *Her time? What time?* Then he quickly realizes, *Oh, that time! She has missed that time!*

---

[12] Proverbs 5:19.

"You have?" he blurts, not wishing to misunderstand.

She smiles and nods her head, the tears coating her cheeks. "Since I arrived in Wittenberg, my time always comes at the proper hour. I can depend on it. But now, it has failed to come. I am with child!"

How these words seize him! He feels himself caught up to the third heaven, so great is his joy. *A child! We are having a child!* One breath, two breaths, three breaths—he struggles to take it all in. *She is pregnant. My love is pregnant!* Everything within him pulses with life, awakened by prospects that leave him dizzy.

He pulls her head against his chest, and they weep together as he exclaims, "Oh, Lord God in heaven, how can this be?! How could such a miracle happen to me?"

She pulls back, wiping the tears from her cheeks and laughing softly. "I think we both know how this miracle has occurred."

"Even so—I am to be a father?" he asks, still adjusting to the idea.

"Yes," she replies, her face transcendent with joy, "and what is just as strange, I am to be a mother."

"Infinitely strange is this thing to me," he breathes, shaking his head in amazement, "yet I feel a joy such as I have seldom known. My love—oh, my love! My Käthe!" he cries, cradling her face in his hands. "How precious you are to me, and how precious is the child you bear!" For the first time, he looks down at her belly. He touches it with his hand, in awe of the miracle residing within her. "I feel as if I will burst from happiness."

"Please don't, Herr Doktor. I prefer you in one piece," she jokes.

"Very well, but you will not keep me from rejoicing."

"Nor do I wish to," she says, placing her hand on top of his. "When I realized it, when I added the days—I was filled with happiness." Her expression changes, becoming more serious. "But now I find myself also afraid: afraid for all this child will face, that it will not survive, that I could lose my life, or what is even worse, I could lose you. Afraid of war and poverty. Afraid of everything."

In this moment, Martin thinks of the tumult of the previous year: the threats posed by the new radicals, the invading Turks, the intransigent magisterium in Rome. *Will my child live in a world I would recognize?* The tension seizes him in his neck, his arms, his legs. But he knows he must be strong for his wife as she has been for him. He embraces her again, cherishing her against himself. She seems to melt into him, as if she could draw from his form the strength that will sustain her. He speaks to her tenderly.

"The promises of God are as sure now as they were before, and yet I understand your meaning. I too fear for this child, though I am also filled with hope. The fear and the hope exist side by side."

"Yes. I suppose that is what it is to be a parent," she says, her voice muffled against his chest.

"Likely so."

As he gazes down at her, he sees what people so often talk about: a kind of glow of happiness and expectation, an aura of hope sprung from the granting of life itself from on high. The sight of it stokes his breath. Overwhelmed, he whispers in awe, "Käthe, you are so beautiful. So very beautiful."

She blushes deeply, looks down for a moment, then back up into his eyes. "This is the kindness of the Lord, Herr Doktor: that this miracle has occurred not only after our hands were joined, but our hearts as well. This child has been conceived in love. It will be raised in love."

"Yes. Yes, you are right, but you are usually right."

He touches his forehead to hers. Their eyes close and noses rub.

"'The love of God does not find but creates what is pleasing to it,'" she whispers. "You wrote that."

"It was not an original idea," he admits.

"And yet it awakened hope in me."

He kisses her forehead, pressing his lips against her skin, then rests his hands on her shoulders. "That love will carry us, come what may. And you must be filled with the love of God to love me."

"I never loved another so well," she says with deep sincerity.

It is not the moment to tell a joke, but he cannot help himself. "Not even Herr Baumgartner?" he inquires.

Her eyes fill with a sudden fire. "Especially not Herr Baumgartner! Evil man to remind me of that!"

She slaps him playfully, and they both laugh. He doesn't dare admit that somewhere in a crevice of his soul, so deeply buried that he was barely aware of it, he has been worried about this very thing, for, after all, it was Baumgartner who first won her heart: a man far younger, much better looking, and from a greatly esteemed family. Yet, as he gazes into her eyes now, he knows there is no need to fear, for he shares something with her that Baumgartner could not possibly understand. *What kind of man would trade my Käthe for a girl who barely knows her right hand from her left?!* No, he need not worry about Baumgartner, nor any other man, for she is entirely devoted to him, and he to her. The knot in his soul loosens—he is free.

"I would rather have you, my Käthe, than all the riches of Croesus," he says. "Your kindness to me is great, for you have not gone after the younger men, even as Scripture says. In the end, you chose me."

She takes his hands in her own, kissing them gently. "There is still life in you, and now that life is passed to another—one that resides in me."

"God be praised for this gift!" he exclaims, shaking his head in wonder. "I can scarcely comprehend it. It is the goodness of God—the goodness of God in the land of the living."

He feels the beat of his own heart, already strained by years of cares. Another heart now beats, pumping blood through a tiny body, so fearfully frail. *How long will it live to beat?* His heart, it seems, is tied to another. *Might they beat with the same rhythm?* He could almost believe it, so bound does he feel to this child. If his heart ceased to be his own when it was bound to Katharina's, now doubly so. He thinks of what that tiny body will suffer and the trials that heart will be forced to endure. He cannot know them: that is the fear. The fear lives beside the hope. The love is tied to the suffering. The point where they meet—

"Käthe," he whispers.

"Yes. What are you thinking?" she asks, her eyes alight.

"God became a little boy."

She smiles. "Yes. Yes, he did."

"I cannot comprehend it. It overwhelms me! He entered into our suffering. He gives himself to us fully. He strives with us—for us! Could there be anything stranger?"

"Not that I can imagine," she whispers, shaking her head.

"A boy who would be crucified."

"I suppose we think less about that this time of year. It will soon be the hour of rejoicing."

"The hour of rejoicing and the hour of lament are one and the same. That is what the cross means. 'For the joy set before him.' That is the meaning of faith. That is why we struggle. He is for us, Käthe!

He struggles with us, and beside us, and for us! We are joined to a victory we could never achieve. The Son of God took on human flesh so we would not tremble alone."

She gives him a knowing look as her lips raise into a smile. "Are you planning another book, husband?"

"Oh, I don't know. I just—" For a moment, the words fail him, then he finds the clarity to say, "I must never forget this moment. I must never cease to be in awe."

"Nor I, my love," she says, clinging to him. "Nor I."

Martin breathes deeply: in and out, in and out. He spent so many years telling himself he didn't need children—indeed, thoroughly convinced that he had no desire for them. Then came a brief period when he wanted them for his parents or his wife. Only now, as he receives this news, does he realize just how desperately he has desired this for himself. Indeed, he wonders if he has always wanted children, so powerful is the longing in his heart. It seems a strange thing that after so much fear and trembling, the years of trials and failures, and the breaking and remaking of all he is, he should come at last to this most common and unforeseen moment.

"Miraculous!" he whispers. "I am overwhelmed by the miraculous now. Everything that exists is a miracle."

15 November 1525
Basel, Swiss Confederation

Desiderius Erasmus stands at the correspondence desk in his private study, his spirit in agony. For the past two weeks, he has lacked the will to answer the multitudinous queries which arrive at his door. Though he summons all the powers within himself, he is overcome by angst, for Béda has written. Long was the reply in coming! Erasmus' own letter struggled to find a courier and thus took months to work its way into Béda's grasping hands. When the answer from Paris finally arrived, it struck Erasmus like a thunderbolt, seizing him body and soul.

There is no escape. He will hound me until my dying day, which if he has his way will be rather soon!

He shifts his weight from one foot to the other, his mind distracted by the bells of St. Andreas. It is late in the evening—the hour of compline. In those monasteries that still operate, the monks are chanting their final prayers of the day before embarking on the hours of silence: the deepest darkness that falls upon earth. Again and again, the bells ring. He trembles inside. A rigor afflicts his muscles—an uncertainty leading to paralysis. And still, the bells ring.

My time is running out.

Hoping to gain some peace for his soul, he abandons his efforts at correspondence and stands before the window to the left, staring up at the brilliant stars. Breathing deeply, he begins to recite the words of compline: "The Lord Almighty grant us a peaceful night and a perfect end." But that naturally makes him think of his own end—the dread night that stretches into eternity. He attempts to suppress these thoughts, focusing instead on the confession of sin. He appeals to God as his Almighty Father, but that too troubles his spirit, for he hates the word father: it reminds him that he is fatherless. On he presses to the fourth Psalm. "Know that the Lord has set apart the godly man for himself."[13] *Utterly useless,* he thinks. *No comfort at all.*

"Into your hands I commend my spirit." A terrifying thought! "With your eyes you shall behold and see the reward of the ungodly." His stomach tightens—his bowls ache. He knows what he will find if he approaches the holy one. At least, he thinks he does, for he has felt it all his life. He comes to the prayer of Simeon: the dying wish of an old man. "Now Lord, you are releasing your bondservant to depart in peace, according to your word. For my eyes have seen your salvation—"[14]

He ceases the recitation mid-sentence. Tears are trickling from his eyes. In his mind, the skeletons are dancing, preparing to drag him into the Underworld—the abyss from which no soul returns. *A man ought to depart these days in something like peace,* he thinks, but the closer he comes to his end, the more he longs to flee from it. He feels the twin weights of age and infirmity pressing upon his form, and then there is the possibility of arrest, imprisonment, torture—or perhaps the very worst fate of all.

My time is running out.

Béda has prepared a work attacking him, and it will soon be released. Erasmus had hoped his opponent would restrict his criticisms to those writings that were most critical theologically—indeed,

---

[13] Psalm 4:3.

[14] Luke 2:29-30.

he had sought to influence him in that regard. But the delay has cost him everything: Béda completed the tirade before Erasmus was able to have a say.

"As for your suggestion that I note only those passages in your writings which have a bearing on the Christian faith, et cetera," Béda wrote, "it is now too late: what I have written I have written."[15] Line after line dripped with sarcasm and disdain. "I do not think your writings have led me astray. I only hope that those who approve of them have not been led astray, and that you have not been deluded by their extravagant praise."[16]

Erasmus' concerns about the theological faculty in Paris—that they are more committed to the old way of doing things than the truths of Scripture or basic reason—were utterly dismissed. "What you think, or once thought, of the theologians of the Sorbonne is of no great importance," Béda gloated. "The faculty will survive. Like myself, you will soon be treading the path which all human flesh must tread." Then, just to make the point clear, Béda wrote, "I hope it will lead you to eternal bliss!",[17] implying that he could not be certain of Erasmus' salvation.

We have something in common after all, Erasmus realizes, *for I too am uncertain of my salvation, only for different reasons.*

The bells have stopped ringing, but their warning resounds in Erasmus' head. Whether the breaking of the earth means the ending of all flesh or simply the ending of his, he knows there is no escape. He has been running all his life. Never has he enjoyed a moment's peace, and now he hopes to depart in peace. Impossible!

I am finished. My time is up.

He closes his eyes, breathing in the terror, fully acknowledging its presence. Too often, he has denied it—suppressed it with all his might, refusing to yield. But this night is different: this night, he has no strength left to fight. Having reached the end of himself, he is given over to desperation, and desperate men do strange things.

---

[15] "Letter 1642 - From Noël Béda," in *The Collected Works of Erasmus*, vol. 11 - Letters 1535 to 1657, trans. Alexander Dalzell (Toronto: University of Toronto Press, 1994), 368.

[16] Ibid.

[17] Ibid.

To his enemies, he would admit no such weakness. The world can never know the fear that clouds his existence. But here and now, in the privacy of his study, he can admit to himself that which he denies to others: he longs to know the love of a father.

For he is not so different from that boy who approached the altar, hoping to receive the blessing of one who grants him his name, nor has he escaped the young man who waded deep into icy waters, seeking in death's embrace the closeness he was denied in life. He received a glimmer of hope that day—the possibility that he could rest, not in the arms of death, but those of God. *A ridiculous thought!* A blistering sentimentality, not unlike his boyhood wish to "live together like a real family."

These are the things for which he has always hoped, and which life has proven absurd time and again. But tonight, with the specter of death hanging over him, he senses he has no choice: he must approach the altar again and seek the forgiveness and acceptance of a son. For years, he has been too afraid to ask the questions—to force answers from the Ancient of Days. *Are you my Father? Do you love me as I am?* Far easier not to test the one who kills and makes alive, for uncertainty is a kind of hope. But if he wants the peace of Simeon—the salvation for which he so desperately longs—he must risk the death of that hope.

He turns his back to the wall, pressing his head against it in frustration. In his uncertainty, he is at least half loved, half graced, half saved, even if that half feels like almost nothing. But to pursue the overflowing grace—the complete filling of body and soul, the union without limit or end—he must take the chance of losing it all: of discovering that he is, in fact, a soul rejected and damned. The rewards of certainty might be high, but the cost is unbearable. Few men, he suspects, would be willing to pay it—to buy certainty by the price of death. *Am I such a man?* He must find out. He must confess it all and seek absolution.

In the end, there is no great deliberation, nor does he tell anyone where he is going. He simply dons his fur coat and flat cap, entering a night both dark and cool: one in which he hopes to find that the ultimate truth is not darkness, but light. His body seems to be moving automatically—he struggles to acknowledge the reality of what is happening. He is drawn inescapably, as if his entire existence were pointed toward this moment. So strange does it feel to be given over! He treasures every beat of his heart, which increases pace along with his feet—but his fear increases as well.

It must be done. I have no choice.

Turning and twisting through the streets of Basel, he comes at last to the west front of the cathedral, its twin towers of red stone only partially visible in the scattered torchlight. *This cannot be real. I cannot be here.* And yet, his senses confirm it. To the right of the main portal is a statue of Martin of Tours, the saint who once cut his cloak in half and gave part to a beggar. The story has always struck Erasmus as odd. *Didn't Christ command you to surrender your whole cloak and nothing less? Now you both will be cold!* No one else seems to notice the absurdity. *What good is a saint too perfect to abide by the rules of logic? But no one cares about logic as long as his relics stand ready to heal them and his merits are there for the taking.*

These thoughts are interrupted: the great doors swing open before him, and a small crowd of worshippers departs for their well-earned rest. But there will be no rest for Erasmus if he returns home now, for there was none all the nights before. His insides are screaming, attempting to hold him back, but he strides through the portal by a power incomprehensible, knowing as he does so that it will result not in his physical destruction, but one more fearsome still.

The church is lit only by the candles that line either side of the nave. Their light reflects upon the arches high above him, tracing the vault lines that crisscross the ceiling. The air is heavy with incense. Every niche belongs to a saint—every cranny to a martyr. The walls and ceiling are awash with colors he can barely see, so great is the darkness. *How many times have I trodden this red tile floor? What good has it done?*

Standing just before the altar, nearly fifty yards away, is Bishop Christof von Utenheim, locked in conversation with one of his deacons. Erasmus can just see them through the doors of the elaborate choir screen: they seem to be the only persons left in the building. He takes a few steps forward, protesting internally with every cautious placement of a foot. The air feels hard against the walls of his lungs—his every fiber is piqued. *What will become of me here?*

Christof notices Erasmus and dismisses the deacon with a flick of his aged hand. *There can be no turning back now,* Erasmus realizes.

The bishop then gestures for him to approach, which he does, though he has little sense of what he is moving toward. The old man descends the few steps to the floor of the nave, still wearing his cope, though his head is unadorned. His hands are clasped together within the sleeves of his cassock, even as Erasmus' hands flex irrepressibly at his sides, the fingers curling in and out in turn. The two men meet not far from the altar.

"Brother Erasmus!" Christof greets him. "You are come after dark."

"Is there any other time?" he responds, even as he thinks to himself, *I can't believe this is happening. What has come over me?!* Whatever it is, his heart is pounding.

Christof nods thoughtfully and says, "I take your meaning, for I know what troubles your spirit."

This causes Erasmus to bristle. "You have no idea—no concept of the immensity of what troubles my spirit," he objects, the words so bitter, he practically spits them out. As the bishop raises an eyebrow, Erasmus clarifies, "This is not about Lutheran dogs or the harpies of Paris and Louvain. It is a far greater darkness."

At this, Christof's gaze seems to soften—he is visibly filled with concern. "My son, you speak as if you were tortured."

"I am tortured," he admits softly. "I have become so accustomed to torture, it is like my daily bread."

"Why have you never spoken of this?" Christof asks, his brow furrowed in consternation. Then he seems to check himself. "Forgive me. It does not matter why. Can you find the strength to speak about it now?"

Erasmus shakes his head despondently. "Many times, I have tried to tell you, but always my strength failed." He lifts his eyes to the heavens, staring at the distant images above. Angels play upon a field of gold, the paint shimmering ever so slightly in the distant candlelight.

You can trust him, Erasmus tells himself, or rather a voice in his head seems to say. *You have been brought here for this very reason.*

He looks again into Christof's ancient eyes. The bishop stands silently, waiting to receive whatever vexes Erasmus' heart. He gains a sliver of strength and tells the old man, "I have something I wish to confess."

"Then you may do so freely," the bishop replies, making a sweeping motion with his hand. "Do you wish to go to the vestry?"

"No," he says. "I would hide in the vestry. I am always hiding. It must be this way."

Why are you saying these things?! a voice protests within Erasmus' thoughts. *Have you lost your mind?!* But another voice seems to say, *Don't be afraid. You have come this far.*

"Then speak, Erasmus," the bishop encourages him. "Tell me what it is you fear."

Very well. I am committed, Erasmus decides. Taking a final breath to steel himself, he admits, "I do not know God. I never have."

A few seconds pass as the bishop scrunches his face, tilts his head, and finally inquires, "What do you mean?"

"I do not feel things as a Christian should. The sacraments grant me no peace. Prayer is like walking through a barren wilderness."

"Oh, my son!" Christof exclaims, stepping closer to him. "Nothing afflicts you that is not common to man. Many dear saints have experienced the same thing: seasons of spiritual darkness, striving without progression, doubting the goodness of God. In time, these feelings will pass. I have seen it happen for many people."

He still doesn't understand, Erasmus realizes. *I must make him understand.*

"I have been waiting for it to pass for fifty-eight years," he explains, each word coated with passion. "This is not a season, father: it is my very existence! I follow the commandments. I do all I can—everything that is in me—but I have never felt myself the subject of the grace of God."

It is the first time he has admitted this out loud, and the force of it shakes him from head to toe. He is surrendering vast swathes of territory that have been closely guarded for decades, but he must do so: he is out of options.

Christof touches his shoulder kindly. "The grace of God is a fact, son. It does not depend on your feelings. You can have done nothing so bad—"

"Can I not have?" he interrupts. "You have no idea who I am."

The bishop drops his hand, looking upon Erasmus quizzically. "You are Erasmus of Rotterdam, are you not?"

"I barely set foot in Rotterdam. I am from Gouda. That is where my father served as priest for many years."

"But surely the world knows this! His Holiness granted you the dispensation."

"I lied to His Holiness," he admits, taking no pride in the fact.

"What?!" Christof exclaims, recoiling ever so slightly. "Why?!"

"I told him my parents were betrothed until my father was forced into the priesthood—that they only sinned out of expectation. That was false. I have a brother, after all."

"A brother? You never mentioned him."

"Of course, I didn't. His name was Pieter. He is dead these many years. You see, there was never an understanding between my parents. My father was not forced into the priesthood. He chose to carry on in sin with my mother for years." Even as he speaks the words, he feels a stab of shame within his breast.

Christof nods his head slowly and stares at the floor, seemingly overwhelmed by what Erasmus has divulged. "I see. Well, one could perhaps understand why you did not wish to publicize the fact." His gaze returns to Erasmus as he concludes, "You can apologize to His Holiness. I'm certain he will show mercy."

He still does not understand, Erasmus laments. The fear seizes him in the chest, for he knows what he must confess next: the thing that fills him with more shame than any other. *Do it,* he urges himself. *You can trust him.*

So, he admits, "That is not the half of what I have done. When I went into the monastery of Steyn, I developed a strong attraction to another man."

Good Lord, I've said it! Erasmus thinks, the chill of panic setting in. *I have said it, and I cannot take it back!* He gazes upon Christof's face intently, attempting to judge the effect of this revelation. The bishop does not seem shocked, but simply confused.

"What type of attraction?" Christof asks, his brows wrinkled.

Oh God! He's going to make me spell it out. There is a strain of annoyance in Erasmus' voice as he asks, "What type do you think?"

"I did not want to assume," the bishop replies, holding up his palms to indicate his peaceful intent.

Erasmus shakes his head grimly. "Of course, you didn't. Even if you had no respect for me, you would not want to assume such a thing, and even less to hear the details. Any man would be disgusted to hear the things I've thought: the fantasies that filled my mind in those youthful days."

"Well, I am not pleased to hear it, but I won't pretend you are the only person I know with such a thing in his personal history," Christof replies, as if it is not such a great matter after all.

The words may mean little to Christof, but they are hugely significant for Erasmus. He is not as alone as he thought! There are others like him who suffer under the same burden. Of course, he has always known it—he spent time in Italy, after all—but he has never truly felt it. Yet here it is confirmed: *I am not unique.* This thing over which he has obsessed for years is not such a thing after all. *Who am I?* He ought to feel comforted, but he finds himself growing angry—yes, terribly angry!

Then comes another question from the bishop. "Did he sodomize you, or did you sodomize him?"

This is something more like the pain Erasmus expected. His lower lip quivers, but he refuses to break into tears. "He rejected me," he explains simply—deliberately. "Our friendship was broken. He thought me more accursed than the devil himself."

"Then at least you were spared from committing that sin," Christof concludes.

Erasmus shakes his head bitterly and whispers, "I committed it a thousand times in my heart."

"Even so, there is forgiveness with God," the bishop insists.

He still does not understand! Erasmus bemoans, his anger growing. *Must I repeat every detail for him? Does he not see how this tortures me?!*

"I did not stop there!" he presses on. "When I was in Paris, I visited a prostitute. I walked into the cathedral still wearing her sweat, waiting to feel the shame of a son, but it did not come. I felt nothing at all from God."

"Why do you assume you must feel something?" Christof asks again.

Erasmus can no longer bear the tension. Like the bursting of a dam, the feelings pent up for years rush forth, and he is powerless to stop them.

"Because that is the sign!" he cries, the tears finally releasing. "The children of God cannot sin in such a manner without their consciences being tortured. Even in disobedience, they know that God is their father! But I am not certain that God is my father. He seems no keener to acknowledge me than my father of the flesh. Don't you see that I'm a fraud?! I write about a God I do not know: a God who denies me the light of his countenance! He has chosen against me. How else is one to interpret the tragedy of my life? Every time I feel the light of the sun upon my face, even just for a moment, it is snatched from me, and I begin to wonder if it is worth enduring this present darkness for those few moments—the false hope of the light. Well, say something, father! Have I shocked you?!"

He has delivered this speech with a fervor that could rival any of the radicals preaching in the market square, yet Christof stands unmoved in body or spirit, his expression serene. With a voice thoroughly under control, the bishop replies, "Not in the least."

Erasmus shakes his head, utterly exasperated. "You ought to be shocked! I have worked very hard to keep these facts secret. I am regarded by many as the greatest writer in Christendom and even something of a theologian, though I am in no way worthy of the title. Did you think me guilty of heinous sin all this time?!"

Again, the bishop refuses to be drawn, but speaks to him gently. "All men are guilty of heinous sin, and although you are most august, you are still a man."

"A child of Adam and heir to his curse," he replies bitterly, feeling as if all his efforts—the revelations he has spilled like blood upon the floor—have been for nothing.

As Erasmus stands there breathing heavily, Christof makes a new inquiry. "May I ask—why do you confess this now?"

"Because I can no longer bear it," he laments, staring at the floor in disgust.

"Then why confess to me?"

"Because you are one of the few men on earth whom I can trust to be discreet."

"Maybe so, but you really ought to bring this to your prior. Unless—"

The bishop stops mid-sentence, giving way to a silence of excruciating heaviness. Erasmus looks up slowly into eyes that transfix him with their potency. "Unless what?"

"Unless he already knows," the bishop says, seeming to drop the words in horror. "Oh, my dear Erasmus! What happened to you at Steyn? Is this why you stay away?"

His eyelids flicker against the tears. The destruction is total. "I can never return—you understand."

"No, I don't understand," Christof states, shaking his head in confusion. "Have they refused you forgiveness?"

Erasmus is barely registering these words. In his mind, he is beneath that tree again, standing before Servatius, declaring all he feels, kissing his beloved's lips. But all he hears is, *You disgust me!* Forever, the words repeat. *Repent, Brother Erasmus, if you can.* Blow after blow bruising his conscience. *Beg for mercy, son of iniquity!* Stretched out upon the rack, he surrenders to the pain.

"The prior and I—He was there all those years ago," Erasmus explains. "We were brought in only a year apart."

"Have you discussed this with him?" Christof asks.

"That would be quite impossible now. Not after what took place. Not after what he said."

There it is: the dawning of full recognition. The bishop's eyes widen in horror—he lets out a stuttered gasp, as if the breath is catching in his throat. "Oh, sweet Jesus! Do you mean what I think you mean?"

"Now you see why it is impossible for me to receive absolution from that quarter," Erasmus explains, his cheeks wet with the tears. "I was damned long ago! Damned from birth for things beyond my control!"

These words seem to work a strange magic upon Christof. The muscles in his face grow taut—his gaze hardens. "And is that what you desire: absolution?"

"Of course," Erasmus replies, annoyed at the repetition.

"Then do you repent of these sins?"

"Would I be here if I did not?

"I don't know," Christof says quietly. "You say things are beyond your control. Did you choose to come here?"

How dare he?! Erasmus fumes. *How dare he make this into a game?! Can't he see what this is doing to me?!*

"Of course, I did!" he explodes. "Don't be ludicrous!"

"Are you angry with me now?" Christof inquires, his voice steady and calm.

"I just don't see why you feel a need to stretch this out when I suffer!"

"I ask you again, are you angry with me now?" the bishop repeats, placing particular emphasis on the word 'me.'

Swept into a fury, Erasmus blurts, "Don't treat me like a fool!"

The words circle through the vast chamber, bouncing off every surface. Desiderius Erasmus has snapped under the weight of inquisition, the screws tightened to the breaking point. Having been thoroughly chastened, the bishop breathes deeply—stands up straight, folds his hands.

"What would you have me do, my son?" Christof asks.

"Grant me some penance," Erasmus requests, staring down at the red tiles below him. "Assign me some prayer. Tell me what to say, and I will say it." *I must have done with this,* he thinks. *I never should have come here.*

"No," comes the response, quiet but firm.

Erasmus looks up slowly, the flame igniting within him. "No?"

"You heard me correctly," Christof assures him, completely unmoved.

"May I ask on what basis you refuse my request?" Erasmus asks, the words laced with venom.

Christof sighs. "I will not assign you penance, nor will I put words in your mouth. They would do you no good in your present state. Instead, I place a task before you. Walk this place seven times round and see what you see, then do whatever seems right to you."

The odd request catches Erasmus by surprise, momentarily dousing the fire within him. Then he realizes it may all be a ruse. "Are you laughing at me?" he demands to know.

"Far from it," the bishop promises, his tone and expression seemingly sincere.

"And if I refuse this strange request?"

"That choice is open to you, but you would never know what might have happened if you had taken my advice, and I must remind you that you came here seeking something like my advice."

Erasmus shakes his head in despair, overcome by all that has passed between them. The bishop places a hand on his shoulder.

"For what you have suffered, friend, I am truly sorry," Christof says. "I will leave you to your thoughts and come back later to see how you do."

With that, the bishop walks away, leaving Erasmus to stew in his despair. Then Christof turns back, offering words strange and new. "There may be other voices here that would speak to you if only you would turn from yourself and listen."

As soon as the bishop is out of sight, Erasmus commences an internal debate. *Should I submit to his odd request and risk further humiliation, or accept my losses and return home in the hope he never mentions this again?* Nothing about their conversation went the way he expected. He was prepared to be utterly pulverized, but instead he feels deflated. *Circle the church seven times?!* He does not believe Christof's prescription to be utterly worthless: after all, there are few persons more optimistic about the benefits of walking than Desiderius Erasmus. But his punishing confessions have drained him of life, leaving him utterly exhausted. Jericho might have surrendered to encirclement, but he struggles against a force far greater.

He has almost made up his mind to leave when, to his great surprise, he finds himself making for the southern end of the transept. Passing the font, he descends into the crypt, weaving his way behind the altar in a counterclockwise direction. There is hardly any light here, and it is so cold that he folds his arms across his chest, pulling the folds of his robe inward. His path straightens as he ascends to the Gallus Portal and begins walking along the northern side of the nave, passing chapel after chapel. *What am I meant to discover here?* he wonders. *I hear no voice but my own—always my own.*

The greatest treasures of the cathedral are locked away, only to make their appearance on high feast days, but there are plenty of adornments to be seen in the faint candlelight: a painting of John the Baptist here, a stone carving of the Apostles there. Every chapel has an altar on which sits a crucifix. Above each one is the image of a saint, some in blissful contemplation, others suffering unspeakable tortures—yet even the ones being tortured appear serene. Something within Erasmus hardens as he passes image after image, their eyes staring at him, seemingly in accusation. The contrast between himself and the saints of old could not be clearer.

He has completed one circuit and begins a second, his agitation increasing with every step. *Did Christof hope to shame me by sending me on this odd pilgrimage?* The saints gaze upon him as if to strip him bare. There is a fire in their eyes that burns him to the core. His legs are weary—his joints ache. But he is committed to what he began: he walks the unforgiving road knowing there is no hope. Try as he might, he can do no other.

It is during his fourth circuit of the cathedral that he pauses for the first time in front of an image of the Magdalene. Here are two eyes pointed not at him, but heaven. Her hands are clasped together—crimson tresses peek from beneath her veil. She is bent down on her knees, as if her very being depended on the act. He suspects those knees are rubbed raw with the effort.

No wonder the Lord deigned to appear to you, he thinks. *Your devotion was total: even I can see that. You did not hold back your love.*

He turns to continue along his way when he suddenly feels something odd, almost as if a hook had caught him by the stomach. A brief rush of excitement moves up his breastbone—the beginning of some thought. Then the words come to him: *Look at me.*

This is not the miracle that came upon the prophet Samuel, for it has all happened inside his head. Yet, he senses he is not the sole author of this thought. As he looks into the eyes of the Magdalene, he can almost imagine them focusing on him, making some plea to his soul. Of course, they are not really moving—that would be ludicrous—but he feels somehow connected to her in a way he cannot describe. Now, another thought: *I was possessed. I was overcome by demons.*

It is an odd detail of Scripture—one to which he has never given much thought—but now it seizes him, wrenching his soul in its grasp. Here is no serene woman, but one driven mad by the evil within her, biting and foaming at the mouth. Here is a woman whose whole existence was darkness: who knew nothing but the scourge of evil day after day, night after night. A woman without hope in the world, who had nothing to offer that men might esteem her. A woman who was a very enemy of Christ.

At last! he thinks. *A saint for me!* How strange that the Lord chose this woman of all women. *But she must have loved him the most, for she was forgiven the most.*

He leaves her alone and continues on his way, though he could have lingered a good deal longer, so warm was the feeling in his heart. As he begins a fifth circuit, he stops in front of an image of St. Lawrence standing with a book in hand. A deacon of the ancient church, Lawrence refused to turn over the purse when the Empire demanded it, granting the money to the poor instead, then presenting himself for martyrdom. "Nothing remotely sinful about that," Erasmus mutters. "You would make a poor banker, Lawrence, but beyond that, I find no fault in you."

No sooner has he spoken the words, then he finds himself interrupted by another thought unbidden: *When they demanded the money, I shook in terror! I doubted everything I knew. May you never suffer what I suffered! I don't know how I survived it.*

Again, the image is static: there is no sound issuing from the saint's lips. The thoughts are Erasmus', yet they are somehow unearthly. Despite the distance in years, he feels an odd communion between himself and this man, for here is one who also doubted. *Well, there's two saints who possessed something of flesh,* he concludes, resuming his walk.

He crosses to the other side of the nave and looks upon the statue of St. Maurice, a soldier of ancient Rome who refused to massacre the innocent. "Did you tremble too?" he whispers, and this time it does not surprise him when the words reveal themselves: *I killed countless men with my own hands long before I refused to kill. It was only the Lord who freed me from bloodshed.* Erasmus sighs as he realizes that, of course, it must be true. He shudders to think of how it must have felt to walk under the weight of that shame. Here is a man who understands what it means to reside in darkness—and yet, he found the light.

Erasmus' feet feel lighter now: his steps come easier despite the late hour. On his sixth circuit, he begins to view all the images differently. Coming upon the altar dedicated to St. Eustace, he gazes at the man on a tall horse with a spear in his hand and a red cloak hanging from his shoulders. Eustace was a Roman general of old—like Maurice, a man of war who came to value the shame of the cross over the fleeting glories of this life.

"I do not have your strength," Erasmus whispers. "I do not think I could sacrifice it all and live like a vagabond in the wilderness, glorifying in my humiliation."

Then the eyes of Eustace speak to him powerfully. *I was sent to Egypt in fear and trembling. I dragged my sons across a river as they gasped for breath. And I doubted God in that moment—I doubted that I had taken the right path. It was only by the divine comfort that I survived. I never felt a moment of glory.* Yes, it must be true. Erasmus is deeply moved—his breath comes forth in spurts. His entire being is quickened, and as he continues walking, he feels he is upheld by a thousand hands.

He has come to it now: the final trip around the cathedral. He pauses before a statue of St. Paul, the man whose words he has translated for hours on end, treasuring the deposit that the apostle left for the Church. He senses immediately what will come, and soon it does. The voice resounds in his head: *I spilled the blood of the saints and was an enemy of Christ. Had he not seized me, I would have died in that state.* Erasmus nods his head, pinching his eyes shut, and the tears flow freely—waters that have been stored up for long years.

Wiping his eyes, he stumbles more than walks toward an image of St. Peter, the rock on which Christ elected to build his Church. Here is a man who was truly great: the first bishop of Rome, the one from whom the popes take their authority. And yet, the voice says to him, *I forbid my Savior to go to the cross. I denied him three times. What would I be without Christ?* Erasmus' heart churns within him.

He has made it to the western end of the nave and stares at an image of the coronation of the Virgin displayed above the portal. *Here is one saint who has nothing to fear from close inspection!* he reasons. How regal she looks in her blue robe with a golden crown on her head, placed there by the Savior of the world himself! He accepts that he will find no commonality with the Queen of Heaven, but then he sees something in her eyes which he never saw there before. The voice comes. *I was so young. I was terrified.*

Just like that, he is undone. He buries his face in his hands, feeling a hundred things at once. He strives to bring order to this chaos of emotion: to find the one point in his existence that makes sense of everything else. He breathes deeply—in and out, in and out. Then he hears the voice clear and sure: *God loves you, Brother Erasmus!*

In this moment, he becomes fully aware of what was staring him in the face all along. The value of the saints is not in the supernatural, but the natural. They were not more righteous than other men and women, but equally unrighteous. *That is the point!* Not that they became something so holy as to be inhuman, but that they were thoroughly and utterly human from beginning to end.

They were embodied. They feared and trembled, stumbling and falling. They threw themselves upon the mercy of a righteous God. They are not to be valued for the holiness of their flesh, but because they ate the holy flesh as their daily bread, time and again, year after year, placing their faith in the one who offered himself to them. They are not saintly due to miracles they worked, but because God worked a miracle in them: they persevered to the end.

They kept the faith, and thus they became witnesses to the grace of God. Their witness went out to the ends of the earth, and though they are dead, they speak by faith. He does not draw hope from them because they are unlike him, but because they are entirely like him—born in sin, driven to repent, they became pilgrims on the way, struggling with God and man, keeping the faith until the end. That speaks a better word to him than all the saints' lives he has ever read. *If there was hope for them, then there is hope for me.* He treasures it as a pearl of great price. At last, he knows beyond a shadow of a doubt what he must do.

He turns to the left, looking down the length of the nave: the safe harbor for his soul. At the end is the altar, and Christof is standing before it with his hands folded. Erasmus feels that he is once again the boy at his first communion, readying himself to approach the altar, hoping that when he does so he will find acceptance.

With his wrinkled hands, he removes his heavy outer robe and sets it on the floor. He takes off his rings: the presents of gold sent to him by the great and good. He removes every article that might set him apart as something of worth, until he is standing only in his tunic, his feet bare upon the cold floor. He shivers reflexively, the chill seeping into his bones, but it is not the chill of death—something very different.

Taking a final breath for courage, he begins to move forward. *Am I walking or floating?* He cannot be certain. There is a great change in the air: the wall within him has given way. He presses on with hope in his breast, believing that when he reaches the destination, he will receive what has been promised. For the Church triumphant is with him: the saints of all the ages walk beside him, strengthening his weak hands and feeble knees. He passes through the opening in the screen and comes at length to the base of the stairs. On the first step, just a few inches above his position, Christof stands with tears in his eyes and a brilliant smile on his face.

Erasmus kneels upon the painted tiles and forms a fist with his right hand, beating his chest thrice. "Vader," he whispers, looking desperately into the bishop's eyes. "Through my fault, I have sinned. I cry out for mercy. Mercy!"

Christof places an aged hand on the crown of Erasmus' head. The warmth flows through him as if it were the very touch of God awakening him to life.

"My son," Christof says, his voice filled with determination, "I absolve you from your sins in the name of the Father, and the Son, and the Holy Spirit."

As the words enter his ears, Erasmus is utterly overcome. The burden of years has been lifted! He weeps uncontrollably, but for once, they are not tears of sorrow. Then, to his astonishment, Christof drops to his knees and captures Erasmus in a powerful embrace. They are both crying, leaning upon one another, gaining strength from the meeting of persons.

Erasmus catches his breath and declares, "They are with me, Christof. I felt them."

The bishop takes Erasmus' face in his hands and says, "See what a great cloud of witnesses the Lord has raised up to assure you of your faith! You are not alone, Erasmus. The world is a darkened wilderness in which we are all laid bare before the blinding light of the Almighty, but we have this treasure that sustains and purifies us—that enables us to go on. Believe that. Take comfort in that! If you doubt the Lord's calling, you need only look at how he has blessed you with so many spiritual gifts—how he has worked his righteousness in you, making you his instrument. The very choir of heaven, the assembly of the saints, confirms your faith and strengthens it. No, my son: you are not alone, and you never shall be."

20 December 1525
Wittenberg, Electorate of Saxony

Philipp Melanchthon sits at the desk in his study, head in his hands, the final light of day seeping through the windows on the opposite wall. It is the darkest time of year—the great departure of the sun. Lying open before him is a freshly printed copy of *On Bound Will*, Martin's response to Erasmus. For the past two days, Philipp has been poring over it with every free moment, attempting to judge how the work will be received. Despite his requests to view the material ahead of time, he was never given more than bits and pieces. Now, the full weight of it has struck him like a tumbling boulder, and he is smitten—crushed and bleeding.

He promised me, Philipp laments. *He promised he would be civil!*

Glancing again at the book, he sees not a product of tempered academic debate but an absolute hammer blow of a text: an argument of explosive power, unyielding in its vehemence, utterly rapacious in its aims. If Philipp knew no better, he would suspect Martin of instructing a naughty schoolboy rather than the most respected scholar in Christendom.

"Your thoughts about God are all too human,"[18] Martin taunts, casting Erasmus very much as a theologian of glory—which is to say, not a proper theologian at all. "For the operations of God are not childish or bourgeois or human, but divine and exceeding human grasp. But you do not seem to see that these tumults and divisions are marching through the world by the counsel and operation of God, and you are afraid lest the heavens should fall."[19]

Reading those words, Philipp feels very much as if the heavens have already fallen. It is not merely the book's insults that cause him distress. The method of argumentation is concerning enough, but there is also the substance of the argument: the stark vision that Martin provides, far bleaker than any of his previous works, or so it seems to Philipp. Erasmus had objected to the idea of a monstrous God who makes

---

[18] Matin Luther, *De Servo Arbitrio* (On Bound Will), trans. and ed. Philip S. Watson in *Luther and Erasmus: Free Will and Salvation*, ed. E. Gordon Rupp and Philip S. Watson (Philadelphia: The Westminster Press, 1969), 125.

[19] Ibid., 130.

men damnable and then damns them. Rather than seeking to reassure Erasmus of the love of God, Martin seems to revel in the tension.

> "But why that majesty of his does not remove or change this defect of our will in all men, since it is not in man's power to do so, or why he imputes this defect to man, when man cannot help having it, we have no right to inquire; and though you may do a lot of inquiring, you will never find out."[20]

The more Philipp thinks about it, the greater his consternation. The effect of these words is visceral. He has hardly eaten since reading them. Of course, he has always believed that there would be a portion of humankind damned for all eternity, and he has recognized what the Scriptures clearly reveal: man contributes nothing toward his salvation, but receives the work performed by God. The logical implications of this are clear, yet Philipp finds himself shying away from them, trembling at the thoughts that fill his mind. He knows that God is not evil, but he cannot deny that God allows for a great many things that seem monstrous.

"Consequently, how things can be good in God's sight which are evil to us only God knows, and those who see with God's eyes—that is, who have the Spirit,"[21] Martin writes. He might as well have written, "You do not understand, Erasmus, because you are not a true Christian."

He told me he wouldn't do this! Philipp cries internally. *He told me he would treat Erasmus with respect! After everything I have done for Martin, after everything that has passed between us, what could have possessed him to produce such a work?! We will lose many supporters, and we cannot afford that.*

He feels a headache coming on—presses a hand to his temple. At the far end of the desk sits the Greek grammar gifted to him by Reuchlin. He touches it with his free hand, running his fingers along the edge, feeling the grooves of the leather. *I thought the questions were finally answered. I thought my path had been confirmed.* His eyes are moist. He wipes them with both hands. *Does the dream live on?*

---

[20] Ibid., 202.

[21] Ibid., 231.

Do they remember us when we've gone? He looks down at the open volume and reads again the section that has afflicted his bowels more than any other.

> "This is the highest degree of faith, to believe him merciful when he saves so few and damns so many, and to believe him righteous when by his own will he makes us necessarily damnable, so that he seems, according to Erasmus, to delight in torments of the wretched and to be worthy of hatred rather than of love. If then, I could by any means comprehend how this God can be merciful and just who displays so much wrath and iniquity, there would be no need of faith."[22]

Philipp inhales sharply, the tears beginning to flow. Each reading wounds him anew, not only because there is now no chance of engaging with Erasmus, nor solely because he is once again doubting his relationship with Martin, but also because he is confronted with a vision of a truly fearsome God: a Lord of Hosts unleashing himself on humanity, punishing arbitrarily, more worthy of hatred than love. To rest in the embrace of such a God would certainly be the highest degree of faith. To believe in his goodness despite all evidence to the contrary is a scourge worthy of the saints of old. It was the task forced upon Abraham when he was commanded to murder his son, putting God's promise to death. In his head, Philipp hears the words of God as they were proclaimed to Moses: *I will be gracious to whom I will be gracious, and I will show compassion on whom I will show compassion.*

"And I will damn who I will damn," he whispers.

His eyes wander to a corner of the room near the hearth, where the smashed crucifix of Kahla still sits. He has had neither time nor money to repair it, and even then, what would he do with it? But as he looks at it now, it seems to him a symbol of himself: cracked and broken like a clay pot upon the floor. *Was I wrong to believe?* he wonders, for he has bet his whole existence on a vision that seems as broken as himself.

His anxious thoughts are interrupted by the arrival of his dear daughter, now three and a half years of age. She walks timidly into his study, her big blue eyes staring up at him, her lower lip projected in

[22] Ibid., 138.

something like a pout. She is clothed in a simple dress of light brown flax. Her blonde curls trail halfway down her back. Shifting his chair to face her, Philipp breathes deeply, attempting to push his fears aside and be present for his Anna. They have had several poor days in a row, the young girl fighting against her parent's instruction. Only this morning, she received a stern lecture. But as he looks at her—the very image of her mother—he is filled with compassion. She approaches him and places a small hand on his arm.

"Papa," she whispers sadly.

"Yes, love," he replies.

"Are you angry?"

He strokes her cheek with the back of his index finger. "No, Anna. I am not angry."

"You seem angry," she remarks, clearly unconvinced: her eyes are wide and despondent.

Philipp takes her by the waist and lifts her onto his lap, wrapping her in his arms. He leans down and kisses her cheek. *She is so bright already,* he thinks. *I wonder if I could provoke in her a love of Cicero?* But there will be time for that. Right now, she needs something rather different.

He speaks to her kindly, seeking to banish her fears. "The anger a father feels against his daughter is but for a moment. His love lasts a lifetime, and even when he is angry, he still loves her." He cannot be certain how much she understands, but he will keep telling her these things nonetheless, for one day she will comprehend them.

Anna looks up into his eyes and says, "I love you, papa."

Now, his heart is beating full, propelled to life by her words. He holds her tightly, pressing her form against his chest, unwilling to let her go.

"And I love you, Anna," he tells her, "more than you will ever understand, until perhaps you have children of your own."

Then comes the question that has recently become her favorite: "Why?"

He lets up his grip so she can look him in the eye—reaches for the words that will describe all this little girl means to him. "Because you are my daughter, Anna, the flesh of my flesh."

She smiles and buries her face in his robe, giggling softly. It is a rather different reaction than he would receive if he spoke the same words to an adult, but it is an entirely Anna thing to do, and he treasures it. When she has recovered herself, she asks, "Papa?"

"Yes, dear," he replies, stroking her hair.

Her tiny brow furrows and she seems to gain a wisdom beyond her years as she asks, "Will Philipp be alright?"

How deeply her question strikes him, right in the pit of the stomach! How often he has asked himself the same thing in the dark hours of the night, when all is quiet and no one is there to hear! This question is etched on his heart. It stalks him every moment. Still, young Philipp lags behind his peers. He is nearly a year outside the womb but can neither crawl nor stand. *What would I not give to know that my son will be alright?* He never feels more powerless than when he thinks of little Philipp, and yet he must grant her a reply. He reaches quickly for something—anything! The question must have an answer.

As his mind spins, a single tear falls from his eye, trickling down his cheek, settling in his beard. Anna sees it, and like a very ministering spirit of heaven, she wipes it away with her tiny fingers and whispers, "Don't cry, papa. Don't cry," even as he has done to her so many times. This alone grants him the strength to answer her query.

"I hope so, Anna," he whispers, his voice quivering. "I hope so. He is loved by God, which means he will be alright in the end, no matter what else happens."

This explanation seems to satisfy her. She sets herself on the floor, her feet pitter pattering across the wood floorboards as she makes a triumphant exit.

Perhaps it is time to join the others, Philipp reasons. *I am unlikely to gain anything sitting here.*

With a heavy heart, he rises to his feet and makes his way into the passage, descending the stairs slowly. He can hear Anna chattering excitedly in the parlor as she opens the chest containing her toys, the wooden lid squeaking on its hinges. She means to play with her dolls and likely her baby brother as well. Katharina is in the kitchen preparing something for supper: he can hear the wooden spoon scraping the side of a bowl. Much as he longs to bask in their love, his thoughts are captive to what troubles him—the book, the debate, the uncertainty. With a heavy sigh, he completes his descent and enters the parlor, where he finds his children playing in the corner and a fire crackling in the hearth. The trestle table is unfolded, ready to receive their modest meal. He sits on the frayed couch, hands clasped together, pondering Martin's words: *This is the highest degree of faith.*

It was faith that brought him to Wittenberg—faith that he soon placed in a man. Now he knows for certain that no man can ever be worthy of a person's faith, however much one attempts to keep that faith in check. God is worthy of the totality of his faith, yet he finds himself doubting. *Where is the Spirit I saw at the first? I thought it was come in our day: that God was shaking the earth once again.* Surely, the Lord is shaking the earth, but to what end? *I cannot see, Lord. I cannot see the fulfillment of the promise.*

Katharina enters, wiping her hands on a cloth. Dropping it lightly on the table, she looks at him with heavy eyes full of concern. *Do I really look so bad?* he wonders. *I suppose I must.* She approaches him swiftly, navigating the narrow confines of the room and taking her place beside him. Then gently, she takes his hand in her own, rubbing her thumb back and forth against his calloused skin.

"What's come over you, husband?" she asks quietly, presumably to keep from alarming the children.

To tell it all would take a lifetime, so he mutters, "Just thinking."

"Yes, but when you think, it is rather different than when the rest of us think," Katharina says pointedly.

He smiles at her sadly. "You of all people know that, in truth, I am no different than any other." Then his gaze moves to the infant on the floor, who is rolling back and forth happily, clutching a rattle in his hands. "How does our son do?"

Katharina sighs. "He eats well, which is a blessing."

"Anna asked me if he would be alright. I didn't know what to say."

"I'm sure whatever you said was infinitely more profound than I could have managed," she offers.

Again, she praises his intelligence and learning, but after all he has experienced the past few years, Philipp begins to wonder if it is any advantage at all. *How many books of theology have I read? How many hours have I spent poring over the Scriptures? And yet, when it comes to the most fundamental questions—when it concerns my own son—I have nothing of value to offer.*

Pained by the depths of his inadequacy, he tells her, "Sometimes your soft touch is more effective than anything else."

She looks deeply into his eyes and asks, "What is it, Philipp? Something is troubling you, and not only that."

He breathes deeply, attempting to summon the courage to reply. "Sometimes—" he begins, but his strength fails. "You will think me scandalous for saying it."

She leans in closer, wrapping her arms around him, lying her head on his shoulder. Softly, she invites, "Speak. I am listening."

Philipp stares at his children. Anna has sat little Philipp up against the toy chest and is pretending to feed him, lending herself far more amusement than her brother, who is sliding down helplessly, struggling to right himself. *Will he ever walk?* his father wonders. *Will he ever be able to do normal things?* He is pressed into an admission.

"Sometimes I wonder if God is really good," Philipp whispers so only Katharina can hear.

There is a pause in which he trembles profoundly, dreading her response. But all she says is, "I see."

"I know he is good," Philipp assures her. "I know it! But sometimes—"

His voice trails off as he watches Anna take young Philipp in her lap, attempting to interest him in one of the dolls. Katharina releases her husband and sits up straight, a twinkle in her eye.

"I cannot answer your questions, Philipp, but I will tell you a story," she explains, allowing him to glimpse her beautiful smile.

"Very well," he concedes, happy to be distracted from his thoughts of woe.

"You know the first time you came to visit our home—when mama invited you for dinner?" Katharina asks.

"Yes. How could I forget it? That was the night I met you."

She nods. "You know that Doktor Luther and Mama had spoken to one another."

Philipp is deflated by this statement. Of course, he had wondered at the time if the whole thing was arranged, but he was wise enough not to seek knowledge that could only lead to disappointment.

"I always assumed as much, though I was afraid to ask," he mutters.

"You were afraid because you thought our happiness might be the result of a plot hatched by others, and you did not want to think yourself beholden in a matter as important as this."

She's nailed me, he thinks, *and what's more, she's made me realize how prideful I am.* Ruefully, he admits, "Yes, you are right. Very astute."

But Katharina does not chide him. She grins broadly, looking as pleased as a cat who has recently feasted. "I will give you an early Christmas gift, husband: You were not there to meet me. You were there to meet my sister."

It takes him a few beats of his heart to process what she has told him, and even then, he can only exclaim, "What?!"

"My elder sister, Anna, the most beautiful and intelligent of all the Krapp siblings," she explains, as if these were established facts. "Mama was desperate to find her a good husband, and Doktor Luther was equally desperate to find you a good wife."

Philipp's brain and heart are reeling in equal measure. "Do you mean to tell me that the whole thing was set up for me to marry Anna?" he asks incredulously.

"That is what I am telling you," she assures him with a firm nod of the head.

"But I never even looked at her!" he objects, panic setting in.

"Which I'm sure would have greatly disappointed my mother if you had not formed an attachment with me," Katharina continues calmly. "When she saw that, she was happy to adjust her expectations."

"But—Anna?!" he cries, offended by the very idea of it. *But why should I feel that way?* he asks himself. After all, Anna is a wonderful person—just not the one for him. "She's a lovely woman," he stresses, not wishing to create the wrong impression, "but for God's sake, she's my sister!"

Katharina's smile reaches its maximum extent as she revels in his discomfort. "She was not your sister then!"

Philipp sighs, or rather grunts. "What I mean is, we never would have made a good match! Our sensibilities are totally opposed."

"Yes, Anna realized that too, which helped her overcome any hopes she might have had for you."

Philipp stares at the floor, shaking his head in disbelief. Then, a new and troubling thought breaks into his mind. "Wait. All this time, she thought I rejected her?"

"No, no. She understood," his wife assures him. "Don't worry about her. That is not the point I am trying to make."

"Then what point are you trying to make?" he inquires desperately. "Because I'm starting to question everything about my life."

She nudges closer to him and takes his hands in her own, her eyes beaming with love. "The point, dear Philipp, is that despite the efforts of others to control you, you made your own choice. I had spent years listening to others praise my sister while I escaped everyone's notice. Not that anyone was rude to me, but I was never one to seek attention. I was shy. She literally towered over me!"

As she says these things, Philipp sees in his wife a vulnerability—a fear of which he was not fully aware, but which is obviously deeply entrenched within her. He had never thought of Anna as more exalted or favored. Then again, particularly in those early days, he had never thought much about Anna at all. She simply wasn't Katharina.

"But you, Philipp," his wife continues with real feeling in her voice, "you were the first person to walk into a room where both of us were present and focus your attention first and foremost on me. I was flattered by it, but I feared it, for I knew the day would come when you would realize that I was not the best of the Krapp women: that I was in no way worthy of your affection."

He shakes his head violently, refusing to submit to her assessment, but she continues undaunted.

"Only, that day never came. Your love for me was genuine. I felt utterly transformed by it." Her voice breaks—she is overcome. "I have never wished anything but the best for my sister, for she has always been good to me, even as she is to everyone else. Whatever she gains in life, she deserves. But when it came to you, I was selfish: I wanted you for myself. Is that so wrong of me? Am I a terrible person?"

As he sits in wonder, listening to the words pouring from her lovely mouth, he is filled with a sense of goodness: a thing beyond deserving or description. It is a warmth in his chest—a lightness in his limbs. The lifting of gloom, the arrival of hope, the sweetness of human existence! He presses his forehead against hers, her tears brushing onto his cheeks.

"No, my love," he speaks, quieting her spirit. "My heart has always belonged to you, and you knew it from that first glance, even if some doubt remained. You didn't want to lose what we had, and neither did I. You are the goodness of God to me, Katharina."

She takes his face in her hands. "Then let that be your sign: that against all odds, the Lord brought us together, and a God who would do that is not evil, Philipp. Every time I look at you—every time I look at our children—I know that he is good, despite our difficulties and heartbreaks."

Oh, how he longs to believe her words! His heart is fired within him, and he senses that the flame is true. It is not merely his fleshly desire, but the very Spirit of God that moves him to the conclusion that the Lord is good, for he has tasted and seen. He embraces her, treasuring all that she is.

And yet, there is a darkness even in this moment—a speck of doubt obscuring his view. In his flesh, encased in his humanity, he still fears and trembles.

Then he sees something in the corner of his vision: his head swivels to meet the sight. It is his son, perched on his knees, reaching for the top of the chest. As Philipp watches in amazement, the boy grasps the lid and pulls himself upward until he is standing on two feet.

"Look what he's doing, Käthe!" Philipp cries, unable to contain his excitement. "Look what he's doing!"

Katharina turns to see her son standing up and grinning from ear to ear, his few teeth making a delightful appearance.

"Oh, God be praised!" Katharina exclaims, jumping to her feet and racing toward him. "Philipp, you are standing!"

The elder Philipp moves to join them, his heart overcome with joy. *His legs can hold him!* From the time of young Philipp's birth, there had been no certainty of this outcome, even as other children the same age were finding their feet. But now, they have the proof: at the very least, their son can stand, and most likely he will walk.

"Good job, Philipp!" young Anna tells her brother, abandoning the dolls.

Then, in an instant, little Philipp seems to grow tired. He lets up his grip and plops on his rear, exhausted by his effort but still smiling.

Katharina sweeps him into her arms, even as the elder Philipp gathers Anna to himself. The family is joined in a collective embrace.

"You did it, son," Katharina says, kissing young Philipp repeatedly on his bald head, chubby cheeks, and tiny fingers. "Mama is so proud of you."

Philipp remains quiet, too overcome for words. In his heart, he prays two words alone, but they carry an unfathomable weight: *Thank you.*

Winter

30 December 1525
Wittenberg, Electoral Saxony

It is the sixth day of Christmas: a day Martin Luther has looked to with great anticipation, for he has something special planned. This evening, he will take supper with his wife, but it will be unlike their usual meals. He hopes she will approve of what he has done, yet he feels a slight trepidation, for he has never attempted anything like it, and it must be perfect.

Only a day after she informed him she was with child, any doubt regarding her ability to count was rapidly obliterated, for she fell victim to such disturbances of her innards as are the burden of expectant mothers. For almost two months, she struggled to eat, vomiting at the slightest provocation, gagging at seemingly random smells. She was forced to decrease her workload and spend more time in bed, returning their home to something of its former squalor—which did nothing to help with the smells. He expressed his wish to suffer in her stead, but she insisted, "No, Herr Doktor! You are more necessary than me!" He doubted it with all his being, for he had been forced to endure Wolf's cooking again—food he never thought impoverished before, but now judges to be infinitely inferior.

But praise God, his wife is now recovering! Her diet is still greatly limited, but what she does eat, she manages to keep down. The joy she felt at first is returning: she speaks often of her hopes for their child. Yet, she is also filled with fears. When the Elector's chaplain, Spalatin, invited Martin to his wedding, Katharina broke into tears and begged him not to go.

"There are many who wish you ill, Doktor!" she insisted. "They may fall upon you on the road. How could I bear to lose you now?"

He wanted to dismiss this concern as the product of her bodily condition, but he remembers that earlier that year, there was a definite plot to assassinate him, and he has been lately receiving letters from the families of escaped nuns pledging to make an end of him for his crime of setting their daughters free. So, he consented to remain with his Käthe in Wittenberg. Never has he had a stronger desire to live, both for her and for his child.

Now, the days of Christmas are upon them, and he has set his mind to a new matter: procuring a gift for his wife. He understands this is something husbands tend to do, and he ought to have done it long ago. Upon their marriage, they were given many things, some more useful than others. But to his shame, he provided her with no token of his love. He is determined to make amends but has no idea what kind of gift might be expected.

If only they had taught me such things at university, he grumbles, *instead of that one additional day plodding through the Sentences.*[1]

Hoping to remedy this gap in his knowledge, he has consulted several husbands of his personal acquaintance. Bugenhagen recommended a book of sermons: "Perhaps even yours!" That, Martin felt certain, was bad advice. On one of his visits to the Lufft print house, the owner suggested a recently published tome on herbal remedies. *She could write such a book,* Martin reasoned. Ulrich the blacksmith suggested a silver cup, but they had already been inundated with those. Martin's barber, Peter, was likewise quick to recommend his own services. "I will make you look good, Doktor, and that will please her!" At which point, Martin nearly despaired of the whole endeavor.

He made one last attempt with the Cranachs, and Lucas assured him that, "Since I will be giving you both the portraits I painted, there is no need for any other gifts."

Cranach had taken their likenesses shortly after the wedding, and in the months since he had produced numerous copies—both painted and printed—to be sent across the Empire, the better the emphasize the legitimacy of their union. A special pair of paintings

---

[1] The *Sentences* of Peter Lombard (1096-1160) were the standard theological text used to teach students in late medieval universities.

had been promised for the Black Cloister: a kingly grant from the Elector's own artist. However, Lucas had rather mistaken the motivation behind Martin's inquiry.

He shook his head in annoyance. "But this must be my gift to her! The point is to show her how much I care about her."

As always, it was Barbara Cranach who had the best advice. "What brings her joy, Doktor?" she asked him. "That is what you ought to give her: something that will make her soul come alive. It must appeal to her heart, not her head."

At that point, Martin knew exactly what he must give his Käthe, and he secured the aid of both Cranachs to help him accomplish it.

The time is now come to reveal his surprise. The sun has set—the day's activities are done. Katharina has been sleeping for the past two hours, giving Wolf enough time to prepare a sumptuous feast of bone broth and bread: the two items she has been most likely to tolerate. Fortunately, Wolf also caught a hare which he has roasted along with some rosemary from the garden.

"Are you sure you want nothing more, Doktor?" Wolf asked Martin as he prepared the trenchers. "I'm sure the mistress would say we should add some winter berries."

"The mistress would add a great many things, but if she must eat simply, then we should as well," Martin concluded.

This met with Wolf's approval, and he scurried off to set the table for two, adding a bottle of wine gifted by the university. Now, Martin stands outside the door to his and Katharina's bed chamber, attempting to determine if his wife is still caught in slumber. He cracks the door open and peers into the dark room. There he can just make out his wife's form on their bed. She shifts to the left, then the right.

She's awake then, he concludes.

Opening the door fully, he steps into the room, making his way quietly to her side. Light filters in from candles in the space he has just abandoned. As he crouches down, he can see the features of his wife's face coming into focus: her eyes, her cheeks, her lips.

"How long was I asleep?" she asks groggily.

"About two hours," he concludes, placing a hand on hers.

Katharina's eyes widen—she bolts into a seated position. "Too long! You should have woken me!" she chides, twisting her back and raising her shoulders to release the tension. With each movement, she groans softly.

We really must get a better bed, Martin realizes. *She'll never make it through the pregnancy on this one.*

Katharina releases a yawn and asks, "What is that I smell? Rosemary?"

"Is it making you ill?" he inquires, feeling suddenly panicked. After all, he has witnessed her descend into fits of nausea at a rapid pace.

"No, no!" she assures him. "Actually, it smells rather good."

"Really? Well, if you want to try some, you're welcome to. It's cony meat."

"Oh. That doesn't sound very good," she comments, wrinkling her nose in disgust and shaking her head, her twin braids shifting back and forth.

As I suspected, he thinks, but she is so utterly adorable that he must kiss her on the cheek—not on the lips, for he is likely to have consumed something that will upset her.

"Come," he invites. "I have something to show you."

He takes her by the hands, helping her to her feet. She is clothed only in her chemise, so he places a wool shawl around her shoulders for warmth. Then she grips his arm, and he leads her through the network of doors to the entrance of the Aula.

"Shouldn't we be going downstairs for supper?" she asks, her brow wrinkled in confusion.

"No, my gift is in here," he explains softly.

"Gift?!" she exclaims in horror. "But I didn't get you anything!"

"You are giving me a child," he notes. "I think that has rather occupied your time and thoughts."

"I suppose so," she acknowledges, sighing plaintively.

He places his arms around her, unwilling for her to feel that she has let him down in any way. He never imagined that God would give him a woman so capable, intelligent, and beautiful inside and out. Had he become a lawyer in Mansfeld, he would not have married a woman of noble blood, yet it is Katharina's love for the Lord that makes her most extraordinary. *The judgments of the Lord are righteous altogether,* he thinks, *but I certainly do not understand them.* He pushes the door open, his eyes fixed on his wife's face.

As soon as she sees the room, her whole being seems to come alive. Her gaze is transfixed—she places a hand over her mouth, muffling a gasp. She stares in wonder, as if frozen to the spot, gripping his arm tightly. The sensation moves into his heart, speeding his pulse.

"Do you want to go in?" he asks softly.

She looks at him with eyes full of tears and nods her head. At this signal, he releases her, and she moves forward, clutching the shawl tight around her shoulders.

The room she enters is hung on all sides with fir branches cut from a nearby forest. The glorious scent fills the room: she pauses for a moment and breathes deeply, allowing it to fill her lungs. To his relief, it does not seem to bother her. The student's benches have been placed against the walls and are likewise covered in fir garland with candles interspersed—the work of Barbara Cranach. From the ceiling hang paper stars of various colors, all designed by Lucas. There is a single table in the center set for them to eat, and at the far end of the room where he usually lectures, five fir trees are displayed, each decorated with paper birds. The closed portrait case holding Lucas' gifts sits on a stand in front of the trees, ready to be viewed, and on each side of it is a burning candelabra. It is nothing less than a magical forest.

When Katharina has made it to the center of the room, she turns to face him, her tears gleaming in the light of the candles, her face as radiant as he has ever seen it.

"Oh, husband," she whispers. "You remembered!"

He moves toward her, his heart overflowing. She rushes into his arms, burying her face in his chest. This was the memory she first related to him that night at the Cranach house: sitting in her family home, surrounded by the tree branches from which she took her name, resting in her mother's embrace, feeling she was truly loved. Now she is resting in his arms, with a child of her own growing in her belly.

"Katharina," he says, "I can never replace what you have lost, but I swear to you now that this place will be your home—our home. It will be filled with light and love, and children playing happily, if the Lord should grant them to us. Here you will never need to doubt that you are loved, not only by me, but by God. Whatever you need to feel at home, if it is in my power, we will bring it here. Our family will be—" He stumbles, searching for an appropriate word. "Strange, I am certain, but we will love each other always."

She gazes into his eyes in adoration. “Thank you, husband. Oh, how I love you!”

Suddenly, he has a thought that makes him chuckle. “I told you you’d be married within the year, did I not—that night in the snow?”

“It just proves you should be careful what you promise!” she concludes, breaking into a smile. “Can we see the portraits now? I’ve been longing to view them.”

“Yes, it will be my first time as well,” he notes, leading her by the hand to where the stand is located. How strange it is to have one’s portrait painted by the finest artist in the Empire! *Well, except for Dürer, but I would never tell Lucas that.*

The frame is made of oak with gold hinges. Upon the exterior, an intricate floral design has been painted in hues of red and blue. Katharina runs her fingers over it as he works to open the lock. At last, it springs free, and he swings the double doors open to reveal the likenesses taken the previous summer and now copied for them to keep. As he steps back to take it all in, he looks first at Katharina’s portrait and then his own, both set against a blue backdrop.

As he stares at them, he begins to find himself oddly disappointed, for the level of detail is not equal to many of Cranach’s other works. The colors are somehow wrong: the features do not match what he has seen in life. He tilts his head to the right, then the left, attempting to make sense of what he is viewing, for if he is not mistaken, these are not exceptional paintings. *That doesn’t make sense. Cranach’s works are always excellent!* True, he is no expert in the modern arts, but surely what he is seeing must be visible to anyone.

He looks over at his wife, whose brow is wrinkled as she examines the portraits. She steps closer and leans forward, pushing her face within a few inches of the subject. After another half minute or so of observation, she straightens up and turns to face him, her expression pained.

“Are you thinking the same thing as me?” he asks, fearing the answer.

She scrunches her nose. “That they leave something to be desired?”

“They’re awful,” he concludes stepping next to her to judge the shortcomings in greater detail.

"Well, I'm glad you were the one to say it and not me. I cannot claim to know much about art, but you look positively ill in this one," she notes, pointing to the portrait on the left.

Martin takes in the image of his wife. The lips are fairly accurate, he thinks, but the one visible ear seems far too prominent. Every angle has been sharpened: every imperfection removed to such a degree that it seems almost monstrous.

"He's done your eyes all wrong," Martin concludes, his gaze fixing on the slanted orbs that are more off kilter the longer he views them. "Actually, he's done your whole face like one of his Venuses!" he exclaims, repulsed by the thought.

"I'm not as comely as his Venuses?" Katharina asks, crossing her arms in indignation.

"No," he assures her, his stomach tensing. "He's trying to make you fit a particular theme of his. He should have just painted you as you are." When she still appears unconvinced, he insists, "You are far prettier than this woman, whoever she is!"

This seems to satisfy her. Martin sighs in relief as Katharina turns her attention to his portrait again.

"Really, I don't think he could have made you look more miserable," she concludes. "This shows little of the skill in his other works."

"He was probably in a hurry to get them to us in time for Christmas."

Katharina leans her head on his shoulder. "I suppose they are gifts, and we shouldn't complain. I love his other paintings."

"Yes, me too. I can't account for this."

"Perhaps we will hang them somewhere less prominent," she says, grinning mischievously.

"And now, the rest of my gift for you!" he proclaims, directing her away from the questionable art and toward the supper laid out with care.

As she takes her seat gingerly at the table adorned with a vase full of holly, Katharina assures him, "You've already given me everything I desired—everything that a person could give. Only our Lord has given me more."

"Infinitely more, I should think," he comments, making sure she is well situated. Kneeling beside her, he says, "Käthe, I wish I had done better at the beginning. So much of what a new bride would expect, you were denied."

"I never expected to be a bride at all," she notes quietly.

He takes her hands in his and kisses them gently, for he knows full well the price she paid to bring them together. She had desired all her life to be a wife and mother, yet at the moment of truth, she placed those desires on the altar in the hope that he would give them back to her. And now he is determined to place himself on that altar for her every day, for that is what Christ does for his bride.

"Be that as it may," he responds, rising to his feet and striding toward the far side of the room, "I have prepared a gift for you, my rib, the flesh of my flesh and mother of my child."

He arrives at the darkened corner where his lute has been sitting, hidden from notice. He cradles it in his arms as he strides toward the table.

"There was nothing I could have bought you that would have come close to what you deserve, nor anything I could have built for you, as I have no such skills," he explains, taking a seat and fiddling with the strings. "But two skills I do have: I can write and play. So, I sat for a while and thought of you, my love, and I thought of our dear child, and I wrote a song for you—a hymn, really."

"Oh, husband!" she exclaims, face beaming, eyes filled with love. "That is the best gift you could have given me."

"Wait until you've heard it," he cautions, bringing the instrument into tune.

"Play it for me, please," she urges, her voice hushed.

Oh heart of my heart, he thinks as he stares into her hazel eyes. *How I would hate to lose you!* The thought of it cinches his bowels like a vice. But he reminds himself, *The Lord is with us. The Lord is our strength.* He begins to play, plucking the strings according to the pattern he has memorized. It took him several hours to get it right, not because he lacked the skill, but because he was utterly determined that it must be perfect. Then he sings for her, pouring forth his soul, proclaiming the hope that drives him forward.

"A mighty fortress is our God—
A good defense and weapon.
He helps us free from all distress
That now on us has fallen.
The ancient evil foe

Is full of grave intent.
Great power and cunning
Are his dreadful armor.
On Earth is not his equal.

Our might accomplishes nothing.
We would soon be completely lost,
But the right man fights for us,
Whom God himself elected.
You ask who he is?
His name is Jesus Christ,
The Lord of Hosts.
There is no other God.
He must hold the field.

If the world should fill with devils
Who desire to utterly devour us,
We will not be sore afraid.
We will yet succeed.
The Prince of this world,
Though he makes himself fierce,
Can still do nothing against us.
It is finished. He is judged.
A little word can fell him.

The Word will still stand,
And no thanks to them.
He is with us and will fulfill his plan
With his Spirit and his gifts.
Should they take my body,
My goods, my honor, my wife and child,
I must let them go,
For this is not the ultimate gain.
The Kingdom will still be ours."[2]

---

[2] This is not an exact translation of "Ein Feste Burg," although it is far closer to Luther's meaning than the most commonly sung English translation. I have attempted to retain most of the literal meaning and intent while also smoothing it out a bit. I have also changed the second to last couplet in this way: I use the first-person singular rather than the second person plural, as this seems more natural in the context of the scene.

As he shares the song, her cheeks are wet with tears. She nods at times, closing her eyes, feeling every beat of the music. He can see all that it means to her—the same as it means to him. For as he speaks of letting go his wife and child, she thinks of letting go her husband, and it fills her with fear and trembling, even as it does him. But with the final line—the promise that Christ's kingdom will last forever—she is filled with the same hope as he, for they belong to the same Savior.

When he has finished, he sets the lute aside and kneels before her again, wiping the tears from her face, even as his own eyes grow moist. She shakes her head in wonder and whispers, "Perfect. It's perfect."

"You liked it?" he asks, though he has already received the answer.

"Yes," she assures him. "Will you publish it, Herr Doktor?"

It is a question he had not yet considered. Somehow, he does not like the idea of sharing his gift for her with everyone else.

"Perhaps," he replies, "when the time is right."

Then she kisses his mouth and embraces him with a contented sigh, and he can't help but think that right now, at this most sacred moment, his life really is perfect.

"I want you to know that I will do all I can to care for you, to protect you," he whispers. "Now, let us enjoy this feast that Wolf has prepared."

Katharina cannot help but chuckle as she raises the bowl of broth to her lips, for it is something less than the feasts in Burgundy of old.[3] Taking his seat, Martin fills his beaker with wine and raises it to his lips, savoring the taste: neither too sweet nor too dry. As Katharina begins nibbling on her bread, he tears into his meat—but alas, it lacks flavor.

"I must fetch some salt," he decides. "I'll be right back."

"I will miss you," she replies, smiling sweetly.

He rises to his feet and walks toward the door. Suddenly, his left ear begins ringing. As he moves into the passage, he applies pressure to it for a few seconds—a remedy that nearly always works. Sadly, it makes no difference on this occasion.

That's annoying, he thinks.

---

[3] The dukes of Burgundy who ruled in the 14th and 15th centuries were well known for their outlandish feasts that featured extravagant and expensive foods.

As he nears the stairway, the ringing becomes louder. It is sharp, like a blunt instrument against his skull. He massages his left temple with his hand, attempting to release the pain.

Arriving at the top of the spiral staircase, he gazes downward, watching the steps make their turn to the left, spinning around the central pillar. The stairs are moving, but he has not yet begun his descent. He places a hand on the wall for balance: this seems to restore his vision. He breathes deeply, allowing the dizzy spell to pass. But the noise in his head—the buzzing of a thousand bees—continues unabated.

I really must get more rest, he decides.

He descends the stairs, the pain in his head increasing by the second. *What is happening? Am I sick?* Then everything spins at a rapid pace. He is no longer certain which way is right or left. His foot misses the step, and he is falling, tumbling down the slabs of stone, receiving blows to his shoulders, hips, and back. *Sweet Jesus, help me!* The pressure in his head is now unbearable. He collapses on the floor of the foyer, bellowing in pain. There are flashes of light across his vision—bursts of fantastic color. The very sight of them is like nails driven into his forehead. *What is happening to me?! Am I dying?! I can't die now! They need me!*

He lays flat on his back, staring up at the spinning ceiling, his whole body aching. "Help!" he cries, his voice hoarse. "Please, help me!"

Someone is coming: it is his wife racing down the stairs, rushing to his side. She bends over him, her face coated with fear—every muscle is strained, her eyes are wide and desperate. It is a sign of how frightened she is that she cries, "Martin! Martin, are you hurt?! Are you bleeding?!"

"I—" he mutters, raising his shaking hands for examination, attempting to make sense of his scattered thoughts. "I don't think so."

Katharina sits on the bottom step and lifts him up to rest on her lap, making a careful study of his head for any signs of injury. He pinches his eyes shut, the tears hot and stinging. Was he not singing to her just a few minutes ago? Was his life not perfect? *What is happening?!* He strains to remember the words—the promises he is meant to recite to himself. Yet, his mental grasp is as feeble as the legs that were meant to hold him upright. Anxiety coats him in thick waves, rippling across his skin, washing away his hope.

"What can I do for you?" Katharina asks, clutching him in her arms. "Is there anything I can do?"

He can think of no remedy to aid him, for he knows not what is wrong. So instead, he requests, "Speak truth to me."

For a moment, he hears only the ringing, as ceaseless as the wars that rage. Then her voice pierces through the darkness within him, and she recites the words of a man at the end of himself.

"As for me, I know that my Redeemer lives,
And at the last He will take His stand on the earth.
Even after my skin is destroyed,
Yet from my flesh I shall see God;
Whom I myself shall behold,
And whom my eyes will see and not another.
My heart faints within me!"[4]

31 December 1525
Basel, Swiss Confederation

Erasmus of Rotterdam sits before the hearth in his study, holding a book in his shaking hands. Its author is Martin Luther. Its purpose: the utter destruction of all he is.

A single month has passed since he stood in Basel's cathedral and dared for once to step out in faith. When Christof placed his hand on Erasmus' head—when he bestowed the blessing, the outpouring of divine love—Erasmus felt himself resurrected if only for a moment. A precious, fleeting moment, like the final hope in Pandora's box. But with the morning's light, his doubt was reborn.

The questions bombarded him. Was he really forgiven? Could one man truly grant such a thing to another? Had exhaustion dulled Erasmus' senses? Was it the unearthly light of the candles that caused him to give way to sentiment? Can a feeling, even one as powerful as that, be all it declares itself to be, or was this the last and cruelest deception of an aging man given over to desperation?

With each day, the light within him dimmed. *I am a fool! A damned fool!* He clung to the remnant of that feeling: the fading echo of hope, growing more distant by the hour.

---

[4] Job 19:25-27.

Then it came—this monstrous thing, this devourer of his peace. Barely had Erasmus' wounds had time to bind than Luther poured his invective upon them. Oh, how it burns! Every caustic word scorches to kill. *Yes, he would kill me. Worse: he would destroy my soul but leave me in this body of death, a wraith and a vagrant, without purpose or pleasure.* The shadow has fallen now. He can never have his peace.

Line after line, Luther insults and demeans him, treating his carefully considered arguments as if they were the witless musings of schoolboys. Not only has Luther refused to treat him as an equal—he has refused to treat him as a Christian. It is written out in black and white: "I wish the defenders of free choice would take warning at this point, and realize that when they assert free choice, they are denying Christ."[5]

The rules of engagement have been utterly ignored. To read it is to be attacked not by skill but utter brute force. He did not want to read it, of course: not after making it through the first three pages, for there already he found the following.

> "Your book struck me as so cheap and paltry that I felt profoundly sorry for you, defiling as you were your very elegant and ingenious style with such trash, and quite disgusted at the utterly unworthy manner that was being conveyed in such rich ornaments of eloquence, like shit being carried in gold and silver vases. You seem to have felt this yourself, from the reluctance with which you undertook this piece of writing."[6]

It is a truly shocking statement, particularly given how careful Erasmus was to show deference in his own work. Again and again, the question echoes in his mind: *What have I done to deserve this? What is it about me that offends him so?*

---

[5] Martin Luther, *De Servo Arbitrio* (On Bound Will), trans. Philip S. Watson in *Luther and Erasmus: Free Will and Salvation*, ed. E. Gordon Rupp and Philip S. Watson, The Library of Christian Classics (Philadelphia: The Westminster Press, 1969), 321.

[6] Ibid., 102. The translation reads "refuse or ordure being carried in gold and silver vases," but I have changed the text in this one instance to better reflect Luther's intended meaning.

It has taken him two days to make it through the thing, for Luther was not content to hit him once or twice, but insisted on assaulting him hundreds of times, any sense of proportion abandoned. Now, Erasmus has made it to the final page—proof, perhaps, that God is still remotely merciful. The hour is late. He should have gone to bed hours ago, but he was determined to have it over and done with. For this attack upon his honor cannot be allowed to stand: silence would imply that Desiderius Erasmus was defeated. No, he will have to write against Luther again, and this time he will grant him nothing at all. *The man does not deserve it.*

Practically seething with anger, Erasmus looks again at the text printed before him, its letters glowing in the light of the fire. His joints are exceedingly sore—his stomach overturned, his head consumed by ache. *How did this man come to haunt my entire existence? Will I ever be free of him?!* He presses on to the next paragraph, knowing full well that he will loath whatever he finds. There he reads the following.

> "Moreover, I praise and commend you highly for this also, that unlike all the rest you alone have attacked the real issue, the essence of the matter in dispute, and have not wearied me with irrelevancies about the papacy, purgatory, indulgences, and such like trifles (for trifles they are rather than basic issues), with which almost everyone hitherto has gone hunting for me without success. You and you alone have seen the question on which everything hinges and have aimed at the vital spot, for which I sincerely thank you, since I am only too glad to give as much attention to this subject as time and leisure permit."[7]

Erasmus inhales deeply, the book trembling in his grip. *You and you alone.* The words penetrate deep into his chest. Could this be, at the last, an acknowledgement of the strange and obscene bond between them? An admission that Desiderius Erasmus is something greater than a flea? *No, it cannot be.* For even as Luther attempts to praise him, he condescends, the arrogance dripping from his pen. *There is nothing true in him—nothing at all.*

---

[7] Ibid., 333.

Erasmus tosses the book aside, sending it sliding across the floorboards. Utterly exhausted, he rises and moves toward the hearth, resting his hand on the mantle, gazing into the flames. His whole being is seized by an inquiry.

How was I beaten so severely?

He closes his eyes, allowing the bitterness to take him. For a single moment of his life, he had enjoyed some peace. That night in the cathedral: it all seemed so real! He believed for once that the saints were with him—that God himself was with him! But now he sees once again that the game is rigged. *Luther was not fighting fair. He never does.*

Black are these musings! He has lost all trace of the light. *First Béda, then Louvain, and now this: the cruelest blow of all!* The anger has gripped him fully. He is almost shaking with rage, his spirit one with the flames before him. *How did he beat me?! He is nothing!*

Then, a moment of revelation, as if God himself had granted it from above: *Melanchthon!*

Yes, it had to be Melanchthon. That is the only possible explanation. The form of argument, the range of allusions, the arrows hurled with such skill: it all bears the mark of the greatest scholar in the Empire. A man whom he had tried to help—for whom he placed his own good at risk! A man he would have taken to his bosom as his successor, whom he forgave again and again, always granting him the benefit of the doubt!

"You fiend!" he fumes. "You betrayed me!"

For there will be no Savior for Germany—no great reform of Christendom. If Philipp Melanchthon can become his enemy, then all is lost. Yes, only time stands between him and the destruction of all he loves. Of all the betrayals he has suffered in his life, this one stands alone: the peak of his purgation and the nadir of his spirit. For in losing Melanchthon, he has lost his hope once and for all.

The hour is late. The world is cruel. Erasmus watches the flames dance, cursing himself for his carelessness. *Why did I think things could be different? Why did I ever believe?* A single phrase boils within him, rising to the surface, burning a path through his flesh.

"Damn you!"

1 January 1526
Wittenberg, Electoral Saxony

Philipp Melanchthon sits at the desk in his study deep in thought. He has done so every day for the past few weeks: every day since he first read Martin's book and felt his foundation shaken. The memories torment him. The pain is as sharp as ever. *So much striving, and yet I make no progress!*

How many times has he gone for walks to work through his thoughts? How many times has he recited the Our Father, willing God's kingdom to come? He has looked everywhere for the fruit of the Spirit—for signs of the goodness of God. Yes, he has witnessed a few: the sacraments are still offered, the Word is still preached, and he still enjoys the communion of those he loves. But every time he is filled, the joy seems to leak, leaving him parched and desperate for more. Never does his joy remain. *How could it when the whole world is in upheaval?*

The Great Conjunction,[8] the warning of divine wrath: everything he feared has come to pass, for this deluge has struck him with no less power than that endured by Noah. He has witnessed the breaking of the earth, and it has changed him irreversibly.

They say Martin was taken ill, but is recovering after some rest, with only a few bruises to remind him of his trial. *If only I could emerge from my calamities thus unscathed!* he thinks. Philipp is finding it difficult to forgive Martin for his treatment of Erasmus: it still defies his skills of comprehension. *For what have I lost so many friends? What else will I be asked to sacrifice for that man?* Though he remains as committed to the gospel as ever, Philipp knows in his soul that his bond with Martin can never be quite what it was. They will never have another moment like they had before the trial—before his colleague went away and the world became a whirling chaos.

It cannot be only Martin, and it cannot be only me leading the way, he reasons. *It cannot be any of us. We need a miracle.* The tears run bitter from his eyes. He slams his lids shut, attempting to endure the pain, but it is a pain no man can endure except the one who descended to ascend.

---

[8] The Great Conjunction was an astronomical alignment that occurred in 1524 and was seen by many as a portent of great events.

A branch brushes against one of the windows, the breeze directing its path. There is a storm coming. *Strange for this time of year—very strange.* Soon, the rain will fall. He wonders if the clothes were left out to dry. *I should warn Katharina lest her work be undone.* Then something else catches his eye: the silver cross of Kahla, an object that will forever fuel his ache, for it is tied to both Karlstadt and Luther.

Does the dream live on? he wonders. *Is there life and hope beyond all this? Is the Spirit still at work?*

Suddenly, a powerful notion strikes him, and before he has time to think, Philipp is descending the stairs to the lower level, the cross in his hand. He steps boldly toward the back door, seized by a single object. *There by the Elbe—there I will find my answer.*

"Where do you think you're going in this weather? You'll make yourself sick!" Katharina calls after him, but he does not stop to answer. "Philipp! Husband, come back!" she cries. Too late—his course is determined. He shuts the door behind him.

Retrieving a hammer from the shed—a tool of which Martin would approve—he continues on his way. The wind is whipping up dust, papers, straw. It sends forth all in its path, directing even the great Philipp Melanchthon to obey its call. The sky is darkening fast: within minutes the storm will arrive.

He passes the Black Cloister and exits the town through the Elster Gate, making for the hill overlooking the river. The air is thick with moisture—it seems to tingle with expectation. Philipp's heart pounds as he experiences a final doubt. *Is this really a good idea?* After a moment's debate, he concludes, *I am far beyond such considerations.*

Within minutes, he reaches the hill in question. A few drops of water are released from the sky. The eternal Elbe stretches gray before him, bending with the contour of the earth. As the thunder begins to roll, he pounds the cross into the ground, with each stroke releasing the tension he feels inside. Once it stands upright, he drops the hammer, steps back, and falls to his knees upon the brown grass. There, for what seems like an eternity, he waits, closing his eyes, absorbing the moment.

The storm is moving closer, and the rain begins to fall in earnest, but all is quiet upon the hill. Here he takes his stand in the valley of the shadow of death—the wilderness of the soul, the graveyard of faith. What he thought he knew has been belied. What he built lies in rubble, and here amid the charred remains, he seeks some solace: a final bit of hope among the dry bones. There is a holy yearning within him. *This will be my going under.*

He is filled with fear, but his fear is not that of the weak. Rather, he dreads what it would mean to be fully alive: that the truth itself will be his undoing. With a cry, he casts a lament to the heavens. "Lord, I pray you, show me your glory!"

Nothing. Silence.

The wind overthrows all in its path. He knows not where it comes from, nor where it is going. It has forced him along, through triumph and tragedy, and now it has brought him here. He sheds a single tear. *Must I endure the trial?*

He calls out again to the sky above, "Oh, that you would rend the heavens and come down! Oh, that you would grant me what I seek!" Only God knows how long he waits there in the fading light, as alone as any man can be. He is stiffened, tensed, stretched to the point of breaking. *Do not be silent,* he prays. *Do not leave me here alone.*

Then suddenly, all is changed! A piercing flash of light descends, so loud it shakes the very ground beneath him. He is toppled and lands flat on his back, heart pounding, blood forcing its way urgently through his veins. The silver cross has been struck from on high, and the ground around it smokes. Philipp tilts his head to look upon it, gasping for breath, astounded by what has occurred.

The sky is aflame—the great storehouses open. Peals of thunder: again, again, again! It is the end and the beginning. *This is not a dead place. This is holy ground.* And there he is, still flat on his back, confronted with a reality beyond the power of man to tell. The rain pelts him from head to toe, seeping through his robes. He has never been so broken, and never more alive.

Then rising, he is swept up in the torrent. He kneels before the smoking ground, thoroughly humbled before the Ancient of Days, but he does not fear, for he knows he is called by the divine name. He is captivated by this maddening thing, and all else fades away. A consoling force, a consuming fire: the Lord of Hosts who burns the chariots.

Lifting his hand toward the sky, he cries, "God! My God!"

"For now we see in a mirror dimly, but then face to face;
Now I know in part, but then I will know fully just as I
also have been fully known."

—1 Corinthians 13:12

"And all shall be well and
All manner of thing shall be well
When the tongues of flame are in-folded
Into the crowned knot of fire
And the fire and the rose are one."

—T.S. Eliot, "Little Gidding"

Acknowledgments

Thank you to my husband for supporting me as I wrote these novels. To my family, who loved me first. To all my teachers, especially those who opened my eyes to the wonders of Reformation history and theology. To my son's babysitter Willow, his teachers, and his therapists. Not only have they helped him immeasurably and given us hope, but they also provided me with time to work on projects like this.

God has blessed me richly. My basic needs have always been met, and I have enjoyed a world-class education. I live in a country where I have freedom to write, to speak, and to worship. Despite the numerous difficulties I endure on this earth, I cannot help but stand in awe at the goodness of God to me. May he be ever praised.

I am once again indebted to the publishing team at 1517—Steve Byrnes, Sam Leanza Ortiz, Elysia Brewer, Grant Klembara, Mai Choy, Zach Stuef. Thank you for seeing goodness in this project. I have received goodness from you all. I am also grateful to our sister organization, Mockingbird, and its founder David Zahl, for showing unwavering support for this project.

Two characters in this book are named in honor of real people of later eras. The bookseller Dietrich whom Erasmus briefly visits is named in honor of Dietrich Bonhoeffer, Lutheran pastor and theologian, as an exemplar of all those in the Confessing Church. The baker Scholl is named in honor of Sophie Scholl, who was raised in a Lutheran family and became an important member of the White Rose resistance movement.

Last of all, I am immensely grateful to you the reader for stepping into this world with me. I know you have many demands on your time, and that you chose to grant some of it to these novels is a tremendous gift. I hope that the story has granted you strength and encouragement, even as it has me.

May God be praised in all the works of my hands and heart.

Pax et gratia.

About the Author

Amy Mantravadi lives in Dayton, Ohio, with her husband, Jai, and their son, Thomas. She holds a B.A. in biblical literature and political science from Taylor University and an M.A. in international security from King's College London. She is a 1517 contributor and author of the *Chronicle of Maud* series of historical novels. When she is not writing, she enjoys geeking out about history and theology, filling the internet with GIFs, and spending time with her family.

www.ingramcontent.com/pod-product-compliance
Lightning Source LLC
LaVergne TN
LVHW040558210825
818979LV00004B/10